Sign up for our newsletter to hear
about new and upcoming releases.

www.ylva-publishing.com

OTHER BOOKS BY
MICHELLE L. TEICHMAN

The Space Between

RESCUE ME

BY MICHELLE L. TEICHMAN

ACKNOWLEDGEMENTS

Special thank you, Nicole, for the emergency police procedural information and for being the first person to read this, as always. Thank you, Luciana, for all of the paramedic information and checking the content when I needed it. Lisa, thank you so much for the wealth of RCMP information that is very hard to come by. Josh, thank you for the medical content and allowing me to call between surgeries to get it. Sonia, thank you for filling in all of the police and emergency services information in between. Thank you, Sheri, for always pushing me to make my books the best version of themselves. I could not have written this book without all of your knowledge and expertise.

DEDICATION

Nicole, my best friend, thank you for always supporting my writing and being the first to read all of my books. Thank you for giving me constructive feedback as well as the praise you know I need not to throw out the first draft. I always feel better once a story is in your hands and I get that first excited message from you. You keep writing fun for me, and for that, you have no idea how grateful I am.

Sonia, my beautiful wife, thank you for the support you have given me these past couple of years. Even though I don't always show it, it's helped me persevere and make some difficult choices. Thank you for putting up with my less-than-stellar moods and backing up my decisions. It helps knowing there's someone in my corner.

Ally, my sister, thank you for always supporting me as a writer and for being there with a glass of wine (well, let's be honest, a bottle or two) when I need it. Your belief in me is boundless, and when mine falters, it's amazing to know there's someone out there who thinks the world of me.

CHAPTER 1

"ASHLEIGH?" HER MOTHER STOOD AT the stove, wearing the Wonder Woman apron she'd received as a stocking stuffer last Christmas from Ashleigh's father. Her light brown hair, so close to Ashleigh's in colour, was pulled up and out of the way, but she'd let it down for supper in a few minutes, just like she always did. The room smelled like the salmon baking in the convection oven, but it had a nice spice to it and was actually pleasant. "There's someone I'd like you to meet."

Ashleigh groaned. *Not this again.* "Mom—"

"Now, before you protest, he's a doctor."

So what? "That's great, but that doesn't make me any less of a lesbian."

Her mother stomped her kitten-heeled foot. "I wish you wouldn't use that word."

This again.

It was time to move out. She'd been back home for two years, and it felt like if she didn't leave now, she would never get out again. She loved her parents, but twenty-five and employed full-time meant she was too old to be living at home with her mom who refused to accept that she was gay. Ashleigh had finished undergrad three years ago, taken a job with Global Vision International, and moved to Kenya with her university boyfriend, only to realize two things—she hated working abroad and she was a lesbian.

Having the talk with her parents when she returned had been the most difficult conversation she'd ever had, and she wasn't thrilled to keep having it over and over with her mom.

Her father walked into the kitchen, his dark hair covered with a Blue Jays baseball cap. The crack of a bat and cheers entered the kitchen from the TV in the family room. Ashleigh hoped the discussion might improve now that her father was here. Even though he had fought her on it initially, he had been marginally better about accepting the news of her sexual orientation the first time. Of course, he'd also told her that she had just gone "bush-queer" in the jungle and assured her that he'd had a similar experience as a teenager when he'd gone on a forty-five-day canoe trip with a group of boys through Algonquin Park. It was just a phase, something she'd grow out of as he had.

"Dad, tell Mom to stay out of my dating life."

Her father froze, his arm halfway in the fridge as he reached for a beer. After a brief pause, he grabbed the beer, closed the fridge, and popped the top on the can of lager. "What's going on?" he asked in his most neutral voice.

"Nothing," her mother said, her back to Ashleigh as she stirred the potatoes.

"Mom's trying to set me up with another guy," Ashleigh said quickly. She felt like a child, tattling on her mother, but living at home sometimes made her feel thirteen all over again.

Without warning, her mother began to cry. Her father took his wife's hand, gave it a squeeze, and said, "Oh, honey, come on. She's our daughter."

Her mother wiped her eyes on the backs of her hands and sniffed. "Well, maybe if our daughter had become a doctor, I wouldn't be trying to set her up with one."

Ashleigh's face burned. Somehow, her mother had managed to pull the two biggest bones of contention between them into one conversation. "I help people," she said through her teeth.

"She helps people," her father repeated, patting her mother's back in an effort to soothe her.

"Oh, yes, chasing ambulances."

"That's a lawyer. I drive the ambulance."

"With what you make, you might as well be driving a cab."

"Sure, Mom. Give me the keys to the Cadillac, and I'll quit my job and become an Uber driver. Would that make you happy?"

Her mother turned around to look at her. Her brown eyes were glassy and red. "I was proud of you when you went to Africa. I thought when you came back you were going to go to med school and join Doctors Without Borders."

As if the high risk of malaria, constant fear of Somalian pirates, and black market human kidney harvesting weren't bad enough, the poisonous snakes and venomous spiders she often found in her residence and shoes were sufficient to send her running back home. Still, she wanted to help people. The medical training that she had learned with GVI and the time leading up to that had been enlightening, fascinating, and had given her a sense of immense satisfaction. Her attraction to Laura, on the other hand, made her question everything she thought she knew about herself and left her with an overwhelming emptiness, a yearning to be fulfilled by…something. She didn't know what, exactly, but she somehow understood that it was missing. Whatever it was, when her arm had brushed against Laura's, it felt like fire on her skin.

"Africa wasn't for me. Neither is MSF, and neither are men." Medecins Sans Frontieres, or Doctors Without Borders as her mother referred to it, had seemed like a great idea in theory, as had both Africa and men, none of which had worked out for her.

"What about Colin? You were with him for years. You loved him."

Colin's touch, unlike Laura's, hadn't felt like much of anything. Still, they both wanted the same things, valued the same things—a house, kids, kindness, and a family. Because they agreed on the important stuff, Ashleigh supposed she just forgot about their relationship somewhere along the way.

When Ashleigh had first told Colin that she didn't think she wanted to continue their relationship, it had been the hardest conversation she'd ever had until, of course, the one when she told her parents that she was moving back home because she'd broken up with Colin and thought that she was gay. In hindsight, she should have come to them with some proof. The fact that she'd never mentioned anything of the sort before, didn't have any experience with women, and had been with a boyfriend for the previous five years had brought her parents to the comforting conclusion that it was just a phase.

"Yes, I loved Colin, but I was never in love with him, not the way I should have been, not the way you're supposed to be when you marry someone."

"Ha!" Her mother laughed mirthlessly. "Like you would know. You're a child."

"I'm not a child!"

"All right." Her father put his hands up in a defensive stance, then gestured them toward Ashleigh first and then her mother. "This reminds me of that summer I thought I was bush-queer—" her father started.

"James, honestly, enough with that! You're only encouraging her. You're not queer."

"I'm just trying to say, well, I guess you can take the queer out of the bush, but our daughter is still a lesbian." The comment was so absurd that the three of them couldn't help but laugh, and it was the break in tension they needed.

Her mother pulled a paper towel from the roll and wiped her eyes. The tears stopped, and she looked to Ashleigh. "I just want you to be happy, and you're not."

That much was true. After she quit GVI, returned from Kenya, and moved back in with her parents, she'd spent the last two years going through the process of becoming a paramedic and establishing herself as a lesbian. The first part was easy. She had similar medic training from her time abroad, and she'd always had a knack for tests. Proving to herself and everyone else that she was a lesbian had been a little messier. If she'd been less naïve, she would have approached things with Denise differently.

She thought back to the night she met Denise at Tango, the only women's bar she knew of in Toronto's gay village. She hadn't known where else to go to shake the lesbian tree and hope some forbidden fruit would drop in her lap. Unwittingly, she'd been looking for love in the wrong place, but she'd fallen for Denise regardless of the numerous red flags.

While Ashleigh was looking to find a partner, Denise had been looking for nothing more than a challenge, but her bad girl demeanour had sucked Ashleigh in. Her entire life, she'd been careful, done what was expected of her, played on the safe side. She'd gotten together with

Colin in first year because he was her best friend. She'd followed Colin to Kenya for similar reasons. He felt safe, comfortable, like an old robe she simply slipped on because she knew it would fit.

"You're right," Ashleigh said. "I'm not happy, but I plan to be."

"That's all we want for you," her father said, giving her mother a stern look. After a moment's hesitation, her mother conceded with a nod.

"I know, and I'm working on it."

Her mother untied her apron. "Dinner's ready."

Her parents might not bug her on the issue any more that evening, but she couldn't stop her mind from revisiting it. When would she meet someone who made her heart race and her head spin? Someone nothing like Denise. Someone warm and caring, who took relationships and commitment seriously. Somebody she could make a home with.

———— ··· ————

Parade was lackluster as usual. Sure, it helped for Kristen to learn about the cases, the beats, and the local gangs in the mandatory morning meeting and debrief, but learning all that and more was part of her prep work for the undercover position inside the Toronto Police Service. She'd had the names, colours, designs, and insignias of every local gang memorized before she'd stepped foot into 52 Division for the first time. Her rather carefree attitude was not just part of her Constable Kristen Bailey persona, it was simply who she was. One thing she did take seriously, though, was her job, and she excelled at it. Her RCMP rank, medals, and decorations attested to that, and the Mounties did not hand them out lightly.

As 52 Division's Staff Sergeant King droned on, Kristen let her gaze wander. The only cop who was giving his undivided attention was his son, Charles King. With only two years under his belt, he was still looking to earn his dad's favour. Her gaze continued around the room until it rested on her training officer, Henry Hackett. Cop extraordinaire. He was half-asleep, slumped over in a chair that looked a size too small for him. *Jackass.*

Hackett was a typical I'm-just-here-collecting-paycheques-till-I-retire kind of cop, and that didn't sit well with Kristen. If he carried a badge, then he better respect it. Lives depended on it. Veteran police constables like Hackett, who still worked patrol, were often made training officers for rookies. There were several TOs in 52, and Kristen was quite certain she'd been saddled with the worst one.

Sure, it was common in Toronto to have a TO ride with a new cop for six months, even a year if a rookie's superiors didn't think the constable was ready sooner; however, part of Kristen's cover was that she was a veteran transfer from Montreal, so why was she stuck with this oaf after three months? Training officers like Henry Hackett might have been a contributing factor in the death of rookie constable Ricky Oslowe, whose murder was the reason she was in Toronto in the first place. Hackett hadn't been Oslowe's TO, but curiously, he'd been the training officer of another rookie who'd gone missing six months prior to Oslowe's death. That officer had never been found.

Hackett was lazy. That one was obvious. What she'd not-so-subtly learned during their first fifteen minutes together was that he was also somewhat of a misogynist and a racist. Any cop who wasn't strictly a white male had to work twice as hard to earn his respect. As a lesbian with a black sister-in-law, Henry's prejudice concerned Kristen, but she wasn't there to teach tolerance. Her mission was clear: find Oslowe's killer, bring the perp to justice, collect another accolade, and with any luck, the keys to the Banff branch of the RCMP, along with a sizeable salary bump.

Positions in the Banff office didn't come up often. They were highly coveted. The fact that her staff sergeant major had even dangled one in front of her still stunned Kristen. Banff was a retirement post, the location where most RCMP dreamed of finishing their careers. Being offered a position in that office at only thirty-two years old told Kristen just how highly her superiors thought of her.

"These two gangs have been at it for years. We need to make sure we know who's in their territory before they do." Staff Sergeant King finished off with a quick recap of what happened on the overnight shift when the Italian Mafia infringed on the Chinese *Lǎohǔ* gang's territory in the west end. It ended in a sloppy storefront shooting in Little Italy. No one was killed, but gunshots were never good. "The more we know, the fewer people get caught up in things they don't understand. Neither of these organizations has much patience for the other, and the summer heat isn't going to help with that. We need to stay vigilant." He looked down from the podium at the sheet he held there and flipped to the last page. "Oh yeah, we're coming up on the August long weekend. That means illegal fireworks sales in Chinatown. If you're in the area, stop, get out of the car, and just walk the beat. Police presence should be enough to scare off most civilians looking for kicks."

King put his papers down and wiped the sweat off his head with the back of his hand. His stiff, starched, white collar and his epaulettes set him apart from the rest of the officers in the room, and Kristen wondered with amusement if it bothered Henry Hackett that his commanding officer was black. It would probably blow his mind to know that Kristen was a staff sergeant in the RCMP and outranked him by miles. She would have her own white shirt if the RCMP handed them out to staff sergeants the same way they did to local police, but she was still a few promotions shy of inspector, and not everyone reached that desiderated rank.

Kristen looked over just as Henry's head drooped down. The motion woke him abruptly, and he looked around, clearly startled, and almost fell out of his chair. Kristen suppressed a snicker as King pinned her TO with a warning look.

"There's one last thing before we head out there today." Staff Sergeant King continued as if he'd never been interrupted. "We're coming up on one year since Constable Richard Oslowe was found dead at the scene of a routine drug bust. For those of you who didn't know Ricky, he was a class act. All cop, all the way. When we lose one of our own, it's personal, so let's get out there and catch this guy already." There was a cheer, and Staff Sergeant King motioned to them for quiet. "His young widow suffered the most, and this year we will be having a fundraiser in her honour. FiteNite. If you want to participate, I'm leaving a sign-up sheet outside this room. I know you guys, and I know we won't lack for volunteers. Just remember that it's for fun and for a good cause. Please come if you can, and open your wallets as big as the hearts buried somewhere inside you." This garnered a few laughs. "That's it for today. Serve, protect, and don't screw up."

Hackett met Kristen in the hall outside the parade room. "Ready, rook?"

"You know I'm not a rookie, right?" Kristen did her best to appear amused. "Anything special you wanted us to get started on today?"

"Yeah." He straightened his belt. "Tim Hortons is having a sale on doughnuts for some charity. Let's grab a box."

"Yes, sir." She held the door open for him as he passed through.

"You're driving," he said and tossed her the keys. "I don't like getting powdered sugar on my uniform."

"Could have fooled me," Kristen mumbled under her breath.

It was the beginning of rush hour, not the best time to be driving down Spadina Avenue in Chinatown. As she slowed the car to a stop behind a long line of traffic, Hackett looked out the window, an expression of ennui on his face.

"So, it's been almost a year since Ricky Oslowe was gunned down," she said, almost out of boredom at this point.

"He wasn't gunned down. He was strangled."

"Right." She feigned ignorance. "I can't believe they haven't arrested any paramedics yet. I mean, there's that video evidence, right?"

"No one to arrest." He cleared his throat and looked back out the window. When he opened it for air, Kristen wrinkled her nose. She'd never quite gotten used to the stench of seafood and sewer that seemed to permeate the Spadina and Dundas area, especially under the hot summer sun. "Why do you say that?" she asked, trying to sound casual instead of like she was gagging.

"It wasn't a paramedic."

That surprised her. The first time she'd questioned him three months before, Hackett had said somebody would pay for Oslowe's death. When she'd asked who, he told her it was none of her business. She thought that good ol' boy Hackett would have jumped on the easiest solution, like the rest of the force, and blamed the paramedics for murdering Oslowe at the response call. The video of unidentified EMS workers approaching an injured Oslowe just before his death that had been leaked around the department certainly made it look that way. "You don't think the paramedics killed him?" she asked. Did he know more than she'd thought? Had she misread him?

He tightened his jaw. "Where he was killed?" he said rhetorically. "Mafia territory. Probably some wop did it."

No. She hadn't misread him.

"You think some mobsters just happened to walk by on the street and kill him?"

Hackett shrugged. "The wop thought he saw something. Made sure no one would ever know what that was."

Well, at least it was a theory, which she admitted was more than she had at this point and more than what SIU had when they'd called her in after failing to catch the killer for nine months, which had created a stain on the special investigations unit's reputation.

"Wasn't he killed in *Lǎohǔ* territory? And why kill a cop and make a mess? Seems kind of pointless. Also, how did they get the ambulance there so quickly for the cover-up? I saw the video," Kristen said.

"Good for you. Hell if I know why anyone does anything. A gang's a gang; don't matter much which one. They're all impossible to pin down with any one crime. Why are you always going on about this case anyway? You were still in Quebec when he was killed."

"It just doesn't sit well," she said.

"Yeah? Well, get used to it. A lot of what you see ain't gonna sit well, rook."

"I'm not a rookie," she said for the fiftieth time that summer.

"And those doughnuts ain't gonna materialize out of thin air. For God's sake, take a side street. You drive like a boob."

Kristen bit her cheek and took the next turn up Cecil Street. "I don't buy that it was a random gang hit. It doesn't make any sense."

"New cops always have lots of theories. All full of ideas and rainbows in your eyes. You can't see the world in front of you because you spend too much time trying to fix what you can't. Hotshots, hotheads, glory chasers." He shook his head. "That's how you end up dead."

Did Oslowe being a rookie—albeit near the end of his first full year with the force—have anything to do with his own death? Would a veteran cop have fared better? The video didn't show the altercation, so it was hard to tell.

"And what would you have done?" She put the car in park outside of Tim Hortons.

"What I always do: seen through the bullshit, kept my head down and my nose clean, and stayed alive." He opened his door, and it took two tries to heave himself out of the opening and onto the street. "I'm getting a box. You want anything, *Bailey?*" He looked back at her through his still-open window.

She smiled. "Medium coffee. Black."

"It'll put hair on your chest, rook." He smirked to himself, and Kristen's smile fell.

Inside Tim Hortons, Henry showed his badge and moved the queue aside as he walked straight to the front of the line to order his box of doughnuts. From the privacy of the car, Kristen almost laughed at how official he made it seem. Almost, but she couldn't quite muster up the energy. It was going to be another long, uneventful day, much like the last three months. The prospect of ever solving this murder was beginning to fade into the distance, along with her promotion.

CHAPTER 2

IT WAS A TWO-ALARM BLAZE, and as usual, the EMTs were second to arrive after fire. Ashleigh unbuckled her seatbelt and readjusted the collar of her shirt. The smoke from the building was dark grey, which meant the fire was almost out. With large hoses connected to a nearby hydrant, firemen doused the last of the flames.

"Ready, Paige?" Rodrigo asked Ashleigh from the seat beside her. Since she'd become a paramedic a month ago, Ashleigh hadn't heard her first name used once at work. She felt kind of silly about it, as if they were pretending to be a hockey team. She called her partner by his first name, regardless of precedent.

"Lead the way, Rodrigo."

Rodrigo gave her a crooked smile as he stepped out of the ambulance. Ashleigh jumped down after him. They took a moment to find the fire captain, and when Rodrigo recognized him, they made their way over.

"Hey." Rodrigo stepped up to him. "What's the rundown?"

The captain's forehead was smooth, and his body was relaxed, sure signs things were going well inside the building. His face was clean shaven, and there were no soot marks on him. Ashleigh didn't recognize him, and by the looks of it, he hadn't even gone into the low-rise apartment building; the fire was under control. The structure was old brown brick, not unusual for Chinatown, and black smoke poured out of the top corner unit on the fourth floor, but the rest of the building looked okay. These were the kinds of calls she hoped for.

"Nothing much yet," the fire captain answered. "There are a few people inside, but none of them appear to be injured. Stick around, though; we might have a few mild cases of smoke inhalation to bring to you once it's all cleared."

"Sure thing." Rodrigo turned to Ashleigh. "Let's go back to the truck."

Ashleigh nodded. Rodrigo liked to be more involved in the action, but she was happy to be on standby.

Just as they were about to get back into their vehicle, a sole police car finally arrived on scene. Ashleigh shook her head. Good thing they didn't actually need police assistance on this call.

"You guys get lost?" Rodrigo asked. His voice had a hard edge to it.

Two cops, a male and a female, lackadaisically made their way out of the cruiser. The driver was pushing fifty and had salt-and-pepper, crew-cut hair; tanned, leathery skin; and what Ashleigh's mother would call a pot belly, visible even through the bulletproof vest that covered the rest of his torso.

"Har-har," the female officer said, a wicked smirk pulling up the corner of her dark red lips. "It turns out all-you-can-eat doughnuts eventually has its limits."

She was tall for a woman, as tall as Rodrigo, and she leaned against the cruiser with a sexy confidence that made Ashleigh smile. Her nametag read *Bailey*. Now that was a last name she could get behind. She liked it. A lot. Bailey wore classic aviators that were big enough to cover not only her eyes but part of her striking cheekbones as well. Her dark hair was down and disheveled in that sexy just-got-out-of-bed look. It was a look Ashleigh had never been able to pull off with her own long, light brown twists. Bailey's hair rested just above her pronounced clavicle, nicely complementing her golden skin. The two top buttons of her uniform shirt were unfastened and showed off her tan, which was almost as dark as Rodrigo's, before the Kevlar hugged the rest of her torso. She was thin and fit, with wiry muscles on her arms.

The residual heat from the fire combined with a blistering hot summer day made Ashleigh sweat, but the sight of Constable Bailey in her uniform made her hot in a completely different way.

"Toronto PD at their finest," Rodrigo said loud enough for the cops to hear.

The older man spat, and Constable Bailey's grin grew even wider.

"Fine and dandy." She pushed herself off the cruiser and took a step toward the fire before turning her head back to them. "Any criminals hiding up in there, or is this another social call, Cruz?" she asked, her tone matching Rodrigo's.

In her month on the job, Ashleigh hadn't seen either of these cops, but with her short tenure, there were always new faces.

"Not sure," Rodrigo said curtly. "Why don't you do your job and find out?"

"Whapsssh!" The woman mimed a whip. "You're feisty today," she said to Rodrigo.

"It's just a kitchen fire," Ashleigh said.

Rodrigo glared at her, and Bailey turned around and glanced at Ashleigh's name tag.

"Well, hello there, Paige. Haven't seen you before," she said with that easy smile still painted on her lips. Bailey moved toward her and leaned in conspiratorially. "You should be careful. If you're too nice to us, your buddies will start calling you a doughnut-chaser."

"Okay, enough." Rodrigo moved between the two of them, placing himself protectively in front of Ashleigh. "There's no crime here. Why don't you two run along and let the professionals handle things?"

"Ooh." Bailey cooed and looked to her partner, but he was busy picking something out of his ear. The woman sighed and focused her attention back on Rodrigo. "We need to stay and make sure there wasn't any mischief here, sir." She gave him a mock salute. "I think I'd feel more comfortable standing in that fire than out here with you, so I'm going to head up, but do me a favour? If one of us gets hurt in there, call someone qualified to help us out, would you? I'd hate to succumb to injuries without a competent medic around."

Ashleigh's mouth opened in surprise as the woman walked away brashly. Cops, EMTs, and firefighters were supposed to be on the same team, and although the woman had said everything with a lilt of humour in her voice, Rodrigo vibrated with anger.

"Who was that?" she asked.

"Fucking cops." He kicked the ground and sulked back to their truck. He sat on the ledge of the open back door, next to their gear. It was ready and accessible, just in case they were needed. The truck's red and white lights were still flashing, but not much else was happening on the scene as the firefighters put out the last of the small blaze.

"I don't understand." Ashleigh joined Rodrigo on the truck's ledge. "I thought we were all on the same side."

He scooted over and made room for her to sit beside him.

"Used to be," he said under his breath. "Until a year ago."

"What happened a year ago?"

Rodrigo looked down at his feet and kicked the pavement again before letting out a long breath. He glanced over at the older cop still standing next to the cruiser. "I'll tell you later."

Ashleigh opened her mouth to ask him to explain now, but Bailey strolled back to her partner.

"Okay, guys, it's all clear," Bailey said. "No need to thank us. Keeping Toronto safe is just what we do."

The muscle in Rodrigo's jaw flexed and released. Clearly he wanted to comment but bit back the remark.

Bailey started to slide into the passenger seat but stopped. With half her body in the car and the other half hanging out, she turned back to them. "Welcome to the fold, Paige, and good luck. You're going to need it." With that, she slid the rest of the way in, her partner's foot already heavy on the gas as the door swung shut.

"She doesn't seem so bad," Ashleigh said. The attractive curve of her smile and the easy way she carried herself more than made up for the sass she gave Rodrigo.

"Are you kidding me? Bailey's one of the worst. I've never seen anybody so cocksure in my entire life. Everything's a fucking joke to her, a game. I'm sure if she ever needed it, she'd refuse treatment from an EMT, just like the rest of them."

"You mean, like, refuse medical treatment?"

"Yep. Almost every last one of them refuses now. Won't let anyone touch them until they get to the hospital. That makes us just glorified sirens, and they already have their own on their vehicles."

In hindsight, every time she'd offered cops treatment, they'd always refused, saying it was just a bump or a scratch. Ashleigh hadn't thought anything of it. Cops were proud and liked to think they were invincible, so she'd let it go. Rodrigo had certainly never pushed PD to accept medical attention.

"That's just... That's totally fucked up." She looked off to where the cop car had sped away. "I don't understand. Someone could die like that, refusing help on scene."

"The way they see it, someone already died accepting help."

The condo was hot and dark when Kristen got home, if home was even the right thing to call this place. She'd been living here for the last three months, and still, the unit felt stark and unfriendly. She wasn't happy about how long this case was dragging on.

Her phone rang, and she groaned at the name on the call display. Couldn't her staff sergeant major give her one day without needing a briefing?

She picked up. "Bailey."

"It's Ouellette."

"I know." They only did this every time he called.

"So, what's the status?"

"Nothing new since yesterday." She hung her keys up in the foyer and moved to the small adjoining kitchen. There was little in her fridge, but a Mad Tom IPA was all she wanted. She popped the cap and waited for Ouellette's reprimand. He did not disappoint.

"Come on, Staff Sergeant." Clearly, he was in a mood, because he knew she hated being addressed by her rank. "I put you in there to make me look good, not bad."

Kristen moved the phone away from her mouth and let out a long breath. "My TO only lets us respond when dispatch already knows we're in the area of the call, so I don't get to see all that much outside of our daily drive. We answered a call with some EMTs today, but it was Rodrigo Cruz, whom we've already pumped dry for information, and his partner is new, so no leads to be had there."

"I didn't think getting around an aging training officer would be so difficult for you," he said without humour. "Who's Cruz's new partner? What did you learn about him?"

"He was a she, and nothing more than her last name. Paige."

"I'll run the name."

Kristen nodded. "Sounds good, sir."

"Have you been able to get close to anyone since Maria Cruz?"

"Not in that way, no." Kristen swallowed the neck of her beer. Tracking down Maria Cruz and sleeping with her had been a disaster.

Rodrigo Cruz had been one name in a roster of hundreds who had travelled the 650-kilometre radius of Toronto Paramedic Services' jurisdiction that day. Breaking it down only to those who had worked shifts the afternoon Ricky Oslowe died had narrowed the field some, but dozens still remained as suspects. The trouble was that background checks on all the paramedics had been performed before she'd arrived, and none of them showed much more than some debts in collections or unpaid parking tickets. Rodrigo Cruz stood out when his dispatch log showed him in the area where Ricky Oslowe had been found within the one-hour window of Oslowe's call to dispatch and the subsequent official finding of the officer's body.

Unfortunately, Kristen's investigation into Cruz found him guilty only of making an unsanctioned stop to visit his sister, Maria, whose daughter was celebrating her fifth birthday that day. Maria had even provided the video of Rodrigo singing "Happy Birthday" and presenting his gift to his niece at the same time that Ricky Oslowe's murder video was timestamped. Of course, Maria hadn't known at the time that she was handing over evidence on her brother to the RCMP. Kristen had merely asked Maria to get her a glass of water from the motel washroom after they'd slept together, then taken the opportunity to put a chip in Maria's cell phone and copy the memory to her own device while she was in the washroom running the tap.

The earlier investigative work by SIU into pulling all the traffic feeds, local business surveillance footage, and red light cameras in the area confirmed the validity of the video Kristen copied from Maria. Kristen had turned the evidence she found on Rodrigo over to her cover team two months ago, which had resulted in Rodrigo Cruz and his then-partner receiving unpaid suspensions, as well as the severing of their partnership. If Cruz hadn't been running his mouth about how much he hated cops over the past year, Kristen might have felt bad about splitting him and his partner up or even about what she'd done with his sister, but to Kristen, both acts had been nothing more than a part of the job.

"What about at fifty-two? Made any new friends in the division?" Ouellette asked.

"Not recently, no."

"Damnit, Bailey. You're not giving me anything to work with here. I don't know what else I can do for you. You need to start delivering on this case, or I'm going to have no choice but to yank you. That won't look good. We've spent a lot of time and pulled a lot of strings to get you in there."

With the help of Staff Sergeant Major Ouellette and the Royal Canadian Mounted Police's resources, they'd manufactured a story for her and all the right paperwork to get her transfer pushed through to Toronto Police Service's 52 Division, supposedly as a transfer from a Montreal precinct that had too many officers for its payroll. The problem was she hadn't arrived soon enough. Rookie constable Richard "Ricky" Oslowe was killed months before she reached the precinct, reportedly by an EMT, and by the time she put on the Toronto uniform, the animosity between the cops and paramedics was so thick that a lot of the EMTs had shut down and wouldn't talk to her, regardless of the fact that she hadn't been part of the force when Oslowe died and the bad blood began.

"What about Detective Ortiz? Tell me you've got him talking to you by now."

Kristen winced. That she hadn't been able to get the lead detective to talk to her about Ricky Oslowe remained a huge disappointment to both her and Ouellette. Usually, her charm worked easily, but Ortiz had been closed off from the start. She'd chalked it up to the responsibility that must be weighing on the man who was charged with catching a cop killer and who kept coming up empty month after month, but still, it irked her that after three months, he'd said little more to her than an occasional gruff hello.

"No, sir. He's still not talking."

"I don't have to tell you that it should have been the first relationship you cultivated when you arrived."

Her eyes narrowed as she remembered all the times Hackett had been derisive and dismissive of her around the precinct. She was supposed to be a seasoned transfer, but he regarded her as a bumbling rookie, so how were the rest of the cops supposed to respect her?

"There are still avenues that I haven't investigated, sir," she said, trying to steer him away from her failure with Detective Ortiz. "I think pulling me now would only make us lose the headway I've made."

"What headway is that?"

"We know this isn't the first time something suspicious has transpired at Fifty-Two Division. Take Constable Jenna Bradley, for instance. She's been missing eighteen months, and no one at the precinct talks about her."

"Talking about her would just be bad form, Bailey. Cops die; it's an occupational hazard, but gossiping about it like schoolchildren is not the way police officers are expected to behave."

Kristen let out a deep breath. Maybe Ouellette's opinion of her wasn't far from Hackett's at this point. "I don't believe in coincidences. Constable Bradley went missing after going in to break up a drug bust on her own. Ricky Oslowe died the same way. They were both rookies at fifty-two. They were both out on their own when there were more than enough officers for them to have been with partners. I've done a nationwide search; this division is the one that keeps pinging the most with results in suspicious police activity and strange protocol of this nature. If nothing else, something strange is going on at this precinct."

"You are not there to find Constable Bradley or expose some citywide conspiracy into police activity. Henry Hackett was Bradley's TO; if you haven't found anything suspicious about the guy after riding around with him every day for three months, then I think it's time to drop your theories on the cases being connected. You've rattled enough cages already, don't you think? You're there to catch Richard Oslowe's killers, nothing more."

"Give me more time and I will."

"With what? Admit it; you've got nothing solid on this case, Bailey. Little more than the information we gave you when you first went in. I'm starting to think you like it a little too much there."

Yeah, right. This wasn't the longest she'd ever immersed herself in a job, but still, the ennui of it was starting to wear on her. It was trying, the obscurity of being undercover. She could make friends while she was UC, but they weren't real friends. Everyone was a suspect or a potential lead, and no one knew who she really was, not even 52 Division's Staff Sergeant King, who had signed her transfer paperwork.

The RCMP set her up with a one-bedroom condo and a Toronto Police Service badge, and she'd ceased to be RCMP Staff Sergeant Kristen Bailey. Her looks helped. A lot. Mounties used whatever assets they had available. In her case, her astute mind and slammin' body weren't interchangeable, but she used both for leverage on different cases. Neither seemed to be working too well on *this* case, though, and she wanted out of Toronto as soon as the job was done.

"Give me another month. If I don't have something solid, I'll pack my bags." Kristen scratched at the imprint of the beer logo on the bottle as she waited for his response. He wouldn't pull her yet. For now, he was making a threat, but she needed to come up with something soon, or his threats wouldn't be so idle.

"Next month will make a year since Richard Oslowe was murdered. If you don't have a solid lead by his anniversary, I'm putting you on a plane back to Ottawa, and you can kiss Banff goodbye."

She swallowed. As much as she wanted to leave Toronto, she didn't want to go back to Ottawa. A position in Banff was a once-in-a-lifetime opportunity, and she desperately didn't want to miss hers. "Understood, sir."

She'd done her tenure with headquarters in the nation's capital, put forward an unmatched solve rate, and shown that her methods were both solid and honest, which was why Ouellette had requested her for the Toronto job in the first place. One more job well done, Ouellette had told her, and she would be made staff sergeant major herself in the Alberta branch.

Unfortunately, this Toronto case was taking much longer than either of them had hoped, and after three months of playing beat cop, Kristen had yet to come up with a single solid suspect. Her hunches so far had been mostly glorified guesses, all of which had led nowhere.

Ouellette let out a long breath on his end of the line. "This isn't a punishment, Bailey. I just don't know how much longer I can postpone things. I have people to answer to as well, and they're getting impatient. This isn't good for first response morale, and it doesn't look good on us. SIU called us in because they weren't making any progress on their own, and they needed someone in custody yesterday. Don't make them regret their decision, and don't make me regret mine. Get me something I can use."

Ouellette was right. It had been very big of the Special Investigations Unit to reach out for help; a great deal of pride must have been swallowed. They needed the offending parties caught and put behind bars, and Ouellette had entrusted Kristen with the task.

"Will do. Goodnight, sir."

"Goodnight, Bailey. Don't disappoint me."

She ended the call and held the phone to her forehead. How was she supposed to come up with a solid lead in one month when the last three had proven fruitless? She moved to the couch, opened her laptop, and selected the video file that she'd seen so many times she had it memorized.

The scene began with Ricky Oslowe, a close-up of his bright blue eye before he moved the camera back a couple of inches and addressed his wife.

"Hi, babe. So, I don't want you to worry, but I've been shot." Here he winced, but the smile came back to his face. "I'm okay, but I wanted to send you a message, you know, just in case."

The background was dark except light coming through the damaged slats of wood from a second-storey window that had been boarded up and then broken.

"I was taking down a drug bust. Probably should have waited for backup." He laughed and winced again. "That's me, though, right? Always going in guns blazing."

A noise sounded behind him, and he turned. In the distance, a door opened. "Just a sec, babe. The paramedics are here," he whispered into the camera. Two people wearing dark uniforms entered the frame. The light filtering in from behind made their features unclear. Oslowe put the phone down. It now captured only the dilapidated roof of the building—an abandoned co-op where the drug deal had gone down—but the audio remained clear. "You guys finally made it. I took a good shot to the stomach, but I don't think it's done any major damage."

"Let's have a look," a man said.

"Okay, but I think we should wait f—" His voice was muffled, and there were sounds of a scuffle and someone gasping for breath. The camera was knocked during the commotion, and caught the final struggle, the last kicks of Ricky Oslowe's legs, before all movement in his body ceased.

In the background, sirens began to wail, the sound getting louder as it came nearer to the building.

"Is it done?" a man asked hurriedly.

"It's done," the other man replied.

The camera caught the men as they turned and ran out of the building. A car door slammed, tires squealed, and the camera timed out just over a minute later. Ricky Oslowe did not speak or move again.

The surrounding traffic and surveillance cameras had both incriminated Rodrigo Cruz of breaking the rules and then exonerated him of being involved in the murder. None of the feeds had picked up a second ambulance arriving at the scene. It was a shoddy back alley with dilapidated buildings, most of which were boarded up. The one surveillance camera that faced the entry had been dead for years, and the videos further out on the streets didn't pick up any ambulances entering the area except the one that had reported into dispatch and found the body.

Kristen leaned back on the couch. In the unit next to hers, the front door closed, and a woman called out that she was home. The squealing voices of her two kids and the bark of her golden retriever soon followed. What would it be like to have a normal life? A job she simply left at the office and someone to come home to instead of the quiet darkness and cold case files? Just the thought of the complications of a relationship had always seemed far more arduous to Kristen than coming home to an empty suite.

When she'd first started meeting women outside of the Depot, it didn't take her long to realize that dating wasn't for her. She'd had a girlfriend in high school—that had been a long month—but as a Mountie, she had a lot of secrets and little personal time.

It was late, and Kristen was too tired to even finish her beer. She was on the last night of her rotation, and four twelve-hour days combined with the heat of midsummer took its toll. It made her next four days off sound blissful.

Her cell rang again, and she closed her eyes before looking at the call display. A relieved smile quickly spread across her face.

"Hey, Jared, what's up?"

As much as Kristen dreaded her nightly call with her staff sergeant major, she loved hearing from her brother an equal amount.

"Want to come up here? The fish are biting like crazy right now," Jared said from the Algonquin cottage he and his wife lived in, about three hours away.

Kristen looked at her watch. "You want me to come up right now?"

"Well, in the morning. We're actually going to head to bed soon, but we could go out early tomorrow and catch some dinner."

She couldn't think of a better way to spend the next few days than out on the water, fishing, drinking beer, and catching up with her older brother. Ouellette had just expedited her deadline, though, and she was cognizant of the slipping sand in the hourglass. Four days was too long to leave the case on hold, so she'd have to bring her laptop with her. The RCMP-issued computer had all the reports, files, recordings, and notes from both before and after she'd been handed the case. Clearing her head outside of the city often helped her add some clarity to her thoughts, but it meant going easy on the beers. She would just have to spend a little more time on her laptop and a little less in the boat this trip.

"Are you sure Cyn won't mind?" Kristen asked.

"Are you kidding? She suggested it."

Jared's wife had always been more than accommodating of her visits. She'd liked Cyndi from the start, which was probably why Kristen had hit on her first.

"Do you want to bring someone up with you?" he asked.

Jared asked her the same question every time, and every time she gave the same answer. "Nobody to bring."

"Just thought I'd offer. So, we'll see you tomorrow?"

"Mmm-hmm." She swallowed a mouthful of beer. "Anything I *can* bring?"

"The usual. Booze. Illegal firearms. Strippers."

She laughed. "See you in the morning."

Kristen ended the call and let out a long sigh. She dumped the last third of her beer down the washroom sink and pulled out her toothbrush. There wouldn't be too many more weekends like this. It was only a matter of time before Jared and Cyndi got pregnant. They'd been talking about it a lot lately. Beyond the fact that the next few months might be the last they had together before a possible new arrival from the stork, Kristen also had to admit that she didn't know how long she would be able to stay this close to Jared geographically. One way or another, this job in Toronto would wrap up in a month, and although the three-hour drive to Algonquin seemed daunting the next morning, it was nothing compared to the five-hour flight Banff would be.

Sleep didn't come easily, but then, it rarely did. She groaned and turned over, trying to ignore the sound of her own heartbeat in her ear as she laid her head against the pillow. It was irritating, like the sound of someone crunching with a steady rhythm through fresh, packing snow. Her thoughts drifted, strangely, to the pretty paramedic from that afternoon. The one with honey-brown hair that fell in shining twists, the one with pale pink lips and possibly the greenest eyes she'd ever seen. They weren't as light as the typical mossy-green eyes most people had, but a fierce, natural green, like the first leaves of grass in the spring.

She turned over in her bed again. With the call she'd just had with Ouellette, she should be thinking about the case, not girls. What was it about this case? Why was nobody talking? She needed the murderers exposed soon, or she'd be stuck here with nothing keeping her in Toronto but an unsolved case and too much time on her hands. That's when she could waste her nights thinking about pretty women, but right now, Banff was calling, and she couldn't wait to answer.

CHAPTER 3

"WHY DO WE ALWAYS GET the crazies?" Rodrigo said under his breath as he stopped the truck.

"We're just lucky, I guess." Ashleigh tried to lighten his mood. "Come on, it looks like this is going to be our last call of the day." She unhooked the radio and brought it up to her mouth. "Ten-seven at Augusta and Cecil." She replaced the radio and Rodrigo laughed. "What?"

"Only greenies say 'ten-seven.'"

"What do you say?" she asked with mild embarrassment.

"I say 'on scene,' like a human being." He laughed and nudged her to show that he meant it good-naturedly.

"I'm not green," she argued weakly.

"One month on the job?" He shook his head. "You'll be green for five years, Paige."

"I was a medic before I started with EMS, you know."

"You're still a greenie here, though." He flashed his smile one more time before a shout on the street interrupted their banter.

A dangerously skinny woman stood outside the window on Ashleigh's side of the truck. She had scraggly, blonde hair that managed to look dry and greasy at the same time. She waved her rail-thin arms around and appeared to be in her sixties, but Ashleigh knew her to be younger. It was amazing how drugs could steal the years away from a person, the ones spent in the spiral and those it shaved off from the end.

They exited the truck to tend to the woman for the third time that month. "How can we help you today?" Ashleigh said with the friendliest smile she could muster.

The woman bared her teeth in response and motioned to her wildly. "What the fuck do you want?"

Ashleigh jerked her head back, actually afraid that if she got closer, the woman might bite her. "We don't want anything," she said soothingly. She held her hands out, palms up, in what was intended to be a calming gesture.

"Don't fuckin' touch me!" the woman screamed.

"Whoa, easy now." Rodrigo came around from his side of the truck, talking to the woman as if he were approaching a bucking mare. "We got a call to come out here, so we have to do our jobs. You know that. Now, we can see nothing's the matter," he said in a placating voice, "so, why don't you help us out here and just tell us why we might have been called so that we can leave."

"Don't know anything about that," she said with a rasp, but she seemed to have calmed a little.

Her eyes were more jaundiced today than the last time Ashleigh had seen her, and she had dark circles around them. There were bruises on both her arms, and her teeth were turning brown. She was an addict for certain, but what she was high on that day and what would calm her down was unclear. She had the right to refuse medical treatment, and if PD ever got there, they would need grounds to detain her and get her off the streets. Even then, throwing her in a group cell, only to be released by Court Services a day later, wouldn't be any more beneficial to her than letting her slink back to whatever hovel she'd crawled out of.

"Is there anyone else here who we might be able to talk to?" Ashleigh asked.

"Ya can ask Frank, but he's the shit who stole my stash." The woman covered her mouth, realizing she had given herself away. It didn't matter. Ashleigh looked around. There was no Frank to be seen.

"Come on, CeCe." Ashleigh used the woman's name to remind her of their standing acquaintance. Did she have any recollection of who they were or how many times they'd been called out to check on a disturbance she had caused? CeCe made a show of sealing her lips and offered a childish smile that made her look ghastly with her rotting teeth. CeCe hadn't looked this rough the last time they'd been called

25

out here, or the time before that. It was like she aged a year every time Ashleigh saw her.

"The cavalry's here." Rodrigo sneered as a cruiser with its lights flashing came into view and pulled up a few feet behind their ambulance. "Let them deal with her."

Ashleigh's face flushed when Constable Bailey stepped out from the driver's side of the squad car. It wasn't normal for someone to be that attractive. Today, Bailey wasn't wearing her aviators, and Ashleigh found herself falling into beautiful, laughing, blue eyes.

"Paige, Cruz, what a pleasure." Bailey quirked her head around them. "Ah, CeCe, what have you done now?"

CeCe pouted and crossed her arms, the wildness in her dissipating under Bailey's gaze. CeCe may not have recognized Ashleigh and Rodrigo, but it was clear that Bailey's presence affected her.

"I've met her a few times before. Is she dangerous?" Ashleigh asked, since Bailey seemed to know her.

"No, not if she's on her meds." Bailey moved her focus to CeCe. "You wouldn't hurt anyone, would you?"

Ashleigh couldn't help but smile at Bailey's casualness. She found it comforting, and relaxed just being in her presence.

"Do you know if she has her meds on her?" Bailey asked.

"We're not friskin' her," Rodrigo said, as if disgusted by the idea. "It's much funner to watch you do it."

"All right, take it easy, Captain Grammar." Bailey walked around him to CeCe. "How are you doing, honey?" Ashleigh was taken aback by the sudden change in her tone, by the kindness in it.

"I don't feel well," she said sadly.

"I know," Bailey said sympathetically. "Where are your pills?" CeCe shook her head in response. "You know you need to take those. Now, did you pick up your last cheque from Ontario Works?"

"I lost it." The woman's eyes filled with tears, and her bottom lip began to tremble. For the first time, Ashleigh's heart ached for the addict, and she felt like a complete jerk for having judged her.

"Shh, it's okay."

If Ashleigh had been surprised before, she was dumbfounded when Bailey pulled the strung-out drug addict into her arms for a hug.

"Shh." Bailey rubbed her back gently, then did a surreptitious pat-down so quickly and smoothly that CeCe didn't even seem to notice it. "It's okay. We're going to help you find it."

"We?" Rodrigo said from beside her. "Fuck that. You're here now. We're leaving."

Ashleigh's eyes narrowed. When she turned toward Rodrigo, there was hatred and disgust etched on his face, and she wasn't sure if it was directed at Bailey, CeCe, or both of them equally. Bailey's partner, on the other hand, hadn't even gotten out of the car yet, and on closer inspection, he was eating a rapidly melting soft-ice-cream cone.

"Don't listen to that mean old monkey," Bailey said with a kind smile. She slowly pulled CeCe away from her until she was at arm's length in front of her. "Now, do you remember picking up the cheque?"

CeCe nodded.

"Good. Was it today?"

CeCe looked like she was about to start crying again.

"It's okay. Let's just try to retrace your steps. Where did you go after you picked up the cheque?"

Ashleigh was sure they weren't going to get a straight answer out of her, but with a few more soft rubs to her arms, Bailey managed to finesse one.

"I went home."

Ashleigh was surprised she had a home.

"Why don't we check there and see what we can find, then?" Bailey said.

"No." CeCe shook her head.

"No? But how are we going to find your cheque if we don't look for it?"

"I don't want the monkey to come."

Bailey threw her head back and laughed. It was a beautiful sight. "I wouldn't let that mean old monkey anywhere near your fine home," she assured her.

CeCe seemed to find that acceptable, because she began to walk in the direction of what Ashleigh assumed was home, with Bailey following closely before the officer turned back to look at Ashleigh. "Are you coming?" Bailey's gaze met hers, and Ashleigh was drawn in.

She looked to Rodrigo, who gave a curt shake of his head.

"Yes," she said.

Rodrigo's gaze hardened.

"I'll be right back," she whispered to him before sauntering off to catch up with them.

"I knew it," Bailey said so that only she could hear.

"Knew what?"

"That you had a backbone in there somewhere, Paige."

Ashleigh wasn't sure if she'd just been complimented or insulted, but the fact that Bailey had thought anything about her at all made her grin. "How far does she live?" she asked.

"Just at the end of this row." Bailey nodded her head to indicate the rundown apartment buildings they were passing. Most of them were low-rises and had windows that were either broken, boarded up, or covered. The brick buildings were stained, and the whole neighbourhood stank of urine. "When we get in there, don't touch anything that isn't you. She's as clean as a whistle when she's manic and on her meds, but when she's in a low or on street drugs, the place can be a real hellhole. I've seen as many roaches there as I've seen strangers. The sober her would be sick if she could see herself."

That comment made Ashleigh sad. "How do you know all this?"

"She was one of my first calls. When I first saw her, she was high and unkempt, but it wasn't so bad then. A lot of cops think you have to be hard with everybody to get respect, but I learned pretty quickly that people respect kindness a lot more than fear or cruelty."

"Catch more flies with honey," Ashleigh said.

"Something like that."

She was surprised to hear a cop talking this way. Maybe she'd been a little judgmental, not only about CeCe but about the police as well. Ever since Rodrigo had told her about the divide between the police and paramedics, she'd wondered how it had ever eluded her. The animosity was almost palpable some days, and being an EMT, she found herself growing closer to her department and allowing the margin of that divide to grow. Being around Bailey, on the other hand, made her wish it wasn't so.

"She hates men, though," Bailey laughed, bringing Ashleigh back to their conversation. "Unless she's sleeping with them, and even then I think they get shit treatment from her. It's just up here." She put a hand out in front of Ashleigh to stop her. CeCe turned up a flight of stairs, and Bailey grabbed the heavy door and held it open for Ashleigh to enter. Ashleigh looked up. It wasn't one of the boarded-up brick buildings. It was a glass and steel condo. A new build. She hadn't expected that.

"Thank you," she said to Bailey as she passed her.

At the top of two flights of stairs, CeCe made a turn down a well-maintained corridor, going about her business ahead of them, trailing her hand along the paint on the wall as she walked, and Ashleigh wondered if she even remembered that they were there with her.

At her unit, Bailey stopped CeCe before she opened the door. "Why don't you let me take a look around first?" After a moment, CeCe nodded her head, and Bailey turned to Ashleigh. "Sometimes she has guests, and they don't exactly remember each other. I'm going to clear it." She opened the door and slipped inside, then closed it behind her.

Ashleigh's heartbeat quickened. Bailey shouldn't be in there alone. Anything could happen to her. She was armed, but they had no idea how many people were in there. Beside her, CeCe whimpered. When she looked at her, she was crying again.

"I'm sorry," CeCe said.

Ashleigh wasn't sure what to say, so she said nothing.

"You were right about him, Jenna. I should have listened."

Ashleigh opened her mouth to answer, still unsure of what to say, when the door to the apartment opened again.

"All clear," Bailey announced.

CeCe went in, but Ashleigh stopped Bailey at the door. "Who's Jenna?"

"Her daughter. Why?"

"She said that she was sorry and that she should have listened to her."

Bailey shrugged. "Who knows what she meant. I don't know if she's still in contact with her daughter or not. She has these moments of lucidity where she's here, you know, but they never last."

"That's so sad," Ashleigh said quietly.

"Yeah, well, welcome to every day of the rest of your life."

"What do you mean?"

Bailey pointed at her. "Wearing that uniform in Toronto means dealing with crack addicts and indigents half of your day, every day." Bailey looked around. "Now, let's see if we can find her cheque."

Inside, the home reflected a strange dichotomy of character. There were old family pictures on the wall in beautiful frames, but they hung crookedly, and on two, the glass panes were broken. There was a picture of CeCe that looked to be taken a few years ago, but God, did she look different. She looked happy, healthy. If the photograph hadn't been in her home, Ashleigh wouldn't have even made the connection. There was a young woman beside her in the photograph, somewhere close to Ashleigh's age, with light brown hair and a kind smile. *Probably Jenna.* What had happened to make them stop speaking? *Probably the drugs.*

She continued to peer around the room. CeCe's couches were leather but worn and cracked and stained. The wood coffee table was warped and looked like someone had recently made a bed of it. Ashleigh walked into the kitchen, where a cockroach scurried into the sink.

"Paige, get in here," Bailey whispered harshly from the washroom. "What's wrong with her? I mean, medically, what are her conditions?" She handed her four empty pill bottles to examine. "I took them from the garbage."

They were standing close together in the small washroom, so close that Ashleigh could feel the warmth of Bailey's skin. She closed her eyes for a second as she breathed her in. It was both feminine and masculine at the same time, earthy and clean, and it made her light-headed.

"Do you know what the pills are for?" Bailey asked, which forced Ashleigh to open her eyes.

She swallowed and studied the small, empty bottles in her hands. "She's bipolar," she said after reading the first, then moved on to the next. "She also has borderline personality disorder." She turned the next bottle to read it.

"Borderline personality disorder? I don't think I like the sound of that."

"Psychosis and psoriasis," Ashleigh said, determined not to smile at Bailey's words.

"What's psoriasis?"

"Basically, chronic dry skin and scalp."

"Oh, is that the dandruff du jour? I'll have what she's having then; sounds a lot sexier than saying my Head and Shoulders ran out."

This time, Ashleigh did smile. "It's not a good combination, that's for sure, but if she's on her meds, then she should be okay...and dandruff-free," she added good-naturedly.

"We need to find her cheque, then."

"Isn't it likely she's already spent it?"

"It is," Bailey agreed. She put the bottles back into the garbage. "You carry drugs in the truck, don't you?"

"Not for all of these things. I mean, we're not a drug store. I have an antipsychotic and some lithium, but not knowing what street drug she's on now, I wouldn't want to give her anything that could cause a reaction."

"Well, she needs something. We can't leave her like this."

"I found it!" CeCe called from the other room. Ashleigh shared a bewildered look with Bailey before leaving the bathroom to find CeCe holding a flyer from Walmart.

"That's...great." Bailey took it from her. "You stay here, and I'll make sure to get your prescriptions filled with this money, okay?" CeCe smiled proudly, still enjoying her victory. "I mean it, CeCe. If I come back here and you're gone, I'm going to be very sad, okay?"

Outside of the apartment, Ashleigh hurried to keep up with Bailey. "Where's the fire?" she asked, narrowly sidestepping a dumpster in the alleyway.

Bailey laughed, never slowing her rhythm. "You sound like an old man."

Ashleigh reddened. That was so not how she wanted Bailey to see her. Come to think of it, though, it was an expression her dad used and no one else she knew of.

"We have about fifteen minutes until she forgets we were ever there," Bailey said, thankfully not referring to her in any other unflattering way before getting back to business. "I want to get her medication to her. Then you can figure out what she can and can't take."

"And you're going to pay for it with that half-price Salisbury steak coupon?"

"Heh, I wish." She turned to her with a smile as she rounded the corner. "The pharmacy on her prescription bottles is just on this block. I'm going to see if they'll fill them for us."

Us? Ashleigh mused, following her into the drugstore. When they reached the counter, it took a little cajoling, but the pharmacist knew CeCe well enough. After a check of both of their government IDs—as if the uniforms weren't enough—he agreed to fill the bottles for them.

The pharmacist also had her government reimbursement information on file, so the pills came to just under fifty dollars. When Bailey pulled her wallet from one of the cargo pockets in her uniform pants, Ashleigh could not contain her astonishment. "*You're* going to pay for them?"

"Well, like you said, I don't think they're interested in the Salisbury steak coupon. Though I must say, two for five dollars sounds like a good deal." Bailey took the white paper bag but interrupted the pharmacist when he started to explain what to take when. "I've got a medic with me. We're okay."

The confidence in Bailey's voice surprised Ashleigh. If she didn't trust the paramedics to provide adequate healthcare, then why the assurance in her training now? Was it because the care was for a welfare case and not a cop? Nothing of her treatment of CeCe so far had led Ashleigh to believe that Bailey thought she deserved subpar service, so could it be that Bailey really did have faith in her abilities?

The walk back was actually a sprint, and Ashleigh was out of breath from trying to keep up with Bailey, who climbed the stairs two at a time ahead of her.

Inside, CeCe was asleep on the couch. She'd left the door unlocked. Bailey motioned for Ashleigh to step back when she approached her and leaned down to wake her.

"CeCe, time to wake up now," Bailey said softly. When there was no response, she tried giving her a little shake.

CeCe woke up in a flash, taking a swing at Bailey. Unfortunately, she had a bottle of vodka in her hand. The bottle crunched against Bailey's skull, and nausea roiled through Ashleigh. Bailey dropped to the ground. Ashleigh rushed to Bailey's side as CeCe got to her feet and rounded on Ashleigh now as a predator would its prey.

"Now, now." Ashleigh stood up slowly, trying to calm her. "We're only here to help you. This officer has your medicine. If you just let me check on her, I can—"

CeCe raised the bottle to strike her, and Ashleigh threw her hands up instinctively to protect her face, but the bottle never made contact.

Bailey launched to her feet and knocked it out of CeCe's hand, then grabbed for her outstretched arm and twisted it behind her back. When CeCe lashed out and tried to scratch her, Bailey pinned the woman's arms to her sides. CeCe began to spit at her, and Bailey wrapped an arm around her chest and squeezed tight, binding her lungs until the fight left CeCe. She slumped forward in Bailey's arms, unconscious.

"What the hell did you just do?" Ashleigh asked wide-eyed.

"I suppose I could have let her clobber you with that bottle," Bailey said flippantly as she gently lowered CeCe to the ground. "Would that have been preferable?" Ashleigh was speechless. "We need to take her down to your truck. We can't leave her here now."

"No kidding." Ashleigh pulled the radio from her belt up to her mouth. "Rodrigo, bring the stretcher down the alleyway. I'll come meet you at the bottom of her building."

"Ten-four," Rodrigo said, a smile in his voice as he teasingly supplied the numbered code.

"Cute," Bailey said from beside her. "You use codes like you know what they mean."

Her words stung, and Ashleigh wondered at the change in her countenance. Getting hit over the head with a vodka bottle might sour one's mood, though. She paused for a moment, trying to think of something to say back, but it was more important to get the stretcher upstairs before CeCe woke again, so Ashleigh left Bailey in the unit to rub her head while she went to meet her partner. She found Rodrigo just as he approached the condo.

"We need to hurry."

"Why? What happened up there?"

Ashleigh opened her mouth to tell him, then thought better of it. Bailey would have to fill out a report for what she'd done, and it would come into question if she had used excessive force, and they would be questioned as to what they were doing up in CeCe's condo in the first place. She might be new on the job, but she was sure that buying drugs and giving them to a drug addict was probably not strictly to code.

"CeCe passed out," she said and refused to answer any more of his questions on the way up the stairs.

Inside, Bailey had moved CeCe to the couch. "Thank God you're here." Bailey feigned wiping sweat from her brow as she spoke to Rodrigo. "I was so worried she'd die before you got off your ass and made it up the stairs."

"Bite me," he grumbled.

"No thanks." Bailey slipped by them to the doorway. "I assume you can handle it from here?" The question must have been rhetorical, because she didn't wait for an answer before leaving the unit.

"Fucking bitch," Rodrigo said absentmindedly as he strapped CeCe's legs to the bottom of the stretcher.

"She's not... She's not that bad," Ashleigh said, doing the same with CeCe's upper body. "She seems pretty kind, actually."

"She's PD," he said flatly. "She doesn't do anything unless she expects something in return."

If Rodrigo was right, she didn't know what Bailey expected from anyone after shelling out fifty bucks for a drug addict's medication and then taking a whack from a liquor bottle.

Once they had CeCe strapped in, they carefully carried the stretcher down the stairs. When they got to the truck, Bailey was rifling through the back of it.

"Hey, get out of there!" Rodrigo yelled at her as if she were a raccoon in his garbage bin.

"Take it easy, big guy." Bailey hopped out of the truck with a smile that did not reach her eyes. "Just taking a look around."

Bailey had several large gauze compresses fisted in her right hand, and when she turned, the back of her head was matted with blood. Ashleigh's insides quaked, and her knees wobbled. For the first time, she was sick at the sight of blood. "Let me look at that," she said unevenly as she fought off a wave of nausea.

What's happening to me?

34

"No," Bailey said quickly. "I'll take care of it myself."

"It looks bad." She swallowed. "With that much blood, you likely have a concussion."

"I'm fine."

"She's fine," Rodrigo echoed, a warning in his voice to Ashleigh.

"She doesn't look fine."

"Just a scratch. A scratch! Ask for me tomorrow, and you shall find me a grave man!"

"What the fuck are you talking about?" Rodrigo asked.

"No one?" Bailey looked at Ashleigh who shook her head. "*Romeo and Juliet*. Geez, don't they make you guys go to school before giving you your Fisher Price medical certificates?"

That one stung. Ashleigh was tired of hearing people ask her why she hadn't become a *real* doctor. She was proud of what she did, but she was not immune to the disdain of others, no matter how hard she tried to be.

"Are you capable of taking anything seriously?" Ashleigh asked her scathingly.

"You show me a serious problem, Paige, and I'll take it seriously." Bailey looked to her partner, who was finally getting out of the car. "Great, the backup's awoken."

"Not enjoying your partnership?" Ashleigh asked. This time, she was the one who was amused.

"Oh yeah, he's a gorgeous TO. Dumb as an ox and slow as a mule."

"TO?" Ashleigh tilted her head to the side. "Why are you riding with a training officer?"

Bailey's jaw tensed for a moment before her easy smile replaced the expression and she quipped, "He's fallen in love with me. Now, don't go doing the same, Paige. I see the way you look at me."

Ashleigh flushed from her neck to the tips of her ears. She found Bailey irritating and aloof; she hadn't been looking at her in any other kind of way—had she?

"If you've had your fun, we need to get her to the hospital," Rodrigo interrupted, looking between Ashleigh and Bailey in disgust. "I assume she isn't being charged with anything?"

"Just tell her to start taking her meds. I hate to see her like this when some counseling and a few pills could put her back into society." She shook her head, then winced before her eyes took on a mischievous glint. "Who knows? Maybe with the right prescription cocktail she could have your job in a week, Cruz. That's about how long the training to become a fake doctor takes, right?"

A scowl was her reward. "Fuck you, Bailey."

CHAPTER 4

If Kristen thought her head hurt when the bottle cracked it, she hadn't yet met pain. Two hours later, it was so bad that she had to pull her car over. She had just left Mount Sinai, the hospital CeCe had been taken to. Hackett hadn't made a big deal about her head injury, thankfully. After he asked her if she was okay and Kristen explained that she didn't want the EMTs touching her, he shrugged and told her she should get it checked out at a hospital. Their shift had just been ending, and that was exactly what she'd done. Only, she'd gone into Mount Sinai after she was sure Paige and Cruz had left. First, she asked the nurses about CeCe's condition. Given that CeCe's lungs had collapsed, Kristen wanted to make sure that she was okay. She followed up that enquiry with one about her own head trauma. The look of betrayal on Paige's face when she refused care had been hard to take, but she had to keep up appearances in front of Hackett. Had she been alone, there was no doubt she would have let Paige examine her. She would have welcomed it.

What she hadn't intended to do was put CeCe in the hospital, but her adrenaline had kicked in. When the bottle had connected, she'd seen a shower of lights cascading before her eyes, like fireworks exploding inside her mind, as the excruciating pain ripped through the back of her head. She'd dropped to her knees and wished she could just lie down and die. Her first attempt to stand had made her waver, but when she'd seen CeCe closing in on Paige, bottle still in hand, she'd found the strength to get up off her knees.

At the hospital, she'd waited impatiently for the paramedics to leave. A quick flash of her Toronto Police Service shield to the ER staff got her right through for an MRI, which confirmed the pretty paramedic's suspicions of a concussion. The doctor told Kristen that it wasn't too severe, but that she should keep an eye on it and come back if her headache or nausea worsened or if she started showing other signs such as vomiting or amnesia. When asked if she had someone to wake her every hour, Kristen nodded, thinking that her phone's alarm clock would have to do.

Kristen got out of her car and walked into the nearest establishment on College Street, a bar and grill. She hadn't much of a plan except to get out of the sweltering heat of summer and into some air conditioning while her head cleared. As she waited for the bartender, she contemplated the events of the afternoon. It wasn't like her to be so friendly with the EMTs in front of Hackett, and she wondered if her so-called TO would say anything to the other cops about it. He certainly hadn't been quiet about his disdain for her before now.

"I'll have a Blanton's." She pointed to the bourbon on the top shelf. "Pour it with a heavy hand." It was a term she'd learned while bartending undercover through one of her first assignments out of the Depot, and she found that it worked in most establishments. The bartender nodded knowingly, and his perfectly styled blond hair did not move in the least. She appreciated the generosity of his pour. "Can you throw a few ice cubes in there?"

He obliged, showing off his handsome smile. The bourbon was cold and smooth on her lips, and she resisted the urge to sigh as it slid down into her stomach and started its slow burn.

"You know, you shouldn't drink with a concussion."

Paramedic Paige was smiling beside her, leaning over the bar in a seductive manner—or at least that's how Kristen saw it. She had changed out of her uniform, and Kristen found her equally—if not more—attractive in a pair of slim jeans and a tight, white V-neck T-shirt. She wore a thin silver chain around her neck, which fell into the dip between her clavicle. It was a hot day, and Kristen wasn't sure if the gleam on Paige's skin was from sweat or the shower she'd obviously just taken. The smell of her fresh shampoo wafted over, and her hair was still a bit damp. When Kristen took in a deep breath, it was sweet, feminine, and extremely enticing. She gritted her teeth. There was no way she was going to let Paige guess at the direction of her thoughts.

"If I need medical advice, there's a hospital down the street," she said into her glass. Her tone was more acerbic than she'd intended, but she hadn't expected to have her head filled with Paige's tantalizing scent.

Paige dropped her smile, and she looked hurt.

"I'm sorry, that was rude. Let me buy you a drink. We both had a hard day," Kristen said.

"No, thank you."

"Don't be pissed. Please, have a drink."

"I don't drink."

"No? Too many wild parties in your past?"

Paige shook her head, and those light brown locks swayed around her face. They released more of her soft, sweet scent. "If you were in my line of work and saw what that stuff really does to you, you wouldn't drink it either."

"And if you were in mine and saw the things I've seen, Paige, you would."

"Fair enough." Her smile easily returned. "It's Ashleigh, by the way." She extended a hand.

"Kristen." She shook her hand and smiled, noting the unexpected firmness in Ashleigh's grip. Not so strong as if she had something to prove, but firm enough to tell her that the soft curve of her bicep wasn't just for show.

Kristen was pleased that Ashleigh Paige was offering her first name up. In their industry, it was strictly last names, and although she'd insulted her a few times that day, Paige—no, Ashleigh—still made a kind effort to talk to her.

"So, what's a nice girl like you doing in a bar if you don't drink?"

The bartender reappeared, this time with a glass of sparkling water and a smile that was clearly meant exclusively for Ashleigh. "You want the usual, or are you going to change it up on me now?" he asked flirtatiously.

Kristen noticed for the first time that his smile was exceedingly charming—if you were into nice, good-looking guys with teeth so white you could navigate the wilderness with them.

"The usual." Ashleigh mirrored his grin, and a wave of nausea came over Kristen.

"So that's why you come here," she said. Before Ashleigh could answer, Kristen rolled her eyes and finished her drink.

"How many of those have you had?"

"Not enough." She shook her glass at the bartender. He obliged, this time putting it on the rocks before he poured. Kristen polished off half the glass in one long sip, holding the ice back with her teeth as the bourbon slid down her throat.

"I really don't think you should be doing that," Ashleigh said.

"And I really don't remember asking for your opinion." Kristen felt like a jerk the second the words left her mouth, but she couldn't help herself. If Ashleigh Paige was there to flirt with the bartender, then she should get on with it and leave her alone. She couldn't remember ever having such a bad headache, and this conversation was exacerbating it.

"It's not an opinion," Ashleigh said tersely. "You've—" The rest of her sentence died on her lips when Kristen fell to the side, almost slipping off her chair. "Shit, Bailey." Ashleigh caught her and steadied her on her stool. "You need to go home and lie down. I'm sure you have a concussion, and drinking is just about the stupidest thing you could be doing right now." When the bartender appeared with Ashleigh's food in a to-go container, the paramedic threw a credit card onto the bar. "That's for the food and her drinks. I'll be back to pick it up tomorrow."

The bartender didn't argue with Ashleigh, and when she pushed Kristen's drink down the bar and out of her reach, neither did Kristen. Ashleigh put a hand on her cheek and forced her to meet her gaze. Kristen tried to face her, but it was a struggle. Her vision was blurry. She felt like she'd been drugged. Ashleigh's hand was warm on her skin, and suddenly much too hot. She shirked away from her and lost her balance again, but Ashleigh reached a hand out and steadied her on the stool once more.

"We have to get you home. Now." Ashleigh looked around. "Did you drive here?"

Kristen's mouth felt thick, like she couldn't talk, so she nodded, which turned out to be the worst idea in the world.

"With a concussion this bad, you need to be woken up through the night. Do you have someone at home to watch you?"

She didn't answer. Why wouldn't Ashleigh just leave her alone and let her fall over?

"Give me your keys."

"What?" She squinted at her. "No."

"Give me your keys, Bailey." Ashleigh's voice was stern. "You may not be drunk, but you'll be driving like you've had a full bottle, and you look even worse. Give me your keys and your address. I'm going to take you home." When Kristen made no move to acquiesce, Ashleigh's voice grew more commanding. "I'm not going to let you kill somebody. Give me your keys."

Swallowing hard, Kristen handed them over.

Kristen slumped forward in her seat. Only her seatbelt kept her in place. Her head hung low and to the side. Her headache was unbearable. She was vaguely cognizant of the fact that she was slipping in and out of consciousness. In one of her moments of awareness, her throat constricted. She was going to be sick.

"Pull over," she groaned. Before the car stopped, she had the door open and was throwing up out the passenger side. Everything was foggy. She wiped her mouth and closed the door and was surprised to see Ashleigh Paige there in the driver's seat. "What's happening?" she asked, barely able to stay awake.

"You all done?" Ashleigh asked in response.

Kristen let her head hang. It was all she had the energy for.

"The GPS says we're almost there."

Almost where? They pulled up to her building, and in her half-conscious state, she knew the unthinkable was happening; someone was coming into her condo.

"You have to go," Kristen said weakly.

Ashleigh ignored her and parked the car. "What's your suite number?"

"You can't come up," Kristen said, unwilling, even in this state, to break her rules.

"I'm not going anywhere until you're inside and in bed, so tell me your suite number, and we can get on with it."

She couldn't do it. No one knew where she lived. She'd never brought anyone home with her. Ashleigh huffed and reached across her into the glove box. She must have found what she was looking for, because she opened her door, walked around to Kristen's, and wrenched it open.

"Let's go." Ashleigh reached down and unbuckled her seatbelt for her. She was holding the insurance papers to the car in her other hand. Kristen's address and suite number were there.

She didn't want to go in, but she was barely hanging on to consciousness, so she grudgingly allowed Ashleigh to help her out of her seat and onto her feet. Ashleigh slammed the car door closed, and Kristen winced as the noise assaulted her eardrums.

"Lean on me," Ashleigh instructed, and this time, Kristen didn't argue.

At her unit, there was fumbling with some keys until the fob was swiped and finally the door opened. She stumbled into her condo, leaning heavily against a body. It smelled sweet and familiar, and then there was nothing.

———•••———

Ashleigh found the light switch just inside the entryway. There was a small kitchen to her left, and a living space in front of her that opened up to two doors on the right. She made her way to the door on the left, supporting almost all of Bailey's weight. She'd made the correct door choice and found her bedroom. Ashleigh helped ease Kristen onto the covers. She thought of helping her change her clothes, but the inappropriateness of it stopped her from even trying. She did, however, slip Bailey's running shoes from her feet and took them with her when she left the room.

It was only just after seven in the evening, which meant she had a really long night ahead of her. She opened her phone's alarm setting and set one for every hour until six the next morning, when she'd have to leave for her shift.

In the kitchen, she found drinking glasses and filled one with water. When she brought the glass to the bedroom, Kristen was sound asleep.

Ashleigh spied a bottle of Advil by her bed and wished she could give her some, but this was a concussion, not a headache. She took the bottle and moved it onto the dresser, out of reach. After she set down the water glass, Ashleigh checked to make sure Bailey was breathing all right. She watched her chest rise and fall in her black tank top. Her eyes were closed, and her dark red lips were slightly parted, showing straight, pearly teeth. Somehow, Bailey managed to be exceptionally alluring even as she slept.

Her hair looked the same in bed as when she was awake. She sported the messy look well. Just then, Kristen's brow tightened as if in pain, and she turned slightly on the bed, which allowed her tank top to rise up along her ribs and Ashleigh to see a few inches of newly exposed skin around her midriff.

Ashleigh swallowed and deliberately forced her gaze away from Kristen's torso. Ever the medic, she leaned forward and put two fingers to her throat, feeling for her pulse. Kristen didn't react to the contact, and Ashleigh quickly found the steady rhythm of her heartbeat. It was normal, if a little on the low side, but nothing to be concerned about. Given Bailey's physique, she must exercise regularly, so a lower resting heart rate would be normal.

Medically, there was nothing more she could do for her. She'd spent long nights looking in on patients in Kenya who had received concussions from blows to the head with weapons ranging from metal pipes to gun whacks, so why was she lingering, watching Kristen sleep? It was going to be a long night, and soon, she'd be sick of the room, she was sure.

She tried to step lightly on the birch laminate flooring. It didn't seem to match Bailey's personality, but then, what did she know about Kristen Bailey? When Rodrigo had accused her of looting their truck, Bailey had certainly made an exit with her recriminating remarks about paramedics, but still, Ashleigh hadn't been able to stop thinking about her. At first, it had been about what a jerk she'd become after being hit with that bottle. She'd gone from playful and helpful to irritated and scornful in seconds. Ashleigh felt like she was dealing with two different people. The only thing both versions of Bailey seemed to have in common was her wicked grin and flippant comments.

Oh, and that sexy-as-hell way she did and said everything.

Not that Ashleigh had noticed that part. She certainly wasn't going to think any more about it in the threshold of Bailey's bedroom.

Ashleigh pushed thoughts of Kristen from her mind. She was too jacked up on energy to even think about sleep, and the smell of Bailey's room, which was an extension of the warm, musky scent of the woman herself, had an intoxicating effect on Ashleigh. She told herself that her visits to the bedroom would be done quickly and efficiently. The desire to linger was already much greater than she'd anticipated...and again... she was thinking about Bailey.

She groaned and moved to the couch where she flipped through the stations for the better part of fifteen minutes before dropping the controller in frustration. She was restless and still buzzing from being in Bailey's personal space.

She walked the small layout of the condo. She bit her lip as she moved through the open concept living area. She looked inside drawers and cabinets, then closed them with embarrassment, only to open another right after. If Bailey woke up, she would not be happy about Ashleigh snooping, but she couldn't help herself.

She wanted to know the types of plates Bailey had and if they all matched. They did, and they were few. She checked to see if she drank coffee or tea and if she had a favourite mug. She drank coffee, and the mugs were simple and uniform. She wanted to know the weight of her utensils and what items stocked her fridge. The cutlery was from IKEA, and there wasn't much at all in her fridge—five bottles of Muskoka Mad Tom IPA, a carton of eggs with three left in it, ketchup with no sugar added, a glass jar of grainy mustard, an old piece of manchego cheese, a head of lettuce that was badly wilting, two apples, one of them fatally bruised, and a bag of celery that had seen better days. *Cops.* She closed the fridge.

In the living area, she found one picture in a frame. It was of Bailey and a man that bore a striking resemblance to her. It looked recent, and both were holding up a big fish with a body of water in the background. They were grinning the same beautiful, wide smile. As she looked at Kristen, Ashleigh wished that smile were turned toward her.

The alarm sounded, and the vibration of her phone in her pocket startled her. Surprised an hour had passed, she turned off the alarm and returned to the bedroom.

The blinds were closed, but the summer sun in Toronto was still as bright as day, even in the evening. Bailey might freak a little when she woke her, but she knew she had to do it.

"Bailey," she tried, but the word caught in her throat. She cleared it and tried again. "Kristen?" She put a hand to her sinewy shoulder and shook her gently. The skin where her hand made contact was firm and warm.

"Hmm?" Bailey made a noise but didn't open her eyes. For a cop, she certainly was not a paranoid sleeper, but maybe that was the concussion.

"Kristen," she repeated, trying to acclimatize herself to saying her given name. "Hey, you need to open your eyes for a minute, okay?"

Bailey made a similar sound to the first, but this time, her eyelids flitted open briefly before closing again.

"That's it," Ashleigh encouraged. "Open your eyes, and look at me a moment."

Bailey let out a small, irritated grunt before opening her eyes. This time, she stared at Ashleigh. Her expression cleared after a few moments. "What are you doing here?"

"You have a concussion," Ashleigh said quickly. "We ran into each other, and I took you home. You're okay."

Kristen nodded her head slowly and swallowed audibly. "The doctor said I shouldn't sleep too long." Her voice was gravelly as her eyes closed again.

So she had seen a doctor? That would explain why she'd run into her in the hospital district. The knowledge irked Ashleigh, and she was again reminded of the comments that Kristen had made about seeing a *real* doctor after she'd refused her help. She tried to push the thought away. This was no time to argue.

"How are you feeling?" she asked instead.

Bailey's eyes opened again, but the effort looked strained. "Tired."

"Okay, go back to sleep. I'll be back to check on you in an hour. If you need anything, I'm just in the other room. Is there anything I can get you now?"

Kristen swallowed slowly. "Water?"

"It's right here." Ashleigh picked up the glass and placed it in Kristen's hand. When Bailey had a grip, she let go. Kristen took several large gulps, leaned back again, and let Ashleigh take the glass from her.

"Thank you," Bailey whispered, her eyes closing.

Ashleigh put the glass back onto the nightstand and couldn't stop herself from putting a hand to Kristen's cheek. It was warm, and Kristen turned her face into her hand.

"Mmm," Bailey murmured, and the sound made Ashleigh's stomach stir. She removed her hand from Bailey's face and hurried from her bedside.

In the living room, she replayed in her mind the sound that Bailey had just made, and her stomach flipped again.

No, no, no. She was not going to fall for Kristen Bailey. Bailey was a cop, an incredibly arrogant one at that, and Ashleigh was not attracted to women like her. A flashback of Denise brought an abrupt halt to that train of thought.

Ashleigh's stomach grumbled, and this time, the activity was something she could agree with. She remembered the supper she'd brought with her from the bar.

She ate her salad out of the takeout container while playing with a Euchre app on her phone, but soon tired of it. She was getting anxious to see Bailey again, and that unnerved her. She refilled her glass of water, wishing that Kristen at least had club soda, but she was forced to drink it flat, which she hated. She pulled out her phone and stopped the alarm before it was to sound in two minutes. Finally, it was time to check on her again.

The room was a little darker this time, but the sun had not yet set, so she didn't need to turn on any lights to see her. She entered the room slowly to test if Kristen would wake. She didn't, so Ashleigh approached the bed.

"Hey." She gave her shoulder a gentle shake. Bailey didn't stir, so she tried it again with a little more force.

This time, Kristen's eyes shot open, and surprise registered when she saw Ashleigh.

"It's okay," Ashleigh said with a friendly smile. "You have a concussion from an altercation this afternoon. I was there with you, and now I'm here to check on you."

Bailey still looked confused.

"You got hit in the head, but you're okay," she said. She didn't want Bailey to have to think too hard. "I'm going to be here through the night to wake you up every hour, so try not to be alarmed when you see me, okay? You're doing just fine."

Kristen looked like she might argue, but her fatigue won out. She closed her eyes and drifted back into sleep. Ashleigh sighed in disappointment. She had been hoping for more time with her, which was ridiculous. She didn't even know this woman. From the doorway, she watched Bailey for a moment. There was nothing wrong with finding her attractive, as long as she took it no further, and how could she help it? Bailey was gorgeous. Ashleigh wasn't naïve enough to think Bailey was unaware of her own charm. Images of Denise using her and kicking her out in a drunken, post carnal haze flashed before her. She turned from the room and pressed her back against the outside wall. This was as far as it would go. Bailey was hot. She'd noticed. Good for her. That would be the end of it.

She returned to the living area and looked around a moment before she approached the single bookshelf in the corner by the small breakfast table. She wasn't sure what she had expected to find but smiled when she saw what looked to be twenty books in the same murder mystery series. The author was Anne Perry, and all the books looked well loved. For some reason, it amused her that a cop would read crime fiction. She ran her fingers along the titles and along some others she didn't recognize. She had never been a huge reader, but her fingers stopped when they came across *Where the Red Fern Grows*. It had been at least ten years since she'd read it.

She pulled the paperback from the shelf and tried to remember if this was the same cover as the copy she had read so many years ago. It definitely looked familiar. It had been the first full-length novel she had ever read on her own. She remembered staying up late, hoping her parents wouldn't notice that her light was still on as she read long into the night about Old Dan and Little Ann's adventures. She took the book back to the couch with her and opened the first page.

Ashleigh had been reading steadily when her alarm went off again, and it startled her. It was amazing the way a book could take her out of where she was and into a whole other world. An impressive feat for Billy and his dogs, considering she was just one room away from Kristen Bailey. It was getting darker in the apartment, and her eyes must have adjusted while she was reading. She put the book face down at the page she had reached, not wanting to dog-ear someone else's copy, and turned on the floor lamp by the couch before going in to check on Kristen. It was darker in the bedroom. Next time she came in, she would need to turn a light on, but she could get away without it this time.

"Kristen," she said softly, trying to wake her gently. She didn't stir, and Ashleigh realized with the faint light in the room that it might startle her to have a shadow leaning over her when she woke. She took a seat on the edge of the bed and tried again. "Kristen?" She put a hand on the blue-jeaned leg next to her and gave it a little shake. Kristen's eyes opened slowly, but there was no surprise in them this time.

"Hey." Kristen's voice was hoarse from sleep.

"Hey." Ashleigh smiled. "How are you feeling?"

"Tired." Bailey blinked slowly. "I remember," she said and left it at that.

"Good," Ashleigh replied, but Kristen's eyes had already closed again. "I'll be back in an hour," she whispered, and got up off the bed.

Back in the living room, Ashleigh picked her book back up without hesitation. She had just been getting to the part where Billy was on his way to town with fifty dollars, and she couldn't believe what a fast read the story was as an adult. When her alarm went off near midnight, she wasn't sure if it woke her or just startled her. She looked at the book and could not remember what paragraph she'd been reading.

She wiped her eyes a little and returned to the bedroom. It was completely dark. Ashleigh clicked the bedside lamp on. Again, she took a seat at the very edge of the bed.

"Hey there," she said and stifled her own yawn as she waited. "Bailey, are you up?" She gave her side a little nudge.

Bailey opened her eyes, and her lips curved into one of her easy, sexy smiles. "You haven't ditched me yet," she murmured as her eyes closed again.

"Not yet." Ashleigh laughed softly. Bailey's water glass was empty. It was good that she had woken up on her own to drink it. "I'm going to refill your water. Is there anything else I can get you?"

"No, thank you," Bailey said softly and nuzzled her face further into her pillow.

Ashleigh left the room and returned with the water, but she did not wake her again. She still had six wake-ups to do before she woke her up for good and left for work. When she returned to the couch, she did not try to read. What she needed now was sleep and to forget how enticing Bailey's smile was, and how badly she wanted to see more of it.

CHAPTER 5

Kristen wasn't sure if the smell of coffee entered her brain before or after she awoke. She opened her eyes and looked around. Things were hazy, but this was definitely her room. If she was in her bed, who was making the coffee?

She sat up in a panic and was greeted with searing pain in the back of her head.

Her number-one rule was not to bring women home. She didn't want any of them knowing where she lived. Women were a one-shot deal. They met, they slept together, and she left. There were no maybe-next-times or when-can-I-see-you-agains. Phone numbers, e-mail addresses, and social networking handles were not exchanged. So, who the hell was clanging around in her kitchen?

"Hey, you're up," said a warm, honeyed voice.

Kristen looked up, and there, standing in the doorway with a cup of coffee, was the beautiful paramedic, Ashleigh Paige.

Kristen remembered.

Ashleigh had stayed through the night. Most of the times Kristen had seen her, she'd convinced herself she'd been dreaming, but then Ashleigh was still there. She looked over at the glass of water on her bedside table. Every time she awoke during the night, no matter how many times she drained it, a fresh glass waited for her.

Ashleigh was dressed in her medic uniform, her light brown hair pulled back into a ponytail, and Kristen had to admit she didn't mind the sight of her first thing in the morning.

"How are you feeling?"

"Better." She took the proffered cup of coffee from Ashleigh's hands. "Thanks to you. I can't believe you stayed the whole night."

"You don't have any milk or cream or sugar anywhere, so I figured you drink it black."

Kristen smiled and took a sip of her coffee. She wasn't sure what to say, and the truth was she was becoming increasingly embarrassed by the situation. She'd allowed her pride to get the better of her the day before and then jeopardized her investigation by having Ashleigh stay at her place. There wasn't much to find, but if she'd cracked the password on her computer, Ashleigh would know a whole lot more than she should about her. As much as she was able to trust anyone, she thought she could trust Ashleigh, and that alleviated her fears a little. She was good at reading people and was prone to mistrust—it was an occupational requirement—but she didn't read anything sinister or suspect in Ashleigh Paige. That was all well and good, but it didn't change the fact that she was an undercover Mountie and had been careful not to let a soul inside her condo since arriving in Toronto three months before, and now an EMT had spent the night there.

"You really didn't have to stay," she said, as if the words could undo the past.

"Ah, but that's what we fake doctors do. We make house calls," Ashleigh said, and Kristen blushed.

"You know, I was only teasing when I said that. I'm sorry," she said, truly chagrined.

"That's just the way it is, right, between PD and EMS?"

Kristen paused. If she said no, it would be a lie, but to say yes would strengthen the divide between them, and she didn't want that. "We weren't around then," she said evasively. "We're not part of it."

"I'm an EMT with Toronto Paramedic Services, and you're PD. We're a part of it whether we like it or not." Ashleigh returned to the bedroom door. "I have to get to work, so you need to stay up now, hence the coffee." She pointed at the mug in Kristen's hands. "I'll see you around."

"Hey, wait."

Ashleigh stopped just outside the doorway, but she did not turn around.

"I wanted to thank you for not saying anything yesterday. I checked in on CeCe, and I know you didn't tell the hospital what really happened."

Ashleigh shrugged. "You were trying to do the right thing. I didn't think you should be punished for it."

"Thank you. I know you must be tired, and I'm sorry if I ruined any plans you had or something," she added as an umbrella apology. She didn't know anything about Ashleigh's life. Was she married? Living with someone? "Did I do something to upset you?" she finally asked, trying to suss out whatever it was she'd done that had Ashleigh acting so aloof this morning.

"You didn't do anything." She still didn't turn around. "Your brother called," she added, then continued her walk out of the room. The front door opened and closed a few seconds later.

Confused by her last comment, Kristen reached over to the side of the bed for her phone.

She opened her call history. Jared had called three times in a row. The last call had been picked up at 4:53 a.m. and had lasted less than a minute. She pushed his name and waited for the phone to ring.

Jared picked up almost immediately. "Finally," he said, letting out a loud breath on the other end of the line.

"What's up?" She leaned back into the covers. The pain in her head was beginning to register now that she was awake. "Is everything okay?"

"Not really, and since when do your flings answer the phone?"

Kristen's breath caught. "What?"

"I had to take Cyn to the hospital this morning." His voice cracked. "She was pregnant."

A weight dropped in her stomach. She didn't have to ask what that meant. They'd lost it. "Oh God, Jared, I'm so sorry." They had wanted to get pregnant so badly. It was common for women to lose their first child in the very early stages of the first trimester, but she didn't say anything. He didn't need to hear that right then. "I'm sorry I wasn't here for you."

"Yeah, well, I didn't appreciate having to talk to the girl you're fucking while you slept it off."

Jared was hurt, but he never talked like that, especially not to her.

"I have a concussion. I got cracked on the back of the head with a vodka bottle yesterday while answering a disturbance call. One of the EMTs took me home and stayed to keep an eye on me. That's who picked up my phone."

"Oh," was all he said. There was a pause. "Are you hurt?"

"I'm fine. What did you say to her?" She cringed in anticipation. In the mood Jared was in, she knew that whatever it was would be foul.

"Look, I'm sorry. Tell her I'm sorry when you see her again."

Kristen wanted to push to find out what he'd said, but Jared was dealing with his own shit. He needed her support, not questions about Ashleigh.

"Is Cyn okay?" she asked.

"Yeah, she's back home, but she's upset."

"What if I come up there later today?" she offered.

"Should you be driving with a concussion?"

"No, but I can take the bus if you'll pick me up from the station." She held the phone away from her ear for a second to check the time on it. "How about if I come around two or three? I'm off the next four days, so I can stay for as long or as short as you need me to."

Jared exhaled a long breath. "That would be great, Kris."

"Can I bring anything?" She sat up and reached for her coffee. She couldn't fall asleep again. The first twenty-four hours after a concussion were crucial, and she wasn't in the clear just yet. Not only was Jared counting on her, but Ashleigh was no longer there to keep an eye on her. She'd felt safe with Ashleigh. Trusted her with her health. Her life. She'd been half-conscious, but still, trust was not something she gave up lightly, especially over her own person.

"Bring booze," Jared said. "Lots of booze."

Even with all the time she had, Kristen just barely made the twelve o'clock bus. Having to walk everywhere, and slowly at that, made everything take three times longer. Now that she was on the bus, she could relax for a few hours. *Where the Red Fern Grows* had been sitting on her coffee table, so she'd brought it with her. She'd brought her laptop as well, but her mind was in no condition to be processing the case just then. Any complex thought worsened her headache. The children's novel was an easy read, and it would give her something to focus on to keep her from falling asleep during the bus ride.

Ashleigh must have read the book while she kept an eye on Kristen during the night, otherwise it would have still been on the shelf. For reasons she did not care to explore, she really liked the idea of Ashleigh reading her favourite childhood book, as if the book were now somehow recommending her as a person.

She tried to read but couldn't keep her mind from wandering back to Ashleigh and how reserved she'd been when she left that morning. If she had Ashleigh's number, she would call to apologize for her brother and to thank her once more. For one insane moment, she toyed with the idea of creating some kind of social media account and contacting her that way. Thankfully, she came to her senses. When had she ever gone through the trouble of trying to find a girl the next day? Sure, this was different, but the idea of going through all that just to find a way to talk to Ashleigh Paige again was crazy.

When the bus pulled into the station, she was no closer to solving her Ashleigh Paige problem. She wished that the two twenty-sixers of alcohol she brought with her could numb her brain like it would do for her brother, but after the way her body reacted to a drink and a half last night, she wouldn't partake in liquor again until she had been given the all-clear with her concussion.

Jared was waiting on the platform, and he pulled her into a tight hug, not letting go for long after he normally would have. When he pulled away, she looked into his blue eyes. The whites were glossy and bloodshot from crying.

"It'll be okay." She gave his shoulder a reassuring squeeze.

He nodded. "Do you have any bags?"

"Just this one." She hiked her leather travel bag a little higher up on her shoulder. "Come on, let's get some booze into you and put that brain on ice for a while."

He let out a stifled laugh and led the way to the car. She was surprised to see Cyndi sitting in the passenger seat. Kristen opened the passenger door to greet her, and Cyndi pulled her into a fierce hug, much like the one Jared had given her.

"I didn't expect to see you at the station."

"I couldn't stay at the house alone." She sniffed and wiped the back of her hand across red-rimmed eyes. She had no makeup on, and her cinnamon cheeks were blotchy from crying.

"I understand." Kristen gave her another squeeze.

As good as Jared and Cyndi were together, every relationship had its weaknesses, and theirs had always been their inability to console one another. They loved each other so much, so deeply, that they were unable to stand one another's pain. When something tragic like this happened, they were unable to draw strength from one another, and that's where Kristen often came in. Jared had grown up leaning on her for support, for protection, and when Cyndi came into their lives, she'd quickly followed his example.

Jared often joked about what a shitty brother he was, always being the one to turn to his sister for protection instead of the other way around, but when Kristen moved into law enforcement and Jared to art and sculpture, the issue became a moot point. Kristen had always been the stronger one, like when their parents died. She hadn't thought of them in a long time, but as she looked at Cyndi now, seeing how distraught Jared was, she couldn't help but be reminded of how Jared had howled and clung to her that night.

The drive back to the cottage was made in silence. Once inside, Cyndi went back to their room to lie down, and Jared walked out onto the back porch. Kristen left her bag in the guest room, dropped the bottles of hard liquor off in the kitchen, and grabbed two beers from the fridge. She didn't want her brother to feel like he was drinking alone, so she figured she could slowly sip on a beer to be social without doing much brain damage.

Outside, he took the beer with a half-hearted smile and downed the neck, but he didn't say anything. He just stared over the horizon. It was a beautiful late-July afternoon, and on any other occasion, they probably would have been out on the boat pretending to fish while downing half a dozen beers in the sun.

"I know it's hard to hear this right now," she said, and his jaw clenched. "But what happened is very common. I know that nothing can make up for the loss that you're feeling, but that doesn't mean this is it for you guys," she said gently.

He stared off for a few more minutes before he answered. "Remember when Grandma died and you told me that we were each other's family now but that she'd always be in my heart?" Kristen nodded, and he continued. "How am I supposed to keep the baby in my heart when I didn't even get to know him or her?" His lips began to tremble, and he covered his mouth with his hand.

Kristen reached forward and took that hand in hers, letting him know he had nothing to be ashamed of. "The baby will always be in our hearts. If you want, we could have a memorial, so there will be a place that he or she will be remembered. We could do it here and plant something." A thought came to her. "We could plant a red fern."

Jared turned his gaze to her, and understanding passed behind his eyes.

"That's a great idea." He smiled through some tears. "I'll go tell Cyn. We can go into town and pick it up right now."

Kristen waited for Jared to go back inside before she covered her mouth to hide her sob and let her own tears fall for the loss of the niece or nephew she'd never know and for her brother's grief that she could not help but share. She hadn't felt it at first, but being here now, she knew they'd all lost something sacred. The red fern would honour that, and with its presence, the loss might feel less acute over time.

When Kristen returned to the city three days later, she was exhausted. Planting the fern had been hard, as had the emotional service that had ensued. She'd spent the following two days going between her brother and her sister-in-law until finally, they were able to speak to one another and comfort each other. She hadn't slept well, paranoid about her concussion and having trouble bearing the headache it continuously brought on. She wished she could call in sick to work, but being on an RCMP assignment didn't work like that. You were the job; there were no such things as sick days or vacation time.

The first few days back were rough, and luckily there was not too much action going on that week in Toronto, because Kristen didn't know if she would be quite up to the task if anything dire were to come across their car. Henry was his usual grumpy, lazy self, and between the two of them, they made one half-decent cop. Thankfully, the highlights so far had been an exorbitant speeding ticket and a domestic disturbance call that they'd arrived at second, so they hadn't had to deal with much of it. When the ambulance had showed, she'd been disappointed that it wasn't Ashleigh's truck, but she didn't know what she would have said to her anyway.

When she got back in the cruiser, she was surprised to find Henry on the radio with dispatch.

"Just got another call." He hung the receiver back up. "Break and enter two blocks from here. We're heading in." He started the car and gunned it before she had her seatbelt on.

"Got any more information than that?" she asked him as he sped around traffic with their lights and siren on.

"Two males, considered armed and dangerous. One victim inside. Gunshot wound."

"Great," she said under her breath. When they arrived on scene, Ashleigh Paige and Rodrigo Cruz were already pulling their empty stretcher out of the back of their truck. The sight of Ashleigh made Kristen hesitate for a moment.

"You coming, rook?" Henry said, already outside.

She got out of the car quickly and took two long strides toward the ambulance. "Wait right there," she called to them. "We need to secure the building before you go in."

The sun was coming down strong and pulling out every natural highlight in Ashleigh's hair. She was back in her uniform, and Kristen noticed for the first time what an attractive uniform it was.

"There's someone bleeding out up there," Ashleigh said, her tone frosty.

Kristen tried not to let it bother her.

"Yeah, and there'll be two more if you don't let us do our jobs first. Stay out here until we give you the all-clear," she ordered. The look in Ashleigh's eyes told her that she did not like being told what to do, but this was her job, and she sure as hell wasn't going to let any emergency response team go in when there could be a gunman still lurking.

They cleared the building quickly, and Kristen was incredibly relieved not to have to subdue anybody or be shot at. In a hallway, she found the woman with the gunshot wound. "Get the paramedics," she said to Henry. When he left, pulling on his radio, Kristen returned her attention to the woman.

"What's your name?"

"Anna."

"You're going to be just fine, Anna."

"I feel cold." The woman reached out.

Kristen took her hand and held it in her own. It was chilly, but not deathly so. "It's just the shock." She took a second to assess the wound. It was through her stomach. "Do you feel pressure pain anywhere else or dizziness?" she asked.

"No," the woman answered.

That was good. There might not be internal bleeding.

"The medical team is on its way up, and we're just a few blocks from the hospital. They'll have you high on drugs and singing songs in the recovery room before you know it."

The woman tried to smile, but it turned into a wince. The sounds of the paramedics arriving and the stretcher being rolled down the hall reached Kristen. "They're here now." She stood up and allowed Ashleigh and Cruz the space they needed to do their work.

For the first time in a while, she watched with appreciation as the paramedics bandaged up the woman, checked her vitals, and moved her to the stretcher. Ashleigh demonstrated the gentleness that Kristen remembered from the night she had taken care of her.

"You think you two can manage to keep her alive till you can get her to a real doctor?" Henry asked tersely.

"They're doing all they can. Let's just get out of their way," Kristen snapped at him.

Ashleigh shifted her green-eyed gaze to Kristen for a moment, but too quickly she returned her attention to the patient. Kristen wanted to say something to her, but now was not the time. What would she say anyway? Ashleigh was a paramedic, and Kristen was posing as a Toronto police officer. Even without the blood feud between their departments, what did she hope to accomplish with her? Why did she care if Ashleigh liked her or not?

The rolling of the stretcher drew her attention back to the scene and to the fact that Ashleigh was leaving without so much as a word to her.

CHAPTER 6

"What do you know about Kristen Bailey?" Ashleigh asked Rodrigo. They'd been sitting in their truck drinking pop and waiting for a call for nearly two hours.

"More than I want to. Why?" He took the last swig of his Sprite and dropped it in the cup holder.

"I don't mean as a cop. I mean, like, as a person."

Rodrigo studied her a moment. "I didn't take you for a lesbian, Paige." His voice didn't hold any malice, but she cringed just the same, and he was quick to apologize. "Sorry, I mean… I just didn't know."

"Neither did I until recently."

"Please don't tell me you have the hots for her."

Ashleigh looked away, but her blush told him all he needed to know.

"For Christ's sake, what is it with you women and that asshole?"

"Why do you hate her so much?" Sure, he showed disdain for mostly all the police on the force, but he seemed to hold a special place in hell for Kristen Bailey.

"Why do you like her so much?"

She tilted her head. "Come on. I asked first."

He let out a sigh of frustration before answering. "Isn't being PD and a pain in the ass enough for you?"

It would be, but still, it seemed like it was more than that. "Is that it?" she asked.

"Okay, if you need more, she slept with my sister."

The blood drained from her face. "Maria?"

He nodded.

She'd met Maria. She had a husband and two kids.

"How did that happen?"

"Hell if I know. I just get a call from my sister one day, asking me for Bailey's number. Saying all kinds of crazy shit. She scared me. I think she would have left Marco if Bailey would have returned her calls. The one decent thing she ever did was not give my sister the time of day afterward."

"She sleeps around a lot?" Ashleigh asked, but she knew the answer.

"She's fucked more girls than me and my three brothers," Rodrigo said crassly. "Trust me, Paige, she's not someone you want to be wasting your time on." He shook his head. "A nice girl like you, you can do better."

Ashleigh bowed her head. Rodrigo was right. It was time she grew up and stopped having feelings for people she wasn't compatible with. She was too smart to get involved with someone like Kristen Bailey, someone who only cared about sleeping around and having a good time. Nothing about Bailey hinted at monogamy or even maturity. Her entire countenance, the way she carried herself, the way she laughed and teased at every occasion, all spoke to a cocky kind of confidence most people only garnered from knowing how attractive they were and not caring what anyone else in the room thought of them. Women like that were dangerous.

It had taken her months to get over the way Denise had treated her, like a discarded piece of trash, used up and worthless the morning after. She'd resolved that she would never let herself be treated like that again. The knowledge that this was how Kristen treated women, had treated Rodrigo's sister, sickened her.

Her phone buzzed. She smiled and opened the message from Amanda, whom she hadn't spoken to in a while.

Erin and I have a bet. She thinks we haven't heard from you in months because you moved back to Africa. I told her it's because you're a jerk. Who owes who $20?

Ashleigh typed off a quick message, still grinning.

Why don't I split the difference and buy you each a drink? Tango tonight?

Let me check with E.

Ashleigh didn't have to wait twenty seconds before she was pulled into a group text with Amanda and Erin.

Hey babe, I found Ashleigh. She's alive! Are we free tonight? She's buying at Tango.

Ashleigh smiled and typed back.

I'm buying one round. You two are on a dual income, you can pick up your own tab.

Erin was quick to join the conversation.

I'm in. I'll message Dawn.

Amanda followed up with the next message.

The foursome is back together!

Keep it in your pants, babe. Erin wrote.

Ashleigh laughed. She hadn't been out with them in months. A year and a half ago, they'd picked up the pieces of what Denise left behind when she met Erin and Amanda her next time at the bar. She smiled as she remembered the newlyweds excitedly introducing her to their friend Dawn, with the hopes that they would hook up. Five minutes had shown that they had absolutely nothing in common, but the four of them had been bar buddies ever since.

This was just what she needed. Whatever she thought she had seen in Kristen Bailey, whatever kindness or compassion she thought was there, she would forget about it that night. Bailey was a womanizer, and she wasn't going to waste another minute on the person she'd hoped she was when the real woman wasn't worth her time. Tonight, she would go out with the girls, and maybe she would meet somebody special.

If it had been just another bad week on the job, Kristen would have been able to handle it. No, what was really nagging at her, more than her unsolved case, was that paramedic Ashleigh Paige seemed displeased with her. Sure, she had made an ass and an inconvenience of herself by getting a concussion, not reporting it, refusing to let Ashleigh look at it, going drinking, and then needing Ashleigh to take her home and give up a night to play nurse to her; but Ashleigh didn't seem like the type to even get angry at all that. She was too kind, too good-natured. In fact, she hadn't seen such a sanguine disposition since her grandmother.

One thing was certain; she could not go on obsessing like this. She would find out why Ashleigh was upset with her, fix it, and then enjoy watching her life go back to normal. She sure as hell wasn't going to allow some rookie paramedic to spin her head for much longer. Ashleigh was probably just pissed at her because she'd cancelled her plans with her boyfriend because of Kristen that night. She'd tell her she was sorry, give her a good bottle of wine, and be done with it. She didn't even need her phone number. She'd just drop by the station and catch Ashleigh when she was returning the truck for the night. It was a simple plan, and it wasn't going to wait another day.

Kristen called the station and found out that Ashleigh was working. Her shift was supposed to finish at seven that evening, and having just finished herself, Kristen ran home to get a quick shower, then booted over to the liquor store to find a decent bottle of wine. Going through the aisles at the LCBO—trying to pick between an old world Bordeaux and a California Cabernet—she remembered that Ashleigh didn't drink. So she didn't want a drink at the bar, did that mean she really didn't drink at all? Like never? *Oh well.* She grabbed the bottle of French wine. *Her boyfriend can drink it.*

She arrived at the station just before Ashleigh's truck pulled in. With the animosity between the police and the paramedics, she didn't want to wait inside the building, so she remained parked in her black Mustang across the street. Fifteen minutes later, Ashleigh emerged, her hair pulled up into a messy bun, wearing dark jean shorts with designer holes and threading, and a flowing, light pink tank top. She had a bicycle helmet in one hand, and she was pushing a mountain bike along beside her in the other hand by one of the ram's horn bar ends.

Kristen's stomach fluttered. She looked down at her abdomen. *What was that?* It looked perfectly normal. That sensation, though… It was something she hadn't felt for a woman in a long time, not since she'd been a teenager with her first and only girlfriend. She'd been thinking about Ashleigh a lot, more than a lot, but that didn't mean she *liked* her, did it? Another look at her as she walked around the corner of the building caused the butterflies to take flight again. This was so not cool.

She got out of the car, closed the door, and took a step toward Ashleigh.

"Does that thing come equipped with a siren, or does the little bell do the trick in a real emergency?" she asked, forcing one of her renowned smiles onto her lips.

Ashleigh turned, and the disbelief on her face was unmasked. "What are *you* doing here?"

Kristen had hoped for a warmer greeting, but she would not be deterred. "Listen, I wanted to thank you again for what you did for me the other night. It was obviously unnecessary, and I just wanted you to know that I really appreciated it, especially after I'd been kind of a jerk that day." She lifted the bottle of wine in the gift bag toward Ashleigh. "Here. I'm sorry if I kept you from anything that night. I know you don't drink, but I didn't know what else to get you, so I figured that your boyfriend or your cat or whoever could have it."

Ashleigh took the bottle and gave her a small smile, looking up at her through her soft, brown eyelashes. "I don't have a cat," she said.

"Your boyfriend, then?" Kristen asked cautiously.

"I don't have one of those either."

Those words should not have felt as good as they did as they washed over her.

"Okay, well, give it to a distant uncle, then, and, again, thank you. I hope you won't still be mad at me anymore." She ran a hand along the back of her neck and through her hair. She couldn't remember being nervous like this around anyone since her corporals in the Depot.

"I'm... I'm not mad at you," Ashleigh said.

"Oh, well, what is it, then?"

"It's nothing," she deflected.

"Please?" Kristen gave her a sheepish smile. "If I don't know what I did, I might do it again."

"It's not anything you did," Ashleigh said, and Kristen waited, the pressure of the silence building in her chest. "It's stupid. It was just something your brother said. I picked up the phone when he kept calling, and I told him you were asleep and that if he could wait that you'd be getting up soon, but he didn't want to wait."

"What did he say?"

Ashleigh sighed. "He made a comment about not wanting to talk to one of your...well...to one of your women."

"Oh." Kristen winced. For the first time, she was embarrassed by her behaviour. "I'm sorry. He got some really bad news that morning, and he wasn't himself. He actually asked me to apologize to you. I'm sorry if he offended you by insinuating anything." She rubbed the back of her neck faster now. "He must have just assumed that you were... Never mind."

Ashleigh smiled as though she'd been caught with her teeth around Tweety. "It's all right." Her shoulders relaxed, and Kristen was relieved when Ashleigh's smile touched her eyes. "You're forgiven."

"Phew, thank you." Kristen mimed wiping sweat from her forehead, but she truly was way too relieved at Ashleigh's words. She stood there, admiring Ashleigh's smile, until she realized what she was doing and that neither of them were saying anything. "Okay, well, I just wanted to thank you again and apologize." She searched for something fresh to say. "You have a good night and... Oh!" She clapped her hands as the idea came to her. "Would you like a ride somewhere?" She gestured to Ashleigh's bike. "It's like a million degrees out, and I don't have anywhere I need to be, so I can give you a lift home," she offered. "Or wherever," she added, hoping Ashleigh wouldn't give her directions to some guy's place.

Ashleigh tilted her head and seemed to consider the offer. "Are you hungry? I'm starving, and I know a great Mexican place on Baldwin. It's not ten minutes from here."

Kristen was taken aback by Ashleigh's offer, and her face involuntarily split into a wide smile. "Then I'm buying," she said, before Ashleigh could change her mind. "Come on."

———

Neither of them said much in the car, and Kristen spent most of the time trying to focus on the road and not the pair of bare legs next to her in the passenger seat. The windows were open, and the honking of horns, squealing tires, squeaky brakes, and cyclists telling off drivers filled the car as they made the quick drive to Baldwin Street.

The restaurant was small and quaint, tucked in a long row of dining establishments in the Baldwin Village shopping district. The host led them to the last available patio table.

"Thanks for agreeing to come to dinner with me," Kristen said.

Ashleigh laughed lightly. "I think I'm the one who invited you."

"Right." She swallowed. "Well, thank you for inviting me, then."

The server approached and handed them each a menu. "Can I get you started with some drinks? We have a pitcher of margaritas for fifteen dollars on special."

Kristen was about to say no when Ashleigh answered.

"That sounds great." She smiled at the server.

"Great!" The server returned her enthusiasm and left them to think on their food order.

"I thought you didn't drink," Kristen said.

"Usually no, and definitely not regularly, but it's boiling out, and it would seem a sin to turn down a margarita on a patio in July."

"Give me my sin again," Kristen quoted with a smile, to which Ashleigh tilted her head to the side. "Shakespeare," Kristen explained.

"Ah, yet again. What is it with you and that guy, anyway?" She opened her menu. "I noticed you had quite the book collection at your place. In fact, you had more books than things to eat."

Kristen shifted a little uncomfortably. Ashleigh had likely seen every inch of what she had come to think of as her sanctuary, although it was stupid, pathetic, even. It was a cold, barren condo, but still, it was the closest thing she'd had to a home in quite a while.

"Did I say something wrong?" Ashleigh asked, then bit her lip.

Kristen tried hard not to focus on Ashleigh's beautiful mouth. "No, no. I'm just not used to having people at my place."

The server returned with their pitcher and two salt-rimmed juice glasses. She poured their margaritas and set the glasses down with what remained in the jug. "What would you ladies care for?"

"I think we need another minute," Kristen said. She hadn't even opened her menu.

"I'll start you off with some complimentary chips and salsa then. You can add homemade guac for two dollars."

"Done," Ashleigh said eagerly.

"Be right back then." The server gave Ashleigh a private smile before she left.

What was that? For the first time, Kristen noticed that the server was rather cute, if one were paying attention, which of course she hadn't been with Ashleigh sitting across from her. Was Ashleigh blushing? When caused by the server, Kristen didn't find it very endearing.

"Uh, so, what do you want to eat?" She tried to shake the thought from her mind.

"I don't know. Maybe the veggie quesadillas."

"Are you a vegetarian?" she asked.

"Yes," Ashleigh answered, "but please, don't let that stop you from ordering whatever you want."

Kristen didn't care about getting her chili con carne; what had her attention was that vegetarianism was a common trait in lesbians. "Vegetarian is fine with me." She took the first sip of her drink. It was too salty with the full rim, but it was cold, refreshing, and strong as anything. "Whoa, is that ever boozy."

Ashleigh sucked her cheeks in and shook her head harshly. "Hoo, yeah." She exhaled. "I hope no one lights a match around us."

Kristen smiled politely at her attempt at humour. "Probably a little stronger than you're used to."

"For sure," Ashleigh agreed after a second sip, making a face like she'd bitten into a lime. Kristen laughed, and Ashleigh mirrored her smile, but it faded quickly.

"What is it?" Kristen asked.

"It's nothing."

She smiled encouragingly. "What is it?" she said again.

Ashleigh took a deep breath, and Kristen braced herself. "Did you sleep with Rodrigo's sister?"

Kristen's eyes widened before she could mask her surprise. She cleared her throat and leaned back in her chair before taking a long sip from her drink. "He told you that?"

Ashleigh nodded. "I can tell just from looking at you that it's true."

"It is true," Kristen said. It was better to admit to a lie and manipulate the facts a little than to deny a truth outright. "Not one of my finer decisions." There was no way she could explain to her why she'd done it without giving herself away.

"So, what can I get you guys to eat?" The server reappeared.

Kristen waved a hand in Ashleigh's direction for her to go first.

"I'll have the veggie quesadillas."

"Great choice." The server took her menu with a smile. "And for you?"

"Baja fish tacos with extra cilantro, please."

"Coming right up." She grinned, but it was for Ashleigh alone.

"Why was it not one of your finer decisions?" Ashleigh asked once the server left. She was apparently oblivious to the server's attention. Did that outweigh her vegetarianism for could-be-a-lesbian points?

Kristen sighed. "It's not like I did it to be a jerk to Cruz or something." At least that part was true, but she'd known he wouldn't like it. It was his fault for making a personal visit to his sister that day when he was on duty. All Kristen was guilty of was exhausting the lead by mixing business with pleasure, as she often did, but under Ashleigh's gaze, she didn't feel right about it anymore.

"So it's okay to sleep with a married woman as long as she doesn't have a family member in emergency services?"

"What? No, that's not what I meant." Kristen ran her hands through her hair in frustration.

Ashleigh sounded pretty pissed off for something that had nothing to do with her. *Great.* She'd just gotten back on good terms with her, and now this Maria Cruz thing had come back to bite her. Considering the video had done nothing to further her case and actually exonerated

Rodrigo, someone who hated her, the incident was managing to cause Kristen quite a bit of trouble.

"I didn't know she was married. I didn't know anything about her when I slept with her." Ashleigh had no way of knowing that she was being dishonest, but for the first time in a while, Kristen didn't like how it felt to lie.

Ashleigh leaned back and poked her tongue into the side of her cheek. "That's supposed to be any better?"

"What does that mean?"

"Nothing. Just confirms what your brother said about you."

Kristen drew her eyebrows together in confusion. Was Ashleigh upset that she was gay? So, maybe Ashleigh wasn't a lesbian, but she didn't seem like the judgmental, narrow-minded type either. Then again, she barely knew her.

"Is it true?" Ashleigh asked.

"I don't know what you're asking." Kristen said honestly.

"He made it seem like you might go through a lot of women. Do you?"

Oh. Kristen let out a quick breath of relief. "I suppose."

"You suppose? Have you had a lot of girlfriends?"

This time, Kristen laughed. "No."

"But your brother said... Ohhh." She paused. "Does that make you happy?"

Kristen swirled the liquid in her glass back and forth, concentrating on the rapidly melting ice as she swayed the cubes from side to side. It was an extremely personal question.

"I'm sorry, that's not my business."

Kristen stopped midswirl, her drink still tilted, and lifted her gaze to Ashleigh. "I guess I wouldn't know, with nothing to compare it to. It's easier, though."

"Easier than what?"

"Than the alternative." She lifted her drink to her lips and finished it in two long gulps, then crunched the two small ice cubes in her teeth and swallowed. "I haven't the time for anything else."

"Or the interest?" Ashleigh asked carefully.

What the hell did Ashleigh care who she slept with, and why did she feel the need to justify herself to her? Her deliberations went on long enough that Ashleigh was the one to answer her own question.

"I'm sorry. It really is none of my business." She took a long sip of her drink.

"It seems you know a lot about me. Why don't you tell me something about yourself?"

"Oh, I don't know that there's much to tell."

Kristen grinned. "You slept at my place and know a whole lot more about me than I do about you, so start spilling. How old are you? That should be an easy one."

"I'm twenty-five. You?"

"Thirty-two. Where are you from?"

"Here. You?"

"I'm supposed to be asking the questions." Kristen bit into a chip with guacamole.

"This isn't an interrogation, officer." Ashleigh smiled coyly. "I get to ask too."

Something about the way she said *officer* had Kristen's insides standing at attention. She tried to ignore the feeling in her abdomen and readjusted her aviators with a smile. "Fine, we'll go question for question, but don't ask anything you wouldn't want to answer yourself, then, girly."

"Girly?"

"You're twenty-five. I get to call you 'girly.'"

"I don't think so." Ashleigh grinned.

"So, why an EMT?"

"I know it sounds trite, but I just wanted to help people. Why a cop?"

"I just wanted to shoot people." Kristen was rewarded with Ashleigh's sudden laughter, and the sound slid down her body like a long drink of smooth bourbon. "No, I don't know, it's just all I can really ever remember wanting to be. I knew a desk job wasn't for me. I wanted to do something where I got to move around and see things, but I also wanted to use my brain. I was always rooting for the good guys, and I wanted to become one. I guess I do the job for the old-fashioned reason."

"To save the day?"

"To get the girl."

Ashleigh bit her lip. "I take it that works out for you most of the time?"

"Most of the time," Kristen said carefully, swatting a fly away from her drink.

"Here we go." The server returned and unceremoniously dropped their wicker plates onto the green, plastic patio table. "Can I get you anything else? How about a refill on that pitcher?"

"We're good." Kristen would have loved a whole bottle of tequila, but with the heat and with Ashleigh not being a drinker, she wanted to keep herself in check. When the server left, Kristen resumed the conversation. "How about you?" she asked as Ashleigh bit into a forkful of veggie quesadilla dipped in sour cream. "Anyone special in your life?"

Ashleigh swallowed and shook her head. "No. I find it's hard with the job, and I guess I'm looking for something a little more than what *other* people are looking for, so it's harder to find."

"And what are you looking for?"

"Someone to share my life with."

"At twenty-five?"

"Is there an age requirement for happiness?" She arched one eyebrow. "What are you looking for?"

"Nothing." At least that answer was honest.

"I guess you wouldn't want someone to share your life with, then? They'd probably just get in the way of all the girls you bring home."

It was a low blow, and it landed with force in Kristen's abdomen. "I don't judge you for waiting around for Prince Charming to come and sweep you off your feet, so why does it bother you what I do or who I sleep with?"

Ashleigh looked uncomfortable. "It doesn't." She cleared her throat and finished her margarita. "So, you have a brother. Any other siblings?"

"No." Kristen relaxed at the subject change. "You?"

"Only child. You're close with your brother?"

"Very. I spend most of my time off back home with him. It's gorgeous, right on the lake."

"Back home? Where is home, exactly?"

Kristen paused. Had she really just been that careless, even after deflecting the earlier question of where she was from? She had unintentionally let her guard down. No, Ashleigh had slipped past it. What the hell was happening to her dozen years of RCMP training?

"Muskoka," she answered honestly, followed by a long exhale. She'd told Ashleigh a truth about herself, one of the first ones she'd told in a year, and it felt inexplicably good.

"Sounds beautiful. I love Muskoka. Where exactly?"

"I guess it's not exactly home anymore. We grew up in Muskoka, but Jared lives in Algonquin now, just outside Huntsville, off Highway Sixty. It's a nice break from the city and only half an hour from where we grew up. What about you? What do you do to unwind?"

"Well, when I was with GVI, I used to spend my free time online, looking things up about home, trying to keep in touch with everyone here. Now that I'm back, I find that I just like to get away from it all. Go biking, take a hike, whatever. Winter is my favourite, though. When I was a kid, we used to go up to Collingwood every weekend. From December to March, skiing is basically my life. I just love getting out there."

"That's cool." Kristen nodded. "So, GVI, eh? That's pretty hard core. Where were you?"

"Nairobi."

"Africa?"

"Kenya."

"What were you doing there?"

"Building homes outside the city, bringing in medicine, and teaching the women how to use it. There was a strong emphasis on teaching women skills and how to use what they had to make money so they wouldn't be reliant on a man."

"Were you a medic there?"

"Yeah, but I felt more like a palliative care nurse than a triage medic. Most of what they had you can't cure, and what you could there was never enough medicine for, or the right kind."

"So, you really do care about helping people?"

"I do."

"I'm sorry about those jabs I made when I first met you. They weren't personal. It's just, well, I'm sure you know that Rodrigo isn't crazy about me, and the cops and EMTs in the city have some bad blood."

"Yes, I've heard plenty about it recently."

"What have you heard?" Kristen asked.

"That you don't seem to trust paramedics. The way Rodrigo tells it, you have a strong dislike for us, just like the rest of the cops."

It seemed odd to Kristen that Ashleigh would answer with something personal about her instead of the feud as a whole. It certainly hadn't been the answer she'd hoped for.

"Ricky was a rookie. He shouldn't have been doing more than writing traffic tickets on his own, but he wanted to be a hero. We all do when we first start out. He shouldn't have died like that."

"I'm sorry."

"He'd only been on the job a year, barely long enough to be out on his own, but long enough to know to wait for backup before going into something like he did. He made a bad decision; there's no denying that, but he might have lived if someone he trusted hadn't killed him."

Kristen didn't want to talk about the strife between their departments anymore. Her job may be to figure out who killed Ricky Oslowe, but the last thing she wanted was to drive the wedge between her and Ashleigh any further.

"My turn," she said. "Have you ever had anyone die on you?"

Ashleigh looked down into her drink. "In Nairobi, a lot of people died. It was just the way things were there. I tried to get used to it, but I never really did. I don't think it's something you should get used to. Dying, no matter how many times you see it, should mean something." She looked at Kristen. "Have you ever killed anybody?" she asked, barely above a whisper. It seemed she knew that it was something you were not supposed to ask of someone in law enforcement, just as she shouldn't have asked Ashleigh her last question.

"Yes." Kristen didn't want her to ask how many. "Come on, our food's getting cold."

Kristen took a big bite into one of her fish tacos and looked away. What was it about Ashleigh that had her armour cracking between the plates? It didn't matter. She'd accomplished her goal. The paramedic was no longer mad at her. She would finish her meal and put her from her mind like she should have done weeks ago. Ashleigh may not know much about the quarrel between the cops and EMTs, but someone out there did, and it was time she started digging deeper if she was ever going to get away from this damned city and her confusing feelings for Ashleigh Paige.

CHAPTER 7

THE BAR WAS BUSY WHEN Ashleigh walked into Tango, the only place left on Church Street that could still be considered somewhat of a women's bar—if you avoided all the men at the front watching the drag show. The air conditioning was broken, and despite the huge fan that blew over the dance floor, there was sweat running down her back within minutes.

Amanda, Erin, and Dawn were already there, drinking Heinekens and standing at one of the few small, round, tall tables—the rest of the floor was reserved as a large dance space.

"Hey!" Erin saw her first and pulled her into a tight hug. She'd cut her hair shorter since the last time Ashleigh had seen her, and she now had dark bangs sweeping to the side over her face. It wasn't Ashleigh's favourite hairstyle on her, but with Erin's sky-blue cat eyes, it didn't matter what she did with her hair. Her face was always stunning.

"Okay, let me in too," Amanda said after a few seconds. She pried her wife's arms from around Ashleigh and pulled her into her own hug. Amanda, contrary to her wife, had grown her hair out, and the dirty-blonde, messy bun suited her well.

"Hey, Dawn." Ashleigh smiled at her, pulling her into the final hug.

"I missed you," Dawn said quietly in her ear, and it made Ashleigh slightly remorseful that she hadn't shared Dawn's initial feelings. Things would have been a lot easier for her if she reciprocated the sweet brunette's attraction, but despite her trying, she'd just never developed any desire for her. She was good-looking, but there'd never been a spark between them.

"We thought you were going to be here a while ago," Amanda said.

"Sorry, I was having dinner with someone. I kind of lost track of time." If by "lost track of time" she meant stretched out every last possible minute she could spend with Kristen, then her apology rang true.

"Well, I've been asked to remind you about the round you owe us," Erin said once Ashleigh had disengaged from Dawn's hug.

"How polite of you to have let me say hello before sending me off to the bar," Ashleigh said with a smile. "What'll it be?"

Amanda held up the last of her green beer bottle and gave it a shake. The other two nodded in agreement with her order, and Ashleigh made her way to the bar to get three beers and a bottle of water. The bartender came over quickly, and she gave her order. She put a twenty and a five on the bar and looked around as she waited but stopped when she saw *her*.

Kristen Bailey was standing at the bar, a Corona in one hand, the other tucking a strand of blonde hair behind a remarkably attractive woman's ear. Kristen wore tight jeans and a torso-hugging bright blue tank top. Her hair was down and styled in that messy way that Ashleigh loved. She had applied a generous amount of black eyeliner and mascara to her eyelids and lashes. The look was finished off with some thick sterling silver bracelets, a large, black watch, and long, black leather riding boots that came up over her jeans. Her tanned skin glistened, her strong cheekbones were accentuated by the dim lighting, and she was the sexiest thing Ashleigh had ever seen.

The knife of jealousy twisted in her solar plexus when Bailey gave the attractive blonde one of her easy, charming smiles. The blonde laughed at something she said, and the phone call with Bailey's brother ran through her mind again. *I didn't call to talk to one of my sister's whores.*

She had to get out of there before Kristen saw her. It shouldn't bother her to see her there, but it did, and she recognized the green-eyed beast as it came alive inside of her. She had to tame it. It was none of her business who Bailey spent her time with or who she slept with, but standing there, picturing Bailey in the arms of this blonde, in the bed where she had tended to her, caused a heaviness in her chest as if she were suffocating. It was ridiculous for her to feel this way; she barely knew her, but when Bailey leaned in and whispered something to the blonde that made her smile coyly, the constriction around Ashleigh's heart tightened. *How many women has she been with?*

She turned away, not wanting to know the answer.

"Hey, can I buy you a drink?" An attractive woman approached her. "That is, if you're here alone." Ordinarily, this would have been the exact outcome she would have hoped for walking into Tango, but seeing Bailey had made her lose her appetite.

"Thank you." Ashleigh tried to look contrite. "But I'm with some friends."

"I'm sure they won't mind if you have one drink with someone."

"I really don't drink, but thank you."

"I just heard you order three beers."

"And a water. The water is for me," she said, realizing she'd been about to walk away from the bar without any of the drinks. Seeing Kristen had her all out of sorts.

"What's the big deal? It's just one drink."

The bartender deposited Ashleigh's order on the bar, and she moved to grab the drinks, but the woman moved in front of her. "How about a shot?"

Just then, a hand pushed gently into the small of her back, and warmth spread through her entire body.

"Babe, what's taking so long?" Kristen said from beside her, but her gaze was on the woman who stood in Ashleigh's way.

The woman looked Kristen up and down. "Not worth it," she said and walked away.

"Hey," Kristen said now that they were alone. She still hadn't removed her hand from her back.

"Hey." Ashleigh looked around her, but she could not see the blonde Kristen had been talking to before.

"So, is it *Princess* Charming you're looking for, then, or are you just here with friends?" she asked, a coy smile on her face.

Ashleigh blushed. "It's princess, and I'm sorry for not telling you earlier. I don't know why I didn't. It was dumb."

Bailey shook her head and removed her hand from Ashleigh's back. She missed the warmth instantly. "It's fine. You don't owe me anything."

"Well, speaking of, thanks for the rescue."

Kristen shrugged. "That was Carla. She's harmless, really, but she can be a pain with her persistence. So, who are the drinks for?"

Ashleigh turned and pointed to her group, which apparently was watching her. "Just some friends. Who are you here with?"

"No one. Want some help getting those drinks back to your table?" Bailey asked, then raised one finger at the bartender and was handed a fresh Corona. She took a sip. Apparently, she didn't have to wait for her drinks.

"Sure, thanks," Ashleigh said, again unwilling to part from her company.

Bailey picked up two bottles of Heineken in her free hand, then jerked her head toward the table. "Lead the way."

"Right, okay." Ashleigh took the last beer and her bottle of water, which right then she wished was a beer. She tried to ignore the expressions on her friends' faces as Bailey deposited the bottles in front of Dawn and Erin. Ashleigh pushed a bottle into Amanda's hand.

"Hey," Kristen said to the table.

"Sorry." Ashleigh swallowed. "Amanda, Erin, and Dawn, this is Bailey. I mean Kristen. Kristen, these are my friends."

Despite being usually chatty, her friends mumbled something that resembled a hello and then just kind of stared.

Finally, Erin broke the silence. "Sorry, did you two just meet at the bar?"

"No." Ashleigh laughed, and it came out awkwardly. "We work together. Kristen's a cop."

"We just ran into each other," Bailey said. "Which is kind of funny considering we had dinner together an hour ago."

"You're who she had dinner with?" Dawn asked, her expression dropping.

"Mmm-hmm," Kristen said into her beer. She took a sip and looked around. Was she bored with them already? "Well, I should be getting back," she said.

Back to what? She'd said she wasn't there with anybody.

"Stay for a drink," Ashleigh said. She shuddered at how much she sounded like Carla from the bar. When Bailey didn't respond, Ashleigh followed her gaze. The woman Kristen had been flirting with before was back. "Unless—"

"I'd love to have a drink with you," Kristen said. She cut her off and met her gaze. "Let me just settle a tab first." She put her half-empty beer on the table. "Excuse me."

Well, at least leaving the beer meant she was probably coming back.

"You had dinner with *her*?" Erin said incredulously as soon as Bailey was out of earshot.

"Yeah, why?" Ashleigh turned back to her friends.

"She's sex on legs."

"Apparently." Amanda nodded in Bailey's direction at the bar. She was saying something to the blonde who slipped an arm around her waist.

"Yeah, she's..." Ashleigh began, but her voice trailed off. What she was, was way out of her league.

"Ashleigh, you're not..." Amanda left the question hanging.

"No." She shook her head quickly. "We just work together."

"Good." Erin said.

"Why?"

"A girl like that..." Erin shook her head. "She'd break your heart."

"Didn't what happened with Denise teach you anything?" Dawn asked.

Ashleigh returned her gaze to Kristen, still at the bar, still talking to the blonde. That must have been one hell of a tab to take this long to settle.

A song came on that had Amanda grabbing at Erin excitedly. "Dance with me, babe, please?"

"Only if Ashleigh and Dawn come."

"You guys go," Ashleigh said. "I'll watch the table."

Dawn looked like she was going to argue, but Amanda was already pulling her away. The bartender appeared, dropping off three tequila shots and another bottle of water. When she stepped away, Kristen was behind her. "Where're your friends?" Bailey picked her beer back up.

"Dancing."

"Oh. I got them shots."

"You didn't have to do that."

"Yes, I did."

"What do you mean?" Ashleigh knitted her brow.

"They didn't like me, but now I'm their new friend with tequila shots. Everyone likes their friend with tequila shots."

Ashleigh smiled easily. "Just three?"

"Well, I figured you're not drinking tonight, hence the water, and I've had enough. You've already had to drag me home unconscious once. I figured I'd give you the night off."

Ashleigh's body buzzed, remembering what it had been like to be in Bailey's home, in the bedroom full of her musky scent.

"So, I don't mean it to sound like this, but I don't really know how else to say it; do you come here often?" Kristen asked, and Ashleigh laughed lightly.

"Not really. Maybe once every few months, when I feel like going out."

"You mean when you want to meet someone?" Kristen raised an eyebrow.

Ashleigh played with the label on her water. "Isn't that what you're doing over there?" She tilted her head in the direction of the blonde at the bar, who watched them.

Kristen shrugged. "It was."

"And now?"

"And now I'm talking to you."

Ashleigh's friends came huddling back around the table, reaching for their cold beers to quench their thirst in the sweltering heat of the bar.

"Shots?" Erin looked at the three tequila shooters on the table.

"Yeah." Ashleigh cleared her throat. "Kristen bought a round."

"Awesome." Amanda picked up one of the glasses. Erin and Dawn did the same, but Dawn's mouth was a tight, straight line. "Cheers!"

The three of them clinked glasses and downed their shots.

"Thanks for the shot," Erin said.

"Yeah," Amanda seconded.

Dawn, still tight-lipped, said nothing. Apparently not everyone liked their new friend with tequila shots.

"So, how do you guys know Ashleigh?" Kristen asked. "Got any embarrassing childhood stories to tell me?"

Ashleigh nudged Kristen, who winked back at her in response. It was one of those really natural, quick winks, the ones that actually looked cool. How was everything she did so damn sexy?

"We haven't known her long enough, unfortunately," Erin said.

"No?"

"We met a year ago, maybe two," Ashleigh said.

"It's summer, so yeah, almost two." Erin looked up and mentally did the math.

"How'd you meet, then?" Bailey asked as she leaned one elbow against the table and took another swig of her beer.

"Here." Amanda picked up her beer. "The three of us have been friends since high school, and one night we met Ashleigh. She'd just—"

"Moved back to the city," Ashleigh interrupted. Bailey did not need to know about her breakdown over Denise and how Erin and Amanda had found her, depressed and cynical, and invited her to join them.

"No, you'd already been back a while," Dawn said, her stare boring into Ashleigh. "It was right after Denise dumped you."

Ashleigh's stomach dropped. She looked to Kristen to see how much damage had been done. She was greeted by a compassionate smile. "Denise sounds like an idiot," Kristen said, and her hand returned to the small of Ashleigh's back. The warmth of her touch burned through her T-shirt as if she were touching her skin.

"She was," Erin said in agreement.

"Yeah, and Ashleigh was a mess over her. Sometimes people can't see what's right in front of them," Dawn said.

Kristen removed her hand from her back and looked at Dawn, then Ashleigh. She finished the rest of her beer in one long swallow. "Well, thanks for the company." She put the empty bottle down. "Enjoy the rest of your night. I'll see you around, Paige."

Ashleigh wanted to ask her to stay, but Bailey was heading back to the blonde at the bar, and she couldn't compete.

"Why did you say that?" Erin whispered harshly to Dawn.

"Because you said it yourself: a girl like that is only going to hurt her."

Ashleigh turned to them. "I can hear you, and I'm perfectly capable of deciding things like that for myself."

"Yeah, right," Dawn scoffed. "You were looking at her like a lost puppy."

Ire and embarrassment kindled in Ashleigh's chest. She had not been looking at Kristen like that. Did Kristen think she was looking at her like that? Is that why she left? "What's it to you?"

"Ashleigh, stop," Amanda said.

It was then she noticed the hurt on Dawn's face. Did Dawn still like her? Yeah, Denise had been an asshole and not right for her, but Dawn being generally nice didn't make her right for her by default. She didn't want to settle for nice or good enough. She wanted... Her thoughts abruptly came to a halt when her gaze drifted to Kristen. The blonde—who seemed to get more attractive every time Ashleigh looked at her—had her hand inside Kristen's tank top, touching her back while she said something in her ear. Jealousy slipped its chains, coming loose inside of her. Kristen smiled, and for the first time, Ashleigh hated that smile.

"I'm sorry. I'm tired," she said to the table and avoided Dawn's gaze. "I think I'm going to call it a night. I'm on earlies this week."

"Ashleigh..." Erin started to argue, but Amanda's hand, laid gently on her wife's arm, stopped Erin from saying anything further.

Dawn's voice stopped her as she turned to leave. "I'm just looking out for you," she said, but Ashleigh knew she'd really only been looking out for herself. She didn't turn back to Dawn, but she did cast one more glance Bailey's way. She and the blonde were gone.

CHAPTER 8

"So, I heard something interesting." Rodrigo said as he lifted up an old cardboard box and let it drop back down in the alleyway.

"Oh yeah, what's that?" Ashleigh asked. Her gaze scanned their debris-laden path. They were looking for the source of a domestic disturbance call but so far had been unable to locate the address. They'd parked the ambulance and were walking down a back alley in Chinatown, looking for a side- or sub-building number, 1-11B, whatever that meant. "God, how do these people ever get a pizza delivered?" she muttered derisively.

"I think you mean pork fried rice and eggrolls," Rodrigo said. When Ashleigh didn't laugh, he stopped. "Someone said he saw you and that shit Bailey talking outside the station the other day."

"Whoa." She rounded on him.

"What, are you going to defend your girlfriend to me?" The anger in his voice was almost palpable.

"Jesus, I'm allowed to do what I want with my personal time. I'm your partner, not your wife."

"No, it wouldn't matter whose wife you were, would it? Or whose sister."

Ashleigh didn't need a reminder about the way Bailey was with women. She'd barely slept the last couple of nights thinking about it, driving herself crazy with the image of the woman's hand inside Kristen's shirt and wondering how Bailey's flesh would feel against her own skin.

"For what it's worth," Ashleigh said, and tried to steady her voice, which was hard under the intensity of Rodrigo's glare, "I don't think she did what she did to hurt you or your sister. I think it was an accident."

"An accident? Like what? She tripped and fell onto my sister's *concha*?"

"Ew, do you have to be so crass?" Ashleigh drew her eyebrows together. "She didn't even know it was your sister." That was a mistake.

"You talked to her about it." He wet his lips and sucked them in as if barely restraining his rage. "I told you that as my partner, in confidence, not so you would run to that asshole with it."

"Stop calling her that." Ashleigh asserted herself as much as she dared. Why was she defending her? Ashleigh pushed away thoughts of Bailey's kindness with CeCe, of how she protected her from the swinging bottle, of how beautiful she looked, even in sleep, and most pressingly, how wickedly sexy she'd looked at the bar, beads of salty sweat rolling down her neck and clavicle in the sweltering heat.

She was about to apologize to Rodrigo, but a horrible stench hit her nose and stopped her. "Oh God, what is that smell?"

They moved slowly, cautiously, following the odour into what appeared to be an abandoned low-rise just ahead of them. This was a gang zone, and Ashleigh was nervous. They were the first to respond to this call, and it had been so long ago that it either meant they'd gotten lost in the zigzagging back alleys of Chinatown or the others weren't coming. It was gangbanger territory, run by the *Lǎohǔ* crew, a Chinese gang well known for their carnage and brutality. She wished they had not responded to the call.

They found a door, half off its hinges, and slipped through into the dark, dank building. It appeared to be abandoned. The smell was worse inside. Rodrigo pulled out his small flashlight, and Ashleigh did the same. The beams shining around the old building provided the only visibility. The boarded-up windows afforded little light even at midday. Ashleigh reached into her pocket and put her facemask on, unable to stand the foul stench any longer. They were silent, and the leaking of a pipe echoed from the other side of the room. The floor was a mix of dusty concrete and old, rotting wood. The air was stale and damp and thick in her throat, coating her lungs as she drew it in.

"I can't breathe," she said and turned to leave, but Rodrigo was right behind her, standing in her exit path. Undeterred from getting the hell out of there, she impatiently went around him and hurried back to the door. In her haste, she tripped on something in the darkness and lost her footing. As she fell, she moved her arms out instinctively to break her fall. Instead of hitting the hard ground as she'd anticipated, her body broke through some barrier. She heard snapping as the ground seemed to open up beneath her, and she fell several more feet. Finally, she hit bottom, and her hands—followed by the rest of her—landed in something cold and squishy.

Rodrigo turned his flashlight toward the commotion and lit up the area.

Ashleigh had fallen through old, wood slats and was lying on a decaying body.

She wanted to scream, but that was cut off by the rush of vomit that spilled from her mouth. She scurried back, away from the body, unable to catch her balance, and landed on her ass in the shallow hole.

"Paige!" Rodrigo called down and rushed to her. He grabbed her by the arm and lifted her out of the hole with her help, back onto solid ground. "Are you okay?"

She shook her head and reached for the hand sanitizer she kept in her cargo pockets. She wasn't sure how much she would need to disinfect the globs of gooey, gelatinous blood and liquefied organs from her hands and wrists, so she squeezed almost the entire bottle into her hands, rubbed them together, and retched again when the combined odour of the decaying body and the alcohol flew up her nose.

"We need to get you out of here." Rodrigo took her by the arm, and she let him lead her outside the building. She was never so happy to see the light of gangbanger territory. "Did you see what I saw in there?" he asked once they were outside.

"You mean the dead body I have all over me? Yeah, I saw it," she said acerbically.

"Paige, he had a badge on. He was a cop."

⁕

Ashleigh looked down at her hands, surprised they hadn't cuffed her yet. They might as well have, considering the treatment she'd received since the police arrived at the building. The first two cops on the scene had listened intently, but when their superior arrived and told Ashleigh and Rodrigo they needed to be separated and that they were each being taken into the station for questioning, Ashleigh couldn't remember if this was all part of protocol.

It had been hours since then, and she'd had time to realize this wasn't normal. For starters, since when did they take other first responders into the two-sided-mirror interrogation rooms? Why weren't they telling her anything? Instead, she'd spoken to two detectives so far, Whiley and Ortiz. They'd both been into the room three times but never at the same time. It hadn't taken her long to realize that they were both asking her the same questions, just in different ways, seeing if her story stood up to their different interrogation tactics.

Whiley returned, his long blond hair now pulled back into a slick ponytail, and sat down in the empty seat across the cold, metal table.

"Why am I still here?" she asked.

In answer, Whiley pulled two photographs out of a manila envelope and slid them toward her. She looked at them. Two different pictures of the same dead body, a young man with short, dark hair. He was lying on his back, blood streaked across his cheek that appeared to have come out of his ear, and his eyes were open, blankly staring up. He was wearing a Toronto Police Service uniform. She looked from the pictures to Whiley.

"Do you recognize anything?" he asked.

"No," Ashleigh said. "I don't recognize him, but I'm sorry for the department's loss." A little good will couldn't hurt. Then the realization hit her. "Was that the body?"

"Do you think if we had crime scene photos that the body would still have been there?" he asked rhetorically as if she were stupid.

"Then I don't understand. Are you trying to tell me that was done by the same person who did this?"

"Are you?" Whiley countered.

Ashleigh tightened her brow. Was he accusing her and Rodrigo of something nefarious? "I don't know who this is. I don't know who the body belonged to in the building. I don't understand why I'm still here." There was a quaver in her voice and a stinging behind her eyes. She looked down at the grey police sweatsuit that she was wearing. It was at least two sizes too big for her. She supposed at this point she should be happy it wasn't an orange jumpsuit. "You've taken my clothing for analysis, and I've been in here for hours. I'm here to help you guys, so why does it sound like you're accusing me of something? All I want to do is take a shower and get whoever this is off of me." She pointed to the dried, brown blood on her forearm.

"The body from the building today was that of Jenna Bradley. She was a rookie who went missing a year and a half ago," he said.

The idea that the body had been so badly decayed that she'd been unable to tell it was female made her feel ill again. She was tired and weary and drained, and she just wanted to go somewhere she'd feel safe.

"I'm very sorry to hear that, but I don't know anything. I've told you everything that happened from the second we noticed the smell up to calling in the body."

Whiley grabbed the photos, shoved them back into the envelope, and stood. He left without another word to her, only to be replaced by Ortiz five minutes later. He entered the room, stroking his dark goatee.

"Oh, come on," she groaned.

"We have only a few questions left for you. You've explained what happened after you found the body several times, but what you still haven't told me is what you and Rodrigo Cruz were doing snooping around abandoned buildings in the back alleys of Chinatown. Was it his idea?"

"I told you before, we got a call," she said exasperatedly. "Check with dispatch. If you guys were ever there first, you'd know what it's like to find the disturbance for yourselves."

That had been the wrong answer. Ortiz gave her a hateful look and moved back to the door.

"Please, just let me go. Honestly, I don't know anything. We were answering a call. That's it. We didn't mean to find what we did. I didn't intend to fall on a body!" Her voice went up several octaves.

He gave her another questioning look and left the room without saying anything. Once he was gone, she took a few deep breaths, but they were shaky. She didn't want to turn into an emotional wreck. Clearly, they were being accused of something, but she didn't know what. She closed her eyes. The man in the pictures, who was he? She saw him again in her mind's eye. She tried to remember the surroundings, but she hadn't looked at the pictures well enough. Then one thing came to her: a cell phone. Rodrigo's story about the rookie cop who'd made a cell phone video for his wife and started this whole mess between the cops and paramedics came to her. Had she just been looking at Ricky Oslowe? Fear buried itself in her stomach, and her armpits broke into a cold sweat. She hadn't even been part of EMS at the time. *But Rodrigo had.*

Hadn't someone from EMS told her about how Rodrigo lost his last partner and was suspended for some kind of inappropriate behaviour while on duty? It had been her first day, and she couldn't even remember the name of the woman she'd spoken to. She'd never suspected it was something serious, and the woman had said it so conversationally that she hadn't even bothered to ask more. She hadn't wanted to be seen as a gossip on her first day, but if the cops were questioning her about Rodrigo, maybe he really had been involved somehow. Her legs went numb. The door clicked open, and her heart stopped.

It was Bailey. In the state she was in, seeing Kristen made Ashleigh weak. If she'd had anything to tell, it would have all flooded out of her at the sight of Kristen. There was wetness on her cheeks, and it took a moment to register that she was crying.

"Kristen," she barely breathed.

Dark clouds of concern crowded into Bailey's blue eyes as she took in Ashleigh's appearance. "What's going on? Are you okay?" Bailey asked in her confident, smooth voice. Ashleigh had an answer prepared, but when she went to speak, more tears came out instead. "Hey, hey, hey," Bailey whispered. She moved forward swiftly, knelt down to Ashleigh's level, and pulled her into a strong hug.

Ashleigh's breath caught. It was the most contact they'd ever had. Bailey was warm and comforting, and in that moment, she couldn't believe how just the nearness of her could make her feel so safe and protected. She had been running on adrenaline and fear for the last few hours, and now that Bailey was here, Ashleigh's body went limp, all the anxiety and apprehension rushing out of her in waves.

"I'm sorry," she said. She should let her go, but she couldn't move her arms from around Bailey's strong neck.

"Don't be sorry," Kristen said by her ear. "Just tell me what's going on."

"I..." She hesitated. "I don't know, but I think they're accusing us of something."

"Okay, start from the beginning. How long have you been here?"

"I don't know. They won't tell me what's happening. They just keep asking me more questions."

"Why?"

"Rodrigo and I found a body. It was a cop," she said, her voice uneven.

"It's okay," Bailey said soothingly, stroking her back. The panic seemed to dissipate at her touch.

Someone cleared his throat in the doorway, and Kristen pulled her head away to look behind her. Ortiz was back, and he had a disgusted look on his face as he watched one of his fellow officers on bended knee with a paramedic in her arms. Kristen slipped from Ashleigh's embrace, and Ashleigh felt the loss acutely, as if someone had taken the warmth from her bones.

Bailey stood, her eyes hard, and turned her ire on Detective Ortiz. For someone who was usually so flippant, Bailey looked mad as hell. "Are you in charge of this charade?" she asked. Ortiz tightened his jaw but said nothing. "What the fuck is going on here?"

"Miss Paige was the witness at a crime scene. We're asking her some questions. Seeing as this isn't your case and homicide isn't your field, Constable, I think it's best you leave this to those in charge."

If Bailey understood he was trying to use her rank to put her in her place, she didn't show it. "How long has she been here?" she asked.

"A couple of hours, not long."

"How long?" she asked again.

Ortiz shrugged. "Three hours."

"Three hours?" Kristen repeated with much less indifference than Ortiz had delivered the news. "Has she been brought anything to drink? Where are her clothes?"

"Her uniform was covered in DNA from the crime scene. We had to take it to the lab for evidence."

"She's a fucking EMT, not a criminal, for God's sake. She's one of us."

Ortiz stiffened before he spoke again. "I suggest you remember yourself, Bailey, and where you are."

Ashleigh's stomach dropped when a second man entered the doorway. It was Staff Sergeant King—Bailey's top boss at the precinct—and he didn't look happy. She reached a hand forward to touch Kristen's arm and let her know it was okay, that she didn't have to get herself into trouble for her. Although Bailey didn't shirk her off, she didn't back down either.

"I assume after three hours of questioning that you've exhausted her and all she knows. Will that be all?"

It was clear by King's expression that he was stunned by Bailey's insolence. "This is not your concern."

"You do know that you have to let her go eventually, right? She hasn't committed any crimes, and you can't hold her against her will. Is she being charged with anything?"

King's face hardened. "No."

Kristen turned back to Ashleigh. "They can't hold you here against your will. You don't have to answer any more of their questions. You never did." She turned back to Ortiz and King, both her superiors, and both looking rather small as Bailey berated them. "Witnesses have the right to leave whenever they want to." She turned to Ashleigh. "Come on, it's time to go."

"They have Rodrigo too." She felt like she was telling on a bully in the schoolyard. With Kristen next to her, she no longer doubted Rodrigo, and she was ashamed she'd even let her fear push her thoughts in that direction.

"I assume you're going to cut him loose now as well?" Kristen asked them.

Ortiz gave an almost imperceptible nod. Kristen turned from him to help Ashleigh up out of her chair. Ashleigh stood and started to walk, but the look of pure hatred in Ortiz made her shrink back and stumble. She might have fallen, but Kristen's hands moved to her waist and gripped her firmly. Her touch was warm and soothing, but strong and sure at the same time.

"I got you," Kristen whispered.

Ashleigh closed her eyes a moment, allowing her words to comfort her. It didn't matter how the detective felt, Kristen wouldn't let anything happen to her. She nodded, took another step forward, and moved past the two men as quickly as she could. When Bailey went to follow, King grabbed her arm forcefully.

"I'd be careful if I were you, Constable. Not everyone takes kindly to being called out and questioned in front of an audience," he warned. "Especially those who outrank you."

"Frankly, the level of your rank means you should know better," she said. He tightened his jaw but said nothing further, and Bailey ripped her arm out of his grip. Kristen moved her hand to the small of Ashleigh's back again, adding gentle pressure to guide her forward. Warmth spread through her once more at the contact.

As she moved through the police station, she tried not to notice all the glances coming her way. She felt naked, exposed, and she wouldn't have been able to get through it without Kristen. Never breaking the contact between them, Kristen kept her moving and stood tall beside her. Ashleigh could feel the weight of their stares, but Bailey cut through the tension with ease. Her unwavering confidence gave Ashleigh strength, and she moved with her, trying not to let anyone make her feel small.

Outside, Bailey escorted her directly to the passenger side of her Mustang and opened the door for her before going around and getting into the driver's seat. Once inside the car, Bailey stared forward a moment and banged the steering wheel hard, twice, with the heel of her hand. Ashleigh jumped in her seat, and Kristen let out a long, steady breath.

"I'm sorry," she apologized without looking at Ashleigh. "I'll take you to your station to get your things, and then I'll take you home." This time she did face her. "Just tell me that you didn't do anything wrong."

It occurred to her that Bailey had just put her job on the line for her without even questioning her innocence. She didn't know many people who would do that. "I didn't do anything wrong," Ashleigh assured her.

Kristen nodded once and pulled the car onto the road.

"I don't want to go to the station," Ashleigh said. "I don't want to see anyone."

"I understand. Where's home?"

The thought of facing her parents right then was just as unbearable. "I don't want to go home either."

Kristen looked at her out of the corner of her eye. "Where do you want to go?"

All she knew in that moment was that with Kristen, she felt protected, and she didn't want to lose that feeling. At the police station she'd felt....violated, and it was only being around Kristen, leaning on her strength, that she was starting to feel whole again. There was only one place she wanted to go. One place she'd feel completely safe. "Can I come to your place?"

Bailey's whole body stiffened, and Ashleigh was about to take back her words—it had been stupid to ask—but before she could say anything, Bailey glanced in her rearview mirror and made a U-turn, wordlessly heading back in the direction of her condo.

"Thank you." Ashleigh exhaled forcefully, more relieved than she had anticipated.

Bailey swallowed and nodded but kept her eyes on the road. "You can tell me what the hell is going on when we get there."

Ashleigh wasn't looking forward to that, but she'd have to tell her eventually, and besides, for some reason, she wanted Bailey to know. Kristen had put herself on the line by standing up for her, and she deserved an explanation for it. If she was going to tell her what happened, it might as well be that night. The sooner she spoke about it, the sooner she hoped to forget it.

CHAPTER 9

"You remember where everything is?" Bailey asked without waiting for an answer. "The washroom is through there." She pointed to the door with one hand and hung up her keys with the other. "There are fresh towels in the vanity below the sink. Please, go ahead. You must want to get clean." Kristen was kind enough not to comment on the dried pieces of Constable Bradley that were still all over her.

It was the best shower of Ashleigh's life. She wasn't sure how long she stayed there, the water temperature so high it scalded her skin and turned it a bright pink. She lost herself for a while under the hot spray and wished she could cleanse her feelings and memories as easily as her skin. She turned the water off and opened the door to reach for her towel. The police-issued baggy, grey sweatpants had been replaced by a smaller navy blue pair and a plain, white, V-neck T-shirt. They were a welcome sight. She pulled the T-shirt over her head. It had Bailey's musky, vanilla scent. She pulled the fabric up to her nose and took a few deep breaths of it, letting the comfort of her smell wash over her as cathartically as the water from the shower had.

When she emerged from the bathroom, Bailey was in the kitchen, stirring something at the stove that smelled divine. The sun had set, but the ever-present bright lights of the city skyline shone in through the floor-to-ceiling living room windows. Kristen had the drapes pulled open, and the sight of the city lights imposed over the darkness of the night sky stirred something strange within her. It was like when she'd been a child in the back seat of the car on the drive home from Collingwood. Hundreds of headlights on the 401 lit up the inside of the car as she drifted off, warm and safe with her parents in the front seats.

As she looked out over the city, the nostalgia she felt for her childhood got all mixed up with the here and now. With Kristen, she had the sense that somehow she belonged here and everything was as it should be.

"Are you feeling better?" Kristen asked. It pulled her from her reverie.

"Much," Ashleigh said with a contented smile. "What smells so good?"

Kristen smiled. "Vegan chili. I can't take credit for it though. I got it at the convenience store downstairs. Prepackaged, but you're right; it smells pretty good." She turned the knob on the stove. "I don't know how to cook, and I had no groceries. Plus, I extra don't know how to cook for a vegetarian, but I thought you'd be hungry."

"I'm starving. Thank you," Ashleigh said, touched. In all her fantasies about Bailey, none of them had included Kristen cooking dinner for her. She'd have to add that one in the future.

Kristen gave her one of her winning smiles. "I'll just grab a couple of bowls. Cheese on yours?"

Ashleigh hesitated. "Is it the same piece of cheese from the last time I was here?"

Bailey paused. "It might be."

Ashleigh let out her first laugh of the day. "I'll pass."

"Probably a good call." She handed her a steaming bowl. "I hope it's edible."

Ashleigh took a seat on the couch, and to her surprise, Bailey took a seat on the coffee table right in front of her instead of sitting next to her or in the nearby armchair.

"It's amazing." Ashleigh said after her first bite. It truly was good, but she would have said the same even if it tasted like plastic. What she'd really wanted to say was that Kristen was amazing, but the compliment seemed safer served on the food.

Kristen tried a bite, swallowed, and put the bowl aside. "Yeah, doesn't really taste like meat."

"Ugh, that's not the point." Ashleigh took up the old argument. "If people keep expecting soy to taste like meat, they are going to be disappointed. Instead of trying to make it into something it isn't, appreciate it for its own flavour and texture. Enjoy how the spices and flavours hit your mouth and forget about trying to turn soy into beef. Just enjoy it for what it is."

"Rubber?"

Ashleigh tried to scowl at her, but she couldn't help grinning, and Bailey smiled in return. The sight warmed her through. That smile could melt icebergs.

Kristen cleared her throat and inched back on the coffee table. It put a little more space between them, and Ashleigh worried she'd stared too long.

"So, why don't you tell me what happened today," Kristen said.

Ashleigh let out a long breath. "Okay." She put her food down. The bowl was near empty anyway. "Rodrigo and I were out on a domestic disturbance call, looking for an address. I don't know how long we'd been out there, but we were the only unit to respond. Anyway, we came across a foul smell and followed it into a building to investigate. Inside, the building looked abandoned, and when I tried to leave, I tripped up and fell on a body. We called it in. The police arrived, took our statements, and then took us down to the station. Turns out the body belonged to a cop."

Kristen stiffened slightly. "I know this is difficult, but do you remember what kinds of questions they were asking or anything they told you at all?"

"They just kept asking me the same things. Where did we find the body? How did we find the body? Why were we there? Did we touch anything? Did we see anyone? Did we tamper with anything?"

"They asked if you tampered with anything?" Kristen cocked her head to the side. "That was rude."

Ashleigh let out a small, hollow laugh. "Yeah, it was."

"So, what did you tell them?"

"Pretty much exactly what I just told you, over and over again."

"Do you know the name of the deceased?"

"Jenna Bradley. She was a rookie who went missing a year and a half ago. That's all I know."

Kristen looked thoughtful. "They didn't tell you anything else?"

"No."

Bailey nodded.

"Wait," Ashleigh remembered, "they showed me pictures of another dead police officer. I think it was Ricky Oslowe."

That gave Kristen pause. "Ricky Oslowe," she repeated. "What makes you say that?"

Ashleigh shrugged. "It was just a feeling I got from the way they were asking their questions, like they were angry at me for it all, and that's when I remembered Oslowe's murder and how it had started this whole thing between paramedics and the police. I realized that was probably who I was looking at."

"What do you know about Ricky Oslowe?"

"Just what Rodrigo told me."

"And what did he tell you?"

Ashleigh sighed. "That a cop went into a call alone, a drug bust, and got hurt. His injuries were significant but non-life threatening. He had a laceration to his right forearm from a defensive wound and internal hemorrhaging in his spleen from a gunshot wound, but the bullet came out the other side and didn't puncture any other major organs. He died on scene anyway.

"The ambulance was first to get there. For once, we beat fire that time. Things looked normal at first, until the coroner's report. Rodrigo said Ricky Oslowe died of asphyxiation. When I asked him if one of the bad guys strangled him to finish him off, he said all the bad guys had been dead already when Oslowe made the call."

"Does Rodrigo have any idea who the EMTs were who took the call?" Kristen asked.

"No, and I don't even know how it's possible that no one has found these guys. We're all tagged and registered, and we have to respond to all our calls through dispatch. When I asked him about it, he said that a team did respond, but when that team arrived on scene, the cop was already dead. He told me the only reason we know there were two teams is that the officer had been making a video for his wife. Apparently they were newlyweds, and he was showing off his first war wounds. Supposedly, in the video, two paramedics pull up, kill him, and leave before the ambulance that responded to the call makes it on scene."

"Have either of you seen the video?" Kristen asked.

Ashleigh shook her head. "No, he said it was covered up quickly, wrapped up along with the whole ordeal, and kept from the public, which explains why I never heard anything about it on the news before I became a paramedic. I've seen some pictures now, though, I guess. The ones the detective showed me."

"This is important." Kristen shifted on the table, leaning forward, coming closer to her. "What did you see in the pictures?"

She wanted to ask why this was all so important to Kristen. Instead, she answered as best she could. "There were two pictures. Pretty much the same picture, really, just from different angles. It was of the police officer's body. A young male. He was lying on the ground."

"Good. What else?"

Ashleigh closed her eyes and tried to recall the image. "He had dark hair. There was blood on his face. His eyes were open, bulging almost. His face was discoloured. Darker than it should have been. He was wearing his uniform." She paused. "There was a cell phone in one of the pictures. That's what first made me think it was the murdered officer Rodrigo told me about."

"That's good. Anything else? Do you remember what was in the background? Anything in the pictures around his body?"

Ashleigh thought for a moment then shook her head. "I'm sorry. I didn't see them for long."

Kristen nodded. "Listen, if they tell you that they need to speak with you again, I want you to call me. Where's your phone?"

"It's in my purse." Her gaze wandered to the front door.

Kristen was quick to get up and grab it for Ashleigh to fish out her phone. "I didn't think you'd want me rummaging through your things," Kristen said. "Plus, I'm afraid of what I might find in there."

"Cute. Here you go." She held it out.

"Put in your password." Bailey waited for her to do so, then took the phone from her hands. "This is my number." She handed it back. "If anyone contacts you in any way about this incident, you call me, okay?"

Ashleigh warmed at Bailey's words. She couldn't help it. She was only human, and the fact that gorgeous Kristen Bailey seemed to care about her made her feel good all over. "Okay, and, well, you should probably have my number too."

"Sure." Bailey pulled her phone from her pocket and handed it to her.

Ashleigh's hands trembled slightly as she entered it into her contacts. Since when did her hands shake while operating a phone? *Get a grip.* She was merely giving Kristen her phone number for safety purposes, not so that she could call her up for sex one night. *Whoa.*

The errant thought was way out of line, and it caused a tightening down low in her body. She should not be having those thoughts. She knew how Bailey treated the women she bedded, and she wasn't interested in becoming one of her one-time trysts. She pictured Bailey at the bar, the same confident smile Denise had given her, the same cocky countenance that had seduced her into her first time with a woman. Bailey was just like Denise. She'd seen it in her demeanour, in that unwavering confidence and cavalier coolness that told Ashleigh that Bailey was not the kind of woman she should give her heart to.

"I won't use it unless I have to," Kristen assured her.

Ashleigh was disappointed. Romantically, Kristen was off limits, but repeating that mantra did little to slow her rapid heartbeat. "Of course."

"Well, I'm sure you must be exhausted." Bailey got up from the coffee table. "You know where the bedroom is, and if you need anything at all in the night, I'll be right here." She nodded to the couch.

"No, Kristen, I couldn't—"

"Please." She interrupted her with a raise of her hand. "It's my turn to take the couch. You did it for me not too long ago. I'm happy to return the favour."

"Thank you." It was time to get up and go to bed. After all, Kristen couldn't until she did. The sound of a phone went off, and it took her a second to realize it was hers. It was sitting on the coffee table with Rodrigo's name in the call display. "Sorry, I should get this." She picked it up. "Hey."

"Hey, where are you? I waited for you at the station."

"Sorry, I had to get out of there," she prevaricated.

"Are you okay?"

She smiled. "I am. I'm okay."

"What the fuck did those assholes want? We told them everything we knew at the scene."

Ashleigh looked up. From Kristen's raised eyebrow, she knew she could hear him too. She surreptitiously lowered the volume on the side of her phone with her thumb. "I know. I don't know. They kept asking the same sort of questions. I'm just thankful it's over."

Rodrigo breathed harshly. "Me too. Fucking cops." There was a pause. "McClaren says we can have a few days off. Stress leave. We don't need to be back until Monday."

"Thanks for letting me know," she said.

"You sure you're okay?"

"I'm sure. I just..."

"What is it?"

"Why were you suspended? Why did you get a new partner? I mean, I'm not complaining. You know I like riding with you, but I never asked before, and you never told me."

There was a long pause before he spoke. "They were asking you about me?"

"No, not exactly."

There was another pause, shorter this time. "It was Daniela's birthday. I went to visit her on duty. It was a slow day, and my partner came with me. I shouldn't have done it, but I swear that's all it was."

"Okay," Ashleigh said.

"Wait," he said loudly and then continued in a softer tone. "There's something else. It was the day that rookie police officer was killed. I was in the area."

"Oh," Ashleigh said quietly. He didn't have to say more. If he hadn't been visiting Maria and her daughter, he might have gotten to that call first, and Ricky Oslowe might still be alive. It made sense now, his loathing of police officers. It wasn't just Kristen Bailey; it was all of them, because deep down he didn't blame them at all. He blamed himself.

"It's not something I like to talk about, and I swear, I haven't done it since."

Ashleigh nodded. "Okay. Thanks for telling me, and thanks for calling."

"Call me if you need anything."

"I will."

"Goodnight, Paige."

"Goodnight." Ashleigh ended the call. She turned to Kristen. "Sorry, that was Cruz."

"I know."

"Did you... You must be wondering what that was about."

Kristen looked at her thoughtfully, as if wrestling with something. "No," she said finally. "I heard enough to know."

"So, you already knew why he lost his last partner?"

Kristen nodded. "With all the aftermath of that day, yeah, the rumour reached the police. As far as I understand it, he's not suspected of anything, though," she said.

Ashleigh nodded slowly, unsure of where to take the conversation from there. "What time do you want me out of here tomorrow?" she asked.

"What do you mean?" Bailey creased her brow.

"What time do you want me to leave in the morning?"

"There's no time. I mean, you can stay as long as you want to."

The answer surprised her. Kristen was going to have to stop being so nice to her, because it was wearing her barriers down. "Don't you work tomorrow?"

"Oh, no, day off, actually. First of four. What time's your shift?"

"Day off too." Ashleigh smiled. "First of three, apparently."

"Nice. You can sleep in then."

"Kristen..." Ashleigh nervously twisted a thick lock of hair between her fingers. "Are you sure it's okay that I'm here? I mean, I don't want to intrude. I wasn't really thinking at the station with everything that happened, and I don't want to put you out."

"You're not. Half the time I fall asleep reading on the couch anyway, so don't even think about it. Just rest. You had a shitty day."

Ashleigh laughed. "I appreciate your candour."

Kristen smiled. "Goodnight, Ashleigh."

Ashleigh took the dismissal and started for the washroom.

"Oh, wait," Kristen said, and Ashleigh turned around. "There's face wash, toothpaste, floss, and all that in the washroom. Hang on a sec." She went in ahead of her and pulled open the medicine cabinet. She took out an extra head for her toothbrush and took it out of the cardboard and plastic. She threw the packaging into the garbage, popped the head off her electric toothbrush, and stuck the new one on. "Here you go." She handed her toothbrush to Ashleigh. "Do you need anything else?"

"No, this is awesome. Thank you." She hesitated a moment. Her words didn't sum up the true gratitude she felt for everything Kristen had done. She'd rescued her, fed her, clothed her, given her a place to stay, and was even sharing her toothbrush with her, for God's sake. "I wish I could tell you how much I truly appreciate all of this."

Kristen's warm smile touched her eyes, and in Ashleigh's weakened state, it broke through the last of her defences. Kristen reached forward and squeezed Ashleigh's wrist affectionately. Ashleigh's gaze dropped to the contact, the warmth of it spreading up her arm like fire. She'd only felt that once before, in Kenya, when Laura touched her. She swallowed hard, the heat of Bailey's skin rushing through her veins.

Kristen let go of her wrist. "I'll be here if you need anything."

"Okay." It was time to stop staring, to stop longing for her, and to get ready for bed. "Goodnight."

Kristen nodded and stepped past her, back into the hall. As Kristen left, her breasts rubbed against hers in the small space of the doorway, and Ashleigh suppressed a moan as the contact cut deep into her core. God, she felt good against her.

"Remember, if you want anything, I'm just out here."

Ashleigh swallowed, trying to find her voice. What she really wanted, Kristen couldn't give her.

Ashleigh had closed the washroom door, but Kristen remained there, breathing heavily. She could still feel where her body had brushed Ashleigh's. She closed her eyes, trying to steady her breathing. She wouldn't be getting any sleep that night.

It had been a long day for Ashleigh, which in turn had become a troubling day for Kristen. She'd been out of line at the precinct, way out of line, and there was a chance she'd made a powerful enemy in Staff Sergeant King. Worse, her behaviour was not going to help her find Ricky Oslowe's killer, which she reminded herself was the only reason she was there. Since she'd arrived in Toronto, she'd held her tongue in check and kept quiet when things went down in ways she didn't approve of. At the end of the day, she wasn't a cop of 52 Division. Today, however, she'd let herself ruin the rapport she'd spent the last three months building.

She should have just stayed out of it, but they'd had no right to treat Ashleigh so uncivilly. It was like they were enjoying Ashleigh's discomfort, her fear and naivety of proper protocol, and that made Kristen furious. Sure, RCMP Staff Sergeant Kristen Bailey could report King for his treatment of Ashleigh Paige that day, but in the Toronto Police Service, Constable Bailey was the new transfer and low on the totem pole, and making accusations like she'd done was supposed to be way above her pay grade.

The door clicked open, and Kristen moved quickly away from the washroom toward the couch. Ashleigh stepped out of the bathroom and went quietly into the bedroom. Her bedroom. In a few moments, she would be in her bed. Ashleigh closed the door behind her, and Kristen deflated at the exclusion.

Was Ashleigh afraid she would sneak in and try something? She shook her head. *Maybe she just sleeps with the door closed.* It was quite possible that Ashleigh had felt nothing when their bodies made contact and had no idea of the lascivious thoughts that had raced through Kristen's mind. She turned away from the door and went to the couch.

The more she tried not to think about Ashleigh, the harder it was to forget about her. It was just like that night at Tango. She'd tried to go home with the blonde from the bar. What was her name? She couldn't remember, but she did remember following her into her apartment building and kissing her on the ride up in the elevator, hoping the act would finally force her sex drive into gear. She'd let the woman pull her into the bedroom of her penthouse suite, where Kristen realized if she wasn't feeling it yet, she wasn't going to be able to perform. She didn't even have it in her to go through the motions. What was the point? She'd only gone home with her for the release, so why fake it?

She'd told the woman she had a migraine and had to go home. The woman tried to offer her services at playing doctor, but Kristen wasn't interested. She couldn't remember a time she'd been less interested in an attractive woman. How was she supposed to strip the blonde's clothes off and take her to bed when her mind was overrun with images of Ashleigh? Why was it that she wanted to know more about her than she'd wanted to know about anyone she'd ever been intimate with? It was as if from the very start, she'd been infected with thoughts of her.

She closed her eyes and moved her mind to safer territory, away from the beautiful paramedic who was just thirty feet away in her bed. She gritted her teeth. She should be thinking about the case. About the dead police officer. That cooled her thoughts.

Why had the detectives brought pictures of Ricky Oslowe into the interrogation room? What had they hoped to gain from showing them to Ashleigh? Like her, did they suspect there was a connection between the two cases? Worse than that, did they *know* they were connected? If so, they knew more than Kristen did, which meant it was time to get in their good graces, but that would be challenging after the stunt she'd pulled that afternoon. *Damnit.* She'd worked too hard to have everything foiled by her feelings for Ashleigh Paige.

She turned over on the couch. This was the first time anything like this had happened to her. She'd never let her personal emotions interfere with a case. She was a professional first and a human being second, and she'd never had issue with that until now. There was no point in dwelling on what she couldn't change. She'd screwed up with Detective Ortiz—a man who already didn't think much of her—and now she needed to come up with a way to get in his good graces and learn what he knew.

Kristen let out a long breath. She should call Ouellette and report that Jenna Bradley's body had been found, but she didn't know how to do it without Ashleigh overhearing her call in the small condo unit. If she left to make the call, Ashleigh might wake, and she didn't want her to feel alone or scared after asking Kristen to take her home, because it was the only place Ashleigh felt safe. She already had all the files on Jenna Bradley's disappearance from before she'd arrived on the case, and the new police and medical examiner's reports wouldn't be loaded onto the police systems until further investigation had taken place, so maybe, just this once, she could let it go for the night. Even as she had the thought, she recognized that she was bending the rules for Ashleigh once again, but that didn't stop her from doing it.

Instead, she pulled out her laptop and read over all the old files she had on the disappearance of Jenna Bradley. That her body had been found in Chinatown added nothing new to the case without the complete autopsy report. There was nothing more she could do now but try to stop her mind from spinning in circles and get a good night's rest. She'd call Ouellette in the morning, once Ashleigh left, and apprise him of the situation. Ouellette would send her the new investigative findings as soon as the RCMP could pull them from the Toronto Police Service's secure database. Sleep was easier said than done, though, and after attempting it for what felt like forever, Kristen decided to read a book.

She picked up several novels, unsure which one to choose. She ran her hands along the spines of some of her favourite pieces of fiction, trying to force the calm that so often came from reading. On so many cases, through so many nights, books had been her closest companions. No matter where her job sent her, she could always count on a book to take her to a place where she *almost* felt she belonged. With Ashleigh in the next room, her novels had their work cut out for them that night.

A book slipped from her hands and landed with a thud. *Jude the Obscure*. She picked it up hesitantly and then sighed with relief. It was not damaged.

"Kristen, are you up?" Ashleigh called softly from the bedroom.

"Yeah, everything all right?" she hollered at the door. It had been hours since Ashleigh had gone to sleep. There was a muffled response that Kristen couldn't make out. She put the books down and moved closer to the bedroom. "Pardon?"

"I don't think I can sleep."

Ashleigh was just on the other side of the door. In her bed. Wearing... She shook her head. It was better she didn't know. "Just try to relax." She leaned her hands and head gently against the door. "You'll fall asleep."

"I'm afraid to fall asleep."

Kristen knew that feeling. Ashleigh was a good person. It wasn't right what she'd gone through.

"I'm coming in," she said before opening the door and walking in tentatively. "What is it?" she asked, taking in Ashleigh's form lying in her bed. She was on the *other* side of the bed—the side Kristen didn't sleep on—her honey-brown hair spilled over the pillow, covers pulled up to her waist. The T-shirt she'd lent her had ridden up and exposed part of her midriff and the dip of her hip bone.

The muscles in Kristen's stomach tightened.

Ashleigh propped herself up against the headboard, which thankfully allowed her T-shirt to fall and cover what it was supposed to.

"I'm afraid I'll see it again in a nightmare," Ashleigh said in a quiet voice.

"You might." Kristen took a step toward her. "It'll be scary at first, and kind of hard to deal with, but eventually you'll process it, and you won't be afraid anymore."

"You sound like you're speaking from experience."

"I am. There've been nights I've been afraid to close my eyes too." She did not elaborate. "It does get easier, though, with time. Right now, you just need to make it through tonight."

"I know it sounds stupid, but I don't know if I can."

Kristen's heart sank. "It doesn't sound stupid." She moved to the bed and sat by Ashleigh's legs. "It's okay to be scared. It's okay not to be okay with what you saw."

Ashleigh nodded. "You're kind of my hero right now," she said with a small smile.

Kristen's heart fluttered. She reached for one of Ashleigh's hands and linked their fingers together. She'd never done this before. Held a woman's hand. Not like this.

The warmth of Ashleigh's hand in hers started a slow burn up her arm and into her chest, and her heartbeat picked up speed. Ashleigh could not look more beautiful than she did in that moment, with her hair half falling over her face and shoulders; her lips curved in a delicate, trusting smile; her vibrant green eyes focused on her. Kristen dropped her gaze and followed the dip of Ashleigh's clavicle to the swell of her breasts. She wasn't wearing a bra.

The heat inside her abdomen rushed lower.

This was not supposed to happen. She knew better than to fall for someone on a case, but her body had done so anyway without her permission. It was one thing to sleep with someone. There was no problem with that, and often it even helped, but this was different. She wanted her, badly, and for more than just a quick turn in bed.

"Will you stay with me a while?" Ashleigh asked. "I feel better with you here."

Kristen forced a swallow. "If you want me to. I can watch over you until you fall asleep."

Ashleigh looked down a moment before meeting her gaze through long, beautiful lashes. "Can you hold me?"

Her words caused a flurry in Kristen's chest.

Ashleigh wanted her to get into bed with her.

She wanted her to hold her.

She wanted her body against hers.

There was a hard pulse between her thighs. Kristen tightened her jaw. She should refuse, make up some excuse, but why? She could control herself. Just because she had never been more attracted to someone didn't mean she couldn't keep things platonic. She swallowed forcefully. Ashleigh needed comfort, a friend. She could be that person for a little while.

She moved to the other side of the bed and crawled in. Ashleigh turned her back to her, and Kristen quickly got the idea. She put her head against her pillow and began to move forward just as Ashleigh inched herself back toward Kristen. Their bodies met, and Kristen's breath hitched. Did Ashleigh hear it?

She slid her arm forward over Ashleigh's side and draped it over her middle. Would it be welcome? Ashleigh put a hand over her arm, laced their fingers together again, and pulled Kristen's arm tighter around herself so Kristen was holding her close against her body.

"I feel so safe with you," Ashleigh said, her silken voice barely more than a whisper.

Kristen closed her eyes. She didn't trust herself to speak. The fluttering in her stomach raged at the closeness of Ashleigh, who was warm and soft in her arms. Kristen inched her head forward slightly, just enough to bury her nose in Ashleigh's beautiful mane on the pillow. She breathed her in deeply. She had never wanted anyone as badly as she wanted Ashleigh in that moment.

She couldn't stay.

She started to pull her arm back, but Ashleigh's grip tightened.

"Just stay till I fall asleep," Ashleigh said drowsily and burrowed back further into Kristen's body. Ashleigh appeared to be in that strange place between sleeping and wakefulness, and when she spoke again, it was so quietly that Kristen had to lean forward to hear her. "You feel so good against me."

Ashleigh sleepily traced her fingers over Kristen's arm. Did she have any idea what she was doing to her?

After a few torturously slow minutes, the touching ceased. Instinctively, Kristen tightened her hold around her waist. Ashleigh whimpered softly at her touch. Kristen wanted so badly to let her own hands wander, to feel more of her, but she dared not. Ashleigh had been through a lot that day. The last thing she needed was to feel like someone was pawing at her when she'd only been seeking comfort.

She raised her head to look at Ashleigh's face. Her eyes were closed, her lips slightly parted, and she was breathing peacefully, the rise and fall of her chest slow and even. Kristen laid her head back down on the pillow and tried to steady her own breathing. After a few minutes, the fire of her desire simmered until just the embers remained, warming her through as she held Ashleigh close. The last thing she remembered before slipping into sleep was that she was about to do something she never had with a woman before. Fall asleep beside her.

CHAPTER 10

Kristen was slow to open her eyes. The heat of a body was pressed up against her, and for a moment, she panicked. She took a quick breath. Ashleigh's unique, soft scent filled her lungs, and she smiled, remembering.

Next to her, Ashleigh's eyes remained closed, her light brown lashes sweeping down and her perfectly winged eyebrows smooth on her forehead. It took all of Kristen's control not to reach out and stroke the soft skin of her face. She had never just lain with a woman before. It felt...intimate in a way nothing else ever had.

She couldn't do this. She had to stop this now before it turned into something else. It was still just... It was nothing. Nothing she couldn't get over, given a couple of days away from her. That's what she needed. Space.

Quietly, she tried to move away, but Ashleigh's grip on her arm did not loosen. A small simpering sound escaped Ashleigh's throat as she opened her eyes.

"Hey," Kristen said softly. Ashleigh's brow tightened for a moment before it smoothed out and she smiled. It was a welcome sight.

"Hey. What time is it?"

"Just after six."

"It's early." Ashleigh nuzzled her face further into the pillow and tightened her grip on Kristen's arm. The moment she did so, her eyes popped open. "I'm sorry." She released her hold on Kristen, her cheeks a lovely shade of pink.

Kristen smiled at her, unable to help being amused at Ashleigh's embarrassment. "It's okay. I didn't mean to fall asleep in here. I guess I was more tired than I thought."

"I'd hoped you'd stay," Ashleigh said softly.

There was a tug in Kristen's chest. She had to get out of there. "Go back to sleep," she said.

Ashleigh nodded and closed her eyes. Kristen was glad for it. She slipped away from Ashleigh's warmth and out of the bed. She grabbed gym shorts and a tank top. Ashleigh would sleep for a while yet, and she needed to release some of the tension choking in around her heart.

The gym was empty. She hopped on the first treadmill and ran with abandon. For once, she didn't turn on the TV or bring headphones. Her racing thoughts were more than enough to keep her occupied and moving until she pushed herself so hard she got a cramp in her side. She took a deep breath, wincing at the pain, and lowered the intensity. She'd been running at over seven miles per hour. Normally, she steadied out around six. She held the stitch in her side and tried to catch her breath, the machine now moving her along at a fast-paced walk.

What was it about Ashleigh? Why couldn't she get her out of her mind? When Ashleigh was around, she was clumsy with her words and inexperienced with her emotions. It was as if she brought out the exact opposite in her than every other woman did. She was in unfamiliar territory, and it worried her.

She was usually a paradigm of control, always the one with the plan, and permanently one step ahead. With Ashleigh, she felt she was always trying to catch up, and her body reacted to her in ways that she'd not experienced with the most intimate of her past lovers. With a look or a small touch, Ashleigh affected her more than any sexual encounter she'd ever had. It was madness, and Kristen had no governance over it, and worse than that, no resistance to it.

She pressed harder at the stitch in her side and quickened her pace, determined to get everything out of her system before she left the gym.

Her feelings for Ashleigh were a problem. She didn't have time for problems. Her promotion was slipping so far away it had become a blur on the horizon. She needed to stay focused. Ashleigh was a distraction. She was getting in the way, clouding her thoughts, and, worse, protecting her yesterday had been detrimental to her limited success on the case.

Involuntarily, she remembered how Ashleigh's body had felt pressed up against hers and felt that tightening in her stomach again.

Stop it.

She increased the intensity on the machine. Sweat dripped down her back. She pushed herself to go faster, holding tight to the stitch in her side.

Feelings were for teenagers. They were for doe-eyed daydreamers. She couldn't help having a sexual appetite, but one-night stands had always been enough. Now it all seemed so hollow. Ashleigh had awoken a hunger in her for something more. How had she ever climaxed without that feeling? That's why she'd left what's-her-name's apartment the other night. The blonde's touch, her kiss, had felt as intimate as if someone were bumping into her elbow. Ashleigh's touch though…

A young couple came into the gym, laughing. That was her cue to leave. She didn't want company, especially not two people caressing and kissing and so clearly enamoured with one another. Public displays of affection had never bothered her before, except when they got gross, but it was not repulsion she was feeling right now. It was envy.

Irritably, she slipped off the treadmill and left the gym. She punched her floor number on the elevator repeatedly. She shook her head and stepped into the car. The doors opened on the seventh floor. She looked up and groaned.

"Hey, you." Amelia stepped into the elevator. "Going up or going down?" She gave her a mischievous smile.

"Up," Kristen said listlessly.

"Me too. It's a hot one today. The pool is going to be perfect."

Kristen nodded. The rooftop pool was one of the main selling features of the condo, but with Jared living right on the water, she found she used it little.

"Why don't you join me?"

"I can't."

Going home with strangers was one thing, but picking up a woman in the lobby of her building had definitely been a lapse in judgment, brought on by too many tequila shots at the end of a long, hard week. The only things she could remember about that night were tripping on computer wires and a hangover from hell.

"Don't you want to get me wet?" Amelia winked at her and flipped her platinum blonde hair behind her large, gold-hoop earrings.

Do people really talk like that? Thankfully, the elevator stopped at the eleventh floor.

"Well, you know where to find me if you change your mind."

Kristen found the courtesy to nod before stepping off the elevator. Was that really what she thought she was worth? Were nights with women like Amelia all she wanted? Amelia had been good in bed, but by the time the act was done, she'd had enough. She'd always had enough by the time it ended.

She reached for her fob, but her cell phone vibrated in her hand before she could swipe the fob against the electronic door strike. She looked at the call display and exhaled forcibly.

Fuck. How could she have forgotten to call Ouellette that morning? It should have been the first thing she'd done when leaving her unit. More than that, it should have been done last night.

She straightened her shoulders and walked a little down the hall, away from her suite. Soundproofing was terrible in new-builds.

"Bailey," she answered, her voice going straight to a business tone.

"It's Ouellette, which I'm sure you know. Why haven't I heard from you?" His tone was accusatory. "How come I always have to call you? You do know that's not protocol."

"Good morning to you too," she said.

"Morning was when I woke up five hours ago. Tell me you have something, Bailey. I feel like you're shooting in the dark over there, and honestly, the higher-ups want me to pull you out."

"What higher-ups?"

"The commissioner."

Shit. It didn't go any higher up than that.

"Just tell me you have something," he said, and she was surprised to hear his voice soften. "At this point, I'll take that you've arrested an EMT for smoking pot."

"I was going to call you later this morning, actually. Yesterday, a team of paramedics found the body of Constable Jenna Bradley, the police officer who went missing eighteen months ago."

"Fuck, Bailey, that's something! Are there any similarities to the Oslowe case?"

"So far, just what we already know. Jenna Bradley and Ricky Oslowe were both rookies with fifty-two. I was hoping you could send me the updated file for Jenna Bradley."

"I'm sending out the request now." He clicked on his keyboard. "The team of paramedics who found this rookie, do you think it could have been the team that killed Oslowe?"

"No way." She blurted out her response. It wasn't her most professional-sounding assessment.

"Why's that?"

"I know one of them, and she couldn't have had anything to do with this."

"What does that mean? You know anyone is capable of anything. What's going on with you out there?"

That was a good question, one she'd been asking herself a lot since meeting Ashleigh Paige.

"I just mean that she's not capable of doing something like this. She doesn't have it in her. I trust her."

"Hmph." He grunted. "Trust." He grunted again. "And her partner? Do you *trust* her partner too?" he said, as if the word were dirty, and the truth of it was that in their line of work, it was.

"Her partner is Rodrigo Cruz, and there's video evidence that puts him at his sister's house at the time of Richard Oslowe's murder."

"And the EMT's name?"

"Ashleigh Paige."

"Paige. I ran her name a couple of weeks ago."

"That's her."

"Right." He paused and clicked on his keyboard again. "Twenty-five years old. Former GVI medic. Been an EMT almost two months. Clean record. So what's her story?"

"Nothing. She's new. Nice."

"And you trust her?"

God, why did she tell him that? "Yes," she answered, unable to take it back now.

"A rookie paramedic could be of use to us."

"How?"

"How well do you know her?"

Kristen shrugged. She didn't know how to answer that.

Ouellette read into her silence. "If you don't know her that well, how can you be so sure she's not involved in this?" He had her there.

"I know her enough to know she couldn't be involved. Besides, she's only been a paramedic for one or two months, like you said, so she can't have been involved in either of those deaths."

"That may be true enough, but we can't say anything's for sure at this point, not until we have a lead in any solid direction. Have you formed any kind of connection with this woman?"

"I guess."

It wasn't much, but it was enough for Ouellette to grab onto.

"I want you to exploit it."

"What does that mean?"

"You know what that means. What's gotten into you? You think you're Constable Bailey of the Toronto police now? You're a goddamn RCMP staff sergeant, Kristen! Act like it." It was never good when he used her first name. It wasn't good when he shouted or threw her rank in her face either.

"I just don't think it'll get us anywhere," she said. Why was she still arguing with him? It was just like at the station the night before, when she should have kept her mouth shut in front of Ortiz and King. This wasn't like her. She cleared her throat. "What do you want me to do?"

"Use the relationship you're building with her to get information. She might not even realize what she's repeating to you if you ask her in the right way."

"But she's a rookie. She doesn't know anything."

"That's what makes her perfect. If she's asking questions that you plant inside her head, people won't be suspicious. She can be our mole without even knowing it." His voice lifted. "Fuck, Bailey, this could be our way in. Tell me you already have a decent rapport with this woman?"

"I do." Bailey said, her bottom lip between her teeth. What Ouellette was saying made sense. She wasn't sure what bothered her more, that he was going to force her to exploit Ashleigh or that she hadn't thought of it herself.

"Excellent. Get close to her. Get so close she doesn't know where her thoughts end and yours begin. You know how to manipulate people; you're one of the best, so don't let me down. You're only as good as your last bust, Bailey, and I handpicked you for this assignment for a reason. Banff is calling; all you have to do is answer."

———————————

Ashleigh jumped when the front door opened but smiled when Kristen walked in and hung her keys on the hook by the door. The scent of coffee and toast wafted through the air as she stirred the scrambled eggs. Soft jazz came from her phone on the counter next to her.

When Bailey came closer, Ashleigh tried to keep her focus on the eggs, but her gaze kept returning to Kristen, who leaned easily against the fridge and watched her. She was wearing a pair of black shorts and had on a tight, black T-back tank top that clung to her torso so tightly it looked like it had been vacuum-sealed on. There was a gleam of perspiration on her skin, and a knot twisted in Ashleigh's stomach as a bead of sweat slid down the side of Kristen's neck. Her face flushed with heat, and she turned her attention back to the task of making breakfast.

"I hope you don't mind." Ashleigh pointed to the new set of borrowed clothing she wore—a pair of jeans and a white tank top—then to the coffee cup she held in her hand. "You were so kind to me last night, and I wanted to do something for you, but I also needed a change of clothes. I'll wash them and bring them back tomorrow or later on today if you want."

"It's okay," Bailey said with a smile. "They look better on you anyway."

"I doubt that." Ashleigh hid her smile in her coffee cup. "So…" She turned and settled her back against the counter, flipped her hair behind her shoulder, and rested on one elbow. "What are your plans for your days off?"

"I was thinking of heading up to see my brother if the weather holds."

"Is it not supposed to?"

"Well, they get a little more rain up north than we do. We mostly fish and go out on the boat, so if it's raining, there's not much to do."

"You said before they live in Muskoka?"

"Algonquin, but yeah, they've got a great place. It has all the modern conveniences like running water and flushing toilets and all that, plus it's right on the water. Their backyard leads into the beach, and they have a big dock for our motorboat."

"Our motorboat?" Ashleigh asked.

Kristen smiled. "Cyndi wanted to spend their savings on getting them from well water to municipal, so I told Jared I'd split the cost of a new boat with him, as long as it was understood that I could take it out whenever I wanted overnight, no questions asked."

"No questions asked?" Ashleigh cocked an eyebrow. "Does the boat double as a bed, Casanova?"

Bailey laughed easily, and the sound warmed Ashleigh. "There is a sleeper cabin in the bottom."

"I guess you've taken a lot of women out on the water then?" She cringed at the jealousy in her voice. Hopefully, Bailey wouldn't hear it.

Kristen shook her head. "No, I just like it for the privacy, actually. It's really peaceful out on the water. I love Jared and Cyndi, but sometimes I just want to go out on my own, escape from everything for a few days."

"That sounds nice."

Kristen turned to look at her. "How about you? Where do you go to escape? I know you said you like to go on hikes and to ski."

"I love skiing, but it's so weather dependent, and it's a lot harder to do now. My parents sold their place in Blue Mountain years ago, so I only get to go a few times a season. I like to run, though. Sometimes I drive up north and hit up some trails, if I can, just outside of the city."

"There are great trails up by the cottage."

"What lake is it on?"

"Canoe Lake, just inside Algonquin Park."

"That's awesome."

"Yeah. Do you have a running partner here?"

"Not really. Lately, Rodrigo comes with me, but not every day."

"So, you guys are pretty close?"

She shrugged. "I haven't been with EMS long, but it's hard not to get close to your partner."

"Unless it's Henry Hackett," Bailey said almost inaudibly.

"What's with that?" Ashleigh asked.

Bailey shrugged. "I'm still new, so I'm being punished."

"Are you serious?"

"No, but it feels that way sometimes. So, how did you sleep?"

"I slept well. Thank you for that." She blushed, remembering how frail she must have come across the night before. "I hope scrambled is okay for your eggs." She changed the subject.

"It looks great. Thank you."

"Oh, and here you go." Ashleigh poured a cup of coffee from the pot and handed it to Kristen, black, the way she liked it. She could get used to doing things the way Kristen liked them.

"So, no nightmares?" Kristen asked and took her first sip.

"No nightmares," she said through a contrite smile. "I'm a little embarrassed about all that. I'm not normally so…vulnerable."

"You have nothing to be embarrassed about." Bailey spoke into her coffee cup and waved her comment off. "Do I have time for a quick shower?"

"Mmm-hmm," Ashleigh murmured through tight lips, not trusting herself to look back at Kristen's tanned, lustrous body without picturing her in that shower.

"Great, I'll be quick." She put her coffee cup down and hurried out of the room.

The lock clicked in the washroom, and Ashleigh let out a long breath. She put the spatula down and leaned back against the counter. It was ridiculous, but she could not stop her attraction to Kristen Bailey.

The way Kristen was with women, she knew better than to be interested in her. She stomped her foot, reminding herself of her mother. She stirred the eggs once more and turned off the heat so they wouldn't overcook. If only overdone eggs were the end of her worries.

She'd behaved so poorly the night before, but Kristen had been so close, and it felt so good to be near her. The problem wasn't that she didn't want Kristen to want her. It was how badly she wanted her to want her. If Bailey were to return her affection, she wouldn't be able to say no to her.

"So, I was thinking," Kristen said.

Ashleigh turned to find Bailey pulling a light blue, thin, cotton V-neck T-shirt down over her flat, toned stomach. There was an answering ache inside her own.

"Why don't you come up to Algonquin with me?"

"*What?*" Ashleigh was abashed by the wonder in her own voice at the invitation.

"To my brother's," Kristen said.

"When?" she asked carefully, trying to determine if this was a hypothetical or real offer.

"Tomorrow. We're both off, and we could be there in a few hours. It's supposed to be a gorgeous weekend."

"Weekend?" She raised an eyebrow.

"I mean, we don't have to stay for more than just the day." She rubbed the back of her neck with her hand. "The weather is supposed to be nice. No chance of rain, apparently. I checked my weather app."

"I…" she paused, trying to think of a reason not to go other than it was the worst idea ever. "I don't have a car."

Kristen grinned. "I wasn't going to make you walk. I'll swing by your place tomorrow morning and pick you up, say, around eleven?"

She should say no, just like she should have left when she'd woken up alone an hour ago, but she hadn't been able to force herself away from Kristen then, and she couldn't now. "Your brother won't mind?"

"Jared and Cyndi could use some new entertainment. Singing for my supper isn't quite as amusing for them when it's the same stories every time. I fear I've become old hat." She gave Ashleigh her most disarming smile.

"I don't think that's possible," she said dreamily, then shook herself out of it. "But you're sure it's okay?"

"Absolutely. We'll make it down there for a late lunch and maybe some fishing. We could go out on one of the trails too, if you want, and I'll take you back whenever you like. Besides, this gives my idiot brother a chance to apologize to you in person."

CHAPTER 11

SOMETHING WASN'T RIGHT. THE CONDO was...what? Empty? Cold? Nothing was different. Nothing was out of place. So why did it feel different?

It wasn't the condo; it was Ashleigh. Or more precisely, the absence of her.

After Ashleigh had gone home, Kristen tried to get on with her day. She'd cleaned up their dishes from breakfast and walked Ashleigh down to the streetcar stop just at the end of her block. She'd wanted to drive her home, but Ashleigh insisted she'd put her out enough already. The truth of it was Kristen didn't feel inconvenienced at all. Despite never having wanted a woman in her place before, she'd liked having Ashleigh there. Was that why she'd invited her to Jared's cottage? Ouellette had told her to get closer to Ashleigh, but was that the only reason she'd spent her morning shower thinking about ways to spend more time with her?

She tried to shake it off. Her feelings for Ashleigh didn't matter. She had just days before Ouellette would pull her out. What she needed was a break.

She opened her laptop, entered the series of passwords required to get through the encrypted software and layers of RCMP security protection, then opened her bureau e-mail. Ouellette had sent her a package of files. It was everything the Toronto Police Service now had on Constable Jenna Bradley, including a transcript and video of Ashleigh's interview and the autopsy report. Most of the files she had seen before, including Jenna's test scores from Aylmer and all of her case notes starting from her first day as a rookie.

Kristen went to the kitchen, poured herself another cup of coffee, and began reading everything again, starting from the first file.

Jenna was the daughter of Michael Stannis and Cecelia Bradley, but Michael wasn't in his daughter's life, and Cecelia raised Jenna on her own in Toronto. Jenna had done well at the Ontario Police College, and she'd been a pretty girl with light brown hair and smiling eyes, not unlike Ashleigh.

She opened the next file. Jenna had been on the force less than a year when she went missing. Most of the cases she worked on were open and shut. A couple of them were homicides, but as usual, the domestic partner turned out to be the murderer, and a quick record check showed that all suspects were in jail eighteen months ago when Jenna went missing, so they couldn't have been the ones to make her disappear.

The scans of Jenna's case notes were straightforward. They were written neatly, intimating that like a lot of officers, Jenna kept a secondary notebook with her for quick notes and saved her official notebook for the second round, once the incidents were over and she was ready to turn in her official version of events. All the names were underlined, which made it easy to pick out Hackett's. The sight of his name gave her pause this time.

She'd always known that Hackett had also been Jenna's TO, but he'd shut Kristen down quickly when she'd first asked him about the missing officer.

Did Hackett have any theories about what happened to Jenna? Did he know they'd found her body? She'd like to ask him about it, but she couldn't without exposing herself, and this information was hardly enough to send her cover team in to arrest and question him over.

She opened the video of Ashleigh in the interrogation room after she'd found the body. Kristen turned her head away when Ashleigh's voice faltered. What did the detectives think Ashleigh could possibly know about an eighteen-month-old case? She was just a rookie EMT. Were they being cruel or thorough? It was hard to tell. She could just ask Detective Ortiz, but she didn't expect him to be too loose-lipped with her after the altercation she'd had with him, which was on the video as well. She flinched at the ire in her voice, first directed at Ortiz, then King. What had Staff Sergeant King been doing there? Sure, his office was at the station, and he had every right to be there, but why this case at that moment? Had he been coming in to interview Ashleigh himself, or had he just been walking by and heard the commotion between two of his officers?

She closed the interrogation video and opened the only audio file in the package. It was Constable Bradley's last dispatch call before she went missing.

"This is car fifty-two-nineteen. I'm just west of Spadina and Dundas, checking out a possible drug deal. We may need ETF down here. How long before I can get backup?"

"That's a read, fifty-two-nineteen," the female dispatcher said. "We can get you a car in ten minutes."

"That's too long. There are civilians out here. I'm going to go in and check it out."

"That's a negative, fifty-two-nineteen. We show you as being alone in that squad car, and we have no cars in your area calling in as available. I need you to stay put."

"No can do, dispatch. These people don't have ten minutes. I'm going in."

That was it. One decision. One heroic and stupid decision had determined Jenna Bradley's fate.

She played the file over. She'd heard it before, but it was always eerie, listening to the voices of the dead. She opened Jenna's police ID picture again. There was something familiar about her. Something she couldn't quite place.

The last file was an autopsy report. The cause of death was internal bleeding. She'd bled out from a gunshot wound to her neck, two inches above where her bulletproof vest would have protected her. It appeared from a sweep of the building where the body was discovered that Jenna Bradley had been moved to the hidden cellar space post-mortem and likely would have stayed decaying a few feet beneath the ground, exposed and unburied, had Ashleigh not literally fallen onto it.

A closer review of the initial investigation report showed that the body of one of the gang members had been found in the same place as Jenna Bradley's above ground, so the blood on the floorboards in that area would have been credited to him. Even if Bradley's blood had been found there by DNA from the blood splatter analysis, she was believed to have gone missing, so that wouldn't have caused any further investigation of that particular spot in the building. Whoever killed her simply got away with it by stashing her body and covering the floor above it with another.

Kristen closed her laptop and leaned back on the couch. With her eyes closed, she finished her coffee as she let everything play back on a reel in her mind's eye.

How were the cases connected?

One, they were both rookies. Two, they died within six months of each other. Three, they'd both gone into drug busts on their own, situations that they really didn't have the training and experience for. Were they hot-headed, or were they heroes? Four, both bodies were found in gang territory. What else?

Kristen had been in Toronto almost four months, and she was still riding with a TO. She was supposed to be a veteran transfer from Montreal, and the scores they manufactured for her from Aylmer were better than Ricky and Jenna's, so why had they been sent out on their own those days when Kristen still wasn't? All Hackett had to do was give the okay for Kristen to be on her own, and she would be.

Henry barely left the car on most calls. Was he keeping her around as his rookie so he didn't have to actually do anything? The way it was, their car got the calls, and she did the work. Were his motives as simple as that? Was it really about Henry's laziness, or was it more personal? Was he not letting her move on because he'd let Jenna loose early and then lost her?

She played Ashleigh's interview back in her mind. There was nothing there beyond some police intimidation. Jenna Bradley's audio clip was short, and because she knew the outcome, it was tragic, but it didn't tell her much. Finally, she pictured a smiling Jenna Bradley in her police photo.

That smile.

The teeth browned in her mind.

Those eyes.

They became jaundiced and bloodshot.

Fuck me.

Kristen knocked on the door. When there was no answer, she kept knocking until she got one.

"What?" The door was ripped open. CeCe stood there, a long, loose, stained, white T-shirt hanging over her skinny frame. Kristen couldn't tell if she had any kind of clothing on underneath it, on the top or the bottom. "Who are you?" Her eyes narrowed a moment before they widened in recognition. "You're that police officer," she said.

It occurred to Kristen that she wasn't in uniform, and that for the first time, CeCe might be sober. "Can I come in?"

CeCe seemed to debate it for a half second before she pushed the door the rest of the way open and stepped aside to let her enter. Kristen did so warily; a sober CeCe was just too good to be true.

The place was tidier than the day she'd gone up there with Ashleigh. Something was sizzling, and she followed CeCe to the kitchen. On the coil-top stove, one julienned red pepper was frying on its own in a pan. On the counter beside it, there was a half-empty bottle of vodka and a full water glass. CeCe took a large sip and turned to her.

"Do you want some?" She pointed to the pepper. Her breath smelled like rubbing alcohol.

Kristen looked from CeCe to the red pepper, then across her countertops. There was no other food. This was her supper, a red pepper and a bottle of vodka, and she was offering her some.

"CeCe," Kristen said softly. CeCe stirred the pepper in the pan. Kristen cleared her throat. "Cecelia," she said clearly, and CeCe turned. "I'm sorry about your daughter."

CeCe dropped the spatula, her eyes slowly filling with tears. "I never..." She shook her head. "I wasn't always like this."

Kristen's heart clenched. "I know," she said softly. "Someone did notify you that we found her?"

She nodded. "Someone came." She walked into the other room, the pepper forgotten. Kristen wasn't sure if she should wait at first, but when CeCe didn't return, she followed her into the bedroom down the hall. CeCe pulled a police cap and badge out of the top drawer of a dresser. "I had them out, but they were too hard to look at."

Kristen nodded. "I need to ask you a few questions."

CeCe sighed compliantly, as if she'd been expecting this from the moment she answered the door.

"First, are you sober?"

"Yes, and I'm sorry." She looked up penitently.

"For what?"

"For hitting you that day. I...I remember."

"You remembered, but you didn't say anything?" Kristen would know if CeCe had reported that she'd compressed her lungs until she passed out.

She put the cap and badge back in the drawer and closed it. "Jenna was always talking about all that paperwork." She shook her head. "I knew it was my fault. I didn't want you to have to go through all that."

Kristen was taken aback. CeCe might have been more lucid all along than she'd realized. She thought about the photographs that hung crookedly in the next room. They didn't look old, but CeCe looked so different in them.

"The drinking and the drugs, did they start after Jenna went missing?"

"It wasn't like this at first, not when I thought she was coming home." She left the room, and Kristen followed again. She returned to her glass of vodka and took a gulp. "After a few weeks, the police stopped talking to me. After a few months, I went down to the station, and they told me they were doing everything they could, but they had nothing. Then it hit me; she's not coming home." She took another swallow. "I always had problems." She waved airily to her head. "But they were under control. After Jenna, though..." Tears brimmed in her eyes. "She was everything to me."

"I understand," Kristen said, "and I want to find whoever did this to her, but I need your help. Jenna went missing fourteen months before I got to fifty-two division, so I need to know if there was anything she ever said to you that made you think someone might want to hurt her. Did she have any issues with anybody?"

"You mean with anyone she arrested?"

"That, or elsewhere. Did she ever mention anyone else?"

"There was one man. She was telling me about him not too long before..." She paused and stared off at the pepper, its skin now blackening in the pan.

"It's okay, go on."

"The officer she rode around with, the one who was training her, they argued over something. Someone was asking her to do some things she didn't think were right. She came to me, asking what she should do."

Kristen knitted her brow. Had they been looking in the wrong direction all along? Should they have been looking for cops and not paramedics?

Of course.

EMTs were mobile medics, for God's sake, not forensics specialists who would know how to cover up the job. Police officers had more training when it came to the science part of evidence collection and would have known the murdered officers much better. They also knew how to tamper with a crime scene.

CeCe moved the back of her wrist to her nose and sniffled against it. "I should have listened to her." She shook her head and closed her eyes, tears streaming out of the corners. "She was right about him. I should have listened better. I should have told her to do the right thing."

Her words were so similar to the ones Ashleigh had repeated to her that first day when they'd gone up to CeCe's apartment. CeCe had called Ashleigh "Jenna" that day.

"What happened? What did she tell you?"

"She was my only child. I was so proud of her when she became a police officer." She turned the stove off and pushed the pan off the element, as if she'd lost her appetite for even her meagre meal. "I didn't want her getting into any trouble. When she told me she was worried about what they were asking her to do, I told her just to shut up and do as they said if she wanted to keep her job. It's my fault." She sobbed into her hand, then lifted the glass of vodka to her lips, her hand trembling as she drank.

"It wasn't your fault." Kristen reached forward and steadied the glass. She needed to get the rest out of her before the alcohol hit her, and there wasn't much time.

"The officer who was giving her orders, do you remember his name? Do you remember what he was asking her to do?"

"She had a funny name for him." CeCe looked off thoughtfully. "I don't remember."

"Do you remember what he was asking her to do?"

"Jenna said they wanted her to take evidence and deliver it somewhere. She didn't want to."

"Do you remember what kind of evidence, or where they wanted her to take it?"

"She wasn't sure, but she thought it was drugs. The man she told me about, he told her to keep her head down and her nose clean if she wanted to stay alive."

That didn't make sense. If her TO wanted her to run drugs from evidence, then why would he tell her to keep her head down and her nose clean? It definitely sounded like a direct quote from Hackett; she'd heard it herself from his lips, but it didn't sound like much of a threat.

"Officer, I'm tired." CeCe left the pepper but refilled her glass of vodka, then meandered to the worn-in and cracked leather sofa. Her furniture made so much more sense to Kristen now. The condo, the pictures, the décor, they were all remnants of another life. A different woman had lived here, a woman who had a daughter. What remained was just a shell, a whisper of who that woman had been.

CeCe closed her eyes. Kristen was out of time, but she was just as confused as when she'd arrived.

"Aitch-two," CeCe called from the couch, just as Kristen was turning the handle to let herself out the front door. "That's what Jenna called him," she slurred.

H2? Keep your head down and your nose clean. Henry Hackett. So, it was her TO who had put Jenna in danger. If he was at the centre of this, why hadn't he asked her to do anything of the sort? Was he lying low now that two officers had been murdered? Had he known where Jenna's body was all along? He hadn't been Oslowe's TO, though. The more the evidence came together, the more this started to look like a police conspiracy, or at least an elaborate cover-up. There had to be more people than just Hackett involved, and wherever there was a ring, there was a leader. Sure, Henry was a misogynistic, prejudiced ass, but was he a criminal mastermind? There was only one way to find out.

CHAPTER 12

THE NEARER THE TIME DREW to eleven o'clock, the more nervous Ashleigh became. Her house was too big for Kristen to believe that she owned it by herself. She was too young, especially for a house this close to Yonge and York Mills, but when she gave Kristen the address, she hadn't been able to find the words to tell her that she still lived at home. She wished more than anything that she had tried harder to find an apartment, that she had made time to go to more showings, that she didn't have to tell Bailey that she was a twenty-five-year-old baby who still lived with her parents.

She waited by the front window, her bag in hand, ready to bolt the second Bailey pulled up in her black Mustang. She'd thought everything would be fine, and that's when her dad decided to go outside and mow the lawn.

Kristen pulled up and parked along the front curb, her hazard lights on. Ashleigh sprang out of her seat by the window and rushed out the door. She tried to hurry past her father, but he noticed and waved her over. The lawnmower was loud, so he didn't speak, but he kissed her on the cheek.

"I'm going to a cottage up north," she shouted in his ear.

"Whose cottage?"

"A friend's."

"Can your mother and I come?"

She laughed. "I should be home late tonight."

"Have fun!" He gave her a smile and a one-armed hug before returning his attention to the lawn.

She waved goodbye to her father and sped down the lawn. Maybe Kristen hadn't seen her talking to him. She opened the door, and Bailey was just putting her phone down.

"So, did you ask your parents' permission to sleep over?" She turned to Ashleigh with a Cheshire grin.

"Oh, shut up." Ashleigh slapped her arm playfully.

"Ow." Kristen feigned pain. "Don't make me tell your father on you."

Ashleigh laughed. "Just drive."

As they drove down Highway 60, Ashleigh was reminded of camping there as a teenager. The windows were open, and the scent of trees and that fresh Algonquin air filled her nostrils in abundance. Did Bailey feel the same freedom she did out here? They'd long since left the 401, the 400, and the scenic drive on Highway 11. Now that they were on Highway 60, it was all rock-cleared, two-lane road looking out over seemingly endless expanses of water.

"This is gorgeous." Ashleigh was almost breathless at the view. "I can't believe your brother lives out here."

"He's lucky." Kristen agreed with a nod. She had her aviators on like the first day they'd met. Her hair was loose and messy. It framed her striking features.

Bailey looked at her again, and she averted her gaze. "What did your brother and sister-in-law do right to get to live out here?" she asked.

Kristen smirked. "Well, he makes furniture from wood and antlers—naturally shed—that he finds up in the woods here, and it's the perfect place for him to have his workshop. Cyndi is a freelance marketing consultant, so she comes into the city from time to time and brings Jared's creations to the stores that buy from him, but she gets to spend most days up here with him."

"That's awesome."

"Yeah, really makes me wish I was better with a drill and sandpaper than I am with a gun."

"He must be proud of you, though?" she asked. Bailey nodded slightly. "You said before that Muskoka was home. Do your parents live nearby?"

Kristen's mouth became tight for a moment before she answered, her eyes never wavering from the road. "They died a long time ago."

"I'm sorry," she said automatically.

Bailey said nothing further on the subject, and Ashleigh made no more small talk. They turned around a long bend and left the town they'd just been driving through.

"We're a few minutes away now."

The enjoyable views of various cabins along the shore kept Ashleigh occupied in silence until Kristen turned the car into a nice, long, gravel driveway. There was a large cottage at the end of the lane.

"Wow," she said. "I'm officially green with envy."

Kristen laughed, and Ashleigh was happy to see her easy smile return. "Wait till you see the back patio."

Ashleigh quickly fired off a text to her dad to let him know she'd arrived safely and that the cottage was just inside Algonquin Park. She put her phone back in her pocket and hadn't even stepped out of the car before a handsome man with a shock of black hair came running down the gravel driveway. He picked Kristen up in a hug and swung her around before she hit his arm enough times to make him put her down. It was strange to see Kristen handled like that, as if for one moment, she wasn't the one in control. It was the first time Ashleigh had ever seen her that way.

The man gave Kristen a long, hard kiss on her cheek with an exaggerated "muah!" and then put her down. His gaze moved to her next. "Who's this beautiful creature?" he asked with the same Bailey charm she had become accustomed to in Kristen.

"Jared, this is Ashleigh, the friend I told you about."

"Nice to meet you," Jared said but lifted his dark eyebrows questioningly in his sister's direction.

Just how many *friends* had Bailey brought up here over the years? Yet another reason to steer her thoughts away from all things Kristen.

"Nice to meet you too," she responded.

"Ashleigh and I met a few weeks ago when I had that concussion. She's actually the one who was at the receiving end of your phone call that morning."

He squinted his eyes a moment before they widened. "Oh, I'm so sorry about that." He took Ashleigh's hand into both of his. They were strong and rough with wear, a bit of a contrast from the well-kempt man in front of her. "We were... I was going through something that day. Please, forgive me. I would never usually use that language. I can't tell you how awful I feel about it."

"It's forgiven." Ashleigh smiled.

"Thank you." His forehead relaxed. It seemed good nature ran in the family. "Let me make it up to you with a mojito."

"Ashleigh doesn't drink," Kristen answered for her, picking up both of their travel bags.

"No?" He looked a little disappointed. "Not even for me?" His smile was a little crooked but no less contagious than Kristen's. What was it with this family and that smile?

"I'll split one with your sister," she said, and Kristen shot her a questioning look. "We can't have you getting drunk if you're going to drive me home later."

"You're not staying the night?" Jared's expression fell, and he looked between the two of them. His disappointment was almost palpable. "I got steak and lobsters and that bottle of Barolo you loved from last summer, remember?"

"That's another thing." Kristen laughed lightly, and Ashleigh could tell she was enjoying toying with her brother's mood. "Ashleigh's a vegetarian."

"Holy shit, you're killing me here, Ashleigh," he said to her, but his grin was as fixed as his sister's. Was there anything that could break the stoicism in a Bailey?

"I eat seafood," she said, hoping that might count for something.

"A girl after my own heart!" he exclaimed, putting an arm loosely around her waist. "Come, Cyndi is going to love you. She's a vegetarian as well. You two can bond over broccoli while Kris and I get the boat ready."

Kris. She liked it. It suited Bailey. Would she ever be close enough to her to call her that?

Jared turned and smiled at her as he led them to the house, his arm still amicably around her. They were making her so welcome, and it warmed her more than it should. Kristen was just a friend who, for some reason, was showing her a lot of kindness. Why was Bailey being so nice to her?

She didn't want to think about that night at Tango, but she did. Kristen had walked away from her at the bar to go home with that blonde, and the memory stung. Her actions told Ashleigh that her feelings were unrequited, so why was Kristen being kinder to her than anyone had been in a long while? It was singularly odd for a cop who had a history of being a troublemaker for Rodrigo.

"Is fishing okay, or do you want to go for a hike?" Kristen asked her, and Jared turned to her as well, his brow creased. It was obvious which of the two he preferred.

"Fishing sounds great," Ashleigh said, and Jared's forehead smoothed out.

"Awesome." He gave her side a friendly squeeze before he released her and opened the door. He gestured for Ashleigh and Kristen to walk through before him. "Cyn!" he hollered for his wife.

A beautiful woman with milk-chocolate skin and gorgeous, tumbling curls of lustrous black hair came out of the large, open kitchen, drying her hands on a tea towel. When she saw her guests, her face lit up in a broad, welcoming smile.

"This lovely young lady is Ashleigh, and she will be joining us for supper. She's a fellow herbivore like you, so don't go falling in love over a head of kale while Kris and I get the poles and gear ready."

"Pleased to meet you. I'm Cyndi." The woman held her hand out to shake Ashleigh's. It was warm, just like her smile. "Can I get you a drink?"

Ashleigh liked her immediately.

"Water?"

"Sparkling or still?"

It was Ashleigh's turn to smile. "Sparkling, if you have it."

"Sure thing. Come join me in the kitchen. I'm just finishing up some salad and wraps for lunch."

"Don't forget what I said about the kale," Jared said over his shoulder as he and Kristen slipped out the back door. Cyndi laughed.

The floor-to-ceiling vaulted windows spanned two storeys and ran all along the backside of the house. The lake sparkled under the bright August sun.

"It's quite a view." Cyndi walked up beside her, tying her long curls into a loose ponytail while she looked out the window. "Come on outside for a minute. Lunch can wait."

They stepped outside, and Ashleigh paused in reverence of the view. The sun was so bright on the lake that she had to squint to take it in. The weeds stood firm at the shoreline, greeting the soft ripples of water slowly running against them. The current was calm but always moving, as if an invisible hand were gently threading its fingers along the surface. The water was a mix of deep indigo and charcoal, with tall trees lining the horizon, bordering the lake.

A red-breasted robin landed nearby, then took off into the riparian woods. It was only then that the tweeting of different birds registered in the background, too many species for Ashleigh to identify. There was the distinct aroma of cedar mixing with the fresh smell of the lake. She breathed in deeply, the air thick and warm as it coated her throat and lungs. A fish splashed in the water not far from where they stood, and the sound quickly blended into the soft rustle of the current along the muddy shore, tickling the few rocks and pebbles that lay there.

An insect buzzed by her ear, but the sound was not unpleasant, given the natural, majestic surrounding. The willows on the banks of the shore stood proud, and even the air had a sound that was calming and relaxing as it rushed by her, the breeze hugging her in its warm embrace. She breathed it in again, this time picking up hints of something sweet, the sap in the nearby trees, maybe?

Dark green pine trees enclosed the shore, some rust and copper-coloured needles shed beneath them, and light green foliage hung over the edges of the lake. There were dry hollows in the trees created by insects and birds for the homes where they took up residence. Beyond the long wooden dock, there wasn't another cottage for miles, and the sky was an endless light blue, reminiscent of the depth and colour of Kristen's eyes.

"It's pretty powerful, isn't it?" Cyndi commented. "I'm used to it now, but some days, especially when I'm with someone who's seeing it for the first time, I remember how moving it can be."

Ashleigh nodded, her gaze focused on the horizon. "It reminds me of how small I am in the large expanse of the universe. Like anything is possible."

"Isn't anything possible?" Cyndi smiled, and Ashleigh mirrored it.

She'd thought it might be awkward being away from civilization with two people she had never met before, and a third she barely knew, but already she felt comfortable, and she was thankful to all three of them for that. Just forty-eight hours ago, she'd been scared and alone in that interrogation room at the police station. Today, she was surrounded by comfort and warmth. This wasn't anything she would have ever imagined after her first meeting with Bailey.

"You guys ready?" Kristen and Jared came around the corner, loaded up with four fishing poles and two tackle boxes. Kristen had a huge, excited smile on her face, and it was quite possibly the cutest thing Ashleigh had ever seen.

Cute. Not a word she thought she'd be using for Constable Bailey. Hot? Sure. Sexy? No doubt. *But cute?* Cute was personal. Too personal for how she was supposed to feel about her.

"Just going to grab lunch." Cyndi clapped her hands and practically skipped inside, her floral summer dress swaying over her long legs.

"Can I help you with that?" Ashleigh asked, gesturing toward the gear and tackle.

"We're good," Jared said, the size of his smile matching his sister's. "Just get your bathing suit on. The water's great out there, and we'll probably stop the boat for a while to jump in. There's a bedroom on the right, just past the hall when you go inside, if you want to change."

"Okay, I'll be right back." Ashleigh went inside, wondering what an afternoon with the Baileys might bring.

"She's smokin'," Jared said and then quickly added, "Don't tell Cyn I said that. Not that I'd be going after your girl anyway." He started walking toward the boat.

"She's not my girl." Kristen walked in step with him.

"Ah...heh." He let out a small laugh. "You sure about that?"

"What do you mean?"

"From the way she was looking at you, I'd say she thinks she's your girl." He grinned.

"What?" She put a hand on his arm to stop him from walking.

"You're not sleeping together?" Jared looked confused.

"No."

"Oh, I guess that makes sense why you brought her here," he said.

"What's that supposed to mean?" she asked.

"Just that I didn't think you talked to girls after you…you know."

"Ashleigh's different."

"But you're not sleeping with her?"

"No," she repeated.

"Are you dating?" he asked.

Kristen gave him an incredulous look.

"All right," he said defensively. "I didn't ask if she has three boobs."

She looked away from him, back toward the house.

"You like this girl," he said slowly.

She turned back to him but didn't argue.

"Holy shit!"

"Okay, calm down," she said harshly. "I didn't tell you she has three boobs."

Jared laughed. "Sorry, sorry, but this is huge."

"We're just friends," she clarified.

"When have you ever brought a friend up here?"

"I've never brought anyone up here."

"Exactly. There's no shame in liking someone, you know."

"I know." She looked down. "I just don't want to like *this* girl."

"Why not? It's about time you found someone you wanted to keep around longer than one night."

"Even if I had feelings for her, which I'm not saying I do, she's an EMT, which means she's part of my investigation."

"She doesn't know you're RCMP?"

"Of course she doesn't know."

"Oh, Kris, you have to tell her."

"I can't. This is my job, and like you said, I barely know her."

"I didn't say that."

She looked back at the water. "Maybe it was a mistake to bring her here. I don't know what I was thinking."

"Why did you bring her up here?"

"My boss told me to keep her close."

Jared shook his head. "I think that's why you allowed yourself to bring her up here, but come on, Ouellette's told you to do a lot of things, and you haven't done them all. I don't buy that you only brought her here on the boss' orders." He put a hand on her arm, bringing her attention back to him. "She wasn't the only one with a dreamy look on her face when you got here."

"Oh, come on." She shook her head. He made it sound so juvenile and embarrassing.

"Fine." He shrugged. "What do I care if you keep lying to yourself? But it'd be really stupid if you blew things with this girl because you can't admit to yourself that you have feelings for her. You can't just let someone in halfway. If you only open one floodgate, the deluge still gets through."

"What the hell are you talking about?"

"Why can't you just admit that you like this girl? That you might want more from her than what you usually look for in a woman?"

"I don't know."

"You don't know?"

"No."

"Okay. Now the real reason?"

Kristen sighed. "I'm not sticking around Toronto, Jared. One way or another, I'm out of here in a couple of weeks. I wouldn't even be here now if my lead hadn't left town for four days."

"You have a lead?"

Kristen wasn't thrilled with the surprise in his voice.

"Yeah, my TO."

"Do you think he skipped town?"

She shook her head. "He has no way of knowing I'm looking into him. I think he just went away. It's summer, and it's a nice weekend."

"Do you think you're getting close to solving the case?"

Kristen shrugged, pretending to be much more nonchalant about the lead than she was. "I hope so, and this one better pan out 'cause

Ouellette's yanking me if I can't catch whoever killed that rookie. Either way, my time here is no longer indefinite, and anything I start with Ashleigh will end with the case."

"How do you figure?"

"Because I'll either be in Banff or God knows where, depending on Ouellette's mood that week. Things are just less complicated if we stay friends and not worry about the rest."

"I thought *the rest* was all you were interested in with girls?"

Kristen stopped and looked back to the house where Ashleigh was talking with Cyndi. How easily she'd just fit right in. As if she belonged. It wasn't right how much Ashleigh already felt like a part of her life in that moment.

"It's different this time, isn't it?"

She turned back to him. "I don't want it to be."

"Do you mean that, or do you mean that you're scared to find out what it means if it is?"

Kristen's shoulders fell. "The job always comes first. It will always come first, so what does it matter? Even if things were different with her, how would that change anything?"

"It already has; you just can't admit it."

They stared at each other for a moment, and Kristen was caught off guard when Cyndi announced their arrival. "We're ready," she said, then looked skeptically between Kristen and Jared. "Everything okay?" she asked.

Jared smiled and nodded at Cyndi, then squeezed Kristen's arm quickly before he let his hand drop. "Absolutely. Let's get out there."

Kristen took up the slow walk with the others, but her mind was racing. What the fuck had she been thinking to bring Ashleigh there? There was so much, too much, that Ashleigh could never find out about. Sure, she had asked her here because Ouellette had told her to get close, to get Ashleigh to trust her, but that could have been done over a short period of time back home. A few more chance meetings, some texting, maybe a phone call or two, and that would have taken care of it. Ashleigh didn't need something as elaborate as this to get her to open up. Even with Cruz's sister, it had only taken two nights to talk her into bed and out of everything she knew about the EMTs and their possible involvement in Ricky Oslowe's murder. So why the hell was Ashleigh Paige at Jared's house? She felt powerless to stop her attraction to Ashleigh. It had started from the very first time she'd seen her.

One floodgate.

Jared was right. From the beginning, it was as if she'd had no control when it came to Ashleigh. She'd gotten inside her mind, her home, her heart so quickly that she hadn't had the chance to build up the walls that normally came so naturally to her. She had never opened her heart to anybody. Never even had to think about it. This was so not the time to change her routine. Despite what she felt two nights ago when Ashleigh had been in her arms, she was nothing more than an EMT and a possible lead, a potential witness in the investigation. After yesterday's revelation with CeCe, Kristen would be damned if she blew an investigation this big over a girl.

"I'm excited," Ashleigh said beside her. "It's been forever since I've been on a boat."

"Well, let's get out there, then." Kristen forced her usual smile onto her face, glad for the sunglasses that concealed her eyes.

"No, yes, just like that," Kristen guided Ashleigh.

"It's too big," she said, trying to angle the fish in.

"Just keep reeling it in."

"He's going to rip my arms off!" she said through a laugh. Kristen came up behind her, put her arms around her, and grabbed the pole with her. Ashleigh's breath caught, and her entire body warmed when Kristen pushed up against her back.

"We got him," Bailey said next to her ear, and Ashleigh shivered. "Okay, now pull!"

Bailey pulled back too, and in doing so, tightened her grip on Ashleigh. She tried not to notice the smell of Kristen's skin, so close to hers, as she pulled on the rod.

Finally, they yanked so hard that the mammoth lake trout was pulled out of the water and came hurtling into the boat.

"Holy shit. That thing is huge!" Jared said. "Looks like those lobsters are going to have some competition tonight." He grabbed the line and expertly pulled the hook from the fish's mouth. Ashleigh turned away at the sight.

"Can't quite stomach it?" Kristen asked beside her. Her small smile showed her comment held no malicious intent.

"I suppose that's the vegetarian in me."

"You two *are* staying for dinner, right?" Jared asked with his most hopeful smile.

"You don't have a curfew or anything, do you?" Bailey asked teasingly. Ashleigh slapped her arm lightly.

"We're staying," Ashleigh answered, her eyes still on Kristen. "That is, if your sister can behave herself."

Jared and Cyndi shared a knowing look, and Ashleigh's cheeks warmed.

"Well, I think that catch is definitely as good as we're going to get for the day," Jared said. "You guys ready to haul in and head back?"

The return ride had more wind, and the day was cooling off, which made the breeze rather chilly in the late afternoon. Goosebumps rose on Ashleigh's arms and legs. "I guess it's a good thing we didn't take a swim." She pointed at her raised flesh when she noticed Kristen looking at her.

"Well, since you guys have your suits on, we can hit up the hot tub after dinner, if you like," Cyndi said.

"I don't know if we'll be here that long," Kristen answered cautiously. It was clear that she didn't want Ashleigh to feel pressured.

"Speak for yourself. I'm freezing, and that sounds amazing right about now." Ashleigh grinned.

"I knew vegetables weren't the only thing we had in common." Cyndi laughed.

"Here." Bailey took off her charcoal zip-up hoodie and offered it to Ashleigh.

"You'll be cold," she protested.

"It's all right." Bailey wrapped it around Ashleigh's arms. "I'm used to the breeze."

"Thank you."

Ashleigh inhaled the scent of the sweater and felt an answering dip in her stomach. Even with the smell of the lake surrounding them, it was all

Bailey, and she wrapped it tighter around herself. God, she was getting pathetic, but what was she supposed to do? Here was this amazing, gorgeous woman giving her all of her attention, even introducing her to her family, and she was supposed to, what, pretend it didn't affect her? Kristen was everything she'd dreamed of finding in a partner. She was beautiful and brave, kind and caring, selfless and sexy; yet at the same time, she was everything she'd promised herself she'd stay away from as well.

"Are you sure you're okay with staying for dinner and all that?" Kristen asked, her mouth close to Ashleigh's ear, obviously not wanting Jared and Cyndi to overhear her. "Whatever you want, I'll do." God damn, did those words ever feel good caressing her cheek.

Ashleigh nodded, unable to speak. She was on dangerous ground. If she let herself, she'd fall hard for Kristen Bailey.

Who was she kidding? In just a few weeks of knowing Kristen, she'd already fallen harder than an Acme anvil.

CHAPTER 13

DINNER WAS EXQUISITE. ASHLEIGH COULD not remember the last time, if ever, she'd eaten such good food. There were two lobsters, broiled with garlic butter, then barbecued with a couple of filet mignons. Plus, there was the fish Ashleigh had caught. Kristen had gutted it, an image Ashleigh would not soon forget.

They were eating outside on the back patio, with the lake as the backdrop for their supper. Jared brought out a bottle of port to finish off the meal.

"I'd better not." Kristen refused the port with a wave of her hand. "I have to drive soon, and I had two glasses of wine with dinner."

"We still have the hot tub," Ashleigh said. "You could have a glass."

Kristen smirked. "You're sweet, but the hot tub will only make all the alcohol rush to my head. You'll be dragging me home if I have some of this before getting in there." She pointed in the direction of the hot tub. It was inlaid into a cedar deck overlooking the water and the stars.

"You're no fun," Jared said, putting the cork stopper back in the bottle. "It was a ten-year." He sighed melancholically, as if the bottle had sadly experienced an untimely death.

"You can still have some," Kristen said to her brother, adamant that he not stop his enjoyment on her account.

"No, it's no fun without you."

Ashleigh looked from brother to sister. Something about the way they were looking at each other made her think of Jenna Bradley and what it was like when a cop lost her life on the job. Did Jenna have a brother who cared for her as Jared so clearly did for Kristen? Did she have a sister? Someone she'd meant the world to? Had she known the last time she saw her loved ones that she was saying goodbye for good? It could happen to Kristen.

A shiver ran through her.

No one ever knew when they left for work if they were coming home that day, and with everything that was happening in her life lately, did she know how many more nights she'd have like this? Life was so short, much too short not to have that bottle of port and enjoy all the company she could with good people like the Baileys.

"Why don't you both have some, and we can spend the night, if that's okay with you, of course," Ashleigh said, looking between them.

"Of course it is," Cyndi said quickly.

Jared was already smiling and pouring the port. "We'd be delighted to have you. Only... There's just the one spare room."

"I'll take the couch." Kristen offered automatically, a smile on her face to match her brother's when she clinked his glass and tasted her first sip.

"You don't have to do that," Ashleigh said. They had spent the night together before, and she liked waking up with Bailey way more than she wanted to admit to herself; but that didn't mean she would pass up the opportunity to do so again.

"I'm okay. You take the room. I could never put a guest up on the couch...knowingly."

"No, I mean we can share the bed."

Kristen's glass stopped midway to her lips, and Ashleigh couldn't help being pleased with the visual. She'd caught Kristen off guard, and it wasn't something she was used to.

"Well, that's settled, then," Jared said, looking meaningfully at his sister.

Bailey managed to draw her eyebrows together and raise one at the same time. She turned from Jared back to her. "Ashleigh, I—"

"This is perfect." Jared interrupted again, pouring his second small glass of port. That was fast. "There are already clean sheets and extra toothbrushes in the room, and it has its own ensuite," he said to Ashleigh.

"Are you sure?" Kristen asked her as if Jared weren't speaking.

Ashleigh pulled her cell phone from her pocket and nodded. She typed off a quick message to her dad, letting him know she wouldn't be home that night as she'd told him earlier, then put it away quickly so as not to appear rude. "I think I'd like to try some of that port," she said and managed a smile, but her stomach was in knots. For once, she wanted to lose her inhibitions. She craved what her mind kept telling her she shouldn't. Perhaps it was time to dull that incessant voice, the one that insisted on reminding her that anything to do with Kristen Bailey was a bad idea.

Jared happily poured two more small port glasses for Ashleigh and his wife. The four of them toasted, and Ashleigh sampled the fortified wine for the first time.

"How do you like it?" Bailey asked. A smile turned up one side of her mouth.

"It's like raisins…and whiskey," she said.

"Ha! Close enough." Jared laughed.

Ashleigh looked to Kristen for an explanation.

"Port is basically wine mixed with brandy," she said.

"Hmm." Ashleigh took another sip. "Well, I like it."

"So, shall we take this to the hot tub?" Cyndi suggested. Already equipped with their suits, there was no changing required for Kristen and Ashleigh. "You guys go on ahead. We'll be right back. Don't wait for us."

By the tub, Ashleigh began to remove her socks but stopped when she noticed Kristen pulling off her T-shirt. Underneath, she wore a black bikini top, and she had stomach muscles to envy. Every part of her was sun-kissed, and when she dropped her shorts, she saw wonderfully toned legs that had a noticeable space between them at the top of her thighs. Every part of the woman was divine, and Ashleigh's heart sped up at the sight of her barely covered body.

Kristen stepped into the hot tub and moved her back against the border. She spread her lean arms out and watched Ashleigh. It was only when Bailey looked at her that she had the grace to avert her gaze and continue with the removal of her own clothing.

"You'd better hurry and grab a jet before Jared and Cyndi steal them," Kristen said.

Ashleigh shed her shirt and shorts, climbed the stairs into the tub, and sank down into the wonderful warmth of the water. She moved across the small space and chose the spot right next to Bailey.

"This is nice." Ashleigh closed her eyes. She knew she should have kept some distance between them. It was torture to be so close to what she wanted but be unable to reach for her. Thankfully, Jared and Cyndi arrived in swim trunks and a one-piece, brandishing four large, fluffy, white towels.

"Oh, this feels good." Jared sank right in, and his wife followed quickly after him. "So, do you girls want to play a game?" he asked.

"What kind of game?" Cyndi asked skeptically.

"Truth or Dare," he said, then avoided a slap from his wife. "I'm kidding, geez." He pretended to be affronted. "How about Would You Rather?"

"What's that?" Ashleigh asked.

"Basically, you ask the group if they would rather do one thing over another, and then the asker answers too, and everyone who answered differently drinks," Cyndi said. "Like, would you rather freeze to death or burn to death? Stuff like that."

"But we don't have any drinks," Kristen said.

"Never fear." Jared produced the bottle of port from between two of the towels. He then reached between the other two and produced a frosty bottle of white wine with a screw top. "Two bottles between the four of us can't do much harm."

He twisted the cork stopper off the port with a pop and handed it to Cyndi, then reached across to give Kristen the wine. She cranked the metal top, and it crunched when the seal broke, then came off easily. She leaned back, put the cap behind her, and took a sip from the bottle.

As if the wine could have looked any better, a cold drop spilled out and down the side of Kristen's mouth before she wiped it away with the back of her wrist. Ashleigh followed the movement of the drop and swallowed.

"I'll go first," Jared said. "Would you rather have a cat or a dog?"

"Lame," Cyndi said out of the side of her mouth.

"Relax, I'm just getting warmed up." He gave another one of the charming smiles the Baileys were blessed with.

"Dog, I guess," Kristen answered.

"Cat," Ashleigh said. "I had one growing up."

Cyndi sighed. "Cat, I suppose."

"Dog. You guys drink," he said to Cyndi and Ashleigh.

Kristen handed her the bottle, and she took a sip. It was a sweet Riesling that slid deliciously down her throat.

"Your turn," Jared said to his wife.

"Would you rather…" she left the sentence hanging while she thought, "eat rotten eggs or rotten fish?"

"Ew, you're disgusting." Jared kissed Cyndi's head affectionately.

"Gross," Bailey agreed. "Fish, maybe… I don't know… That's so disgusting." She laughed. "How about you, Ashleigh?"

Her chest warmed at the sound of Kristen saying her name.

"Fish too, but that's really gross, and I hope I never actually have to make that decision."

"I think we should all just agree that my wife is disgusting and that she should drink?"

"Agreed," Ashleigh and Kristen said at the same time.

"Oh, come on," Cyndi said, but she took a swig of the port and looked at Bailey. "You're up."

"All right, would you rather, assuming you wouldn't die, go a year without food or a year without sex?"

The blood drained from Ashleigh's face. This was not how she'd intended for everyone to find out she basically had the sexual experience of a teenager.

"Food," Cyndi said quickly.

"Sex," Jared said at almost the same time, then deflected a playful blow from his wife. "I'm kidding, honey." He kissed her lips quickly with a smile that said how much he loved her.

It was Ashleigh's turn to answer. "Sex," she said quietly.

"Really?" Cyndi asked.

"Well, it's been longer than that for me, so yeah, I'd say I can live without it." Sitting so close to Bailey, her body belied her words. It was on fire with the knowledge that she would choose sex with Kristen right then over anything in the world.

"Heh, you'd probably die if you had to wait that long," Jared said to Kristen.

Ashleigh's stomach roiled. Instinctively, she pulled in toward herself, turning slightly away from Kristen, but she didn't miss the lethal look

Bailey shot her brother. What he said shouldn't have bothered her. It was none of her business who Kristen slept with, but still, she couldn't help the pit of disappointment that opened in her stomach. It was as if she kept forgetting who Kristen really was. Motivated forgetting, that's all it was. She was trying to convince herself that Kristen wasn't exactly who she was so that she would be okay with her feelings for her, but Bailey wasn't going to change just because Ashleigh wanted her to.

"Jared's just kidding," Cyndi said weakly.

"What about Dawn?" Kristen asked.

"What about Dawn?" Ashleigh repeated, unsure of what Kristen was asking.

"She said she'd known you about two years. Did anything happen between you?"

Ashleigh shook her head. Why would Kristen think that? She tried to recall the conversation from that night at the bar. She hadn't been paying Dawn any kind of special attention, although Dawn had been acting strangely possessive. Kristen had walked away, though, so how would she... That couldn't be why she'd left the table at the bar, could it? No, she'd left to be with that woman.

"My turn," Ashleigh said. "Would you rather have sex with a stranger or spend the night with someone you cared about but not be able to touch them romantically?"

"I'm going to go with spending every night with my wife, the most beautiful woman in the world, even if I could never touch her," Jared said.

"You're such a liar," Cyndi said, but she was smiling. "I'd have to agree."

"What about you?" Kristen asked Ashleigh.

"You have to answer first."

"I think, not being married, that's a difficult question, if I'm being honest."

"You're supposed to be honest," Ashleigh said.

"Come on, Kris. You know you'd go for the sex every time," Jared said, then flinched at his own words.

Ashleigh turned her focus from Jared to Kristen. "Would you? Every time?"

Kristen met her gaze, but she was slow to answer. "Maybe not every time," she said carefully.

"So, if you were at a bar, and this gorgeous stranger was there, wanting to go home with you, would you go?"

"Is there another option?"

Ashleigh's heart sped up. "There's someone you know there, and even though you might not know it, she wants to go home with you too."

Kristen's breath hitched before she spoke. "If I'd known it was an option, I would have gone home with you."

The words carved through Ashleigh's core like a blade on fire. Silence lingered for what seemed like ages as she looked into Kristen's deep blue eyes. "I... That wasn't the question."

"Kris, you're such a sweet talker," Jared said, forcing a laugh.

Ashleigh composed herself and took a long sip of the bottle she still held in her hand.

"My turn," Jared said loudly. "Would you rather continue playing this game or just get drunk?" He followed up his question with a large swig of the port bottle in his hand.

"You two always ask that one just to make me drink," Cyndi said jokingly. She reached for the port and did much the same with it as her husband. "Ashleigh?" Cyndi asked with a smile.

Ashleigh thought of saying she didn't really drink to get drunk, but then she stopped. She took a long sip from the bottle, letting the cool, sweet wine coat her throat before passing it to Kristen.

Bailey reached for the bottle and drank thirstily, draining it down to the last swig, which she passed back to Ashleigh. Ashleigh tipped it back, finishing it in one large swallow. "Empty," she said, turning over the bottle.

Jared laughed, grabbing the port back from his wife and taking another sip. "I thought you didn't drink."

Ashleigh shrugged, and Cyndi yawned, covering her mouth with the back of her hand.

"I think I'm just about done," Cyndi said tiredly, standing up. "I'm ready to turn in. Too much time in the sun makes me really tired."

"Where the wife goes, I follow." Jared stood and dutifully trailed Cyndi out of the tub. He wrapped a towel around her before he took his own.

"Don't forget to turn the jets off when you come in," he said to his sister. "It was a pleasure spending the day with you, Ashleigh. I look forward to regaling you with tall fishing tales tomorrow morning over breakfast."

"Good night." She smiled. Jared and Cyndi were impossible not to like.

"Should I leave the bottle?" Jared turned around and asked the question as an afterthought.

"I think we're good," Kristen said.

He nodded and followed Cyndi inside.

"I think I'd like to get out as well, if you don't mind," Kristen said to her once they were alone.

"Sure." She stood and followed Kristen out of the tub. Like her brother, Bailey supplied Ashleigh with her towel first, opening it so that she could easily wrap it around herself.

"Thank you," she said as she accepted the towel and wished that Kristen's hands had lingered on her skin. "Would you mind if I showered? I don't like going to bed with chlorine on me."

"Yeah, of course. There's a shower in the ensuite." She hesitated. "I'm going to sleep on the couch."

"Don't be silly," Ashleigh said. She *should* just let Kristen take the couch. It would be so much easier.

Kristen hesitated again. "Are you sure?"

It was her turn to vacillate. "What your brother said, about you dying if you didn't have sex for a year, is that true?"

"I don't think I'd actually drop dead, no." She grabbed up her clothing and began to walk back to the patio doors. "He was just messing around with me."

Ashleigh grabbed her own clothes and rushed after her. "How long has it been since you were with someone?"

Bailey stopped just inside the house. They were only a few feet from the room they were about to share. "I don't know... About a month, I guess."

Ashleigh's eyes narrowed before she pushed past her into the room. She went straight to the bathroom, closed the door, and turned the lock.

In the shower, she scrubbed her skin much harder than it needed, considering it was already sensitive from a day in the sun followed by a soak in the hot tub. She'd seen Kristen leave the bar with the blonde that night. There was no doubt in her mind that she had gone home with that woman. She'd even told Ashleigh that was how she operated. What had she been thinking, asking Kristen that question in the game? The fact that she hero-worshipped Kristen Bailey was obvious, but had she really such little respect for herself? Did she want to get her heart broken? Kristen was a user and a liar, so why couldn't she stop wanting her?

Disappointingly, the wine had not done much to dull her senses. Over and over, she pictured the woman from the bar and Bailey tucking her hair behind her ear, and she felt her chest tighten again. Why had Kristen lied to her about it?

<hr />

Kristen was confused about Ashleigh's behavior and was still contemplating moving to the couch when Ashleigh—looking striking in a black tank top, a pair of black underwear, and nothing else—walked out of the washroom and moved quickly to the bed.

"It's all yours," she said, turning instantly over so that her back would face Kristen when she got back in.

She showered as quickly as she could, anxious to find out why Ashleigh was upset with her. She'd wanted to think that Ashleigh wasn't interested in her so that she wouldn't have to deal with the feelings that were building for her. If Ashleigh meant what she said, then that changed everything.

Kristen turned off the shower quickly, afraid Ashleigh might fall asleep. Or worse, pretend to be. She hurried through dressing and brushing her teeth. When she returned to the bedroom, the lights were out, but Ashleigh had courteously switched on the lamp by Kristen's side of the bed. Should she just get in? It would be asinine of her to offer to take the couch again. Plus, this time, Ashleigh might agree.

She climbed into bed and turned on her side, keeping a fair distance between them on the queen mattress. Propped up on one elbow, she asked, "Was there something I did to piss you off?"

Ashleigh's back stiffened. "No, I'm just tired."

She was not going to let it drop that easily, not when she was pretty sure she hadn't done anything wrong. "Why are you mad? You're the one who said…who asked that question."

Ashleigh turned over on her back to look at her. "I'm sorry. I shouldn't have asked that. It was dumb. In that same spirit, are you sure you don't want to change your answer about the last time you slept with someone?"

"I'm pretty sure I would remember."

"Yeah? So, you didn't take that woman home the other night?"

"First of all, I never take anyone home."

"What does that mean?"

"It means I never bring women back to my place."

"Why not?"

"I don't want strangers in my bed. I don't want them to know where I live, and I don't want them to try to spend the night."

Ashleigh didn't have to say it for Kristen to know they were both thinking the same thing. She had brought her home and let her spend the night. Twice. She'd even slept in her bed with her.

"You don't bring women home so that they can't find you again. Is that it?"

It was like everything she was saying was worse than the sentence before. "Why do I feel like no matter what I say, I'm not going to do very well in this conversation?"

"Never mind. Just forget I said anything."

Kristen's eyes narrowed. "I don't get it. What's your game with women? You pretend to be interested, lead them on, and then what? To what end?"

"There's no game. This isn't what I wanted."

"I forgot. You want the fairy tale. So how has that worked out for you? I don't see Princess Charming anywhere. How many women has this little innocent act worked on?"

"It's not a game, and it's been *woman*, singular. It wasn't Dawn, if that's what you're thinking, and it wasn't exactly a fairy tale."

Kristen cocked an eyebrow. She wasn't being coy; she was just surprised. "You've only been with one woman?"

"Yes."

How was that possible? Ashleigh was breathtakingly beautiful and sweet and sexy. Then she realized how it could be possible. "Were you in love with her?" she asked. She didn't want the answer to be yes.

"No," Ashleigh said, and relief washed through Kristen.

"It was that woman your friends brought up, wasn't it?"

Ashleigh sat up in bed, and Kristen did the same. "Yes. Denise." She shuddered when she said her name. "I'd just gotten back from Kenya. I'd gone there with my boyfriend. That's when I met Laura and realized that everything I had been faking with Colin wasn't going to be enough anymore. Laura didn't have the same feelings for me, though, and I wasn't happy there. Not with Colin. Not with any of it. There was too much...just too much.

"When I came home, I didn't know how to meet girls, so I went down to Church Street by myself. I was there for maybe half an hour, getting ready to leave, actually, when Denise approached me. Lacking the confidence to approach anyone, Denise got immediate points for taking the lead. She was attractive, and I thought she was exciting." Ashleigh drew her legs up protectively against herself. "Turns out she was dangerous. Not in an illegal kind of way, but she was careless with me, with my feelings." She looked down sadly. Her fingers picked at pieces of the covers. "For a while, I thought I was falling in love." She looked up and met Kristen's gaze. "Turns out I'd just been falling on my face."

"I'm sorry," Kristen said. She wasn't sure what else to say. Ashleigh had obviously been hurt by this Denise, who sounded a lot like herself. "What happened?" she asked. Even though she didn't like what she was hearing, she wanted to learn everything there was about Ashleigh, and not so she could report it back to Ouellette.

"Denise knew all the lines and how to spot a neophyte lesbian. She was a bartender on her night off. She found out quickly that I'd never been with a woman. She said all the right things. She even made me feel like I was exciting." She smiled self-deprecatingly.

Kristen wanted to tell her that she was exciting, that she excited her, but she couldn't. She couldn't do the same thing to Ashleigh that Denise had done.

"That in itself should have set off an alarm for me, but I had been so desperate to feel for someone the way I felt for Laura. The fact that a woman like Denise—a woman who could have anyone she wanted—wanted me, made me feel good. I know; stupid, right? All Denise had been after was my first time in bed with a woman. For a month we dated, and eventually she wore me down. I had been honest with her about what I was looking for, so she tried to make me think I'd found it. She told me she cared for me, that she'd never felt before how she felt about me. Then she started trying to make me feel guilty. She said I was cruel for driving her so crazy. So one night I went home with her after the bar.

"You know I don't drink much, and I was in really rare form that night, drunk and stumbling, but that didn't deter Denise in the slightest. I know I'm an adult, and it's my fault as much as hers, but I never would have gotten into bed with her if I'd known her intentions."

"What happened?" Kristen asked, a lump in her throat. She wanted to strangle Denise. She wanted to kill her for hurting Ashleigh, for doing to her what Kristen had done to countless women over the years, for lying to her about her intentions, just as she was doing to Ashleigh in that moment.

"Not much. We had sex," Ashleigh said, and Kristen didn't like the way those words sounded coming from Ashleigh's lips. "She woke up a little later and told me to leave her apartment. It was four o'clock in the morning. I couldn't go home. I was afraid my parents would wake up and ask me where I'd been and why I was getting home at that hour, so I slept it off in the stairs to the underground parking lot."

Kristen's jaw tightened. Now, she wanted Denise drawn and quartered. How could anyone do that to Ashleigh? She wanted to take her in her arms, tell her it wasn't supposed to be like that, but how could she? The women she'd been with received treatment that was little better.

"The one good thing that came out of that night was that after making a prized fool of myself, I realized there was no way Denise could have hurt me like that if I hadn't been so blind. I promised myself I'd never be with someone like that again, so I haven't been."

For some reason the thought pleased Kristen. She was happy that no one else had had their hands on her, even if she couldn't either. *She's too good for that.* What the hell did that even mean? Ashleigh was a human being; she deserved love and affection just like everyone else, but Kristen didn't like the idea of someone else sleeping with Ashleigh, of someone being with her just for her body. The thought of a woman using her like that disgusted her. She felt the need to protect Ashleigh, even from consensual sex, apparently.

Now, it all made sense: Ashleigh's revulsion at what Jared had said to her on the phone. Ashleigh asking her about the way she was with women. Kristen had always thought herself so clever, in control of every conversation and its outcome, but Ashleigh had pulled information out of her without Kristen realizing it. Being around Ashleigh made her careless.

Ashleigh had been right to be wary of her. If Kristen had known Ashleigh would have been at all receptive to her advances, she would have already slept with her and dismissed her; there would have been a brief report back to Ouellette on Cruz's new partner, and that would have been the end of it. She'd had similar thoughts the first time she'd met her, and she would have treated her just like Denise had and not given it another thought.

Fuck Ouellette's orders.

She wanted to protect her, to make sure no one ever hurt her again. She wasn't going to use her. Not for the case. Not for anything. She pulled the covers aside and started to get out.

"Where are you going?" Ashleigh asked.

Leaving right at the end of her story probably hadn't been the most sensitive thing. Ashleigh had opened up, and she was likely feeling vulnerable, but what could she do? She was wrong for Ashleigh in every way. She could not heal the wounds Denise had left. Ashleigh deserved so much more than she could offer. Kristen could not give her the affection she needed or the safety and security she was worthy of.

"I should go," she said.

"So, is this what it's like when you go to a woman's place and then leave? She opens up to you—for you—and then you take off?"

What was Kristen going to say? True, she had never lured a woman for weeks just for sport as Denise had done to Ashleigh, but hadn't she done almost the same to Rodrigo's sister and countless others? She had used them for sex, plain and simple.

"That's not what I'm doing. I just need to leave. I can't explain it."

"Just like you can't be honest about sleeping with that woman?"

Kristen creased her brow. "Why do you keep bringing that up? I didn't sleep with her."

Ashleigh paused. "I saw you leave with her."

"I admit I left with her, but I didn't sleep with her," she said honestly. "I'm not lying to you."

"You didn't?"

"No." Kristen sighed. "I couldn't go through with it."

"Why not?"

Why was Ashleigh making this so hard for her? "I had someone else on my mind."

Ashleigh's breath hitched. "Who?"

She wasn't going to do this with her. She moved to get up and leave again.

"Wait." Ashleigh grabbed her arm. "Who did you have on your mind?"

"Are you really going to make me say it?"

"Who did you have on your mind?" she asked a third time.

"You, Ashleigh. It was you."

Kristen's heart pounded with her confession, and Ashleigh stared at her in disbelief, swallowing slowly. Ashleigh's gaze dropped to Kristen's lips, and there was a tightening low down in Kristen's abdomen. She allowed her gaze to lower slowly to Ashleigh's lips as well. They looked so soft, so inviting, and Kristen had never before had such a hunger for someone's kiss.

Ashleigh's breathing became heavy, matching Kristen's. Just when Kristen was sure the ache and wanting inside her could get no worse, Ashleigh spoke.

"What are you waiting for?"

Kristen's heart stopped at the invitation. It was too much, and she could resist her no longer. She reached forward, grabbed Ashleigh by the back of the neck, her fingers threading through her silky hair, and pulled her forward until their lips met. At the first feel of Ashleigh's mouth moving against hers, there was an explosion in her core, and she fought to keep breathing. Ashleigh's lips were so soft, and they moved slowly. She took her time, touching her, tasting her.

Ashleigh's kiss was decadent and indulgent. She tasted of heat and mint and sugar. Kristen couldn't get enough. She deepened the kiss, pulling her closer, testing the boundaries of her lips, but not daring to go further than Ashleigh would let her. A savage heat built inside her chest, and when Ashleigh's tongue pushed against her lips, she opened her mouth to let her enter. Heat erupted through her entire body and lit her blood on fire. Ashleigh moaned as she slid her tongue into her mouth, and the sound sent a jolt deep between Kristen's thighs.

She met Ashleigh's tongue stroke for stroke. Ashleigh's arms came around her, her fingers clenched her hair, and Kristen groaned. She needed to feel Ashleigh against her. Her kiss was no longer enough to satiate the burning, aching desire that had taken her over completely.

She put gentle pressure on Ashleigh's shoulder, and Ashleigh let herself be pushed down against the pillow. Kristen crawled over her in the same movement, and for the first time, she felt the sensation of Ashleigh's body beneath hers. She gasped at the contact, and their kiss broke for the first time since they'd started.

Ashleigh was breathing hard, waiting for Kristen, letting her set the pace. There was such trust in Ashleigh's eyes, an expression that told her Ashleigh would let her do whatever she wanted to her. Ashleigh's heart pounded so hard that Kristen could feel it against her own chest. She wanted Ashleigh more than she had ever wanted anybody, but the guilt crept in with her desire. She couldn't do this to her.

"I can't." Kristen pulled back.

"Don't stop," Ashleigh said beneath her, and there was an answering pull between her legs. She didn't want to stop.

"I have to. You've been drinking. This isn't what you want."

"I've barely been drinking. This is what I want." Ashleigh leaned forward and captured her lips again, so warm, so soft, so wonderful. Kristen kissed her back for one weak moment, drowning in her taste, before she turned her mouth away, this time pushing herself up and rolling to her side of the bed, effectively removing the temptation.

Kristen ran her hands through her hair. "This isn't a good idea." She was sure that no matter what happened between them, she would take whatever Ashleigh gave her and spoil it like she always did. She couldn't be what Ashleigh really wanted. A partner. Someone who stayed.

"Kristen." Ashleigh reached a hand over to touch her arm, but Kristen moved away from her touch.

"I'm going to sleep on the couch," she said and left without turning back.

Ashleigh had never felt anything more amazing than the weight of Kristen's body on top of hers. She leaned back into her pillow and let out a long breath. Her heart was still racing from the feel of Bailey against her, from the rush of her tongue in her mouth. Just the thought of it brought a new ache between her legs. Why had she run from her? The Kristen Bailey she'd heard about didn't care how much her lover had to drink or about anything else, so why had she left her wanting, panting after her in the bed like that?

Kristen said she hadn't slept with that woman because she'd been thinking about her. If Kristen wanted her, why didn't she stay? She couldn't just lie there torturing herself all night. She grabbed her phone from the nightstand and opened her contacts to text her.

Why did you leave?

She waited a few minutes but received no answer. She returned her phone to her nightstand. Denise certainly hadn't cared that she had been almost too drunk to walk and talk. She'd picked her up, taken her home, fucked her, then awakened her by telling her to get the hell out. What she remembered from that night had been awkward and awful. She'd felt used, and she'd vowed that the next time she was with a woman that it would be because they were starting a relationship and that when they slept together, it would be a conscious decision made while she was sober.

So what had convinced her to drink that night? *Being around Bailey.* She'd wanted Kristen more than she knew what to do with and used liquor as the easy way out of her inhibitions. The phone beside the bed vibrated and startled Ashleigh before she grabbed it.

I'm sorry.

Sorry? That's all she had to say after kissing her like that and then leaving?

Did I do something wrong?

The response came quickly this time.

No. I just don't want to ruin things between us.

What do you mean?

Whatever you're looking for, I'm not it.

How do you know?

There was a pause of a couple of minutes.

I'm not the girl who stays the night. I'm not good, Ashleigh, and you deserve someone good.

Ashleigh held the phone against her chest. Kristen was trying to let her know she was just like Denise. Why had she thought she would be any different? She turned over, angry with herself for being so stupid, and put her phone on silent. Bailey didn't return her feelings. She hadn't been interested in anything more than sex. It was better that she had left.

CHAPTER 14

THE LIGHT STREAMED SOFTLY THROUGH the blinds, and Ashleigh decided it was time to get up. She had slept unevenly and unwell, her thoughts repeatedly returning to Kristen and their searing kisses.

While she dressed, she contemplated sneaking out and heading back into town. She knew there was a bus station in Huntsville, but that was miles away. She didn't have much to carry with her, though, and she could use a good run. Even a twenty-mile run, if that's what it came to. Once at the bus station, she would send Kristen an obligatory text, telling her where she was and thanking Jared and Cyndi for their hospitality. Whatever Kristen responded to that, she wouldn't care, and she wouldn't pick up if Kristen called to ask why she had left. After all, it was Kristen who had done the leaving first.

She grabbed her bag and opened the door quietly, intent on sneaking out without waking Bailey.

"Good morning," Cyndi said with a cheerful smile. "Coffee?"

The couch was empty. There were no other sounds in the house.

"Okay, thanks." She accepted the offer absentmindedly. "Where's Kristen?" Perhaps Kristen had exacted a plan similar to her own and abandoned her there, leaving Cyndi to do her dirty work. Well, at least this way, she might get a ride to the bus station.

"Jared and Kris went out early this morning, long before you, me, and the bees woke up." She smiled, handing Ashleigh a steaming cup of coffee. "It's something they like to do together just on their own."

At least Kristen hadn't ditched her there.

"Is everything okay?" Cyndi asked.

"I don't know," she admitted, staring down into her coffee. "Is Kristen always so..." She let her words hang in the air, unsure how to finish her question. What exactly did she want to ask Bailey's brother's wife? Why she was so...what? Difficult? Impossible?

"Closed-off?" Cyndi finished for her.

Ashleigh nodded. That would do.

"How well do you and Kristen know each other?" Cyndi asked.

"Not too well, I guess. Maybe I feel like I know her better than I do."

Cyndi tilted her head, as if considering her before she spoke. "Kristen has the biggest heart I've ever seen, only she doesn't know it." She gave a purposeful pause. "She won't let anyone in, not really, and she doesn't want anyone to let her in." She put her coffee down on the counter. "Besides Jared, she doesn't want to care about anybody. It took years for her to start opening up to me, and still, I know there's so much only Jared sees."

"You don't think she's capable of letting people in, do you?"

Cyndi shrugged. "I think we're all capable of anything, but if you're asking if I think it's likely, I don't know."

Ashleigh nodded and wrapped her arms around herself protectively.

"Hey, sweetie, it's okay." Cyndi rubbed her arm.

Ashleigh looked away, embarrassed. Kristen meant more to her than she wanted her to. "I'm sorry." Tears prickled behind her eyes. "I'm being stupid. I just hoped I might be different, I guess." She laughed self-deprecatingly. "I feel like a huge idiot right now."

Cyndi shook her head. "You are different. I've never seen her the way she is around you."

"What do you mean?"

"Did something happen between the two of you?"

"Sort of."

Cyndi nodded. "I saw her this morning when she came in to wake Jared. She looked wretched."

"She did?" Ashleigh asked, sickened by the hopefulness in her own voice. It was wrong for her to wish for some suffering on Bailey's part, but she couldn't help it.

"She looked like someone shot her dog. I didn't think she had those kinds of emotions in her for anyone but Jared."

"I don't understand. Why is she so closed off?"

"Because of what happened to their parents, I think."

"What happened to them?"

"You don't know?" Apprehension darkened Cyndi's kind, brown eyes. "It's really not for me to tell."

"Please, I just want to understand her."

"You care about her?" Cyndi considered her skeptically, and Ashleigh recognized the love and protection there.

"I do. There's something about her. I just... I want to be a part of her life. Does that make sense? I mean, like, have you ever met someone and just known they're special? That they're going to be important? That's how I feel about Kristen."

Cyndi's face softened. "I always hoped Kristen would meet someone like you."

Ashleigh blushed. Being accepted by Kristen's family was more important to her than it should have been.

"Their parents died when Jared and Kris were just kids, and I don't think she's been the same since. Jared was fifteen, and Kristen was only thirteen. It was a home invasion."

Her legs went numb. "She was there?"

Cyndi gave her a pained look. "It wasn't accidental that someone targeted their house. Robberies are one thing, but in a home invasion where they kill people, those are rarely random."

"Why would anyone want to hurt her family?"

"Kristen had been getting into trouble in school, hanging out with some delinquents who were known to the cops. She even got a ride home from them a couple of times. The night of the invasion, Jared woke to Kristen dragging him out of bed, trying to get him to their parents' room. He says he remembers how hard his heart was pounding. He didn't know what was happening, but the fear in Kristen scared him good. By the time they got to their parents' room, the criminals were already there."

"What happened?"

"It turned out the kids Kris was hanging out with were in a gang. She'd stolen something from one of them. She didn't realize it belonged to a high-ranking member, or if she did, she didn't understand what that meant. She was just a kid."

"What did she steal?"

"A car, of all things." Cyndi gave a sad smile. "She didn't realize there were drugs in it. That's what they came looking for that night."

Ashleigh's heart was in her throat. "They killed her parents?"

"The police found them shot, execution style. Jared told me that he remembers everything from that night. The flash of the guns. His own screaming."

"How did Jared and Kristen get away?"

"Kristen led Jared out the back and to their neighbour's house, where they called the police. The cops came and arrested Kris."

"Why would they arrest Kristen?"

"Well, she stole a car that happened to be full of drugs, although she didn't know that at the time. When the cops arrived and started asking questions, Kristen told them everything she knew about taking the car and not knowing who the car belonged to. The police explained who the man was, and that he had enough drugs in the car to put him away for life. Unfortunately, her stealing it meant she was charged with possession of all those drugs, a huge felony."

"Wasn't losing her parents enough?"

"I guess not." She refilled her coffee and held the pot out to Ashleigh, who waved it away. "Jared says Kristen was never the same."

"What do you mean?"

"He says she became closed off after that. She was always funny and charming, as I'm sure you know, but he says it's only skin deep now. Know what I mean?" Cyndi sipped at her coffee.

"Did she go to jail?"

Cyndi shook her head, lowering the coffee mug from her lips. "Juvie. She was there for a couple of years."

Ashleigh shook her head. "That wasn't fair."

Cyndi shrugged sympathetically. "None of it was. She lost her parents, her home, everything over one stupid teenage mistake. Jared went to live with their grandmother. She died the year Jared turned eighteen. She left him her house, this house. Kristen got out of juvie six months later and moved in with him until she graduated high school. Then she was gone.

"Jared told her the house was half hers. Their grandmother had only left it solely to him so that the government wouldn't try to claim any of it while she was in juvie, but Kristen wouldn't stay. She did community service until her record was expunged, and a week later, she was on a bus. She never came back home to live here again, just to visit."

"Where did she go?" Ashleigh asked.

"To work in law enforcement. She wanted to help people, make sure what happened to her parents didn't happen to other people, but she keeps herself distanced now. Jared thinks she still blames herself for what happened. I think she feels she doesn't deserve to be loved, that she has nothing to offer. When her grandmother was dying, they wouldn't grant Kristen furlough to see her. It was like she went to bed one night a normal kid, then woke up the next day with everything gone. Jared is all she has left. She'd do anything to protect him. When she does love, she does so fiercely."

Ashleigh swallowed her regret. "I understand."

"You're the first person she's ever brought up here, you know that?"

"I am?"

Cyndi nodded. "You're actually the first person I've ever met from Kristen's life, and I've been married to Jared for seven years. I see the way she looks at you and the way you look at her."

Her heart sped up. "How does she look at me?"

Cyndi's smile turned placating. "Come now, you're not going to make me stroke your ego, are you?"

Ashleigh blushed. "No, I just... Well, let's just say last night didn't go as I had hoped."

"You mean after your little question in the hot tub?" Cyndi was kind enough to try to hide her smirk in her coffee cup.

"I didn't want to fall for her, you know? I knew how she was right from the start, so I pretended to myself that we could be friends, but I always wanted more."

"You should tell her that."

Ashleigh shook her head. "I think I tried to last night."

"And?"

"She told me she's not what I'm looking for."

"She probably isn't," Cyndi agreed. "Not right now. But are you going to let her tell you that?"

Ashleigh let out a long breath. "I think sometimes one of the best things we can do for ourselves is to stop feeling things for somebody who isn't right for us."

Cyndi seemed to mull that over as she sipped her coffee. "Maybe." She put the cup down thoughtfully. "Or maybe the best thing you can do for both of you is believe in her long enough for her to become the person you know she is inside."

"I think we've gone far enough. You're trudging through these trails like we're marching into battle. What's going on with you?" Jared's red T-shirt was drenched with sweat.

Kristen stopped and rested her hands on her hips to help steady her own breathing. Her body was damp with perspiration, but she could have hiked another ten miles if Jared hadn't stopped her.

"Can't keep up with me anymore?" She raised an eyebrow.

"I never could." He bent over to catch his breath, then straightened up. "Look, it's obvious that we're not running toward anything, so why don't you tell me what it is we're running from?"

Kristen stretched her arm behind her back until the muscles burned. "I don't want to talk about it."

"Like hell you don't. That's why you dragged me out of bed at five a.m., so spill."

She let out a long breath. "I kissed Ashleigh last night."

A grin spread over Jared's face. "That's great!" His smile quickly faded at the sight of her determined frown. "That's not great?"

"No." She huffed. "I mean, it was, but it's not."

"What happened?"

"What always happens? I left." She turned her anger on herself.

Jared looked confused. "I thought you liked her."

"I do. I actually do. That's the problem."

"As far as I've been led to understand, that's supposed to be a good thing. Did she turn you down?"

Kristen shook her head. "It wasn't that. I just didn't feel like doing that with her, you know?"

"Not really. I love *doing that* with my wife." He grinned but sobered again when he saw her unhappiness. "What is it? There's never been a girl who could hold your interest for more than five minutes. Now there is. I think that's a good thing."

"I've never wanted anyone to hold my interest for more than five minutes."

"Oh, so is this a pride thing or something? I really don't understand you right now. You spend your life in and out of girls' beds you couldn't care less about, and now a sweet, funny, beautiful girl catches your eye, and you don't want her to?"

"That's just it. I have nothing to offer a girl like that."

"Yes, you do."

"You're right." She turned her anger on him now. "I can offer her misery and disappointment."

"Okay, you're starting to sound like your buddy Shakespeare. Easy on the tragedy. You kissed her. It's not the end of the world. Find out how she feels. Take it slow. There's no rule book at the RCMP that says you can't be happy, is there? You have more to offer than pain and disappointment, Kris. Trust me. I've been on the receiving end of your love for the past thirty years, and nothing feels more wonderful than that."

Kristen turned away. Her face coloured from his candour. She collected her thoughts before she spoke again. "Ashleigh is amazing. She's an honest-to-God good person. All I can do is bring her down— the long hours, the work, the things I've done." She looked away and took in a deep breath before letting it out and turning back to him. "I don't want to take something beautiful and make it ugly."

"Why do you think that of yourself?"

"You know why." She looked away again, but he moved into her line of sight.

"You think you're ugly inside. You think all you are is this." He pointed from her head to her toes. "You think all you have to offer

162

women is on the surface. I mean, I think you're gorgeous, but inside, that's where you really shine."

"Jared," she whispered, "you know what I did."

He opened his mouth but paused when he looked into her eyes. "It wasn't your fault. You're still going to tell me you blame yourself?"

"You're still going to tell me you don't?" Tears filled her eyes. "I ruined everything. I took everything from you."

Jared shook his head. "You protected me. You saved me that night. You're a hero, Kris."

She shook her head. "I don't... That's not what I am."

"You say you're not good enough, but—"

"I'm not," she interrupted. "That's what she sees when she looks at me. She sees a saviour, someone who can protect her. I can do that. I can protect her from bad guys. Fuck, I want to...but I can't protect her from myself."

"Maybe this time it doesn't have to be that way. Maybe things could be different with her. You obviously care about her."

"I don't know how to be any other way." She kicked at the ground in frustration. "Even if I could be, it couldn't be here and now. Ashleigh is a part of this investigation. I'm lying to her about who I am and why I'm here. I'm lying to her about everything."

He rubbed the back of his head in much the same way she did when she got tense. "Maybe you just need to trust yourself and take everything slowly."

"If she finds out I'm RCMP and investigating the city's EMTs, she will never forgive me. She'll think I was using her, that I only tried to get close to her to cajole information out of her."

Jared let out a breath and shrugged. "Then don't use her. Don't talk to her about the case. Keep the two separate."

"They're not mutually exclusive. They're all wrapped up together. I just want to catch this guy and move on."

"No one's rushing you into anything. Just take your time with Ashleigh. See what it's like to get to know someone before you bed her. You might be surprised how much more you can feel with a woman if you care about her."

I already do. Too much.

"I told you, I'm going to be out of here in a week or two. She deserves better, Jared."

She deserves someone who can love her.

"Do you ever wonder why they call it French toast?" Cyndi flipped another golden brown piece in the frying pan.

Ashleigh was on her third cup of coffee and starting to think it was a bad idea. Her heart was racing, and when Kristen and Jared walked through the back door, her hands began to shake. She gripped the mug tighter and then put it down.

"Hey," Kristen said to her tentatively.

"Hey," she said back. She could do this. She could be civil with the woman who left her half-naked and begging for it in bed.

"You guys must be starving. Breakfast is almost ready."

"Thanks, babe. I'm just going to grab a quick shower." Jared was already making his way down the hall.

"Be quick. I don't want breakfast going cold 'cause of you," Cyndi yelled after him.

"I'm going to take one too," Kristen said, then walked into the guest bedroom and closed the door.

Ashleigh stared at the closed door a moment before getting up. "I'll be right back," she said to Cyndi distractedly and went to the bedroom.

She took a steadying breath and opened the door. Kristen was already in the washroom. The door was closed there as well. Water was running from inside. She knocked.

"Yes?"

Okay, now what? "Can I come in?"

There was a pause. "Hang on." A few seconds later, Bailey opened the door with nothing but a towel wrapped around her beautiful, tanned body. "What is it?" she asked, concern on her face.

Yes, what was it? Her mouth had gone dry. "Nothing, I..." She shook her head. "I'm sorry." She turned to leave, but Bailey reached out and grabbed her hand.

"What is it?"

Ashleigh didn't know how to explain what she was doing there. She pulled her hand back. "This morning, when I woke up, I was going to leave." Why was she telling her this?

"I don't blame you."

"Then, when I left the bedroom and you weren't on the couch, I thought you'd left me here."

"I don't blame you for that either."

It was hard to be mad at someone who seemed so fucking contrite all the time. "Why did you bring me here?" Before she could answer, Ashleigh saw something in the window behind her, shaking slightly in the morning breeze. "Is that a red fern?" she asked.

Kristen nodded.

"When you had your concussion, I read *Where the Red Fern Grows*. I found it on your bookshelf."

"I know." Kristen swallowed. "That's where I got the idea to plant one."

Ashleigh's brow knitted for a moment before she realized the implication of her words. "I'm sorry," she said, not knowing who exactly she was sorry for but understanding there had been a loss.

"It was a few weeks ago. The day Jared called and you picked up. They had a miscarriage."

"Kristen…" Ashleigh moved her hand to touch Bailey's cheek, but she turned away from the contact. "I'm sorry," she said again and left the room.

———— ••• ————

They drove home in silence. Breakfast had been little better. The few attempts Cyndi and Jared made at conversation fell flat, and Ashleigh could tell that Kristen was just waiting through the pleasantries of finishing up their food and saying goodbye so that she could get the hell out of there. The open, caring Kristen from the last few days was gone. This Kristen was aloof and uncommunicative. She leaned against the driver's side door as if she couldn't get far enough away from her, tearing down Highway 400 at 140 kilometres an hour and swerving around vehicles. It seemed she couldn't wait to get Ashleigh back home and out of her car.

There were a few times that Ashleigh saw something on the landscape that reminded her of her adolescence. She even opened her mouth to share the memory once, but Kristen was so closed off it was like an invisible barrier was between them.

When they pulled up in front of her house, Kristen unbuckled her seatbelt and made to get out and help Ashleigh with her bag.

"I got it," Ashleigh said abruptly. She leaned between the seats to grab it. Once she pulled it onto her lap, Kristen ceased trying to help. It had clearly only been a knee-jerk response anyway.

Ashleigh wasn't sure whether she should apologize to Kristen for what had happened between them the night before or scream at her for being so difficult. Would it be better to close the door on everything she felt between them or beg Kristen to give her a chance? Would it even matter to her? To what end did she want Bailey to reciprocate, anyway? Even if she gave in and they slept together, that was all she seemed capable of giving, and Ashleigh didn't think that her feelings would be abated by spending the night with her. It would only increase the intensity, and that would be stupid. Since when was she a masochist? She needed time away from her, and the first step was getting out of the car.

She opened the door, but before she got her second leg out, Bailey spoke.

"Wait."

Ashleigh paused, neither pulling her leg back in nor stepping further out.

"I'm sorry," Kristen said.

Ashleigh looked at her. What exactly was she apologizing for? Her sunglasses were on, so it was almost impossible to tell what she was thinking, but her usual, easy smile was gone.

"It's just not a good idea for us to get involved. With you being a paramedic and me being a cop, there's too much hassle."

So, that's what she was to her? A hassle? Anger, frustration, and hurt filled her chest all at once, and despite her resolution to keep everything under control, tears pricked behind her eyes. She would not let them fall.

"I'm sorry to have been such an inconvenience to you, then. You didn't have to invite me to your brother's cottage, though, or act like you wanted us to stay the night. You could have just left me at the police station the other day. In fact, I don't even know why you bothered to help me at all if it was such a hassle for you."

"I didn't mean it like that. I just meant…" She stopped and looked out the window. "God, Ashleigh, can't you see I'm no good for you?"

Ashleigh paused. For the first time she wondered if this was about her or about Bailey's feelings about herself. What Cyndi had told her that morning had certainly revealed an extra layer to Bailey that she hadn't anticipated. Was it really any wonder that Kristen didn't want to get close to anybody? Kristen was struggling, trying to tell her she wasn't any good for her, that she couldn't be what she was looking for.

Are you going to let her tell you that? Cyndi's words echoed in her mind. Was she going to allow Bailey to walk away from this? From her? Were Ashleigh's feelings strong enough to try again, even if she knew it was likely to end in her own heartache?

Bailey's jaw tensed. She was waiting for Ashleigh to give some kind of response, and Ashleigh felt the weight of the moment in her heart. Whatever happened here would set the course for their future interactions.

"I think you think you're no good for anybody right now," Ashleigh said, and Bailey swallowed noticeably. "But I don't agree with you. I see the good inside you." She got up and out of the car but turned back before closing the door. "I'm not ready to give up on you, Kristen, even if you are."

CHAPTER 15

Kristen didn't drive away after Ashleigh went inside her parents' house. She stayed in the car, looking at the closed door for a long time. She wasn't sure what she wanted anymore. She couldn't tell if she had been using the case and Ouellette's orders as an excuse to get close to Ashleigh, or if being close to Ashleigh was just a means to solving the case she so badly wanted off her docket.

You're only as good as your last bust.

What Ouellette had said was true. If she didn't close this case soon, it wouldn't matter how impressive her resume was. She needed this case to seal the promotion that was on the table now, or it would go to someone else.

She put her foot down on the clutch and shifted into first gear. She would do what she always did: solve the case, pack up, and move on.

Kristen had a lot of questions, and for once, she knew where to find the answers.

FiteNite.

She wove through traffic, hoping to get to the police fundraiser before the fights started. How was she going to finesse the information out of these cops? She'd put up a wall that day in the interrogation room with Detective Ortiz. He could have spread the story of her insolence, of her siding with an EMT over her own, and it would be damaging to her reputation.

What about Henry Hackett? Could her TO really be involved in this? She'd thought him too lazy and stupid to be a part of anything more lofty or labourious than devouring a pound cake. She'd spent almost every day with the guy since arriving at 52. It made sense why she was slipping up around Ashleigh, but it wasn't as if Henry's charm had disarmed her as well. Was she losing her touch?

Kristen pulled into one of the only spots still open on the street outside of Toxic Nightclub at Adelaide and Portland. She questioned the wisdom in having the police event in the heart of the club district, where weekend shootings and nightclub stabbings had become a regular occurrence. The two thousand-spectator event was almost sold out as usual, though, and they needed a big space to accommodate the boxing ring and a large stage for the bands. It was a controversial event at best and had been earning the scrutiny of public and internal disapproval for years.

As an off-duty police officer, she had to leave her gun in the glovebox. Technically, at her rank, it should be in lockup at the station, and her standard issue police firearm was, but she always kept her RCMP semiautomatic service pistol with her. The trouble was, at an event like this, there would be metal detectors at the door. She didn't like going anywhere without her gun during an investigation, but she had no choice.

It was August, and the Toronto heat was still in full force. Without having pre-purchased an event ticket, she had to pay a twenty-dollar cover charge. Inside, the band was already playing loudly, and people were drinking and dancing around the stage. The ring in the centre of the club was empty, but the first fight would start soon.

She had to do this right. If she asked the wrong questions, she would strike out and miss the chance to gain further insight on the case, but she wasn't sure how to go about it. There were some cops who were loose lipped on the force, but she'd already milked all the information she could out of them. What she needed was a new source of intel. Even if Henry Hackett was there, he likely wouldn't tell her anything, especially not anything that would incriminate himself. She could think of only one person who undoubtedly had at least some information beyond what she'd received in her RCMP files. Sure, the Mounties had access to all of the Toronto Police Service files, but Ortiz was the lead detective on the case. There had to be some elements, suspicions, or unsubstantiated leads that he'd kept to himself and out of his paperwork.

"Bailey!" A drunk Constable Donahue waved her over to the bar. Bill Donahue had been after her since her first week at 52. She hadn't even had to sleep with him for him to spill everything he knew. It was amazing the way people would divulge their secrets for just the chance at sex.

"Donahue, you getting into trouble?"

He laughed and handed her a shot of tequila. There were four people drinking with him. Three of them she knew, the fourth was a woman—a stranger to her.

"What are we drinking to?" Kristen took the shot glass from his hand.

"To Oslowe." Donahue raised his glass.

"And Bradley," the woman she didn't know added.

"To Oslowe and Bradley," Kristen said, then downed her tequila neat, forgoing the lemon. She never trusted where bar lemons had been before her drink. Besides, she preferred it with an orange wedge, and this club did not look like it carried anything with more nutritional value than the bare minimum to ward off scurvy.

"I'm Lucia." The woman put her hand forward, and Kristen shook it. Lucia's dark hair was down, tumbling freely over her shoulders. She was much shorter than Kristen, but that sort of thing had never bothered her, and from the look in Lucia's eyes, it was clear it didn't bother her either.

"Kristen," she said, pulling her hand away.

"Kristen." Lucia smiled. Dimples creased her coffee-with-cream skin. "Can I buy you another drink?"

A month ago, she would have been tempted, but Lucia's warm, brown eyes and pretty face failed to affect her.

"Lucia's a friend from college," Donahue said between them.

Kristen nodded politely, but she'd had enough of this conversation. Lucia was nice to look at, but Ortiz wasn't part of the group, and there was only one woman she had eyes for. "I see someone I need to say hi to," she said apologetically. "Excuse me."

"What about that drink?" Lucia held out a twenty as if she were going to give it to Kristen instead of the bartender.

"Not tonight, Lucia, but thanks."

She turned and walked past the elevated area that was normally reserved for VIP bottle service at a club like this. It was filled with white shirts. The staff sergeants came to FiteNite on principle, but they did not mingle with the blue collars. King was there, which did not surprise her. After all, many of the proceeds from that night would be going to Oslowe's widow.

Unable to find Detective Ortiz among the drinking, shouting cops at the bar, Kristen moved through a wedged-open door that read *Staff Only*. In the back, she found the fighters preparing to box, along with a printout of the lineup. Ortiz was to fight Luke Smith. Kristen grinned. Smith was a monster of a man.

She found Ortiz finishing up his wrist wraps. A few other detectives were around him, giving him advice on how to stay alive against the goliath of a cop he'd be facing.

"Did you draw the short straw?" Kristen asked, squeezing between two detectives and getting in Ortiz's line of sight.

"Well, if it isn't Officer-I-don't-know-how-to-mind-my-own-fucking-business," he said, and the others laughed. He'd obviously shared the encounter with them. No surprise there.

"That's me," she said through an easy smile. "And guess what? I have more not minding my business to ask you about. Do you have a minute?"

"Can't you see I'm getting ready for a fight, Bailey?"

"I can see you're getting ready for a slaughter. When are you up?"

"Second round."

"Good, you have a few minutes then. I need to speak with you. Alone." She'd expected him to blow her off, but instead, he considered her a moment and nodded. The other detectives left them, and Bailey lowered her voice. "I've been thinking over a few things about your investigation into Ricky Oslowe's murder, and I had some questions."

"I don't need to tell you that what you're saying is way above your rank. You have no business looking into anything or even thinking about anything to do with that investigation. The guys at the station may like you well enough, but you've only been trouble to me."

"I just want to help," she said.

He looked her over. "You want to help? Get me out of this fucking fight, and I'll tell you whatever you want to know."

"How?" she asked. "You signed up."

"Not to fight fucking Frankenstein."

Ortiz had reason to be nervous. Kristen had done background checks on the police officers in the precinct. Luke Smith's uncovered one excessive use-of-force charge and two counts of assault filed by the criminals he'd been arresting. Luckily for Luke in all three cases, the criminals had been found guilty, and the charges against him had been dropped and buried, but not so deep that the RCMP hadn't been able to unearth them.

"If I get you out of this fight, you'll tell me what I want to know?" Kristen asked.

"Yes."

She took a deep breath. There was only one way to get him out of the fight, and it wasn't going to be pretty. "If you renege on this deal, I'll tell everyone what a lying, cowardly sack of shit you are, you understand?"

Ortiz tightened his jaw. "Just do it."

Kristen walked back into the heart of the nightclub searching for Luke Smith. She'd seen him by the bar before. She easily spotted him again from across the room. He was that big.

The best way to get under anyone's skin was to insult him, make him feel like he had something to prove. With a guy of Smith's stature, that wasn't going to be easy.

She approached the bar and ordered a beer. Although they were from the same division, she was on a different platoon than Smith, so they'd never met, which meant there was no existing pretense of friendship between them. That would work to her advantage.

"Can I get a cup with that?" She slid over a five-dollar bill and a toonie. The bartender handed her a cup and moved on to the next patron. She poured the beer to the top and left the can on the bar.

Smith had his back to her, which thankfully would make things a little easier. Kristen eased her way over to where he was standing with his friends, took a deep breath, and dumped her beer over his close-cropped blonde hair. It poured all down his back. He turned around quickly, rage contorting his features. Kristen hardened her own.

"You know what that was for." She glared up at him. There were not many people she had to look up at.

He looked at her with loathing, then seemed to remember he had an audience. "If you weren't a girl, I'd punch your face in," he said, his voice a low growl.

"Fuck you, Luke. You know you deserved it."

"Who the fuck are you?"

"Think real hard, moron."

His face went red at the insult. He was trying to remember her or figure out why she would pour a beer on him. "Are you one of Elena's friends?" he finally asked.

There it was. "Good one, genius." She provoked him further. "You and your limp dick better stay the fuck away from her."

Anger flashed in his eyes. "You're lucky you're not a cop, or I'd drag you into that ring and beat the living shit out of you."

She smirked. "Today's your lucky day. I'm Constable Bailey."

The information seemed to surprise him. "I'm already in a match," he said.

"So cancel it. I'll put my name down. Unless you're afraid a girl's gonna kick your ass."

His friends laughed behind him, shoving him playfully in encouragement. It was the perfect fuel for the fire. He glared at her. "You're on, you little bitch."

"In this corner, weighing in at two hundred and forty-five pounds, standing at six feet six, we have the undefeated champion of FiteNite: fifty-two division's Luke Smith!" the emcee said into the mic, and the crowd cheered wildly.

Kristen was already sweating. Her hands were clammy inside her gloves. She was wearing what she'd walked into the club with, a black T-shirt and jeans. At least she'd been in running shoes. Luke wore gloves and real boxing shorts. She'd had to borrow Ortiz's mouth guard. Luke had his own, with his name printed across the four front teeth.

"And in this corner, weighing in at only a hundred and sixty pounds, standing at five feet nine, and soon to be dead meat: also from Fifty-Two Division, Kristen Bailey!"

There were a few claps from the crowd, but mostly everyone seemed horrified at the matchup. She shared their sentiment.

"Let's make this a good, clean match," the emcee said and motioned for them to join him at the centre of the ring.

"Don't think I've never hit a girl before," Smith seethed around his mouth guard.

"I don't." She bumped his gloves.

"You're dead."

He bumped her gloves hard, eliciting an "oooh" from the crowd. They both backed off to their corners.

She was in trouble. Smith was built like a condominium, and while she had wiry strength, she was no match for him in a head-to-head punchout. They both wore boxing headgear, but the small cushioning would do little against his extraordinary strength. Could he hit her hard enough to knock her head off? The bell dinged. She was about to find out.

Smith wasted no time in coming at her. He stamped toward her and opened with a long punch aimed at the side of her head. Kristen ducked out of the way to avoid what would have been a crushing blow. Smith wasn't deterred. He followed it up with a quick jab of his left fist. She turned her body, avoiding most of the blow, but part of it landed on her right side. The crowd gasped. Even at half force, it was a powerful hit. The strength he had in his jab alone would be enough to knock the wind out of her at full force. She danced back, out of his reach.

He came at her again, this time with a left hook, which opened up his frame. She ducked and delivered a hard jab with her right fist square in his solar plexus. Her fist bounced off of him as if she'd hit a wall. He smiled around his mouth guard and thrust his right arm down and up in a shattering uppercut. The full force of his strength sent her flying back in the air. Her body collided with the ropes, and she fell down hard on the ring floor. For a moment, there were only bright lights and blackness before her eyes refocused. She tried to move her jaw but it was painful, maybe even broken. Smith was forced to back off while the ref came over to check on her and got ready to lay down the count. She got onto her knees. She could never win this way. He was going to kill her. If she could just implement her use-of-force or pressure point training, she would stand a chance, but that wasn't allowed in the ring. She had two choices: use her maneuvers to save herself and be disqualified, which risked Ortiz having to take the fight up against Smith after all, or let him beat her, and get the information she needed from Ortiz on the case.

She used the ropes to help her up. The crowd cheered for her.

"Haven't had enough?" Smith grinned. Apparently, he hadn't wanted an answer, because he followed his question with blow after blow to her stomach. The first one took her breath away; the rest were just a sport pummeling. The ropes held her up while he delivered punch after punch. Finally, after seven blows, he stepped back slightly. She started to fall, but not before he delivered the final right hook to her helmet that nailed her to the ring floor.

Distantly, as if in a dream, the referee counted to ten. Smith was declared the still-undefeated champion. The crowd cheered. Two hands grabbed her and pulled her out of the ring. One of her arms was propped over someone's shoulder, and then the same happened with the other. She was dragged away from the crowd. She still couldn't catch her breath.

She was deposited into a chair, and the sitting motion caused immense pain to burn in her abdomen, where several organs had to be bleeding out. A door closed nearby.

"Jesus, fuck, are you okay?"

She looked up, her vision coming back into focus. It was Ortiz. Whoever had helped him carry her in there was gone. It was just the two of them in the room.

"Tell me...what I want to know," she said, gasping for breath.

"You need to go to the hospital."

"Tell me..." she gasped, "what I want to know."

"Fuck, Bailey, I don't know what you want to know."

"Who...killed...Oslowe?"

"If I knew, don't you think that person would have been arrested?" he asked tetchily.

She tried to think, but when she moved her head, it sounded like something was rattling around in there. Her brain cells?

Two hands were on her again, and she realized Ortiz was trying to take off her helmet.

He eased her helmet off and put it on a counter behind him, then returned with a bottle of water. He pushed it to her lips, and she drank. After swallowing down half the bottle, she turned away, and he put the bottle down.

"Jenna Bradley and Ricky Oslowe, you think they're connected?" he asked.

"I do."

"How?"

"I don't know."

"But you...suspect something?"

She nodded, still trying to steady her breathing.

"What?" he asked.

"I don't know. That's why I'm asking you. What do you know?"

"You wouldn't know much about rookie protocol, but—"

"Just keeping talking, assuming I know everything," she said.

He paused and looked at her. "Fine. Neither Bradley nor Oslowe should have been out on their own. Their TOs should have been with them when they were killed. Not only that, both those rookies were right on the scene when the calls came in, as if they'd known beforehand where they should be."

"Or someone else did."

He nodded. "Or someone else did," he agreed. "So who would they listen to? Who would give them the keys to a squad car and tell them where to go?"

"Their TOs," Kristen answered.

"Exactly, only I can't prove anything."

"Hackett was Bradley's TO."

"He was."

"Who was Oslowe's?" She knew the answer but needed to appear uninformed to Ortiz.

"Hans Olafson," he said.

"Did you question him?"

"Of course, for the little good it did me. He retired only a few weeks after Oslowe was murdered."

Kristen thought a moment. "What if I told you that these rookies were being used to move evidence? Possibly to make drug drops, ordered by their TOs, but without knowledge of what they were doing?"

"I'd say that's not a light accusation. Has Hackett asked you to do something like that?"

"No," she said, "but he doesn't seem to trust me all that much. From what I understand about Oslowe and Bradley, they were eager to please. They both wanted to impress their superior officers and make a name for themselves quickly. They may have done these extra favours just to be seen in a better light. Bradley started to ask questions, though. I can only assume Oslowe may have as well. So their TOs sent them out alone. They think they're being promoted—"

"But they're being set up," Ortiz finished for her.

She nodded, some of the fogginess in her head dissipating.

"How are we going to prove that, though? The TOs certainly aren't talking."

"What about one of the other senior officers? Someone who's known them a long time?"

"Their buddies aren't going to say shit." He let out a long breath. "Plus, it's hard for me to make any headway with King breathing down my neck and getting in my way every move I make."

King had been taking an inordinate interest in the investigation.

"Okay, let's go over what we have. Two dead rookies in the wrong place at the wrong time. Both of them sent to that place presumably by people they trusted. Their TOs send the rookies to evidence to check out the drugs so that the heat falls on them if anyone gets suspicious. But then the rookies start asking questions. The veteran cops are close to retirement. They don't want the hassle. They're just skimming off the top, padding their retirement with some extra drug money. They know the evidence is just going to get incinerated eventually anyway, so why not make a profit off it? They keep their names clean by getting the rookies to do the dirty work. So what's King's involvement in this?"

Ortiz thought for a minute. "King's the same age as these guys. He's looking at retirement as well. Sure, the staff sergeant's paycheque is a little bigger, but is it enough? Cops on this job see so much going to waste on busts they bring in, they start to wonder why they shouldn't get a cut. King protects them from the top, gets a kickback on every deal, maybe even gives the orders."

"Christ, he was probably in the same year with most of these guys at the academy."

"But how do we prove it?" Ortiz asked.

"How much does King know that you know?"

"He knows everything. About six months ago, he asked me to keep him in the loop about everything I learned."

"Is that why he was there when you were interrogating Ashleigh Paige?"

"The paramedic?"

She nodded.

"He was on the other side of the glass in that interview."

So that was how he'd discovered the altercation between her and Ortiz so quickly.

"What about the calls to dispatch? Why abandoned buildings in Chinatown?"

He looked thoughtful. "I've asked myself the same thing over and over again. It doesn't make any sense on its own. What do you think?"

A thought occurred to her. "Both buildings are in *Lǎohǔ* territory."

"They are, yeah. What are you thinking?" Ortiz asked.

"The TOs had their rookies take evidence from *Lǎohǔ* lockup, then had it delivered to someone somewhere in *Lǎohǔ* territory they're selling the drugs to, I don't know who. When the rookies wised to what was happening, their TOs took care of them by putting them in gangbanger territory so when their bodies were found, it would look like they were a byproduct of a drug bust gone awry. If the drugs were discovered, it would look like it was all part of the same bust. The only problem is you can't make shootouts happen. Still, if you're into drug dealing, you know where a deal is going to go down. They needed a shootout, so they sent each of them into one. All they had to do was make sure they were dead afterward."

"Jenna Bradley's radio into dispatch said there were civilians everywhere. Wouldn't people notice someone walking into a shootout and then taking off? Wouldn't that cause some alarm?"

The realization hit Kristen like a ton of bricks. "Not if they were paramedics."

Ortiz ran his hands through his short, black hair. He paced away, then back again. "You think the EMTs are in on it too?"

"I don't know." She shook her head. "That or someone's pretending to be them."

"They'd have to look pretty legit to escape scrutiny. How would they get an ambulance?"

"What if they didn't?"

"What do you mean?"

"Well, what if they just had the uniforms? That's all the video of Ricky Oslowe's murder shows. They go in, see if the deed is done, and if not, they finish the job."

He looked at her warily. "How do you know what's in the video?"

"Come on. Is there anyone in fifty-two who hasn't seen that video?"

"Fine." He nodded. "So this team is a cleanup team?"

"That's what I'm thinking." This whole time, she'd been caught up in who was on duty that day, but maybe she should have been looking at who wasn't, who could have pulled up to the scene and dispensed of Ricky Oslowe without their cruiser being tracked by dispatch. "The cleanup crew gets called in by King to make sure the job is done. They probably would have gotten away with it with Oslowe if he hadn't been taking that video."

"And anyone who saw them going in or out wouldn't stop them. They'd just think they were responding to a nine-one-one call."

"Exactly," Kristen said.

"So why hide Bradley's body and not Oslowe's?"

Kristen thought for a moment. "In Oslowe's video, you can hear sirens sounding out in the background near the end of the struggle. Maybe whoever it was intended to do something with the body but ran out of time."

"Okay." He stroked his goatee in thought. "That makes sense."

"But how do we know which is which? Were they EMTs or cops dressed up as EMTs or some outside cleanup crew altogether?"

He paused. "You really think it was cops posing as EMTs?"

"That's what we need to find out."

He raised his eyebrows skeptically. "We?"

"Or you can go in on your own, but I think you've made more progress tonight than you have in the last year."

He mulled it over for a minute. "All right, but no one can know we're working together. Don't speak of this to anyone but me, clear?"

"I wouldn't have it any other way," she said with relief. "You keep an eye on Hackett and the rest of the TOs. I'll work the EMT angle, and on that note, stay away from Ashleigh Paige." He gave her a questioning look. "Just trust me when I say she's not a part of this."

He raised his arms and dropped them. "Fine. What about King?"

"I say we both keep an eye on him and share anything we find out."

"Deal." He stretched out his hand.

Kristen shook it with a smile. She'd gotten way more information out of Ortiz than she'd hoped, and more than that, she'd gained a partner. It had been worth the beating.

CHAPTER 16

ASHLEIGH RAN THE PACKING TAPE along the top of the last box and sealed the cardboard together, then broke the end with her teeth, which left the taste of plastic adhesive in her mouth. She patted the tape down and exhaled with satisfaction. Packing up for both university and Kenya had taught her how not to amass too many possessions, and it had taken only two days to pack everything back up into boxes.

Her phone buzzed on her bed. She picked it up and looked at the call display, and her stomach jolted. It was Kristen. She wished she could have stopped her body's reaction to her name. She took in a deep breath and let it out slowly. How could just seeing her name have such a visceral effect on her? She opened the message.

So, turns out I'm an ass.

Was this her way of apologizing? She texted back.

I figured that one out, actually.

She waited, her attention glued to the screen.

Think you can forgive me?

She wasn't sure what to say. Her plan to forget entirely about Kristen wouldn't work if she forgave her, but she wanted to nonetheless.

I suppose.

Thank you. What are you doing?

Packing.

Are you going somewhere?

I'm moving out next weekend.

Cool. Where?

Leslieville.

That's a good area. Want to come over?

Her stomach muscles tightened. More than anything, she wanted to see Kristen again. She read the text over and over, and couldn't help the smile that pulled at her lips.

Why would I want to do that?

Because I could use a friend.

That wasn't the answer she'd been hoping for.

Why?

Come over and find out?

Ashleigh pretended to debate it for about ten seconds before firing off her response, already heading for the door.

Be there in an hour.

Kristen opened the door on the first knock.

"Don't you ask who it is?" Ashleigh slid past her into the condo.

"Peephole." Kristen closed the door behind her.

Kristen wore a pair of form-fitting black yoga pants, and a black tank top that clung to her. She looked sexy as anything standing there in the Toronto heat, a tear of sweat rolling down her tanned neck, a glass of dark liquor in her hand.

"What are you drinking?" she asked.

"Bourbon. Do you want one?"

"I didn't come here for a drink. You said you needed a friend, remember?" She tried to sound nonchalant. "How many of those have you had?"

"This is my second." She swallowed the rest of the glass.

"Are you drunk?"

"No, but I'm starting to wish I was."

"Why?"

"Self-medicating."

Ashleigh stilled. "For what?" She envisioned Bailey's last injury, a crack to the back of her skull, and her stomach lurched.

Kristen put the empty glass down on her granite countertop, gripped the hem of her tank top with one hand, and lifted it up, revealing blue and purple abs.

Ashleigh gasped and covered her mouth with her hand. It looked bad. Really bad. Her heart constricted as she took in Kristen's pain and felt it as if it were her own. She'd thought her heart was healing in the days since she'd kissed her, but being with her now smarted just as strongly as the raw wounds she saw in front of her.

"What happened?" She reached trembling fingers out to touch her bruises, and Kristen flinched. "I'm sorry."

"It's okay." She dropped her shirt and poured herself another drink. "FiteNite happened."

"You got this in a boxing match?"

"Heh. More like a beatdown, but yeah."

She couldn't imagine any of the officers getting so rough inside the ring. It was a charity event. The cops were supposed to let off some steam and put on a little show, but this was far beyond the philanthropic intentions of the event.

"Who did this to you?" she asked.

"Luke Smith, the prick," Bailey muttered, throwing ice into her glass.

Ashleigh looked to the side, trying to place the name. Then it hit her. "Oh, my God. *Him?*"

Bailey laughed, then winced. "You know him?"

"I've seen him. He's a giant."

Kristen nodded and swallowed.

"Why would you fight him?" Ashleigh asked.

"The truth? I made a deal with someone. I needed information on a case, and the cop who was supposed to fight him wanted out, so I took his spot."

"You did this for information?"

"It was for Jenna Bradley and Ricky Oslowe. I want to find who killed them."

Ashleigh let out a long breath. "You have a lion's heart."

The motion of Kristen's hand stopped halfway to her mouth. She lowered the drink slowly, looking her over. Ashleigh wasn't sure what was going on behind that stoic facade. "That is how you see me, isn't it?" she finally asked.

"It is." Ashleigh reached forward and took the hand that wasn't holding the drink. "You do too much for others."

Bailey finished her drink in one swallow. "I wish you didn't see me that way."

"Why?"

Kristen pulled her hand back and motioned between them. "This isn't a good idea, Ashleigh."

"God, why do I keep letting you do this to me?" She started to walk away, then turned around. "You know, I knew you were wrong for me. I knew it from the beginning, but still, I fell for you. I practically threw myself at you at your brother's. I knew how wrong you were for me, and still, I was going to let you have me, but you rejected me. I don't know why I came back here."

"I didn't reject you."

"What would you call turning away a half-naked girl in your bed? Or is that just Tuesday for you?"

"It's not like that. Don't you get it? I left because you're not just some girl. I want to give you everything you want, but I can't."

"What does that even mean?" She moved toward Kristen and placed a hand on her cheek to force her to meet her gaze.

"Ashleigh, please, you have to go."

Ashleigh's heart clenched. Kristen had called her over just to push her away. Again. How many times was she going to let her do this to her? She dropped her hand, incredulity replacing humiliation. If Kristen was going to kick her out, she deserved to know the reason.

"Why?"

Bailey looked at her, her eyes intensely blue, like the hottest part of a flame. "Because I don't think I have the strength to resist you a second time."

"Then don't."

There was only a second of hesitation in Kristen's eyes before she reached for Ashleigh and pulled her in. Their mouths met in a crushing kiss that moved through her body like electricity. Kristen tasted of whiskey and warmth.

Ashleigh came undone.

Her arms were around Bailey in seconds. One hand wound up into her hair and twisted in, pulling her further into the kiss. Kristen moaned against her mouth. The sound tore through her, and she parted her lips. Kristen did the same as their kiss deepened, their mouths locked around each other to keep the warmth inside. Ashleigh trembled when Kristen's tongue touched her own, and she let it in with a groan.

She should stop, but her body was responding to Kristen like it had to no one before. She should go home, but her hands were already reaching under Bailey's tank top.

Cognizant of Kristen's injury, she moved her hands around her, feeling the contrast of her soft skin against her sinewy back. She pulled the tank top over Kristen's head and returned her hands to her torso. Her fingers moved across her body as if they had the memory of her skin.

Kristen deepened the kiss once more, and there was a corresponding pulse between her legs. Kristen's hands were at her side, gripping at her

T-shirt, and Ashleigh raised her arms in permission. Kristen pulled it quickly from her body.

"Take me," Ashleigh breathed against her lips, and Kristen growled obediently at the command.

Kristen reached her arms around Ashleigh and grabbed her ass with both hands, hiking her legs up around her own waist. Ashleigh snaked her arms around Kristen's neck and slipped her hands back into her hair. Their kiss never stopped as Kristen carried her to the bedroom and laid her down on the bed, where only the two of them had ever been.

In one movement, Kristen lowered herself on top of Ashleigh and captured her mouth again in a searing kiss. The fire ran all the way through her body. Bailey's resistance to her was over; she could feel it in the depth of her kiss. Kristen placed an arm on either side of Ashleigh, holding her weight off her, holding herself in place on top of her, gently tucking Ashleigh between her arms as their kiss continued to burn between them.

Ashleigh remembered little from her first experience, but there wasn't one second of it that could compare to the feelings and emotions that threatened to overwhelm her in this moment. Every kiss, every movement brought her body to life. The incessant pulsing between her legs became painful, and she pushed her body up to feel Kristen. When their bodies ground against each other, Bailey finally broke away from the kiss, breathing hard. Ashleigh struggled to focus her eyes, involuntarily whimpering in frustration at the withdrawal of her lips.

Kristen smiled down at her. It was that sexy smile she'd come to love, but there was more. In her eyes, she saw something else, a tenderness, and it stirred something deep within her. Was it possible that Bailey felt anything like what she was feeling? She'd expected things with Kristen to be over quickly, as they had been with Denise. Bailey had been drinking, so Ashleigh didn't expect much more from her. Her chest tightened. Would this be another mistake? If so, at least she was walking into it with eyes wide open this time. Part of her didn't care because, for a few minutes, she would get to hold Kristen, be close to her, have her as close as her own skin, and that would be enough.

It was too late to stop now. She'd fallen for Bailey so hard and so fast it felt like someone had reached inside her and spun her world around.

No matter what she did, she felt herself being drawn back to her. Her entire life, everything she'd ever done, had been part of a large tapestry. All of her choices were invisible threads, circling around her, catching her up in a web with Kristen, spinning her into a fate that culminated in this moment.

"What is it?" Kristen asked.

"Nothing." Ashleigh swallowed.

"Tell me." Kristen kissed her lightly, then met her gaze in the dim light of the room.

"I love you."

That hadn't been what she meant to say. She wanted to say anything but that. Kristen's eyes widened almost imperceptibly in surprise before she answered her confession with a slow kiss, her lips brushing Ashleigh's softly. Ashleigh moaned when Kristen's tongue slipped past her lips again and moved languidly against her own. This was not how Ashleigh was used to being kissed.

Kristen wasn't quick with her. She kissed her deeply, soundly. Every stroke of her tongue set her body on fire. If just kissing could do this to her, how was she going to handle anything more?

Kristen changed the balance of her weight and rested the majority of it on her left arm. She brought a hand up to Ashleigh's neck. Her fingers were like flames on her skin. They traced down her throat and across her clavicle and dipped slowly between her breasts. Kristen moved her hand underneath them, unhooked Ashleigh's bra, and pulled it from around her arms. She ran her hand over her bare torso and trailed her fingers along her ribs. Ashleigh braced herself for the feeling of Kristen's hands on her breasts, and when Kristen stroked her there, Ashleigh could not suppress her groan. Kristen lowered her head and took a nipple into her warm mouth.

Ashleigh gasped and closed her eyes. She couldn't see clearly anyway. Kristen pulled her deeper into her mouth, adding more pressure. Ashleigh's breathing was uneven, ragged as Kristen set the tempo of her body, building her up. Her nipples were hard and taut, aching more with every touch. Kristen released her, moved her head to the other side, and began the sweet torture all over again, worsening the deep throbbing between her legs. She'd never been touched like this before. She didn't know she could be touched like this.

When Kristen sucked her nipple deep into her mouth, Ashleigh moaned loudly, and Bailey growled in response. "I want to go slowly," Kristen said against her body. "Will you let me?" There was a pleading in her voice Ashleigh hadn't heard before. She was asking permission to love her unhurriedly, deliberately, like only she could.

"Yes."

Kristen's response was to lean forward and place a gentle kiss on her lips. "You're so beautiful." She kissed her again. "I can't tell you how many times I imagined this. How badly I've wanted to touch you."

Ashleigh's body responded to her words, her heart pounding. With every kiss, every touch, every word, she was changing her, pulling her out of her skin, exposing the most tender parts of her.

"I want to see all of you," Kristen said against her mouth, once again asking permission. She nodded, and Bailey thanked her with another slow kiss before she sat up and set to work on her jeans.

Kristen undid the top button and pulled the zipper down slowly, then moved her hands to her waist and gradually pulled her pants over her thighs. She stopped every few inches to explore all the new bits of nakedness she exposed. She did everything unhurriedly, as if they had forever, as if there would never be an end to this night. Ashleigh hoped against reason that there wouldn't be.

When Kristen reached her ankles, she pulled each of her socks off, then leisurely slid the last of her jeans over her bare feet and laid them down gently on the floor next to the bed. Kristen had barely touched her, but her body was overflowing with desire from every caress.

Still on her knees beside her, Bailey lifted one of her legs, brought her lips to the top of her foot, and placed a soft kiss there. She followed it with another, just above the last, and worked her way slowly up Ashleigh's calf. It was just the right amount of pressure not to tickle, just enough force to be painfully erotic. She continued kissing up her knee, and now her hand trailed behind her lips and brushed the skin her mouth had set fire to. When Kristen reached her thigh, she laid her leg back down on the bed and kissed up the outside of her thigh until she reached the hem of her underwear. She left a kiss there on her hip and pulled away. Ashleigh panted under her touch, wanting Kristen to move her lips to where she ached.

Kristen moved back and reached for her other leg, the one further away from her, and started again at the top of her foot and left a trail of kisses up her leg. Ashleigh suppressed a groan as Bailey's lips lit up every inch of her body leaving little torches along a path that lead slowly to the apex of her desire. The pressure there built to a level Ashleigh had never experienced before.

This time, when Kristen reached above her knee, she leaned forward and moved her trail of kisses to her inner thigh. Ashleigh's mouth opened as she tried to catch her breath, and Kristen used more pressure on the sensitive skin. When she reached the end of her thigh, she stopped.

Ashleigh throbbed in anticipation.

Kristen bent her head and planted a long, slow kiss directly over her wet, aching centre. When her lips connected, Bailey quivered against the fabric of her last piece of clothing. "I want you so badly."

Ashleigh gasped. "You're killing me," she said breathlessly.

"No." Kristen raised her head, and her hands slowly slid her damp underwear from her hips. "I'm worshipping you."

Every touch, every word, every sound, every breath was different from anything Ashleigh had ever felt before. It was almost as if she was experiencing it all again for the first time, and in a way, she was. Energy hummed through her, flowing into every vein and sending sparks through her entire body as she lay there, naked and full of anticipation. Kristen's touch lit her up from the inside out.

Kristen leaned forward and took a nipple into her mouth again. This time, she used more pressure, and Ashleigh arched her back, rising to meet the source of the pleasure. Bailey sucked her in harder, sliding her hand over to her other breast and kneading the hard nipple she found there. The pressure continued to build inside of her. Her chest grew more and more constricted. Her breathing came heavier and heavier. She was like a harp string spinning tighter and tighter until she was about to snap. She could take it no longer.

"Kristen," she panted, "I need you."

Kristen groaned against her breast and pulled her lips away slowly. She left a line of kisses down her stomach, coaxing her legs apart with her hand as her mouth reached lower. Ashleigh spread them willingly, and Kristen dipped her hand between her thighs, feeling her arousal for the first time.

Kristen's breath caught. She moved her fingers through her slickness again. "You're so wet." Her voice was husky with arousal and longing, and another surge of wetness leaked between Ashleigh's thighs.

"I can't wait any longer," Ashleigh said, giving Bailey permission not to take things slowly anymore.

Kristen nodded gratefully, and the look of unmasked desire in her eyes caused a pull deep inside Ashleigh.

Kristen lowered her body and positioned herself between Ashleigh's thighs. She pushed her legs open wider, and Ashleigh's heart stilled as Kristen lowered her mouth to her sex. Ashleigh let out a long, shuddering breath as Bailey stroked her tongue across her ache for the first time. With a moan, Kristen licked the length of her. The sound caused Ashleigh's insides to tighten, to pulse, to throb. Kristen's tongue stayed right there, stroking her with just the right amount of force.

She gripped the sheets in her hands, thinking she couldn't possibly take another second before exploding. It was too much. Kristen was there, buried between her legs, bringing her to a crescendo she had never reached before. With each caress, the pressure built in her stomach, cascading lower and lower, until it ached and pulsed in time with Kristen's mouth.

Her breathing became ragged. It was as if Kristen held her entire body on the tip of her tongue. With the desperate, quaking need for release, her muscles tensed, and her upper body shook. The pull in her abdomen became painful, excruciatingly stretched and taut, throbbing against Kristen's mouth so hard she thought she might pass out.

"Kristen," she begged. "Please, I need to come."

Kristen moaned in response and placed the flat of her tongue against her. She caressed her need with force, spilling Ashleigh over the edge. She let out a loud, shuddering breath as the release tore through her, splitting her like lightning as she came again and again, her orgasm crashing like waves against Kristen's warm, wet mouth.

She was still panting long after the flow had ebbed. She had never come like that before. She didn't know that sex could feel like that—that anything could feel like that. Kristen washed away everyone else's touch until her body knew and understood only her. She'd reached deep inside Ashleigh, grabbed hold of her heart, and stretched herself out along it, filling all the emptiness that had been there before.

Kristen moved up her body.

"That was amazing," Ashleigh said.

"Mmm, you're amazing." Kristen kissed her lips.

Her words sent a shiver through her again, and at that moment, she realized that Kristen was still fully dressed, except for her shirt.

"I don't think I fulfilled my end of the deal," she said, taking Bailey's black bra strap between her fingers. "You're still dressed."

"Trust me." Bailey kissed her lips again. "I got everything I needed."

"But—"

"Shh, it's okay," she said against her lips and kissed her more soundly. "My body is kind of out of commission right now."

Guiltily, Ashleigh remembered the awful bruising along Bailey's torso. "Did I hurt you?"

Kristen smiled and kissed her again. Was there always this much kissing after sex? If so, she had found another reason to love it.

"You were perfect."

Ashleigh allowed the words to wash over her. She sighed contentedly at the sight of Kristen still above her. She was looking into Ashleigh's eyes with a gaze that could pierce stone. She needn't have bothered. Ashleigh was hers for the taking, again and again if she wanted her. The thought caused another quickening between her legs. It was Ashleigh who wanted her again. Only this time, she wanted to be the one doing the exploring.

She moved out from under Kristen and turned them over. She now leaned on top of her, careful not to put any pressure on her bruising. "Exactly how out of commission are you?" she asked by her cheek and took an earlobe into her mouth, sucking it gently.

Kristen's breath hitched before she answered. "Not completely," she said, her voice catching, and Ashleigh grinned.

"Well, I'm sorry to do this, officer, but I'm going to have to perform a strip search." She kissed Kristen and warmed when she felt Bailey's smile against her lips.

Unlike Kristen, she didn't take her time. She wanted her now, her need already swelling between her legs again. She started with her yoga pants and pulled them down, along with her tight, black underwear. Her heart beat as hard as a drum as she looked at Kristen naked for the first time.

Kristen didn't protest her eagerness. Without even taking the time to remove her bra, Ashleigh straddled Bailey. When they connected, she gasped at how wet Bailey was. "Is this what I do to you?" she asked, sliding her fingers into her wetness, mesmerized by how it felt coating her own skin.

"You have no idea what you do to me."

Ashleigh's stomach tugged, and the sensation quickly slid lower. When Denise had done this to her, she'd found it vile, but with Kristen beneath her, their wetness sliding against each other, she felt like a shotgun cocked and ready to explode.

She moved her hips slowly at first. Bailey reached around and gripped her, one hand on her hip and one on her ass, and pulled her harder into herself. Ashleigh's breath caught at her wanting. She took her cue from Kristen, grinding with more force. Bailey groaned, slightly repositioned Ashleigh's body above hers, and then pulled Ashleigh's weight across her again. Something hard slid through her wetness. Kristen moaned in response. She took control of Ashleigh's body, gripping her more firmly and moving her faster along her skin. Ashleigh moved her body into the motion, willing to do anything Kristen wanted if it meant she would come against her. Just the thought of it had her on the edge again.

Kristen continued to guide Ashleigh as she rode her body, crashing Ashleigh's weight hard against her. It was too much for Ashleigh. Bailey's wetness felt too good on her still-sensitive centre. She cried out and came hard, spilling herself onto Bailey.

Kristen groaned and pushed harder and faster as Ashleigh came. She slid through her with a few long, hard strokes, then tensed and let herself release, trembling against Ashleigh's skin.

After she finished, Kristen let her weight drop back against the pillow, but she pulled Ashleigh down with her, still holding Ashleigh firmly against her. When Kristen suddenly tensed her abs, Ashleigh realized she was flush up against the injuries. She tried to pull away, but Kristen tightened her grip against her.

"Your bruises," she protested.

"I don't care," Kristen said. "I don't want you to go." She kissed the side of her face, where it was wet with sweat. "You feel so good in my arms. Like honey on my skin."

Ashleigh allowed the words to move through her for a moment, just one moment, before she let reality in. Bailey would want her to go soon. She let the warmth of Bailey's arms fill her heart one more time before she pulled away. "I should go," she said.

Bailey leaned up, closing the space between them again. "I don't want you to leave."

"Come on, Kristen. Yes, you do. It's okay. You were very honest about what this was." She started to move away again, but Kristen wrapped her arms around her, holding her in place on top of her.

"Ashleigh, stop. I can't take my hands off you. I don't want you to go."

"But you said—"

"Forget everything I said. I want you to stay with me."

"I..." she started, but she didn't know what to say. She leaned up and looked deep into Kristen's eyes. There was nothing there, no barrier between them anymore. She swallowed and got off of her. She had to turn away. The look in Kristen's eyes was too intense, too real. She loved Kristen, and she could handle that, but she hadn't prepared herself for the look of longing she saw in Bailey. If she let herself give into it, Kristen would break her heart.

Kristen put her arms around her from behind, and Ashleigh stifled a whimper when she felt Kristen push her warm, wet body up against hers. She let Bailey wrap herself around her. Let her pull her in closer. She couldn't leave now if she wanted to. She tried to steady her breathing and the quickness of her heartbeat.

She closed her eyes. Kristen placed a soft kiss at the nape of her neck, and as her breathing slowly evened out, she drifted off to sleep, wondering if that last kiss was Kristen's way of saying goodbye.

CHAPTER 17

KRISTEN OPENED HER EYES SLOWLY. She breathed in and was greeted by the scent of something sweet and feminine. The room was full of Ashleigh's scent. Her stomach muscles tightened, and she winced against her bruises. There was a warm body pushed against hers, and a quickening between her legs. She tightened her jaw, breathing steadily until it passed.

I love you. Ashleigh's words prickled through her chest once more. How could Ashleigh Paige have fallen in love with her? How could she have let her?

She'd seen it in Ashleigh's eyes, felt it in her touch how much she meant to her. What she hadn't prepared herself for was the full reciprocation of those feelings. She was not supposed to fall for her. She wasn't even supposed to sleep with her, but she couldn't help herself from wanting her, couldn't stop herself from taking her. She had never touched someone like that before. She hadn't just had sex with Ashleigh. It had been so much more.

She wished she could give her what she wanted. What she deserved. She couldn't, though. She was too…broken. The sooner she walked out of Ashleigh's life, the sooner Ashleigh could get over her.

Ashleigh began to shift, then stretched out like a cat, and Kristen couldn't keep the smile from her face. "Good morning," she said.

Ashleigh turned to face her but never left her arms, and Kristen didn't try to make her.

"Good morning." Ashleigh smiled. "I didn't mean to stay the whole night," she said sheepishly.

"Don't be silly," Kristen said. "I didn't want you to leave." It was the truth, but she shouldn't have said it. She shouldn't have even let her stay the night. She should have been working on the case. "I need you to do something for me," she said. "I need to know how easy it would be for someone to get a hold of a paramedic uniform. How many locks are between the front door and where you guys keep your uniforms?"

"Well, there's the front door, but that's not locked. Then, there's the keycard you need to get into the staff area. The change rooms are unlocked, but we have codes for our lockers. Why?"

Kristen ignored her question. "How about extra uniforms? Is there a spot where those are kept?"

Ashleigh bit her lip in thought. Kristen tried not to be distracted by it. "There are a few in my supervisor's cupboard."

"Does he keep his door locked?"

"He's a she, and no, not usually."

"Even when she's not there?"

"No," Ashleigh confirmed.

"What about the keys to your trucks? What's locked up and what isn't?"

"The keys are kept in the sally port."

"Is it easy to get in there?"

"For an EMT. Not for a civilian."

"What about a cop?" Kristen asked.

Ashleigh's brow knitted. "Are you planning on stealing a truck?"

"No. I'm trying to figure out if someone else did."

Ashleigh shook her head. "That would be practically impossible. All the trucks have GPS trackers on them. Dispatch knows where they are at all times. You couldn't just grab a truck and take off with it." She paused. "You're trying to find out who killed Ricky Oslowe."

She nodded. There was no use denying it. There wasn't much point in even asking these questions as she knew most of the answers already, but there was always the hope that there was something she'd missed, something that would lead her further down the investigation.

"How long would it take for someone to realize a truck was missing?"

"I don't know." She shrugged, making Kristen painfully aware of her nakedness. "Twenty minutes, tops."

Twenty minutes wasn't enough time. "What about the uniforms?"

"What about them?"

"How long would it take for your supervisor to notice if a few pieces were missing?"

"Forever, probably. They're just extras for if someone needs anything. We get blood and fluids on them a lot and don't always have the time to wash them. I honestly don't even think she keeps track."

Her theory was panning out. "Is it the same at all the stations?"

"I think so, more or less."

Kristen nodded.

"So, do I at least get coffee with my interrogation?" Ashleigh asked playfully.

Kristen's stomach tensed. Ashleigh was unknowingly helping her get one step closer to leaving her. "Of course you do." She kissed her lips and let the warmth of Ashleigh's mouth spread through her chest a moment before she forced herself away. "You get breakfast too."

The sounds of the family next door disturbed Kristen that day. Their laughter burrowed inside her chest. It made the emptiness there more acute.

Toast, eggs, and two cups of coffee later, Ashleigh had left for work, and Kristen had been both anxious and relieved to see her go. Ashleigh had only been gone a couple of hours, but she felt her absence deeply. How was it, after all the women she'd been with, one girl could turn her inside out like this? There was an Ashleigh-shaped hollowness inside her, and it refused to be filled by anything else.

She would just have to get used to it.

She was closer to closing this case than ever before. She had three prime suspects: Staff Sergeant King, Henry Hackett, and the retired Hans Olafson. Of the three, Hackett was the most accessible, so she would start with him, but not before a call to Ouellette to relay the good news.

"Ouellette," he answered when he picked up her call.

"Guess who?" Kristen said with a smile, checking the bullets in her semiautomatic service pistol.

"Tell me you have the *killerz*," he said, his Quebecois accent coming through at the end of his sentence. This was not a good sign. It meant he was stressed. Forget-to-hide-the-accent-everyone-teased-him-about stressed.

"I've narrowed it down. I don't think it's just two people. I think there's a team behind this."

"This isn't good. Teams take longer to bring down."

This isn't good? It was the best fucking thing she'd reported since the start of the investigation. She was not to be deterred. "Well, you might like this part. I think Staff Sergeant King is at the head."

"Why would I like that? Do you know how hard it's going to be to take down a staff sergeant?"

This wasn't like him. Ouellette normally liked a good intrigue. "What's going on?"

He let out a long breath. "They're pulling you, Kristen."

Her heart skipped a beat. "Why didn't you tell me?"

"I would have if you ever called."

All this work. Her promotion. Ashleigh. All of it. Gone.

"They can't do that." The tremor in her voice sounded pathetic even to her own ears.

"Of course they can. They're them. They can do whatever they want."

"And Banff?"

His silence said it all.

"No." She shook her head vehemently. "No way, not when I'm this close."

"Kristen—"

"No!" she shouted. That shut him up. *Good.* "I need till the end of the week. Give me till the weekend to figure this out. If I don't hand deliver the killers by then, you can yank me."

"You've already been yanked."

"Goddamnit! Just give me till the weekend. Stall. I'm so close."

"*C'est Mercredi,*" he said.

"So, give me till *Vendredi.*"

He let out another long breath. "You think you can solve this by Friday? In two days?"

"Yes."

"I can stall for two days. I can say I could not reach you, but, Kristen, this is it."

"I know."

"The next time we speak, it better be when you have cuffs around the killer."

"I understand."

"Okay. *Bonne chance.*"

"*Merci.*"

She ended the call. Two days was not a lot of time to bust this thing open. She slid her gun into the low profile holster at the back of her jeans. It was time to pay an off-duty visit to her TO.

Henry Hackett lived in a semi-detached home in the west end. If he'd bought it early enough, like fifty years ago, it would have been affordable on his salary. Unfortunately, he wasn't old enough for that, which only confirmed Kristen's suspicions that he'd been skimming off the top.

She closed the door to her car and walked up his front lawn. Nothing seemed suspicious. His Toyota Corolla was parked in the driveway. She knocked on the door, then rang the doorbell. A middle-aged woman with graying hair that was tied back in a clip answered the door. The smell of frying onions wafted out of the house. This must be Mrs Henry Hackett.

"Hello, ma'am." Kristen made a point of addressing her respectfully. "Is Henry home?"

She looked Kristen up and down. "Who's asking?"

"Constable Bailey, ma'am. He's my training officer, and I need to speak with him."

The woman nodded. "Come in."

Kristen stepped over the threshold, and her stomach growled. Whatever she was cooking smelled mighty good. What kind of cooking would Henry get in jail?

"He's out back." She walked deeper into the house, and Kristen followed. "Why don't you grab a beer and join him?" She pointed to the fridge.

"Thank you, ma'am." Kristen grabbed a Coors Banquet tall can from the fridge, then a second for Henry. Why not? It might be his last drink before he went to prison.

Hackett looked up when she stepped through the screen door and disquiet registered over his features. "Bailey? What are you doing here?" he asked.

He was sitting on a patio chair, his feet up on another, looking over his small downtown yard. There were cherry tomatoes and cucumbers growing on vines in a small garden around the periphery. Who was the gardener, Henry or his wife? She handed him a beer. He took it and put it on the glass patio table. She sat down in a wicker chair beside him.

She took her aviators off and looked right into his eyes. "Did you kill Jenna Bradley?"

His eyes widened. His mouth opened, but no sound came out. Then his eyes narrowed. "What?"

Surprise. Fear. Suspicion…but not guilt. Kristen was trained to read men, to see everything they didn't want her to see in the way they walked, the words they spoke, and even in the things they didn't say. Despite her sureness in coming here, she began to have misgivings. She'd wanted to surprise him with the accusation, and she had. It was often the best way to catch a culprit, but there was no culpability in him. Sadness, regret, maybe, but that was all.

"She was your rookie," Kristen said. "Why would you send her out on her own?"

"Not that this is any of your business, but I didn't."

"You're my TO. If I'm working with someone who's going to get me killed, it is my business."

"You goddamn female cops; you can't just keep your noses clean, can you?"

There it was again. "What's that supposed to mean?"

"I say left, you say right. I say stay, you say go. I say don't move the fucking evidence, and you move the fucking evidence."

Kristen jerked her head back. She knew she was RCMP, but he didn't. Why was he telling her this?

"Oh, don't look so surprised. I saw you get the shit kicked out of you at FiteNite, then dragged out of the ring by Ortiz. Why would you be fighting Luke Smith, I asked myself, when everyone knew it was Ortiz's name on the fight? Then Ortiz calls me up this morning, asking questions about Jenna Bradley. Imagine my surprise when you show up, doing the exact same thing. My only question is, what angle are you working? If you're looking to make a quick name for yourself, rook, getting yourself killed ain't the best way to go about it."

He'd put that together fast.

"If you didn't send Bradley out on her own that day, then who did?"

"Why should I answer your questions? You come over to my house, accusing me of killing my rookie, and you expect me just to tell you whatever it is you want to know? I'm nearing retirement. I don't want no part in whatever it is you and Ortiz are cooking up."

"Your rookie was sent in to die. Doesn't that bother you?" she asked. How could he keep his conscience clean, knowing Jenna Bradley had been set up?

"I told her not to go. I told her to stick with me, that I would help her through it. The last time we spoke, we argued about it. It didn't matter. She wanted to listen to her damn boyfriend, and that was the end of that."

This was new information. "And who was her boyfriend?"

"You just don't get it do you?" He popped the top of the beer Kristen had brought out for him. "The more you know, the more you become a target. I've kept you off their list so far, but if you start poking around, it'll be you they're asking for a favour next."

He'd kept her off their list? What the hell did that mean? She'd thought they were still riding around together because he liked to boss a woman around and be lazy. "If you didn't authorize Jenna Bradley to travel solo, then who did?"

"I don't know, Officer Smartass, you tell me. Who would have the authority to go over my head and veto my recommendation?"

She didn't need to think about it. "King."

"Bingo."

"And Jenna's boyfriend?"

He smirked. "King's son." He let the information marinate for a second before he spoke again. "Now you're not so gung-ho to go in guns blazing after these guys, are you?"

She ignored his sarcasm. "The drug busts. How did both Oslowe and Bradley end up in the exact place they were going down, right when they were going down?"

"They were sent out to patrol there. The nine-one-one calls were bogus."

"Can you testify to that?"

He scrunched up his face and shook his head. "I can't testify to shit, and even if I could, I wouldn't. I told them to keep their damn noses clean. They made their own choices. Like hell I'm going to put my life or my pension on the line for that. You want evidence, speak to King. Just don't expect to leave that meeting alive."

He was right. She was wasting her time here. Like most of the men and women she'd met in Toronto police, it turned out Henry was one of the good ones too. The officers she'd worked alongside the last few months and met in the locker room and in parade had been welcoming, with big hearts and astounding courage.

She stood up. "Thanks for the beer."

"Bailey," he said, just as she started to turn away. "You're not a bad cop. I kept you with me because I didn't want the same thing that happened to Bradley to happen to you. If you go out there now, though, if you go after them, after King, I can't protect you."

She turned back and put a hand on his shoulder, surprised by what she was about to say. "I'm sorry I doubted you."

On her way to her car, her phone buzzed. It was Ashleigh. She opened her car door and slid inside as she opened the message.

Hey. I'm sure I'm supposed to wait longer to message, but I can't stop thinking about you.

Her stomach muscles tightened. Even after sleeping with her, she hadn't come anywhere close to getting her feelings for Ashleigh out of her system. This was definitely a first.

I've been thinking about you too.

That's good to hear. So, when can I see you again?

Kristen read the message a few times. She should type out *never* and send it, but she couldn't. Just like when she thought she was giving Henry his last beer, she wanted one last, long drink of Ashleigh Paige.

I'll be home around 7 p.m.

Okay. I'm bringing dinner.

Kristen closed her screen, ignoring the hum in her body at the thought of seeing Ashleigh again. She opened her contacts and pressed on Ortiz's name.

"Ortiz," he answered.

"It's Bailey. It isn't Hackett," she said.

"I know."

"I know you know. You called him this morning. I thought we were going to keep each other informed as to what was going on."

There was a pause on the line. "Look, I'm having trouble with this trust thing. I'm not used to it, and I certainly didn't expect to be working with you. To be honest, I kind of thought you were an idiot."

"Charming," Kristen said, pushing down on the clutch and starting the car.

"I just mean, you're always so...I don't know, happy, chumming around. I just figured you needed to get along because you weren't good at your job. Hackett keeping you under his wing so long didn't help either."

"Apparently he did that to keep me out of whatever it is Bradley and Oslowe got themselves into." Kristen put the phone down as the call connected through the car's Bluetooth. She jiggled the shifter around neutral then pushed it into first gear and slowly let up on the clutch. "Did you have any other luck?"

"Hans Olafson has disappeared. I can't find him. He's moved, far as I can tell. Likely out of the country. I don't have the resources to track him down."

"Sounds like a guilty man to me."

"Maybe. Probably. But we can't prove it."

"Anyone else we should be adding to our list?" she asked, pulling onto Dundas Street.

"I'm sure there is, but there's no point chasing after all the little legs. We need to go for the head."

"King."

"Everything I look into, he's looked into first. Every piece of evidence I go to check out, he's checked it out already. Every lead I turn down, I find him in the middle of it. If it isn't Hackett and we can't get a hold of Olafson, then I say we go after King."

"I don't think we have enough evidence to approach him today," she said, deliberating on how long it would take to get her cover team in place to take him down.

"Don't even bother trying," Ortiz said. "He has his poker game tonight. He won't be home."

"Who does he play with?" she asked.

"Who else? Cops. Did you make any headway with the EMTs?"

"I don't think any paramedics were involved, but I'm still looking into it." *Sort of.*

"I'll see if I can dig up anyone else. Report back if you find anything on the EMTs."

"Sure, and Ortiz, that goes for you too."

CHAPTER 18

How was it possible for jeans and a thin, navy blue V-neck T-shirt to look that good? Ashleigh walked passed Kristen and into her condo, carrying a large box of pizza and a six-pack of Muskoka beer. She didn't recognize the name on the pizza box.

"Regina's?"

"Italian-owned-and-run trattoria in Little Italy. Their food is to die for."

The pizza wasn't the only thing in the kitchen to die for.

"I saw this beer in your fridge the first night I was here, so I figured you like it." She put the six-pack down on the counter next to the pizza. "Will it be weird if I know where your plates are, because I do. But if you want, I can ask you where everything is before I grab for it."

Kristen laughed. "Gave yourself a little tour, did you?"

"Perhaps." Ashleigh grinned and pulled two plates from the cupboard and then grabbed the beer opener from the drawer next to the fridge.

It was a welcome sight, Ashleigh in the kitchen, putting dinner together for them as if they were a real couple. Ashleigh handed her a plate with two slices of pizza on it. It was *quattro stagioni*. She hadn't had this since she was in Naples on an extradition case two years before.

Kristen received the plate gratefully and grabbed a beer from the counter. Ashleigh had already popped the tops off two of the IPAs. Kristen took a bite of pizza before she reached the couch. It burned the roof of her mouth, but it was worth it. The prosciutto was cooked perfectly, and the bite of seasoned artichoke that came with it was heavenly.

"This is so good."

"Glad you approve." Ashleigh joined her on the couch and bit into her slice with a smile. Her pizza was the same, only there was no prosciutto on her half.

"Thank you for bringing this. I was starving." She took another spirited bite.

"It's no wonder, with your empty fridge. There's this new place called the grocery store. If you play your cards right, I might take you there one day."

Ashleigh was doing it again. She was making her feel normal. Making her almost feel like she could belong with her.

"Cute." Kristen took a sip of the hoppy beer. "Tell me about your day."

"To be honest, I spent most of it thinking about you."

Kristen bit down hard on the crust of her pizza, letting Ashleigh's words slice through her stomach. When she didn't say anything, Ashleigh spoke again.

"I asked around today, and there was an investigation into the trucks the day that Richard Oslowe was killed. No trucks were unaccounted for. I thought you'd want to know."

Kristen nodded. This wasn't news, as she'd already conducted the same investigation herself months ago, as had SIU. The killers had uniforms but no ambulance. The surrounding surveillance videos of the area had already proven this. The team had knowledge of where the shootings would be, so they could go in first and either finish the job or move the body. Again, all clues pointed back to the police, to the senior officers who knew the game and wanted a little padding on their paycheques before retirement. To get away with it, they would need someone powerful protecting them, and King fit the bill better than anyone.

As staff sergeant, only those with crowns and stars on the epaulettes of their Toronto Police Service uniforms had the right to question him, and those ranks were mostly inaccessible to lower-level cops, who would need undeniable proof before opening an investigation into a high-ranking officer in the organization. She hoped wherever Ortiz was that he was having better luck. If King wasn't at his card game with his band of police miscreants, she could question him right now, but she'd have to wait.

"How are your bruises?" Ashleigh asked.

Instinctively, Kristen slid a hand under her shirt and felt them. They were less tender than the day before. "Healing."

Ashleigh's gaze remained on Kristen's hand under her shirt, and desire flooded her eyes. Kristen knew what it was like to feel attractive, wanted, but Ashleigh made her feel coveted.

"Then you won't mind if I do this." Ashleigh moved closer, her arms encircling Kristen's torso as their lips met for a hungry kiss.

Kristen's body responded instantly, flaring up at the first touch of her lips. Kristen pulled her closer and pushed her tongue against her lips, sliding into the warmth of her mouth. Ashleigh received it willingly, swallowing Kristen's moan. There was a pulse already building deep between her legs. No one had ever kissed her the way Ashleigh did. It wasn't just passion or wanting she tasted in her kiss. It was longing. It was love.

Kristen pulled away, and Ashleigh looked at her questioningly. "I think we should talk," she said.

Ashleigh sat back, tucking strands of honey-brown hair behind her ears. She didn't say anything.

Kristen took in a deep breath. She didn't know how to say any of what she was about to, and she didn't want to say any of it. "I—"

"Stop." Ashleigh interrupted her. "Whatever it is you're going to say, you don't have to say it. I can see it in your eyes—the guilt, the fear." She shook her head. "I wish you wouldn't look at me like that."

"I can't help it," Kristen said honestly, thinking about Ashleigh's confession during sex. "Last night, you said—"

"I know what I said, and I'm a big girl. I don't need you to protect me. I'm okay with feeling more than you do. I'm not embarrassed by it. I know it's fast, and I can't explain it, but I love you."

Kristen's first instinct was to tell her that she was wrong. Ashleigh didn't feel more than she did. Kristen felt the same.

Her heart stilled.

It was too late to deny it. The truth of it pulsed in every atom of her being. She'd never been in love with anyone before, which was how she knew that this must be it. There was no other way to explain how she felt for Ashleigh. It was inexplicable, incomprehensible, but it was also real.

She reached forward, moving over Ashleigh so quickly that Ashleigh didn't have time to stop her. In one swift movement, she had Ashleigh pinned underneath her on the couch. She lowered her head, tasted her lips, and allowed their bodies to crush together. She didn't care about the pain in her abdomen or the tightening around her heart. All she cared about was being close to Ashleigh, and she realized that no matter what she did, she might never be close enough.

"Wait." Ashleigh pulled away from her kiss, and Kristen backed up reluctantly.

Ashleigh stood, and it took a second for Kristen to register that she was undressing. Ashleigh peeled the T-shirt from her hot skin, and Kristen was mesmerized, her eyes transfixed on the lithe body before her. Ashleigh was lean, but soft to the touch as well. Kristen swallowed uneasily when she undid her jeans and slipped out of them, letting them fall to the floor.

"Do you know what I feel right now?" Ashleigh asked as she slowly peeled her bra straps down over her shoulders, first one, then the other.

Kristen swallowed hard. "No."

"Boiling hot." She laughed. "Come and get it," she said teasingly, then started skipping backwards toward the bedroom.

"Hey!" Kristen tore after her, reaching for her, but she slipped out of her grasp. In her room, she found Ashleigh lying on her back on her bed. It was the most welcoming sight she'd ever seen.

When she reached her, Kristen made as if to crawl over her, but Ashleigh stopped her with a wave of her finger. "You need to undress first," she said. "This is a no-clothing zone."

Kristen's mouth pulled up in a smile. "Then you better obey your own rules." She pointed at Ashleigh's two remaining pieces of clothing.

"Of course. I wouldn't disobey the law, officer." Ashleigh raised an eyebrow, and desire flooded Kristen as Ashleigh slowly removed her bra and underwear. Just standing there, watching Ashleigh, Kristen was more turned on than she'd ever been in her life.

Ashleigh smiled at her invitingly, and Kristen quickly rid herself of her clothing, unable to go another moment without feeling Ashleigh's body against her.

When Kristen moved to join her, Ashleigh sat up and moved away again.

"Come on," Kristen said with a growl.

Ashleigh took her hand and pulled her onto the bed. She maneuvered Kristen onto her back and positioned herself over her.

"Patience." She kissed Kristen's lips slowly. "Last night I was too excited," she said, then took Kristen's earlobe in her mouth. "I didn't get to take my time." She kissed down her neck. "Now it's my turn to touch." She ran a hand down Kristen's bare side, causing her to shiver. "To taste." She wrapped her lips around one of Kristen's nipples.

Kristen gasped at the sensation, and Ashleigh sucked her harder in response. The pulsing between her legs instantly quickened under Ashleigh's ministrations and became more adamant, almost painful. She'd always been sensitive, but it had never felt like this. It was as if Ashleigh's fingers, her mouth, were more than just on her skin. They were inside of her, snaking through every vein, every muscle, bringing every part of her to life.

When Ashleigh sucked her harder into her mouth, Kristen's breath caught audibly, and Ashleigh groaned. "I don't think anything could be sexier than listening to you in bed," she whispered against Kristen's chest. "I want to go slow, but I don't know if I can." She trailed her tongue between Kristen's breasts and down her stomach.

"You don't have to go slow," Kristen said, her voice hoarse.

Ashleigh stopped the movement of her tongue and looked up at her. "Has anyone ever done this to you before?" she asked.

Should she lie? She couldn't count the number of girls who had gone down on her. "Yes," she said.

"Not that." Ashleigh wore a patient smile. "Made love to you."

Kristen's heart stopped for a long moment before it kicked back into gear. Is that what this was? Is that why it felt so different? Ashleigh was right. Being with her wasn't just about the release. It was about everything else. "No," she admitted.

Ashleigh leaned forward, her hot mouth meeting Kristen's, and pulled her into a long, sensual kiss that ended with Ashleigh sucking lightly on her bottom lip before she released it and began to move lower.

"I want to devour you." Ashleigh's hands reached her legs first, where they slowly parted her thighs. "But more than that, I want to savour you." She tucked her long hair back and to the side, letting it all cascade over one beautiful shoulder. "I've never done this part before," Ashleigh said, just inches from her aching centre. "I'm glad it's you."

With that, she bent her head and took her first long taste of Kristen. Ashleigh moaned at the contact. The sound triggered a new surge of wetness between Kristen's thighs. Ashleigh licked her again, bathing every part of her with her mouth, until she found the hard centre of her arousal and gently surrounded it with long lashes of her silken tongue.

A primal pull began inside Kristen, moving lower, tightening, throbbing, winding her up until all she knew was Ashleigh's tongue, promising to deliver her from the agony. The buildup was so quick, too quick. Her body was writhing, trembling with every stroke, until she was on the precipice, forcefully holding back the river of her release.

"You taste so good," Ashleigh said. Her words caused a forceful ache in her core. "I want you to come."

As if on command, a crushing orgasm rolled through her and exploded in Ashleigh's mouth.

Ashleigh stayed there, the pressure of her tongue absorbing the waves of her orgasm until she stopped shuddering against her.

When she was finished, Ashleigh crawled up her body. "I've been wanting to do that since the first time I saw you," she said and pulled Kristen in to meet her lips. Kristen did so willingly, openly, and felt a corresponding pull of desire between her legs all over again at the fervour of Ashleigh's kiss.

Kristen could wait no longer to touch her.

She leaned forward and scooped Ashleigh into her arms, almost cradling her against her body. She switched their positions and laid her flat on her back. Ashleigh responded by wrapping her arms around her neck and kissing her firmly. Kristen lost no time in moving her hand down Ashleigh's body before pulling her lips away from her kiss and using them to follow the same trail as her fingers along her soft, warm skin.

With gentle kisses, she eased further down Ashleigh's body, letting her mouth taste the flesh of her neck, her collarbone, the top of her breasts before she reached her nipple and took it between her lips.

Ashleigh let out a sound that tore through Kristen's body and was answered by a new throbbing between her legs. She sucked harder as Ashleigh lifted her back and rose up to meet the pressure of her mouth. With her free hand, she captured Ashleigh's other breast and squeezed her nipple gently between her fingers, never stopping her lips from drawing her into her mouth over and over again.

"Please, Kristen," Ashleigh moaned her name, and Kristen all but lost control.

With a groan, she released Ashleigh from her mouth and laid her body flush against hers. There were no barriers between them, and her body melted into Ashleigh's. It was as if they were no longer two bodies; they had come together to share the same warmth, the same space, the same skin.

Ashleigh arched up against her, and the movement of her wetness on Kristen's skin was almost unbearable. Her own need throbbed, and with a shudder, she realized how close she was to losing control again.

She lifted her body up a little, moved a hand between them, and drifted it lower until it slid into Ashleigh's wetness, which coated her fingers. She gasped, and her arousal spiraled down deep in her core. She met Ashleigh's mouth and led her into a deep kiss that left her head spinning. Ashleigh opened her legs wider, and Kristen slipped her hand deeper in. She moaned when her fingers met the hard centre of Ashleigh's desire. She slid them through her wetness in slow circles.

"Like that," Ashleigh breathed in her ear.

Her voice sliced through Kristen's body, and she quickened the pace.

"Yes." Ashleigh moaned, her lips close to Kristen's ear.

It was almost too much. Even without being touched, she thought she would come again.

Ashleigh wrapped her arms around Kristen and writhed against her, biting back moans and breathing heavily. She began to move her hips against her, and Kristen did the same with her fingers until Ashleigh arched up, and she cried out, a gush of wetness covering Kristen's fingers.

Ashleigh dropped down on the bed, her breathing ragged. Kristen let her weight fall on top of Ashleigh's, and they lay there for a moment, panting, spent, until Ashleigh moved her lips to her ear, and softly said, "I love you."

Tears pricked behind Kristen's eyes. Wordlessly, she moved her lips to Ashleigh's and kissed her softly, then rolled off of her. Her head hit the pillow beside her.

Ashleigh turned, wrapped her body halfway over Kristen's and slid an arm across her torso. It rested just above her chest, over her heart. She nestled her crown of golden brown hair into the nook between Kristen's neck and shoulders, her hair tickling Kristen's bare chest and shoulders in a delightful way. Kristen, unable to stop herself, wrapped her arms around Ashleigh's warm, limber body.

"Kristen," Ashleigh whispered.

She cleared her throat, still unable to speak under the weight of her emotions. "Mmm-hmm."

"If I ask you something, do you promise to answer me honestly?"

"Okay," she said hesitantly, clearing her throat again at the hoarseness in her voice.

"Why do you hate yourself?"

It was the most poignant thing anyone had ever asked her. The words carved deep, cutting her to the quick.

She swallowed. "Because... I deserve it."

Ashleigh was quiet a moment before she spoke again. "If I tell you something, do you promise not to get mad?"

Kristen let a small grin touch her lips. "You're asking for a lot of promises."

Ashleigh moved her hand over Kristen's heart, gently patting her there. "Cyndi told me about your parents."

Kristen froze.

"Whatever happened," Ashleigh said cautiously, "it wasn't your fault."

Kristen swallowed. "You don't know that."

"You were just a kid."

"You don't understand." She turned away, but Ashleigh softly touched her face, turning it back toward her.

"Then help me understand. Tell me what happened."

Kristen considered telling her to leave. She even considered just getting up and walking out herself, but instead, she started telling her things she'd never told anybody. Things that nobody knew except Jared.

"I was in my room doing my science homework. I was learning about osmosis for a biology test. I thought I would never remember the definition—the diffusion of water through a semi-permeable membrane—it's funny how it's the little things that stick," she said, but she didn't smile. "They came in through the front door. I heard them first."

Why was she telling her this? She'd never told anyone the details of that night.

"It was late, and I knew everyone else would be asleep. Jared's room was closest to mine, so I crept in there first. I woke Jared and brought him out, but by the time we left his room and went for my parents, they were already upstairs." She swallowed. "I still wonder what would have happened if we'd just been faster, or if I'd gone to my parents' room first."

Ashleigh intertwined her fingers with Kristen's. The contact was so simple but so comforting at the same time. "You can't do that to yourself."

Couldn't she? Wasn't that exactly what she'd been doing to herself ever since that night? Trying to find a way she could have stopped it all from happening.

"It was a long time ago." Ashleigh's voice broke the silence of her thoughts. "You did everything you could. You need to forgive yourself."

Kristen took a deep breath. She'd never seen forgiving herself as an option. No one had ever given her permission to. Jared didn't hold it against her, but Jared didn't have the guilt she had. He hadn't carried it around with him for almost twenty years. She'd grown up loving her parents. When they died, her first instance of loving someone died with them. Ever since, she'd never wanted anyone else to get inside. She'd killed her parents just as sure as if she'd pulled the trigger herself.

She turned to Ashleigh. She knew. She had known since before they slept together, and she had stayed. She had wanted her anyway. How could someone as good as Ashleigh see those parts of her and not turn away?

"It's okay. I understand," Ashleigh said softly.

Kristen tried to speak without her voice breaking. "How can I explain this?" she started, then swallowed. "The things I touch, the people I get close to, they turn to shit. That's the weight that I carry around with me."

"It doesn't have to be that way," Ashleigh said. "I could help you carry it."

A tear squeezed out of the side of Kristen's eye and rolled slowly down her temple into her hair. "I wouldn't wish any of this upon you. I wouldn't want any of it to touch you." She looked down at their joined hands, as if she was sullying Ashleigh just by their contact. She tried to pull her hand away, but Ashleigh held it tight.

"No, Kristen." She put more pressure on the hand that was still over her heart. "You can't take everything on yourself. It's too much. You can talk to me. I'm not fragile. I won't break."

Another tear slid down the other side of her face. She tightened her jaw when it fell on Ashleigh's cheek. Ashleigh wiped it away, then kissed the trail of salt on Kristen's face. Kristen closed her eyes tight, and a few more tears squeezed out. Ashleigh was too good to be true. Too good for her.

"You need to leave," Kristen said.

"Why?"

"Because I won't ruin you with me."

"I don't want to leave."

Kristen sat up abruptly and ran her hands through her hair, severing their contact. Her nakedness embarrassed her in that moment, and she pulled the covers up over her chest. Ashleigh did the same on her side but made no move to leave.

"It all happened because I was stupid. I stole a car from the wrong person. The night it happened, they tied us up. They made us watch while they killed my parents. They blindfolded us and said they were coming back for Jared, then for me. I haven't been able to sleep through the night since. I haven't had any dream but that nightmare, living it over and over again, seeing what happens to anybody who gets close to me. If I could have dreamed about something else, I would have dreamed about you. When you're with me, it's like I hide in you for a while, but it's not real. The past is never far behind me. It always catches up with me, and I don't want it catching up to you too."

Ashleigh reached a hand forward and put it to Kristen's cheek. "I'm not afraid of your past."

Kristen turned away from her touch. Why couldn't she just let it go?

Ashleigh moved her hand around to the back of Kristen's neck. It cupped her there, which forced Kristen to meet her gaze. "Your past doesn't change how I feel about you. You have nothing you need to hide from me, nothing to be ashamed of. It wasn't your fault, and it doesn't make you damaged; it makes you strong."

She didn't deserve her comfort. She pulled away from her. "Don't touch me."

"I want to." Ashleigh reached her hand back out to her cheek. "I want to touch you." She leaned forward and brushed Kristen's lips with hers.

Kristen breathed hard, then opened her mouth and kissed her forcefully, her tongue seeking access in her mouth, stroking hers roughly.

Ashleigh pulled away from the kiss and searched Kristen's eyes for some indication of what she needed. The love in Ashleigh's eyes made Kristen's heart jump into her throat. She wanted to tell her how beautiful she was, how special. She wanted to tell her that she loved her back, but she couldn't. With a shaking hand, Kristen reached down and moved the sheet that separated her from Ashleigh.

Ashleigh swallowed and leaned back to let Kristen touch her. Kristen didn't take her time. Her fingers moved quickly and glided through her wetness. She was so soft. So smooth. "I want to know what you feel like inside," she breathed in her ear.

Wordlessly, Ashleigh reached down, took Kristen's hand, and guided her fingers to her opening. Kristen groaned, unable to resist, and used two fingers to enter Ashleigh. Her heart hammered as she slid into her wetness and buried her fingers deep inside her for the first time. Ashleigh gasped, but she held Kristen's hand where it was.

"Ashleigh." Kristen's need was raw in her throat, and Ashleigh raised her hips and moved her body against Kristen's fingers.

"You feel so good inside me," Ashleigh said, her voice throaty. "I want to be inside you too."

Kristen stilled. Letting someone inside her was not something she did. It had always felt too...intimate. Instead of saying no like she always did, she found herself nodding.

She closed her eyes when Ashleigh lowered her hand and reached down between them. Her fingers moved much more confidently than Kristen's had as she found her way to her opening. Ashleigh's fingers pushed between her legs, and Kristen lifted her hips to give her better access. Slowly, she slipped into her wetness, and Kristen bit her lip as Ashleigh found her most desperate ache.

Whatever Kristen imagined this would be like, it was a thousand times more intense. Every place inside her that Ashleigh touched awakened to new, amazing sensations. She was still inside Ashleigh, and she started to move again. Ashleigh tightened around her fingers as she pushed them slowly in and out.

She and Ashleigh moved together now. Their tongues slid against each other as their fingers and hips did the same. She fought to keep their lips connected, her body gliding across the sweat and wetness of Ashleigh's.

Ashleigh pushed herself hard against her and cried out as Kristen pushed her fingers up to the hilt. Ashleigh wrapped her free arm around Kristen's back and pulled her closer. She tried to catch her breath as Ashleigh continued to move inside her, stroking her deeply. It was too much.

Ashleigh moaned loudly, and Kristen almost released at the sound, but she wanted to ensure Ashleigh's pleasure before she gave in to her own. Ashleigh gritted her teeth, her insides tightening around Kristen's fingers, and when she came, writhing against her, Kristen allowed herself to release as well. A shuddering moan escaped Kristen's lips as she spread her warmth over her hand. Ashleigh moved to her mouth and swallowed her cry.

Kristen fell back, panting, the sheets soaked with their sweat and sex. "I've never felt anything like that before," she said, still trying to catch her breath. Ashleigh fell on top of her.

"You're beautiful," Ashleigh said, breathing hard against her chest. "I don't want to move my hand. I want to stay inside you forever. And I want you to stay inside me."

"I want that too," Kristen said breathlessly.

They laid there for a few moments, then Ashleigh laughed lightly. "Okay, I know I said I never wanted to move, but I have to use the washroom." She kissed her lips, and Kristen smiled.

Slowly, Kristen eased her fingers out of her, and Ashleigh did the same. It was the strangest feeling of loss. Ashleigh had taken her over completely. Kristen was hers in a way that she had never belonged to anyone, even herself.

She tried to understand what she had just done. For the first time, she had let someone inside every part of her—every part of her body and every part of her heart—and it felt wonderful.

"Now, I'm not leaving, so stop trying to kick me out." Ashleigh jumped back into bed. "I'm going to stay tonight, and you're going to hold me, and then in the morning, if you still want me to leave, I will." She turned away so that Kristen could spoon with her.

Kristen wanted to say something to her. She wanted her to know how much her understanding, how much *everything* meant to her, but she couldn't muster up the courage. She pulled the sheets over Ashleigh and kissed her back, feeling like, for the first time in almost twenty years, she might sleep through the night.

CHAPTER 19

ASHLEIGH FELT AROUND BESIDE HER in the bed, but before she even opened her eyes, she accepted that she was alone. The other side of the bed wasn't even warm. She quirked her head toward the door, but there were no sounds of Kristen in the condo.

She was disappointed, but she wouldn't give in to it. Kristen had a right to want to be on her own; she just wished that she didn't feel the need to be. Maybe she was just at the gym again.

Lackadaisically, she pulled the covers off herself and left the bed. Her clothing had been folded into a pile and left by the nightstand. She started to get dressed, and when she pulled her jeans up over her waist, she felt something in the front right pocket. It was a note. She took it out.

Good morning, beautiful.

I had to go to work, but there's coffee in the pot. Help yourself to anything you want for breakfast. I won't be home until late tonight, so please don't wait for me.

Kristen

Well, that was one way to get rid of her.

She finished dressing and left the bedroom. The place felt so empty without Bailey in it. How was it that she'd lived here for months and had no personal possessions beyond books and dishware? Kristen appeared to have even fewer belongings than she did. Which reminded her, she really should spend the day finishing up at home and getting ready to move out on the weekend. It was time for a change. Time to leave her parents' house and start a life of her own, but she didn't want to be on her own. She wanted Kristen.

Would Kristen come to see her new place? After last night, would she ever see Kristen again? It must have been so hard for Kristen to tell her what she had. She'd kept all of it inside of her so long that it had started to eat away at her until she felt like she didn't deserve anything better.

It made sense now, the way Kristen was with women. It wasn't that she was callous or cruel; she'd just never thought she merited more. Kristen thought she deserved to be unloved and alone. She didn't want anyone to care for her, afraid that they might see inside her to the shame she carried. She'd spent years staying hidden, not wanting the world to see her, but Ashleigh saw her, and she wasn't afraid.

She would go home and give Kristen her space, but she would keep coming back until Kristen realized that it wasn't loneliness she deserved but love.

"I know, first day back on rotation is always a tough one," Staff Sergeant King addressed the room of officers. "And it's a hot one, so you know what that means. Evans?" He singled out a second-year cop who was dutifully taking down her parade notes. For some reason, he always seemed to pick on Evans.

"Quick tempers, sir," Evans said.

King nodded. "That's right. Now, to keep things fresh, today's changeup day. You're all getting new partners."

Kristen turned around in her seat and darted her gaze to the back of the room. Ortiz leaned against the wall with the rest of the detectives, blocking the row of wanted posters that lined the parade room. There were so many faces, so many unsolved crimes that the pictures didn't even register anymore. Ortiz shrugged. Next, she looked to her TO. Henry was shaking his head almost imperceptibly. Was King onto them?

"That's it for today. Check the board for your new partners. Serve, protect, and don't embarrass me."

Kristen was quick to approach the board. Did this mean she was off probation? It seemed pretty coincidental that just when she and Ortiz started asking questions, she should lose the protection of her TO.

She was paired with Evans. That gave her pause. Evans was known as a bit of a screw-up.

"Hey." Evans approached her. "Looks like we're partners."

Evans was a few inches shorter than Kristen, and her blonde hair was cut to her chin, short enough that she wasn't forced to pull it back. She was pretty in that unassuming way that didn't turn heads, but the people she knew well probably thought she was beautiful.

"Looks like it." Kristen offered her an effortless smile. "Why don't you grab the keys, and I'll meet you in the cruiser? I forgot something in my locker. I'll be right out."

"Okay." Evans nodded, apparently eager to be given a task.

Inside the locker room, Kristen looked around before she turned her lock and opened the small door to her unit. She reached inside and pulled her RCMP service pistol from under a pile of clothes. After a second check to make sure again that no one was looking, she clipped it on the inside of her left ankle, closed her locker door, and left hurriedly.

Outside, Evans waited by patrol car 5232. "Ready?" she asked when Kristen approached.

"Ready." She slid into the passenger seat.

"This will be fun." Evans started the car. "We can girl talk."

"Girl talk?"

"Yeah." She pulled out of the station parking lot. "Talk about guys and stuff."

Kristen sighed. "I'm gay and in love with a paramedic who after this weekend, I'll never see again. Are we done?"

Evans kept her eyes on the road. "That wasn't fun."

They drove in silence for a while until Kristen noticed that Evans wasn't taking the normal patrol route that she and Henry usually took on assignment. She looked behind her at the turn they missed. Maybe Evans just drove a different route. She opened the mobile data terminal on the cruiser's dashboard and pulled up the area crime map. There was nothing glaring that Evans could be heading toward.

A few streets later, she took a turn down Dundas. In another minute, they would be outside their patrol territory.

"Where are you going?" Kristen asked. "The MDT shows us off the map. Patrol's back that way."

"I just have to drop something off. Don't worry; you can stay in the car. It'll only take a minute."

Kristen's heart sped up. "What are you dropping off?" she asked, trying to keep her voice level.

"Just a small package. Won't take two shakes. We're almost there."

Yeah, if *there* was *Lǎohǔ* gangbanger territory.

"Who are you giving the package to?"

"That's not really your business," Evans said guardedly.

"Who gave you the package?"

"It's work related, so don't bother writing me up in your book." She tilted her head toward the memo book next to Kristen on the seat, the one they all carried.

"Is the package from your TO?" Kristen asked.

Evans looked surprised. "I didn't know you were friends with Terry."

Nothing about that morning had been a coincidence. "I'm not, and we're not delivering that package."

"What? Of course we are. It's just up here."

Fuck, why hadn't she driven? There was nothing she could do to prevent Evans from pulling over.

"We can't stop here, okay? We have to keep moving."

Evans ignored her and pulled the car over. "Just wait here a—"

They both turned at the sound of gunfire. Evans reached for the radio and unhooked it. "This is car fifty-two-thirty-two. We've heard gunshots. Requesting backup to our location."

"I read your location, fifty-two-thirty-two, but there are no cars in your area for about fifteen kilometres. You'll need to stay put for about that many minutes."

God, no, this wasn't happening.

"Shots are being fired now, dispatch," Evans said into the radio. "We're going in. Send all available units when you can."

Evans unholstered her gun and got out of the car.

Kristen didn't move.

For once, she didn't want to rush into danger. Not now that she had found Ashleigh.

Inside, there would be a gang shootout. They would get caught in the crossfire, then a team of imitation paramedics would show up. If they weren't dead already, they would finish them off, and she would never see Ashleigh again.

Evans was running into the alleyway, her gun held two feet in front of her like an idiot.

"Fuck," Kristen swore under her breath. She couldn't just let Evans die.

Kristen pulled her gun as she got out of the car and raced to catch up to Evans, who had slipped down the alley and was making her way into an abandoned building.

"Evans," she whispered harshly. Evans kept moving. "Evans!" she said again, a little louder this time, but her partner was high on adrenaline and kept heading toward the gunfire. She tried to catch her, tried to stop her before they got involved, but it was too late.

Evans was inside, and the distinct report of her police-issued Glock sounded. There were more gunshots. Kristen looked in. Evans was on the ground, holding a hand to her shoulder. Red was squeezing through her fingers.

Kristen grabbed for the radio Velcroed to her bulletproof vest. "This is Constable Bailey. I have an officer down. We need an ambulance. Constable Evans has been shot," she whispered harshly into it. As she was releasing the button on the side of the radio, a bullet whizzed by her head, barely missing her left ear. She ducked down and surveyed the room. From the angle the bullets were firing at, there were at least six or seven shooters inside.

She had fifteen rounds in her Glock, two spare magazines on her belt, and ten bullets in the RCMP service pistol clipped to her left ankle. Fifty-five bullets. The trouble was, she could only fire one at a time.

This wasn't her first shootout. The primary thing she needed to do was remain calm and get them out of the line of fire. Evans was putting pressure on her gunshot wound, and for now, there wasn't anything more she could do for her. Kristen tried to steady her breathing. In a situation like this, she didn't have time to figure out if there were any innocent parties in the building other than her and her partner. She needed to diffuse the situation before anything else. The shooters had all momentarily taken cover, which meant she had to shoot at the first movement she saw, but before that, she had to take cover as well.

While everyone stayed hidden, likely reloading their weapons, Kristen pulled Evans behind the doorway and crouched behind it with her. As far as she could tell, she was out of anybody's direct line of sight, which meant they couldn't shoot her either. She peeked her head back in, just enough to get a feel for her surroundings.

The building was old and dilapidated like the ones that Ricky Oslowe and Jenna Bradley had been found in. There were two storeys, and she and Evans had entered through the back entrance. There was a door across the way, maybe fifty feet in front of her. A staircase to the left. Old shipping containers to her right. Upstairs, there was an office with glass windows, overlooking the first floor. It had all the makings of an old sweatshop.

At a glimpse of movement by the stairs, Kristen fired twice. The first one missed, but the second elicited a cry of pain.

Fifty-three bullets left.

There was movement to her right, by the shipping containers. Before she could fire, five shots went off from the second storey, and a man fell forward from behind the shipping containers onto the warehouse floor. He didn't move. Kristen counted herself lucky the drug deal had already gone awry before they'd shown up, and the rival gangs in the exchange had already turned on each other. With the two sides distracted, Kristen took the opportunity to fire at the man who'd shot the other guy. Three bullets. Two missed, and one hit her target in the neck. The man fell from the railing of the second floor and landed with a sickening crunch on the concrete that met him at the bottom.

Two dead, one injured. Fifty bullets left.

Kristen ducked her head and moved swiftly behind the doorframe at the crack of a shotgun. The doorframe splintered, and a piece of shrapnel landed in the soft flesh at the back of her left arm. It was not a bad hit, but the loss of their cover was devastating.

She no longer had time to take it slow, to try to coax them out one by one. She moved Evans further from the door and unclipped her second gun. Kristen held both guns down a moment and took a deep breath. She let it in and out slowly, turned onto her left knee, and launched herself inside the building.

Her loss of cover brought everyone else out, enticed by the wide open target. She could only hope her fingers were faster than theirs. She started where she had discerned the largest concentration of shooters to be, in the upstairs office.

The glass shattered as she fired nine bullets—five from her Glock and four from her pistol—up to the second level. She didn't have time to survey the damage, but as she turned back to the shipping containers, she saw two men fall out of the office. She kept firing and ran to a small door on the other side of the room, praying it was unlocked. Several more bullets flew from her guns, and some were fired in her direction as she ran. Two bullets clanked metallically, and some found their targets. Two more lifeless bodies hit the ground.

She'd emptied the magazines in both her Glock and her pistol.

She leaned heavily against the wall and reloaded her Glock, but she didn't have a spare magazine for her pistol. Her training took over, and she hid the service pistol back in the clip by her left ankle. She had thought there were only seven shooters, but someone was running on the level above her. She hadn't seen the shotgun fall. That must be him. If she could create a distance between them, she could gain the upper hand. Hers was the better weapon, but he was right on top of her.

She stayed quiet, not daring to open the door she had reached and alert him of her exact location. The footsteps above her moved to the left, then the right. He didn't know where she was. She looked up. The floors were steel. If she shot upward, the bullets were just as likely to ricochet back and hit her. She needed a clean shot.

Her chest was heaving, and she tried to quiet her breathing. The only advantage she had in that moment was that he had lost sight of her, but she had a fair idea of where he was.

"Dennis?" the man called from the top of the stairs.

Kristen readied her gun.

"Paul?" he called. His men didn't answer. He cocked his shotgun, and a spent shell fell out, clanging loudly on the second level's metallic floor.

Kristen swallowed. The weight of the gun was heavy after firing so many bullets, and she used her left hand to steady her shot. She trained the Glock on the stairs.

"Elli?" the man asked.

He took his first step down the stairs and paused. Kristen ignored the drop of sweat that leaked down from her forehead, stinging into her right eye.

He took another step.

Her heart pounded in her chest.

He took one more step.

The backs of his legs were exposed through the open slats between the metal stairs. Kristen fired. The first bullet hit him in the back of his left thigh. It took a chunk of flesh with it. The second hit his kneecap as he turned.

The force of the bullets pushed him off balance, and he fell down the stairs, a cacophony of bangs, clanks, and grunts.

At the bottom of the stairs, Kristen approached him warily. Somehow, he had retained his hold on his shotgun. She had thirteen bullets left in her Glock. The man grunted, a grimace of pain on his face, and raised his shotgun.

Kristen fired twice.

The first bullet landed in his left eye, the second cracked his eyebrow open. It was impossible to tell which one ended his life.

Kristen fell on her knees next to the man, trying to catch her breath. She cocked her ears, but there was no more movement.

Getting up off her knees, she returned to Evans. She was still bleeding, but she was conscious.

"We have to go," she said, positioning herself underneath Evans and pulling her up by her good arm. She would have loved to have waited for the cleanup crew to arrive, but she didn't think she had another shootout in her, and it was better that they get to safety. Evans didn't argue.

"I'm sorry," she said, as they left the alleyway.

They hobbled a few feet, and their cruiser came into view.

"Don't be sorry," Kristen said and moved along the sidewalk with her, carrying most of her weight.

A cruiser came into sight. There was an ambulance right behind them. Kristen exhaled loudly with relief. A car just down the street took off, its tires squealing.

The cleanup crew.

"The ambulance is going to take you to the hospital now, Evans. You're going to be okay." She stopped their movement but still held her up. "They're going to be here any second. Before they get here, I need to know who asked you to deliver that package?"

Evans winced in pain, and Kristen could tell that talking was difficult. She sucked in a painful gasp of air. "Smith." She grabbed her shoulder as the pain seemed to worsen. "Luke Smith."

Smith was in on it? She'd never received a beatdown like the one he'd given her on FiteNite. *Good.* The news made her smile. She may not have been able to beat him in the ring, but it would feel satisfying to put cuffs on his massive wrists and see his face when she ducked his head into the back door of an RCMP cruiser.

CHAPTER 20

THE PARAMEDICS SWARMED KRISTEN AND Constable Evans. It was obvious that Evans was in more pain and a more dire situation, but they wouldn't let Kristen wave them away either.

"You have fragments from a shotgun bullet lodged in your arm. Do you have any idea the kind of infection you could get from this, not to mention what might happen if we can't clean it all out?" The attending paramedic who argued with her was young, probably around Ashleigh's age, and he was serious about his patient.

"So, clean it out and stick a Band-Aid on it."

"Heh." He laughed humourlessly. "I could lose my job for doing something so careless. Now hold still, and let me do what I can before we take you to the hospital."

"No." She shook her head. "No hospital."

She didn't have time for this. King was the puppet master behind her and Evans' placement at the shootout that day; she was sure of it. She needed to get away from the commotion of the scene and call Ouellette before King got word that his plan had gone awry.

"I promise not to report you or anything if something goes wrong," she said as calmly as she could. "I don't need to go to the hospital. I'm fine, okay?"

The man shrugged. "You think I want to take you to the hospital for kicks? It's protocol, and besides, what else are you going to do while you fill out the mountain of paperwork that's waiting for you?" He stared at something behind her, and Kristen turned in time to see the Toronto police duty inspector approach the ambulance. "Looks like your day is about to get worse."

"Bailey?" the duty inspector asked. She had short blonde hair, dusted with grey, and a no-nonsense tone.

Kristen sighed resignedly. "Yes, ma'am," she said.

"I'm going to need you to go to the hospital, and as soon as practicable, I'm going to ask you for your completed memo book. You need to write in exactly what happened before you hand that over, do you understand?" the duty inspector asked.

Kristen nodded.

The inspector turned to two officers who had trailed closely behind her. "Take her gun and belt," she ordered them. To Kristen, she said, "This is all protocol, I assure you."

A replacement belt with a new gun was handed to her, and she dutifully put it on.

"You're not in any kind of trouble," the duty inspector assured her, "but we are about to have Homicide Squad and FIS in here. A call has been placed to the staff sergeant in charge, and the media is already on its way. Our media officers will handle any and all questions; is that clear?"

Again, Kristen nodded. There was nothing else she could do. The situation had been taken completely out of her hands by the duty inspector. Homicide Squad and Forensic Identification Services would take over the investigation from here, along with assigned detectives and even the superintendent. If they'd already placed a call to Staff Sergeant King, she'd lost the upper hand there as well and would be unable to surprise him with the news that his plan to kill her and Evans had failed. She needed to talk to Ouellette. Now.

"I want to call my lawyer," Kristen lied, knowing she had a right to speak with one in a situation like this, where any notes or statements she made could possibly incriminate her.

The duty inspector sighed. "New procedure is that the subject officer—you—can no longer wait to consult a lawyer prior to handing in your notes."

Kristen clenched her jaw in frustration. This couldn't be happening. She was not going to have her entire case fall to pieces because Constable Evans had been too headstrong to listen to her and had gotten them both shot. *I've been shot.* She smiled. That was it. Because she'd been injured, the police couldn't force her to go back to the station with them until she'd received official medical clearance from the hospital. She'd have to find an opportunity at the hospital to call Ouellette while she waited to be cleared. She needed to speak with him before handing in her notes and being interviewed by SIU. Sure, the Special Investigations Unit might have been in on this whole plot with the RCMP to immerse her there undercover, but it would be hours before they were cleared to speak with her. She needed to update Ouellette on her situation now, or she'd be forced to blow her cover before she had all the pieces together, effectively destroying her case and the remaining sliver of a chance for the Banff promotion.

"I understand," Kristen told the duty inspector.

"You are not to speak with any other officers until you've been cleared and have spoken with SIU," she said, then turned to the paramedic. "You can take her now."

The man nodded and waited for the duty inspector to leave before he motioned for Kristen to step up into the truck. "Told you your day was about to get worse," he said and slammed the large double doors of the truck, sealing her in the back.

———————

There was no such thing as triage at a hospital when a police officer came in with a gunshot wound. She was forced to lie on the stretcher and feel like an idiot, even though she wasn't injured badly, as they wheeled her directly through the emergency room and into the OR. Finally, someone listened to her that day, and the operating surgeon agreed to use a local anesthetic on her arm instead of putting her under general anesthesia while he pulled the shotgun fragments out of her arm, disinfected it, and stitched her up.

"How are you feeling?" he asked as he snipped the last pieces of stitching from her arm.

"Good as new," she said.

"I'm glad to hear it. Before we can clear you, we need to take a quick X-ray to make sure we didn't miss anything."

She stood up, and a nurse came to lead her to a waiting room attached to the operating room. "An orderly will be by soon to bring you up to

X-ray," the nurse said, rather devoid of emotion, and left Kristen in the waiting room alone.

There was a phone in the corner of the room. Finally, some luck.

Her cell phone had been taken from her before her surgery by a uniformed officer, who assured her it would be returned once her memo book had been handed in and she'd been interviewed by SIU. Apparently, she hadn't been the first person to think of sneaking a call to someone while in the hospital.

She lifted the receiver and dialed Ouellette's cell number from memory.

"Ouellette," he answered.

"Ouellette, it's Kristen. I need help."

"What happened?"

"King knows someone's getting close to him. He pulled me from my TO this morning and sent me and another cop into a shootout. We weren't meant to make it out alive."

"The one on the news right now?"

Kristen cringed. "I'm guessing there weren't two shootouts involving cops today in Toronto."

"Are you hurt?"

She put a hand to the gauze and medical tape on her shoulder. It smarted a little to the touch but was manageable. "Not really, but enough for the cops to send me to the hospital. I have to fill out paperwork now, log the incident in my memo book, complete forms, and go through an interview with SIU. I can't get out of here, but we need to stop King. I don't know how much he knows, and we can't afford to let him run."

"You know there's a cover team there waiting for word from me to move in. The question is, do we have enough to arrest him? I don't want to blow the operation," Ouellette said.

"I know." Kristen rubbed the back of her neck in frustration. "Okay, they took my cell phone, so I lost the video. I need you to play it for me. I think I might be able to ID the voices now."

"Hang on." There was some background noise before Ouellette's voice came booming back onto the line so loudly she had to hold the phone away. "Here it is." His voice was quickly replaced by the sounds of the video.

"Just a sec, babe, the paramedics are here," Ricky Oslowe whispered. "You guys finally made it. I took a good shot to the stomach, but I don't think it's done any major damage."

"Let's have a look," a man said.

"Okay, but I think we should wait f—"

His answer was replaced by the sounds of a struggle.

"Is it done?" a man asked. It was Luke Smith's voice.

"It's done," the other man replied. His voice was familiar as well.

"Anything?" Ouellette came back on the line.

"The first man to speak was Luke Smith. Play that last part back again."

He did so.

"Is it done?"

"It's done."

"Anything this time?" Ouellette asked again.

"I'm not sure," she said, frustrated that she couldn't recognize the second man's voice. They could bring in Luke Smith, though. She was disappointed that she couldn't make his arrest herself, but it would be her work that took him down. That was still a thing of beauty.

"What about King?" Ouellette asked. "Could the second voice be his?"

"I don't think so. He's more likely just calling the shots without getting his hands dirty. I think we should bring him in and talk to him, though. We have enough for that. I can't interrogate him without exposing myself, but I would like to be a part of it."

There was a brief pause on the line before Ouellette responded. "I'll notify the cover team about Smith and King. We're going to have to contact ERT to bring them both in, but I'll ask them to wait on interviewing King for as long as they can."

"Do we really need to involve the emergency response team? If we're wrong, that'll put everyone on high alert."

"Don't worry about that right now, Bailey. We're going to call SIU and make sure the right guys come in to interview you so that you can be released. Once you're cleared, we can mic you up to someone from the cover team when they talk to King, but we need ERT to do the takedown. We can't risk anyone getting hurt, even if it means jeopardizing the op."

"I understand," she said, and she did. No operation was worth intentionally putting the lives of police officers in harm's way. "Can you reach SIU quickly? I still have my service pistol tucked in my ankle holster, and I'm about to be taken in for X-rays. I can't leave it with the uniforms assigned to me."

"Done," Ouellette said. "They're on their way. The cover team will message you with their location. You can head over when you get your phone and weapons back."

Kristen let out a sigh of relief. "I'll call again once I'm on my way to see King."

***

Kristen pulled up to the "O" Division office of the RCMP two hours later. SIU had her jot down her statement and then instructed her to return to her precinct and drop off her loaner belt and gun, where she had picked up her car. It wasn't to make it look as if she was suspended, but normal protocol would have her at least finishing off the rest of the day at a desk filling out paperwork and not back on the road. That meant she was in plain clothes when she arrived at 130 Dufferin Street.

She parked her car between several marked vehicles and noted there were a few unmarked cars in the parking lot as well. She reloaded her RCMP service pistol with the spare magazine she kept clipped underneath the passenger seat in her Mustang and tucked the gun back into her holster. Ten bullets was a far cry from the fifty-five she'd started off with earlier that day.

She left her car and went up to the fifth-floor-reception desk where she showed her badge, her *real* badge.

"They're in room five-nineteen, Staff Sergeant," the civilian receptionist said and pointed down a hallway to her left.

Kristen had never been in one of the interrogation rooms at the Toronto "O" Division before. When she reached the door, she knocked. A man who appeared to be a few years her senior opened the door and nodded for her to enter.

"Welcome to the party," the man said. "The name's Walker." He held his hand out.

Kristen shook it. "Bailey," she said. "Is he in there?" Kristen entered the room and looked across the two-way mirror.

"Wouldn't be much point in doing this if he wasn't, would there?" Walker answered. He handed her a headset with a mic. "Speak into this, and Sparks in there will ask your questions for you," he said.

A Mountie inside the room leaned over a table where Staff Sergeant King was sitting.

"Does he know why he's here?" she asked Walker. "What charges did we bring him in on?"

"We arrested Gregory King for the murder of constables Richard Oslowe and Jenna Bradley, the attempted murder of constables Kara Evans and Kristen Bailey, and the attempted murder of a Royal Canadian Mounted Police staff sergeant. He doesn't know that's you yet."

She nodded and switched the mic on.

"Ask him what precipitated the changeup today," Kristen said into the mic. Inside the room, Sparks made as if he was scratching his ear as he adjusted the speaker there.

"So why the changes in parade today? You moved around everybody's partners. One of those changes affected constables Evans and Bailey, who ended up partnered together."

"Tell him you know Evans was asked to make a delivery by Luke Smith, which sent us into the drug shootout," Kristen said.

"We know you orchestrated this whole event so that Evans and Bailey would die in a gang shootout," Sparks continued. He was a big man who had at least six inches on King, and King looked intimidated, although if it was due to Sparks or his presence in the RCMP interrogation room, Kristen couldn't be sure.

"You seem to know a lot," King said incredulously. "What I'd like to know is why the RCMP is in my backyard without my knowledge?"

"You mean when you should be calling the shots, and Evans and Bailey should be dead?"

"No," King answered. "I mean instead of arresting me, I could have helped you guys. I know why you're here, and I've been trying to stop it alone ever since Jenna Bradley went missing."

The man in the interrogation room looked behind him to the mirror, and it took a moment for Kristen to realize he was waiting for her to give him direction.

"Tell him we know he's been setting up rookie cops to move drug evidence. That he's been in charge of a corrupt ring of officers who are stealing from lock-up and killing rookies when they start to ask too many questions."

Sparks repeated Kristen's accusation to King.

"You don't understand," King said desperately. He tried to raise his arms in a plea, but the cuffs with the long chains held him to the metal table. "Just listen to me," King said. "If you're RCMP, then together we can stop this."

"I'm pretty sure we just did," Kristen said, forgetting she was speaking into the mic.

"You sent rookies out to die." Sparks took over. "You had them running drugs for you and your guys, all so that you could have a more comfortable retirement."

"No, I was under duress."

"Duress isn't a defence for murder in this country," Sparks said. "You may not have pulled the trigger, but you're just as guilty."

"Yes, okay, yes, I was involved, but it wasn't my idea, they weren't *my* guys." King licked his lips. "I started off just like you guys, looking into things. I'd been made aware of some evidence having gone missing. I started to suspect something wasn't right, but before I could do anything about it, Jenna Bradley went missing. I thought it had all died down, and yes, I was happy to bury it, until Richard Oslowe was murdered. I followed the same trail you guys probably did and found out the TOs were sending their rookies out on drug runs. When the rookies wised up, they put them in the line of fire."

"Regurgitating evidence we've already gathered isn't going to help you out of those handcuffs."

"Wait, wait." He shifted in his seat. "I was ready to turn them all in, but then they threatened my son."

Sparks paused and looked back to Kristen again. King's son was a rookie just last year. "Keep him talking," Kristen said, "but keep his leash short."

Sparks turned back to King. "You have one minute. Let's hear it," he said, feigning boredom.

"They told me that if I said anything, if I breathed a word of their operation, they'd send Charlie to the next shootout. Any time. Anywhere. That's what they said."

"Why didn't you just yank your son out of the station and call it in anyway?" Sparks asked.

"I would have, but they showed me pictures. They'd had their failsafe planned all along. Charlie had run drugs for them. And not only that, he'd encouraged Jenna Bradley to join in. If I took them down, he'd go down with them."

"So, your son Charles would get a few years in Kingston, nothing worth letting people lose their lives over."

"Do you know what happens to cops in Kingston?" he said, his voice shaky. "A few years in jail... It might as well be a death sentence."

"So you let other cops die instead?"

"I didn't have a choice. No matter what I did, someone was going to die. At least this way, there was a chance of my son making it out. Those guys are all set to retire in a few years. I thought if I just waited..."

"Ask him about Luke Smith," Kristen cut in. "He's young, in his late thirties."

"What about Luke Smith? He can't be more than in his thirties," Sparks said without missing a beat.

"I...I didn't expect that." King looked down into his cuffed hands. "It was just the older cops at first, then they started pulling in these younger guys, and..." He looked up at Sparks. "Look, I know I fucked up, but *you* can actually stop them. Arresting me isn't going to change anything. The real officers behind this are still out there."

Kristen turned her mic off and turned to Walker. "Where's Luke Smith?"

Walker shook his head. "We couldn't find him. He's not on duty, and he wasn't at his house. His car's gone, and he lives alone."

Kristen turned the mic on. "Keep him talking," she directed Sparks.

"What are you talking about?" Sparks asked King in turn.

"There's a file. It's in my office at the station. I was hoping if something happened to me or Charles, someone would find it. It's locked in my bottom drawer, inside a safety lockbox. I can give you the key and the combination."

"You just left a file incriminating a group of dirty cops in a lockbox in your desk?" Sparks asked distrustfully.

"It's encrypted. Even if they found it, they wouldn't be able to open it. With your resources though, you could use it to take them down."

"Why would you leave that kind of evidence at the station and not on you or at home, where you could keep an eye on it?"

"I was worried if everything went south that they might storm my house, burn it down for all I know. Make it look like an accident. They wouldn't be able to get away with that at a police station. It's safer there."

"This file, what are we talking about?" Sparks asked.

"It's a USB containing dozens of files. If you can decode it, you can take them all down."

"Why don't you decode it for us if it's your encryption?"

"Heh, you're giving me too much credit. I had a contact of mine, not the most savoury individual, encrypt it for me. I paid him not to look and to keep his mouth shut."

"Great. Now pay him to decrypt it."

"I would, but one of his seedy deals went awry. He died a few months ago."

Sparks looked back at the mirror, but he didn't wait for an answer before continuing, "Hold tight," he said to King and then left the room. A moment later, he opened the door where Kristen and Walker were waiting on the other side of the mirror.

"I assume you're the voice in my ear," Sparks said with a smile and extended his hand to Kristen, easily switching from interrogator to colleague.

"Staff Sergeant Bailey," she said and accepted his firm handshake.

Sparks looked between Kristen and Walker. "I'm not a hacker," he said, "so I don't know how long something like this is going to take to decode. I do know that we only have a small window though until someone realizes their staff sergeant is missing."

"We don't have that kind of team set up here," Walker said.

"How long until we can?" Kristen asked.

"A day to get someone here or to get the files to them, if they even exist. Either way, we're looking at a day and a half, maybe two days before we can get it in the right hands and crack it," Walker explained.

Sparks shook his head. "That's too long."

Kristen stopped to think for a moment. Regardless of how long it took to crack the files, she only had one day left in her hourglass, according to Ouellette, and the sand was slipping quickly. An idea came to her.

"There's a hacker in my building. She might be able to do it in a day."

"With all due respect, Staff Sergeant, that's not entirely protocol," Sparks said.

"I know, but it's not like this kind of thing hasn't been done before. We can get her to sign a confidentiality agreement and add her in as an expert resource. We can do it all above the table, pay her, make it legit. If there's a chance she can do it in less than a day, I think we have to take it."

Walker looked to Sparks who nodded, satisfied.

"Okay," Walker said, "but we do this like you said, on the up and up. I'll call it in and get started on the paperwork. I'm going to need a full legal name and address for this contact," he said to Kristen.

"Her address I can give you, but for a name, I only have her given name, or the one she gave me anyway," Kristen said.

Walker narrowed his eyes. "How do you know this woman's address but not her...ohhh." He stopped there, a faint pink colouring his cheeks.

Sparks laughed good-naturedly at Walker's discomfort.

"Just find out where the keys to this lockbox are, and I'll get you the rest of her information later," Kristen said.

It must have been enough for Sparks, because he nodded one more time and left the room, only to rejoin King a moment later.

"The key to this lockbox, where is it?" Sparks asked, his tone once again all business.

"My right pocket," King said, motioning his hip out to Sparks. "The key to the drawer is in there. The code to the safety box is one-nine-one-nine."

Sparks reached forward carefully, likely stepping around his legs to avoid a surprise kick in the gut. He pulled the keys from his pocket and waved them at the mirror before putting them in his own pocket.

"If this evidence doesn't check out, I'm pulling you back in here, and you're not going to like the charges I've added to your list of offences, including hindering an RCMP investigation, you understand?"

"I understand," King said, "and thank you. You just saved my son's life."

CHAPTER 21

GETTING THE USB WASN'T DIFFICULT. It was exactly where King said it would be, and Kristen had no trouble with the lock or combination. The problematic part was going to be getting it decrypted. She'd immediately tried to download it to her phone, but King was telling the truth; the files were well encrypted.

The last thing she wanted was the exact thing she was about to do, but she saw no way around it. She had been sent on this assignment alone and had made few contacts outside of the police station and her one-night stands.

Just before Kristen stepped on the elevator at her condo, her phone buzzed. She took it out of her pocket. It was a text from Ashleigh. If she didn't actually open the text message app, Ashleigh wouldn't be able to tell that the text was read. She left the message unread, put the phone back in her pocket, and stepped onto the elevator.

Instead of the eleventh floor, she pushed number seven. When she reached the seventh floor, she took a deep breath, got out, and walked toward unit 712. She knocked on the door.

A beautiful, busty blonde opened it up. "Kristen," she said with a smile. "I was starting to think I'd never see you at my door again."

"Hi, Amelia. Are you alone?"

"Ooh, getting right to it. I like that, and I am," she said, standing aside for Kristen to enter.

"Actually, I need you to come up to my place. This isn't a social call. I have a job for you, and we'll pay whatever your rate is."

Amelia drew her eyebrows together. "*We*?"

"I need you to decrypt a file." She held up the USB.

"Oh, um, okay." She swallowed.

Kristen couldn't tell if she was embarrassed or just surprised.

"You should come in then. I'll need my hardware and software."

Kristen shook her head. "I need you to use my computer." She held out her badge and showed it to her. "I'm with the RCMP, and the file could be crucial evidence in a case I'm working. I need it decrypted now, and I need it to be done on a secure computer."

Amelia laughed. "Staff Sergeant Bailey with the RCMP, eh?" She took the badge between her fingers as she read it, letting them brush against Kristen's. "Well, Staff Sergeant," she said flirtatiously. "I can guarantee you that whatever grade your government tech is, mine is the same or better."

At the playful repetition of her rank, Kristen's heart ached for the way Ashleigh had called her *officer* in bed. She swallowed, pushing the thought away.

"That may be, but I need it done on mine, and I need it done now. Will you come with me, please?"

"You only had to say please." She winked at her. "Let me at least grab some equipment."

Kristen nodded, waiting dutifully in the hall as Amelia packed a few items into a laptop bag along with a bottle of wine.

"Fuel," Amelia said with a smile. Kristen didn't argue. She didn't care if Amelia drank the whole bottle, so long as she did it after she decrypted the files.

In the elevator, Kristen made sure to stay at the other side of the car, her back pressed up against the mirror.

Amelia regarded her with a curious smile. "I don't bite, you know."

"It's not that." Kristen crossed her arms in front of her, trying to appear more casual. "It's just that I'm seeing someone."

"Oh?" Amelia cocked an eyebrow.

Thankfully, the elevator dinged at the eleventh floor, and they got off.

Kristen opened her unit door and locked it quickly behind them, putting on the deadbolt, the chain, and the two extra locks she'd installed after moving in.

"My laptop's on the coffee table." She pointed to it. "What else do you need from me?"

"The USB." Amelia took a seat on the couch and opened her laptop bag.

"Right." Kristen took it out of her pocket and placed it on the coffee table next to the computer, being sure not to make contact with Amelia.

"So you're seeing someone?" she said, picking up on Kristen's distance.

"Can you just work on the file, please?"

"I can multitask. Tell me about her." Amelia was as good as her word, setting up systems as she questioned Kristen.

Kristen sighed. "Her name is Ashleigh. I met her at work."

"She's an RCMP officer too? That's hot."

"No, she's a paramedic."

Amelia grinned. "Also hot." She connected one of her modem-looking things into Kristen's laptop and then the USB into the modem. "I didn't take you for the relationship type."

"I'm not," Kristen said automatically, then amended her response. "I wasn't."

"She must be special, then," Amelia said.

Kristen was relieved there was no jealousy or malice in her voice. It occurred to her for the first time that Amelia was something like her, or like the old her, before Ashleigh.

The old me? Was she that far removed from who she had been just a few short months ago?

"First girlfriend?" Amelia asked perceptively.

"Yeah, if you don't count the one I had for a month when I was seventeen."

"I don't." Amelia pushed some keys on the laptop, and the computer's fan came to life loudly. The hard drive was definitely working away on something. "So, why her? Why now?"

"It just kind of happened."

"That sounds like a cop out. No pun intended." She grinned.

Kristen smiled as well. "Okay."

She took a seat at the other end of the couch, where she could see the screen that Amelia was working on. It was all code and reminded her of working with DOS when she'd first started at the Depot. It wasn't that she didn't trust Amelia was doing the work without her supervision, but, well, she didn't trust Amelia was doing the work without her supervision.

"It was like I didn't really have a choice," Kristen said, answering Amelia's question about Ashleigh.

"That's not much better than the first thing you said." Amelia's focus was on her computer. "I don't know why you're watching me; if you knew what any of this shit on the screen was, you wouldn't have asked for my help."

Kristen grinned at her astuteness and confidence. Her phone buzzed. It was Ashleigh again. She ignored it.

"Is that her?" Amelia asked, and Kristen didn't like the knowing look in her eye.

"Yes, but it's not like that."

"What's it like then?" Amelia pulled another piece of machinery out of her bag.

Kristen was quiet a moment. "If those files are what I think they are, then I'm turning that USB over to my boss tonight, and when I do that, my case here is finished."

"You're leaving," Amelia said, her focus still on the screen, "and she doesn't know."

"No. I mean yes, I am leaving, and no, she doesn't know."

Amelia whistled. "Doesn't sound like that's going to end well. Technically, after tonight, you won't really be seeing someone then, will you?"

Kristen thought about it. Now that this was all happening, now that she was really this close to solving the case, could she just pack up and leave? It had never been hard for her to do before, but there had never been anyone she was leaving behind. Ashleigh wasn't just some girl. Even though it seemed fast, she loved her, and Ashleigh loved her back. There was no point in pretending that it was anything else, that she wasn't yet sure of her feelings just because they'd come on so quickly.

"Look, I'm not trying to be unsympathetic," Amelia said. She had stopped looking at the screen and was looking at her. "It just doesn't really sound like you know what you're doing, or that she knows what she's gotten herself into, and that's not fair."

"Are you sure you want to be talking about this?" Kristen asked. "I mean, we slept together."

"Oh, honey, *I* knew what I was getting myself into," she said with a wink.

"You did?"

"Please." Amelia turned back to the screen. "There are girls like you everywhere. The dark ones. The sulky ones. The mysterious ones. The sexy ones." She flashed her a quick grin. "You don't go falling in love with those girls, though, not unless you want your heart broken. Looks like someone forgot to send your Ashleigh the memo."

That wasn't fair. It made Ashleigh sound naïve. Was she? No. Kristen may not have been honest with her about her job and the pretenses under which they met, but Ashleigh knew what she was getting herself into as far as getting involved with Kristen went. She'd fallen in love with her, and Kristen had let her, even though she'd known how this would end. How would Ashleigh feel when she found out she'd been lied to all along?

There were too many things standing between them. All the lies. The deceit. Ashleigh had trouble trusting after Denise, and Kristen had gone and done the exact same thing to her. Even if Ashleigh could get over that, it didn't matter. Kristen would be going back to Ottawa, in a worst-case scenario, or out to Banff, if Amelia could crack these files. Ottawa was only a four- or five-hour drive, but Ouellette would let her stay just long enough to pick up her next assignment and board her next plane.

"Open the wine, would you?" Amelia asked. "It helps me think. And join me for a glass."

Kristen wanted to say she could have a glass when she handed her the decrypted files, but if she did, she risked Amelia walking out on her. Right now, Amelia was the only thing standing between a busted ring of corrupt cops and a slap on the wrist from the commissioner.

She dutifully opened the bottle, pulled two wine glasses from the cupboard, and poured. "Here you go." She handed one to Amelia.

"Mmm." Amelia moaned after her first sip. "Red wine is better than sex; did you know that?"

Kristen laughed, then her smile faded.

Amelia regarded her affectionately. "Listen, if you don't want to leave her, why don't you stay?"

Kristen shook her head. "It doesn't work like that with my job. I go where they send me."

"And where are they sending you?"

"Banff, with any luck."

"The other side of the country?"

Kristen nodded.

"Poor Ashleigh," Amelia said, not without feeling.

"It's not like that. I love her."

At this, Amelia paused. "*You're* in love?"

"Don't sound so incredulous," Kristen said, running her hand over the back of her neck.

"I'm sorry. I'm just surprised."

"So was I."

"Well, if you feel this way, why don't you just tell her what's going on?"

"I can't, my job—"

"Yes, yes, your job, your job. The sky is falling. The sky is falling." She waved her glass around dramatically. "Enough about your damn job. Don't you realize that some things are more important than our jobs or anything else? Unless, of course, you don't think she is?"

Of course Ashleigh was more important than her job. She was more important than anything. She pictured a life without Ashleigh and then one without the RCMP. The one without Ashleigh was much less appealing. Amelia was right. Just because she'd always been the job didn't mean she always had to be. When this was over, she would tell Ashleigh the truth.

Her phone buzzed.

Once the cops were behind bars, she would tell Ashleigh everything and let her choose what she wanted. If Ashleigh could forgive her, could still love her, she'd turn in her badge to stay in Toronto and be with her if she had to.

Her phone buzzed again.

"Do you really love her?" Amelia asked.

"I do."

"Then check your damn phone."

It had been four hours since Ashleigh sent her first text message to Kristen. She'd fired off six since and not heard back. Okay, she was being a little stalkerish, but she could see that her messages were received, and she hadn't heard back from Kristen at all.

She wanted to send a message screaming, "I know you read that!" but she kept her cool. This was new for Kristen. She wasn't used to having someone in her life. She didn't know what proper protocol was when dating.

Who are you kidding?

First, no one had said they were officially dating. Second, Kristen wasn't an alien. She sure as hell knew that when someone messaged you seven times, they were clearly getting worried about why you weren't writing back. It was common decency to at least send a courtesy reply.

She's just scared. She's not used to opening up about herself.

How afraid was she, though? So afraid that she was going to run away from this? No. Ashleigh wouldn't let her. Even though Bailey hadn't said as much, she could tell she had feelings for her, real feelings, even if she couldn't admit to them. They'd slept together twice. Bailey didn't do that. They'd spent the night together five times. Although those nights were in varying circumstances, Bailey didn't do that either.

Maybe she had pushed too hard. Perhaps Kristen wasn't ready for this. Now she was feeling vulnerable, exposed. Ashleigh knew how that felt.

She needed Kristen to know that it was okay. Whatever Kristen felt, whatever she wanted to do about what was happening between them, she would respect that, but she wouldn't let her hide away again. If she didn't want to answer her texts, that was fine. Ashleigh would go over there and tell her in person that she didn't want to lose her.

Ashleigh knocked on the door. When no one answered, she knocked again. A moment later, Bailey's door was pulled open by a voluptuous blonde. Ashleigh's stomach plummeted.

The woman looked her up and down. "Can I help you?" she asked.

Behind her, there was an open bottle of wine with two half empty glasses sitting on the coffee table next to Kristen's laptop.

"Could it be any hotter in here?" Kristen said, coming out from the bedroom, pulling a white, ribbed tank top over her head.

Ashleigh's heart squeezed. Kristen froze when she met her gaze. She was definitely interrupting something. That's why Kristen hadn't answered her texts.

"Ashleigh," Kristen said, her voice breathless.

The blonde looked at Kristen, then back at Ashleigh with a mischievous smile on her face, and Ashleigh had to stop the tears that prickled behind her eyes. The woman stepped away from the door and picked something up from the coffee table, then pulled a large, black bag over her shoulder.

"I think I'll just leave you guys to it," the woman said.

Ashleigh didn't move as the stranger pushed past her out the door. She stared at her as she waited by the elevator. The blonde looked back as if feeling the weight of it.

"Yeah, I think I'll take the stairs down," she said, inching toward the stairwell door and slinking behind it, out of sight.

"Ashleigh." Bailey's voice called her attention back inside the condo. She was standing by the coffee table now, next to the wine she'd been enjoying with that woman.

"You've got to be kidding me." Ashleigh laughed humourlessly at herself. "I'm such a fucking idiot." She put a hand to her forehead. "I actually thought I was different," she said, disbelief in her voice.

"Ashleigh." Bailey tried again, but Ashleigh didn't want to hear it.

"Last night... Was there ever anything between us?" Her heart pounded hard against her chest.

"It's not whatever you're thinking, okay?" Kristen took a cautious step toward her. "I can explain everything. I want to. Just sit down and let me start from the beginning."

"Like hell I'm going to sit where you were just fucking some other girl."

Kristen flinched. She opened her mouth to say something, but Ashleigh had heard enough. She'd sure as hell seen enough.

"Ashleigh, wait," Kristen called after her, but she didn't wait.

She turned around, opened the door, and walked out.

The sound of the door slamming echoed in the condo. Kristen was at a crossroads. She had the evidence she needed to put the ring of dirty cops away for a long time, even life in some cases, but she hadn't sent it to Ouellette yet. She had been just about to when Ashleigh showed up. The call would take at least an hour, going over the evidence, explaining everything, then putting plans together for the takedown team to bring in the rest of the officers involved. If she waited that long, would she ever see Ashleigh again? The case would be over, and she was sure Ashleigh wouldn't take her calls, even if it was just to hear her say goodbye. No, she couldn't let her leave, not like this.

Kristen rushed to the door, but before she could reach for the handle, it opened. Ashleigh was there. Kristen started to smile. That's when she noticed the gun pushing into Ashleigh's back. Detective Ortiz was holding it. Her stomach dropped, just as it had when she'd seen all of the evidence against him in King's files. In hindsight, the conversation she'd had with him at FiteNite had been more about him pumping her for information than the other way around. Maybe she'd taken too many hits to the head that night, but she should have seen through him. She'd been too blinded by her desire to put the case to rest to see that the one man who was supposed to be trying to find the rookie cop killers was the head of the operation.

Ortiz nudged Ashleigh, who moved back into the condo without protest. Kristen thought quickly. Her police Glock was at the station, but she still had her service pistol tucked into her left ankle.

Ten bullets.

What were the chances she could reach for it and shoot him before he fired one into Ashleigh? When someone held a gun to a hostage as a bargaining chip, they would nine times out of ten change the target to the person they thought caused them a real threat if she pulled a weapon. If she reached for her pistol, he would move the gun from Ashleigh's back to Kristen, but what if the pistol stuck when she tried to pull it out? What if her hand shook?

She thought of her parents. Of all the things she would have done differently. All the things that might have kept them alive.

What if she wasn't fast enough? Then they'd both be dead, just like on that night.

Ortiz pushed Ashleigh further in.

"Put your hands up," he said.

Kristen did as she was told and winced in pain. The stitching from where the bullet fragment had been removed made itself known. The odds weren't in her favour.

Still, maybe she could get to his gun before he got a shot off. That thought died when behind Ortiz, Luke Smith walked in.

"You set me up," she said to Ortiz.

They'd known she was looking into things. Ortiz had sold her out to King, and that had precipitated changeup day. She'd been meant to die in that shootout, along with Evans.

"There never was a card game, was there?" she asked Ortiz. "You saw I was close, so you bought some time, told King I was on to him, and came up with a ploy. You both had me chasing my tail while you planned how to get rid of me."

"Kristen," Ashleigh said, panic-stricken. "What's going on?"

"King was telling you the truth," Ortiz said. "He is doing this for Charles, which is why he used his mandated phone call to warn me instead of calling his lawyer."

"But the files..." she said. She'd seen them herself after Amelia decrypted them. There was enough legitimate evidence to put them all away.

"Oh, you mean this?" Smith stepped forward and punched his fist down. Not only did it break her coffee table, but it shattered the USB. Next, he took her computer and broke the screen off from the keyboard, ripping it in half. He followed that up with snapping both pieces in two. It was like watching the Hulk lose it in Best Buy.

"Frisk her," Ortiz said.

Smith dropped the electronics with a grin. He stepped behind and started with Kristen's chest, which he squeezed as he moved his way down. It was typical of a man like him and wasn't the first time it had happened to her in a pat down, but her heart fell when Ashleigh turned her head from the sight. It took Smith only a moment to find her pistol, pull it out, and wave it in front of her triumphantly.

No bullets.

Ortiz moved forward. He pulled her hands roughly behind her back and zip tied them there. Next, he did the same to Ashleigh.

"Look, I'm unarmed. You got what you came for. Just let her go. She has nothing to do with this. She's no good to you." Kristen used all her training to keep the panic from her voice.

She was grateful she'd had the foresight to leave a copy of the files with Amelia. The evidence would make it to Ouellette. They could do whatever they wanted to Kristen, but not to Ashleigh.

"No?" Ortiz asked. He looked meaningfully between Ashleigh, the computer, and the two glasses of wine. "Something tells me she knows more than she should."

Shit.

"She just got here. I decrypted it on my own. She doesn't know anything about any of this."

"She's the EMT who found Jenna Bradley's body. We can't let her go now; she's seen our faces," Ortiz said.

Luke looked Ashleigh up and down. "And besides, she's good for something."

Kristen's heart jumped into her throat at his innuendo. She opened her mouth to argue just as Luke raised the pistol he'd confiscated from her. She didn't have time to move before it crashed down against her skull, and everything went dark.

CHAPTER 22

KRISTEN'S HEAD WAS POUNDING. WHERE was she? She tried to focus her eyes, but everything was black. She lifted her head, which only caused searing pain to shoot across her eyes. She tried to move, but she couldn't.

She was tied up.

Her body was pressed firmly into a hard chair, and her hands were secured behind her back, behind the chair. How had she ended up here? She tried to focus again, but everything was still dark. A putrid smell filled the air. Was it her? Was it blood? Material covered her eyes.

A blindfold.

In the darkness, it could have been nineteen years ago. She had to remind herself that she wasn't thirteen, and she hadn't just watched her parents being killed. She'd slipped her restraints that night—loose rope—and gotten her and Jared out of the house.

She wriggled her wrists, but they were pinned tight. *Zip tie.* It allowed no give, and worse, it tightened a click when she struggled against it.

"Kristen?"

She cocked her head. Her heart stilled as relief washed through her. "Ashleigh?"

"Thank God." Ashleigh's voice came from somewhere in front of her.

"Where are we?" Kristen asked.

"I don't know. I can't see." Ashleigh's voice trembled.

"You're blindfolded?"

"Yes." Ashleigh was almost inaudible. "I'm scared."

Kristen wanted nothing more than to comfort her, but she needed to prioritize. Rather than mutter words of encouragement to Ashleigh, she tried to get some kind of bearing on her surroundings. Nothing came to her. Ashleigh's voice hadn't echoed, so they weren't in a large open space. They were inside, as there was no wind. The only distinct thing was the smell, but she didn't recognize it.

"How long have I been out?"

"An hour, maybe."

"Are you okay?"

"No."

"Smith, did he…"

"No."

Kristen exhaled in relief. "Are you tied up?"

"Yes," she said.

"How?"

"My arms are tied behind my back."

"Are you on a chair?"

"Yes."

Okay, so they were in the same predicament. She sniffed the putrid scent again.

"Do you know what that smell is?"

"No."

"Please, think. Nothing is random. Is there anything familiar about this place?"

Ashleigh was silent a moment before she answered. "It smells like where I found the police officer's body."

"Okay, that's good, really good," Kristen said encouragingly. "What do you remember about the building? Doors, windows, rooms, exits? Anything you can remember is helpful."

"I don't know. I was only here for a couple of minutes. What is going on? Why is this happening?"

"Please, Ashleigh, focus. This is important."

Ashleigh exhaled forcefully. "We came in the back entrance. There was open space. There were two doors to the right and a long corridor to the left. There was a stairwell at the front. That's all I remember."

A door opened to her left.

"So, you're awake." It was Ortiz. Now that she was blindfolded, Kristen realized his was the second voice from the video of Ricky Oslowe's murder. He'd been there with Smith. They'd killed Oslowe and Jenna Bradley, tried to kill Evans, and now they were going to kill her and Ashleigh.

The blindfold was ripped roughly from her face.

It took a moment for her vision to focus. Ashleigh was seated in front of her, approximately three feet away. Her chair had metal legs with a wood seat and back. She wrapped her ankles around her own chair. Ortiz pulled Ashleigh's blindfold off next. Her eyes were red. She'd been crying. Kristen's chest squeezed.

"I thought Smith killed you with that blow." Ortiz threw the blindfolds on a table to his right, where there was a pair of plyers and a knife.

The blade looked about four inches long and an inch wide. The plyers were small, just the right size for pulling out fingernails or ripping apart the bones in a hand.

Oh God.

"I meant what I said before," Kristen said. "You can let her go. I'll tell you anything you want. I'll do anything you want."

"And why would we let her go when we know that you would say or do anything to keep her from harm?"

Fuck. She was making so many mistakes. It was hard for her to think clearly when all she wanted to do was keep Ashleigh safe.

"We went through your phone. We know you didn't send anything back to your headquarters at the RCMP." He threw her ID badge on the floor in front of her. It landed open.

Ashleigh's eyes widened in surprise. "RCMP?" she whispered. Confusion traced her features.

"It seems your investigation into the Toronto Police Service is at an end, Staff Sergeant Bailey." He smirked. "We thank you for your time and effort, but you won't be needed anymore." He picked up the knife from the table.

"You're RCMP?" Ashleigh asked.

"I'm sorry." Kristen turned to her. "I wanted to tell you. I was going to tell you."

"You didn't know?" Ortiz paused, amused. "Yes, she was here looking into an internal affairs matter between the police and paramedics." His smile was smug as he turned it on Ashleigh. "I assume that's why she was sleeping with you. It's why she was sleeping with your partner's sister. Let's see, who else? There was Heather in forensics." He used the tip of the knife to count off the numbers on his fingers. "Kelly in Ident, Shannon in SIU. Now *she* was hot."

Ashleigh blanched. "It was all a lie."

If this was it, then she at least needed Ashleigh to know it hadn't all been a lie.

"Ashleigh, it wasn't like that with you, I swear. You were different. I lo—" Her voice was stolen from her when Ortiz struck the knife deep into the top of her thigh, up to its hilt. She cried out in equal amounts pain and shock.

The door opened behind Ortiz, and Smith walked in. He took one look at Kristen, noticed the blade in her leg, then turned to Ashleigh. "Time to go." He pulled her up from the chair by turning a fist in the back of her shirt.

"Where are you taking her?" Kristen demanded through teeth that were clenched in pain.

"Well, I didn't exactly plan on taking your sloppy seconds, but hell, it'll be just as enjoyable as beating the shit out of you, only there's no ref to call me off of her."

Tears were in Ashleigh's eyes. Her gaze never left Kristen's as he yanked her out of the room, his grip on her shirt exposing half of her torso.

"You're so fond of Shakespeare?" Ashleigh said. "How's this: *Et tu, Brute?*"

Kristen's heart sank. She closed her eyes, unable to meet the fear in Ashleigh's.

Luke pulled her out of the room, and the heavy metal door slammed behind them.

She needed to think. She would die before she let anything happen to Ashleigh, which in all likelihood was what was about to happen. There was the sound of footsteps trailing away. Luke was taking Ashleigh down the long corridor she'd mentioned. Kristen opened her eyes. Ortiz stood in front of her. He had a sly smile on his face.

"Why?" she asked, buying time.

"You did this to yourself, you know? Coming up to me at FiteNite, begging for information. Until then, we were no more wary of you than anyone else. But you knew things."

"Why were you fighting Smith if you were in on this together?"

"It was just going to be a friendly waltz to look good. Raising money for Ricky-Moron's wife and all that. When you started poking around, I thought we'd have some fun with you, scare you off; but you're dumber than you look."

"Oslowe's video. It was never the paramedics." The realization dawned on her. "That's why in the video, Oslowe said, 'You guys finally made it.' He wasn't talking about the EMTs. He was referring to his backup. All the video showed was two people entering in uniform pants. Pants so similar to EMT uniforms from a distance. When you got closer, he recognized you, and when you went to have a look at his injuries he tried to stop you. He started to say you should wait for the paramedics to get there, but you and Luke never let him finish."

"Very good." He picked up the plyers and tested them in his hand.

"What are those for?" she asked, as if she didn't already know.

"Well, we need to send a message to anyone else who thinks of looking a little too closely into things they don't understand. If King doesn't appreciate after this that we own him, he and his son are as dead as the two of you."

There was nothing in reach she could use as a weapon. The zip tie held her hands firmly behind her back. She tried to wriggle her wrists, but there was no give.

"You're a fucking coward. Untie me and fight me like a man."

He grinned. At first, she wasn't sure why, but then he came in front of her and pulled the knife from her leg slowly. It tore the ligaments on the way out, and she huffed loudly in pain.

Ortiz cleaned the blood off the knife by wiping it on Kristen's other thigh, sneering as he stained her jeans red. He was standing right in front of her, and she didn't waste the opportunity.

Kristen pushed off the ground with her feet, shoving her weight back with full force. As the chair tipped back, she pulled her knees up and kicked forward with all her strength. Both feet landed square in Ortiz's chest. She couldn't have asked for a better outcome. The momentum of her kick sent him flying back, and he crashed first into Ashleigh's chair, which tangled with his legs, then continued back into the far wall.

The motion of Kristen's chair continued, landing her hard on her back. All of her weight landed on her arms still zip tied behind her. She clamped her teeth together, anticipating the blow to her head on the pavement. She didn't want to accidentally bite her tongue off from the impact.

That had been the easy part.

She didn't have time to see what Ortiz was doing. Either she would be quicker than he was, or she wouldn't be, and wasting precious milliseconds looking around was not going to help her.

She needed to get the zip tie in front of her. She scrabbled up against the wall and leaned on it for support as she climbed to her feet. Once she was up, she took in a deep breath in preparation for what she was about to do. She slammed her left shoulder hard against the wall. The bones shifted painfully as her shoulder dislocated. She didn't have time to give in to the pain. She bent over, favouring her dislocated shoulder, leaned toward it at an awkward angle, then stepped back through the loop of her arms. She brought them painfully to the front of her body.

The next part was going to kill.

She hadn't done this since messing around with a few of the guys after too many beers at the Depot, and her shoulder hadn't been dislocated then. Despite her limited range of motion, she gritted her teeth and raised her arms up. She let out a terrible scream of pain as agony throbbed through her shoulder, but she understood this moment would be the difference between living through this and dying, defenseless. Although she couldn't raise her left arm quite as high as her right, she got it up high enough and slammed her arms down and out as hard and as fast as she could, smashing her wrists against her stomach and ripping out toward her waist at the same time.

The zip tie snapped.

Ortiz scrambled to his feet, his gun in his hand. Her hands now free, Kristen grabbed the chair on the ground. She screamed against the pain as she ran at Ortiz and slammed him hard against the wall. There was a loud cracking of bones as the metal chair leg broke through his ribs and sternum.

The gun dropped. Kristen pulled the chair back. Ortiz dropped, his eyes still open.

Kristen released the chair and tried to catch her breath. She wiped her eyes with the back of her hand and shook her head to shake away unconsciousness. She could not stop now.

The knife wound in her leg throbbed as she stepped. The pain ripped through her thigh with every step as if she were being stabbed over and over again. She picked up the knife and grabbed Ortiz's gun from the holster in the back of his pants. She checked the magazine. It was fully loaded.

She tucked the gun into the back of her jeans and put the handle of the knife in her mouth. She needed to stop the bleeding in her leg. The blindfold that had been around her eyes was on the table, along with Ashleigh's. She picked up the one closest to her and wrapped it around her thigh, about an inch above the stab wound, and tied it tight, then wound it around and tied it again. She winced in pain and bit into the hilt of the knife between her teeth to keep herself from making a sound. Once she was satisfied the field bandage was tight enough and it wouldn't move, she removed the knife from her mouth. Cutting off the circulation to her leg wasn't ideal, but it was life or limb, and she made the only choice she could.

According to the files Amelia had decrypted, there were ten officers in the drug ring, including Ortiz and King. She had to cautiously assume that meant there were at least eight hostile officers still in the building.

Eight armed men. Fifteen bullets. One knife.

Slowly, she slid the metal door open. She needed to make as little noise as possible. When there was enough space to look out, she did so. Her breath caught. A man stood not a foot in front of her. Obviously, he'd assumed the screams from the room were Ortiz killing her, so he hadn't bothered to turn around or investigate. There were two other men at the other end of the hall, at the entrance to the corridor. That's where Ashleigh must have been taken.

Slowly, she raised her right arm until she was just an inch from the man's neck. With precision, she slid the blade into the tender flesh between his neck and shoulder. The steel slid in smoothly and severed his vocal cords and windpipe. He gurgled blood, and when his weight began to fall, she grabbed his body and dragged him back into the room with her. He had a gun on him but no silencer. Her best chance at staying alive and getting to Ashleigh was to do so clandestinely.

She checked the magazine. It was full.

Seven armed men. Thirty bullets. One knife.

She peeked back around the door. She needed to take both men out at the same time and without causing a lot of noise. She looked around the room again. There were only the plyers and the second blindfold. She picked up the blindfold and tested its strength by pulling it hard and fast between her fists. It held. It would do.

She crept out of the room and made sure the metal door didn't scratch the floor. The men had their backs to her. That was a bit of luck, but one sound, and they would turn.

She bit back the pain as she walked on her leg. A small spurt of blood still oozed from the stab wound with every step, leaking down her thigh to her calf and pooling in her sock. Her left shoulder throbbed, and she was thankful it was the same arm that had taken the bullet shell fragment earlier and not her good arm.

She was about ten feet from the men when one of them turned. She hadn't made a sound, but still, he turned. She hurtled the knife through the air, and it landed in his jugular with a gurgling squish. The man grabbed at his throat and ripped the knife out. His partner watched in horror as the man's throat sprayed blood. Kristen had hoped to sever his spinal cord and cause a quick death, but she'd sliced through his artery instead. The man finally fell, both hands wrapped around his throat in an attempt to assuage the bleeding that would in a moment end his life. His partner suddenly snapped out of the horror show in front of him and went for his gun before calling out. It was all the better for Kristen. She launched herself forward and wrapped the blindfold around this neck. When her weight landed on him, she pulled him down to the floor as he grasped at the blindfold. He flailed his arms to no avail. Kristen pulled with all her strength until his struggle ceased. She checked his pulse to be sure he wasn't faking. It beat for a moment, and then it stopped.

She grabbed his firearm and clicked the release to drop the magazine into her hand. She put it in her pocket, tucked one gun behind her back, and held the other two at the ready. The knife was wet, soaked in blood, and she decided to leave it. She didn't trust her aim or hold on the slippery handle.

Five armed men. Three guns with four full magazines. Things were looking up.

She crept along the corridor slowly, cautiously. There was no electricity in the forsaken building, so it was dark, but she could just make out two men at the end of the long corridor, stationed opposite the other two she'd just taken out.

When she could see enough that the room beyond the corridor came into view, she stopped. Two more men stood outside a door, facing her direction, but they hadn't seen her yet. She vaguely recognized them as senior officers from the station. She had no sight on Ashleigh or Luke Smith.

She wiped the sweat from her eyes with the back of her wrist. There was no way she could take out four men in such close quarters with stealth. She was thankful for the guns she'd amassed. Without them, she wouldn't even stand a chance.

Silently, she raised both her arms. One gun aimed at the back of one man's head at the left end of the corridor, the second trained to the right on the other. She took a deep breath, steadied her arms, and fired both guns simultaneously.

The man to her right dropped, a bullet taking out the better half of his head, but she'd missed the shot with her bad arm. The kickback of the gun was too much for her dislocated shoulder, and she'd flinched. That one infinitesimal movement changed everything.

The man ducked at the sound of the bullet that exploded in the concrete just centimetres from his head. He took a large step forward and whirled around with his gun raised. The two men by the door ran forward, their guns out.

There were too many shooters. Too many bullets. She dove for cover under the body of the man she'd just killed, firing as she went down. A few bullets hit flesh, and the man closest to her fell forward, his eyes unseeing. Kristen propped up the body of the dead man as a shield. He took three bullets for her before one hit her side and tore through her abdomen. She dropped the body, raised her arms, and fired with abandon. Both men fell before the rain of her fire, but not before a final bullet smoked out of one man's gun, zipped through the air, and landed in Kristen's chest.

Ashleigh's heart was pounding. Luke Smith dragged her, even when she lost her footing, and hauled her weight as if it were nothing. She fell on the cot like a ragdoll and landed face down. A horrible smell shot up her nose from the mattress.

She tried to push off the bed, but her hands were still zip tied behind her back. Smith came and pushed her harder onto the bed when he saw her struggling to get up. She managed to turn and land a kick in his stomach. It barely moved him, but his face reddened. She couldn't stop the punch as it landed hard across her cheekbone. The force almost knocked her out, and for a moment, she wondered if it would have been better if it had. He flipped her back over onto her stomach. From this angle, she wasn't able to kick him again.

This was it. He was going to rape her, and there was nothing she could do to stop him. Tears streamed down her face.

"Why are you doing this?"

"Shut up."

"You don't have to do this."

"No, but I want to."

Smith's hand grabbed at her waist. He ripped hard at her jeans, trying to force them down over her hips. Without consciously making the decision, she began to scream.

"Keep screaming like that," he said, his lips against her ear. "It only makes me harder."

He grabbed at her waist again and gripped her jeans and underwear, ready to yank them down. Gunshots exploded through the air, even louder than her screaming. He paused and looked back.

The door to the room flew open.

He turned and was instantly caught in a struggle. Ashleigh used the opportunity to get off her stomach. She was able to get her legs on the ground and sit up. She looked at Smith. He was so huge that she couldn't see around him.

There was a knife on the side of the bed. She gripped it behind her back and started rubbing ferociously at the zip tie still binding her. She cut skin and kept going, warm blood coating her hands as she continued her raw scratching, desperate to be free of her bindings.

Smith reached back and threw a hard punch at his assailant. He grunted in pain when his fist connected with the metal door, and Bailey slipped under his arm. Ashleigh's heart leapt.

Kristen was alive.

Her white tank top and jeans were soaked in blood. It appeared to be her own.

Kristen reached behind her back. She grabbed for something that wasn't there. Her face registered her dismay. She shifted her balance just in time to avoid another one of Smith's crushing punches.

Ashleigh's hands broke free of the zip tie.

"We've done this dance before. Don't you remember how it ends?" Smith said.

"This time," Kristen breathed heavily, "there's no ring, no rules, and no holds barred."

He punched again, and Bailey slid back and away, but she caught his fist at the end of its extension and quickly turned it down and out as she ripped it behind his back and up in one swift motion. He fell to his knees in pain. He tried to swing his other arm back to grab at her, but before he could reach her, she brought her knee up hard into the back of his skull.

She continued to twist the hand she had behind his back, and he cried out in pain. She kept twisting and pushing up until there was a snap.

Ashleigh cringed. Kristen had broken Smith's arm. That was when she saw it. The pistol Smith had taken from Bailey at her condo was hanging out of the back of his jeans. He could break Ashleigh in half if he caught her, but she had to try.

While Kristen had him distracted, she lunged forward, crashed into him, and grabbed the gun. She yanked it from his pants and tossed it to Kristen. Smith reached for Ashleigh and lifted her up between his arms. He let out a grunt of pain, presumably from the break to his arm, but still took the ground out from beneath her as if she weighed no more than a pillow.

She followed his gaze to the metal bed frame. He was going to break her back against it.

He lifted her, and she screamed. A gunshot went off, and it was as if her body hung suspended a moment, before he dropped to his knees, and then she tumbled down beside him.

She looked into his eyes. They were wide, terrified. There was a bullet hole, oozing blood, where his heart should be. The seconds seemed to last for hours as with each slowing beat of his heart, he pumped out the blood he needed to survive. Floods of crimson stained his shirt until, finally, his eyes went blank and he fell over on his side.

She scrambled away from the body and over to Kristen. She was slumped against the wall. The pistol dropped from her right hand. Her eyes closed.

"No, no, no!" Ashleigh checked her wrist for a pulse, but her hands were shaking, sweating. She moved her fingers to Kristen's throat, trying to calm her own heartbeat. There was a slow pulse, much too slow.

"Kristen? Kristen?" she said, shaking her.

Kristen winced in pain, coming to. Ashleigh's body flushed with relief. She sat back to survey the extent of Kristen's injuries. She looked like she'd been through a meat grinder. There was blood everywhere. The knife wound in her thigh she knew about, so she started there. Kristen had tied her own field dressing, but it had come loose and was soaked with blood. She turned around and ripped the shirt from Smith's dead body. Once it was free from his heavy, limp arms, she used it to tie a tourniquet just above the wound, implementing the knife that had freed her bindings as the rod to twist the tourniquet. She pulled it tight to control the arterial circulation to her leg.

What next? Her stomach roiled at the gaping bullet hole in her chest, just below her collarbone. Kristen wasn't gurgling blood out of her mouth, as she would have been had her lungs been punctured.

Thankfully, unlike Smith, she had been hit too high for the bullet to have punctured her heart. The fact that she had full mobility of her legs, back, and neck also meant it had missed her spine. It was a ghastly wound, but if any of the major organs had been hit, it would probably have already ended her life. Ashleigh took her own shirt off and applied pressure. The bullet may have missed a life-ending mark when it lodged, but there was still so much blood.

Too much blood.

"Ashleigh," Kristen whispered, her voice barely audible.

"Shh, just stay quiet," Ashleigh said, tears streaking her face. She turned so Bailey wouldn't see them.

Smith's cell phone was popping out of the back pocket of his jeans. She picked it up. It was password protected. She tried pushing a bunch of numbers, then noticed the emergency call button at the bottom left. She pushed it. A number pad came onto the screen. She dialed 911.

"This is nine-one-one, what's your emergency?"

"I have an officer down." She swallowed and tried to remember what she was supposed to say. It was hard being on the other end of the line for the first time. "She's a female, thirty-two years old, with several gunshot wounds and lacerations. She's conscious and breathing. We're in a building at Kensington and Spadina, through the back alley. There are several other officers down, but I think they're all dead. Please, come quickly."

"Can I get your name, ma'am?"

"Ashleigh Paige. I'm a paramedic. Please, hurry. We need an ambulance here."

"Are you in any immediate danger?"

"I don't think so, but she's bleeding out." Her voice cracked.

"Can you stay with the officer until help arrives?"

"Yes." Tears squeezed through her eyes. "Yes, I'm not going anywhere."

"Police and EMS have been dispatched. They should get to you in approximately six minutes."

She dropped the phone. Kristen had a deathly pallour. There was more work to be done.

Blood gushed out of her side. Another gunshot wound. Her breath hitched as she realized just how badly Bailey was doing. Her right hand was still pressed up against the bullet wound in her chest, so she used her left hand, bare, and pushed hard against the gunshot to her side. Her hands were covered in Bailey's blood. She felt it, hot, leaking down the soft skin of her arms.

Kristen sucked in a deep breath, her eyes opening against the pain of the pressure.

"It's okay. The ambulance is on its way."

Kristen swallowed and closed her eyes again.

"No, I need you to stay with me," Ashleigh said, desperation raw in her voice. "I can't lose you."

"I'm just...so tired," Kristen said.

"Kristen, stay with me. I won't let you leave me. You don't get to leave, do you hear me? You came to rescue me, and now I'm going to rescue you."

"Ashleigh." Kristen coughed.

"No, shh. Save your strength."

"I love you," she whispered.

Ashleigh's heart stilled. There was a long silence before sirens sounded out, faintly at first, then louder.

"You're going to be okay. Help is here. You stay with me, Kristen. You stay with me." Kristen closed her eyes again. "You stay with me!" Ashleigh screamed, but there was no answer. The moment seemed to last forever as she stared, and the rise and fall of Kristen's chest stopped.

A hand on her shoulder made her turn around. The paramedics were there, pulling her away.

"She's VSA," one of EMTs said to the others.

Vital signs absent. Kristen's heart had stopped.

They swarmed around Bailey, saying all the things she would be saying, pulling out the AED, and opening her shirt to place the pads on her chest and side.

One of the EMTs got on securing her airway and oxygen. Another pulled out abdominal pads and used them to try to stop the bleeding.

"Where's Fire? We need a scoop stretcher."

Ashleigh's vision blurred.

An EMT lifted one of Kristen's eyelids and shone a flashlight in her unseeing blue eye. Ashleigh was pushed farther to the side as more paramedics and firefighters entered the room, and she faded into the background.

They picked Kristen's body up off the floor, put her on the scoop stretcher, and carried her away.

CHAPTER 23

Eighteen Months Later

Kristen's eyes squinted against the sun. She still wasn't entirely used to seeing clear blue skies almost every day, especially in December. She was also not fully acclimatized to having mountains in her daily landscape. The sun would start setting soon, making a cascade of rainbow skies over snowcaps and ski slopes.

She breathed the open air in deeply. She'd become accustomed to the altitude and no longer got headaches, but the air still smelled different. New, crisp, and somehow thinner.

She took in another deep breath, and there was a smarting in her chest.

Ghost wounds.

She'd regained complete mobility in the shoulder she'd dislocated, but in the Alberta cold, the echoes of her gunshot wounds would sometimes make themselves known. She pressed a hand to her chest, where she'd gone through four hours of surgery to remove the bullet that had almost killed her; not that she remembered any of it. One month of her life, completely gone.

"You sure you're good to finish up alone, ma'am?" Constable Malone asked her.

"Go home." She smiled at him. "It's Christmas Eve."

"Thank you, ma'am," he said with a boyish grin. "Things sure are better around here with you as staff sergeant major."

Kristen laughed. "Go home, Malone, and get your wife a present on your way, for God's sake."

He gave her a salute and headed to the parking lot.

Kristen walked back inside. It was a small branch. When she'd first arrived, she had thought she'd meet some resistance from the local constables, but the Banff station welcomed her easily. It turned out they had never trusted the acting staff sergeant major and had been eager to find new leadership. She was still a couple of promotions away from a white shirt and a permanent desk job, but already she spent much less time in the field and was enjoying her elite position where she could change things from the top and encourage the constables in her charge.

The phone rang from her office, and she hurried to the back of the station to answer it.

"Staff Sergeant Major Bailey," she said into the receiver.

"Sergeant Major Ouellette," he said, a smile in his voice. "Merry Christmas, Kristen."

"To what do I owe the pleasure?" She smiled as well.

"I thought you might like to know that Gregory King had his sentencing hearing today in Toronto. He's going away for twenty years for conspiracy to commit murder on four counts. His plea got him a lesser sentence."

Kristen remembered King's words about what happened to police officers in prison. "It's enough," she said, satisfied.

"So, how's it going in Alberta?"

"It's going well." She sat in her desk chair and leaned back a little. "Things are finally all coming together here."

"And the staff? How is everyone treating you with the promotion?"

"Everyone's been great," she said honestly. "There were only a few who made trouble at the beginning, but everyone else has been really supportive. To be honest, things are going great here. Do you miss me out in Ottawa?" she asked teasingly.

"Like a thorn in my side."

Kristen laughed. "Thanks for calling to let me know about King."

"I knew you'd hear about it, but I wanted you to hear it from me, after everything."

She nodded. "Thank you. I still owe you."

"Nah, you made me look good to the commissioner, Kristen. Sealed my new position for me. I'd say that makes us even."

"*Joyeux Noel*," she said.

"*Joyeux Noel*, and happy New Year."

"You too. Thanks for calling."

"Take care out there."

"I will. You too. Bye."

She hung up the phone and exhaled slowly. Her first four months after the Toronto Police Service drug fiasco ended had been spent in the hospital and in recovery, one of them in a coma. Ouellette had personally appealed to the commissioner and saved Kristen her spot in Banff, claiming she'd earned it now more than ever for the injuries she'd sustained on the job.

It was nearing five o'clock. Time to go home and let the night shift take over. She didn't envy them having to work on Christmas Eve, but she wasn't going to miss going home for anything.

Home.

For the first time since her parents died, she felt like Banff had given her one.

She waved to the constables just arriving at the station, and they waved back respectfully. She'd traded in her Mustang before she left Toronto for an F-150 with chains on its tires. The Alberta winters were cold as anything, and the snow never seemed to cease, but the mountains were breathtaking, and she wouldn't trade the view for a city landscape.

Her drive home was only ten minutes through the Banff village. The sidewalks were full of people with bags in their hands, children laughing as they ran through the snow, and ski bunnies with their skis hiked over their shoulders, poles in hand, as they headed back to their lodges. Kristen waved at a few people as she passed. The snow was coming down thicker on the last kilometres of her trip.

She turned the heat up almost to the point of having to take her jacket off and finished the drive with large snowflakes melting on the windshield. Her home came into view as she left the tourist village and started a little up the mountain. In Algonquin or Muskoka, her home would have been considered a cottage or log cabin. Here, it was a chalet. The sight of the hundred-year-old wood ski lodge never ceased to make her smile.

She pulled into her driveway and locked the truck, though she needn't have with the amount of crime in Banff. At the front door, she banged her Sorels to get the excess snow off them before she left them on the doormat. She hung her RCMP winter jacket up on her coat hook. On her way to the kitchen, she stopped by the large fireplace and threw on a few logs along with a starter one. There were a few hot, orange flames within seconds, and she took a moment to warm her hands by the fire. Once she felt toasty again, she plugged in the lights of the Christmas tree. She'd missed Christmas last year. She'd almost never had one again.

The white lights of the tree sparkled, and the ornaments glistened. Her favourite was a ceramic bear dressed as a Mountie—red coat, beige campaign hat, black riding boots, and all—standing at attention and saluting. The gift shop at the airport carried the strangest things. She ran her fingers along his hat and straightened the porcelain rocking horse ornament to the left. For a moment, she considered positioning the Mountie so that he was riding the rocking horse, as he was really only missing a horse, but it might have looked vulgar. She left the ornaments alone before continuing on to the kitchen.

It was a large space, and it had been modernized with stainless steel appliances. She uncorked a bottle of red wine, pouring herself a tall glass and taking a long sip, involuntarily sighing as the warmth moved through her body. She closed her eyes, thinking about all the years gone by. About how close she'd been to letting go and losing everything.

The front door rattled, the silver bells on the winter wreath jangling, and Kristen moved from the kitchen back to the entryway, her thick socks padding softly on the dark, hardwood flooring.

The door opened, and Ashleigh walked in, her face red from the cold.

"Hey." Kristen's mouth immediately split into a wide smile.

"Hey." Ashleigh smiled back at her. "Can you help me?"

Kristen put her wine down on the credenza and took the brown paper bag of groceries from Ashleigh's arms. She peeked inside at a ton of vegetables and, thankfully, a red-paper-wrapped package from the butcher. Kristen's smile grew. Ashleigh wasn't going to make her eat vegetarian tonight.

"How was your day?" Kristen kissed her lips. They were cold from being outside, but they still caused warmth in Kristen's chest.

"It was good," she said as she removed her boots.

She unzipped her red and white Ski Patrol jacket and snapped off the medical pouch of supplies with the large red cross on it.

"I need to get another sling before I go back to work next week. A little girl broke her arm in two places trying out the snowboard park, but she's going to be okay." She hung her jacket up. "A shame to happen on Christmas Eve, though. What kind of wine is that?" She nodded toward Kristen's glass on the ledge.

"It's the Pinot you like from California."

Ashleigh picked up the glass and took a sip before handing it back to Kristen. "Mmm, that's good. Is there more for tonight?"

"Of course there is."

A buzzing began, and Ashleigh reached back into her jacket for her phone.

"Hey!" she said warmly. "Are you guys here?"

Kristen sipped at her wine and waited while Ashleigh spoke on the phone.

"Oh no, we said we'd come pick you up." She paused, listening. "Like you're *here* here?"

Ashleigh opened the front door and looked outside. There were headlights pulling into the driveway.

"Oh my God, okay, I'm hanging up now!"

Ashleigh stuffed her phone into the pocket of her red ski pants, zipped it up, and shoved her boots back on, then ran down the driveway. The car outside parked and turned off its headlights. Ashleigh didn't wait for the two front doors to open. She was already in the backseat, pulling out little Evelyn, named for Kristen's grandmother. Jared and Cyndi got out of the car, and Ashleigh had Evelyn out of the car seat and in her arms. She was dressed in an adorable pink snowsuit. "She's getting so big," Ashleigh gushed, showering the baby's face with kisses.

"She is," Jared said with pride and kissed Ashleigh on the cheek. Cyndi came over next and pulled Ashleigh into a hug, careful not to squish the baby between them. "So, are you going to stand there or come out and help?" Jared called up to Kristen, who leaned against the doorframe and looked at her family.

"I'm just going to stand here," she retorted, a large, genuine smile on her face.

Ashleigh hurried up the steps with Evelyn in her arms. "Look at her, Kristen. Isn't she beautiful? Look how big she is. How long has it been since we've seen her?"

Kristen leaned down and kissed her niece on the forehead. "Well, she's about six months now, so four months. Go take her inside," she said, putting down her wine and grabbing for her boots. "I'm going to help Jared bring their things in."

"Great." Ashleigh stole a quick kiss from Kristen's lips. "I'll get Evelyn settled."

Cyndi greeted Kristen with a big hug at the car. "I'm so glad you guys are here," Kristen said. "It's all Ashleigh's been talking about for weeks."

Cyndi laughed. "Same with Jared."

"Go on inside. I'll help Jared."

Cyndi gave her a quick kiss on the cheek and sauntered off into the house after Ashleigh. It hadn't taken long for the two of them to become inseparable after Kristen's calamity. The three of them had taken shifts, watching over her in the hospital for weeks, first in her coma, and then until she was strong enough to stay conscious and start healing. The nurses and Jared both told her that Ashleigh had barely left her side that first month, going home only to get a change of clothes and shower every few days, then coming right back. After she'd used up all her sick and vacation time, she moved on to unpaid personal days and refused to leave her side. Cyndi and Ashleigh began a close bond in those months, one that Kristen didn't think anything could break, not even the distance of being four provinces apart.

"Kris." Jared pulled her into a tight hug, and she did the same. "I've missed you."

"I missed you too." She clapped him on the back, then grabbed one of the suitcases from the trunk. "I'm so glad you guys could make it."

"We wouldn't miss it," he said, throwing a bag over his shoulder and grabbing the second suitcase. "Evelyn's finally old enough to travel, so get used to seeing us, especially when she gets big enough to start skiing."

Kristen laughed and closed the trunk. Her chest smarted again, and she stopped, taking a sharp intake of breath. It passed quickly, but it gave her pause, as it always did. A reminder that she hadn't always had this life, that she'd been so close not to having any life at all.

"You coming?" Jared called from the door. She nodded and followed.

Ashleigh and Cyndi were already relaxed on the couch in the sitting room, the open fire roaring now. Evelyn was between them, out of her snowsuit and giggling.

Kristen closed the door and pulled her boots off. She went straight to Evelyn and picked her up. Evelyn grabbed a lock of Kristen's dark hair and squeezed it tightly in her little fist. Kristen laughed and attacked her rosy cheeks with kisses, which only made Evelyn giggle and squeal louder. Ashleigh had put some soft Christmas music on in the background.

"I have a confession to make," Jared said from the door as he pulled out a box from his suitcase. "I have something to declare, Staff Sergeant Major," he said to Kristen, but walked over and handed the box to Ashleigh.

She opened it up, and Kristen was greeted by the scent of Ashleigh's mother's pecan pie from where she stood. She laughed. "You brought a pie on a plane with you?" Kristen asked incredulously.

"At my own great peril." He put a hand to his heart. "I risked arrest and seizure because your mom told me she'd kill me if I didn't get her Christmas pie to you," he said. "She also sends her love and wants to know when you two are coming back to visit."

"This summer, probably, while we still can," Ashleigh said absentmindedly. She carried the pie into the kitchen carefully, as if she could hurt it now after it'd just survived five hours on a plane.

"You have to share that with the rest of us, you know?" Kristen called after her. She turned to Cyndi and Jared. "Are you guys hungry? Should we start making dinner?"

"I'm always hungry," Jared said agreeably.

"I could eat." Cyndi nodded. "I just have to feed Evelyn first."

"Sounds good. I'll be right back with some apps." Kristen left and found Ashleigh in the kitchen, already taking the cheeses out of the fridge for the platter.

Kristen pulled another bottle of red from the wine rack. She put the bottle on the counter but stopped and watched Ashleigh as she took out a cutting board and began to spread the cheeses out. Her heart swelled, as it did so often when the reality of her life hit her.

She had been ready and willing to give up everything for Ashleigh, and in return, Ashleigh had done the same for her. She hadn't thought twice about leaving her life as a paramedic in Toronto and coming to Banff with her. Kristen ignored the water in her eyes and moved behind Ashleigh to take her into her arms and pull her back against her body.

"Mmm." Ashleigh put down the brie and wrapped her arms around the ones surrounding her. "What's this about?"

Kristen shook her head. "I just love you so much," she said.

Ashleigh turned in her arms and slipped her own around Kristen's neck.

"Thank you for coming here," Kristen said. "For leaving your home, everything, for me. I just can't believe how lucky I am."

Ashleigh leaned up and kissed her. "Wherever you are, wherever your heart is, that's my home."

Kristen kissed her slowly, longingly. "I love you," she said again.

"I love you too." Ashleigh rested her forehead against Kristen's. "More than words can say."

"Oh yeah?" Kristen pulled away and slightly raised her eyebrow. "Well, maybe you can show me."

Ashleigh laughed, hit her shoulder playfully, and pulled out of her arms. "Behave yourself. We have company."

"I'll throw them back in the van, then."

Ashleigh smiled patiently and pushed the cheese platter into Kristen's hands. "Be good and serve that, and I might just share my pecan pie with you later."

Kristen kissed her again before she returned to the sitting room and placed the cheese tray on the table. "Wine," she said to herself, remembering what she had forgotten, and turned around to find

Ashleigh not a foot behind her, the bottle of wine and extra glasses in her hand. She handed them out.

"A toast." Ashleigh raised her glass of sparkling water and waited for Kristen to pour the wine for everyone before she started. "Thank you for coming to see us for the holidays. We can't tell you how much it means to see you and Evelyn. Skype just isn't enough. To Christmas, to the holidays, and to family." She turned to Kristen. "You're my world, Kris. Thank you for giving me all of this."

They clinked glasses and drank their first sips, but Kristen hesitated. "To you, Ashleigh," she said, "for giving me my family back. For making me whole again." She reached forward and put a hand on Ashleigh's stomach. She could swear she felt the life inside her move even though Ashleigh had already told her several times it was too early for that.

"Do you know what you're having yet?" Cyndi asked.

Ashleigh shook her head, and Kristen kissed her temple. "We won't know for a few more weeks, but I'm betting it's a girl." Ashleigh leaned against Kristen.

"You better hope she's nothing like Kris," Jared said teasingly.

Ashleigh smiled, looked up at Kristen, and met her lips for a quick kiss. "Actually, I hope she's exactly like Kristen."

The love and adoration in Ashleigh's eyes warmed her through, as it always did. Ashleigh had broken down every last one of her barriers and had filled her with affection and love she hadn't dared to dream of. She kissed her again, relishing in the warmth of her.

"I love you," she whispered, and Ashleigh responded with her knowing smile that told Kristen that no matter how many times she worried this life would be taken from her, Ashleigh would always be there, her words and love a beacon in the night, ready to remind her that she had a home again, a family with their own baby on the way, and a partner she never wanted to stop kissing.

ABOUT MICHELLE L. TEICHMAN

Michelle graduated from the esteemed creative writing program at York University in Toronto, where she studied under notable authors Susan Swan, Richard Teleky, and Shyam Selvadurai. Michelle believes that nothing is more powerful than the written word and that the world is changed by disaster but shaped by art and that there is no greater responsibility than that of the artist to express not only where we are now, but where we've been and where we are headed. She is also a proud Canadian who delights in rich coffee, good wine, smooth bourbon, and football on Sundays. When not writing, Michelle spends her time playing with her wonderful dog, Link, who has proven to be the best writing buddy, throwing dinner parties with her wife, and reading everything she can get her hands on.

CONNECT WITH MICHELLE:
Website: www.michelleteichman.com
Facebook: www.facebook.com/MichelleLTeichman
Twitter: @MLTeichman
E-Mail: Michelle.L.Teichman@gmail.com

OTHER BOOKS FROM YLVA PUBLISHING

www.ylva-publishing.com

THE SPACE BETWEEN

Michelle L. Teichman

ISBN: 978-3-95533-581-6
Length: 280 pages (92,000 words)

Life is easy for Harper, the most popular girl in her grade, until she meets Sarah, a friendless loner who only cares about art. Inexplicably, Harper can't stop thinking about her.

Unsure of her feelings for Harper, Sarah is afraid to act on what her heart is telling her. She can't believe Harper feels the same.

Can Harper and Sarah find a way to be together, or will fear keep them apart forever?

IN A HEARTBEAT
(L.A. Metro Series – Book #2)

RJ Nolan

ISBN: 978-3-95533-159-7
Length: 370 pages (97,000 words)

Officer Sam McKenna has no trouble facing down criminals but breaks out in a sweat at the mere mention of commitment. Trauma surgeon Riley Connolly tries to measure up to her family's expectations and hides her sexuality from them. A life-and-death situation at the hospital binds them together. But can there be any future for a commitment-phobic cop and a closeted, workaholic doctor?

BLURRED LINES
(Cops and Docs – Book #1)

KD Williamson

ISBN: 978-3-95533-493-2
Length: 283 pages (92,000 words)

Wounded in a police shootout, Detective Kelli McCabe spends weeks in the hospital recovering. Her only entertainment is verbal sparring matches with Dr. Nora Whitmore, the talented and reclusive surgeon. Two very different women living in two different worlds. When the lines between them begin to blur, will they run from the possibilities or embrace the changes they bring to each other's lives?

DELIBERATE HARM

J.R. Wolfe

ISBN: 978-3-95533-368-3
Length: 300 pages (70,000 words)

Ever since Portia Marks learned her fiancée Imma was executed in Zimbabwe, she's struggled with grief. Then a stranger tells her Imma is alive, but he's killed before she can ask questions. To learn the truth, Portia teams with two friends in the CIA. Her search takes her across continents and entangles her in a terrorist plot that will rock the globe. Portia's quest becomes a race against time.

COMING FROM YLVA PUBLISHING

www.ylva-publishing.com

BETWEEN THE LINES

(Cops and Docs – Book #3)

K.D. Williamson

Tonya Preston is a psychiatrist that likes dealing with her patients more than her family. Haley Jordan is a rookie police officer trying to find her way. They meet under dangerous circumstances that leaves a lasting impression. As their paths continue to cross, attraction simmers between them, but are they strong enough to power through the obstacles the people around them put in their path?

DARK HORSE

A.L. Brooks

Sometimes, going back is the only way forward. Punished for a crime she did not commit, Sadie is sent away to rebuild her life. Several years later she returns home to visit her terminally ill mother and face up to the past. In the midst of family turmoil Sadie meets Holly and falls in love for the first time. Can Sadie overcome the lies of the past to build a brighter future?

Rescue Me
© 2016 by Michelle L. Teichman

ISBN: 978-3-95533-762-9

Also available as e-book.

Published by Ylva Publishing, legal entity of Ylva Verlag, e.Kfr.
Ylva Verlag, e.Kfr.
Owner: Astrid Ohletz
Am Kirschgarten 2
65830 Kriftel
Germany

www.ylva-publishing.com

First edition: 2016

Credits
Edited by Jove Belle & Michelle Aguilar
Cover Design by Dirt Road Design
Print Layout and Cover by Streetlight Graphics

www.ingramcontent.com/pod-product-compliance
Lightning Source LLC
Chambersburg PA
CBHW031001260626
47169CB00002B/639